Excerpt

"Remember when we were in the simulator, when we first met, and I told you about the two simulations I never could beat? Well here comes sim one. The real-life version."

"Don't dwell on past failures, Darq. Think." Tokoray spoke in a steady, resolute tone. "We must get over the horizon, or the Doyons will know we survived and come after us."

Jewels of the Sky

Catherine E. McLean

RIMSTONE CONCEPTS LLC
Carlton PA, U.S.A.

✧ For information about special discounts for bulk purchases, please use the contact form at Rimstone Concepts: www.rimstoneconceptsllc.com

✧ To book the author for your event or to do a workshop online or in person, go to Rimstone Concepts at www.rimstoneconceptsllc.com and use the contact form there.

✧ Cover: George A. Vrbanic
http://home.comcast.net/~gvrbanic/site/?/home/
e-mail: gvrbanic@comcast.net

✧ To be notified when future books are released, please join the author at
https://twitter.com/#!/CatherineMcLea7

✧ Author's Page for readers: www.CatherineEmclean.com
and for writers: www.WritersCheatSheets.com

ISBN 978-0-9885874-0-3
ISBN-10: 0988587408

See Darq's avatar (a doll!) by going to
Http://jewelsofthesky.wordpress.com

Thank you for always believing in me
and appreciating a good story–

J. D. M.
R. M. M.
J. S.

✧ Chapter 1

Terror seized Darq, waking her, jolting her to sit up, her heart pumping as if the *Dujaki*'s scramble horns blared of an incoming attack. But instead of her eyes focusing on the battlestation's bulkheads, she found an ocher moon hanging three-quarters full against a starry sky.

Not the *Dujaki*, definitely not the *Dujaki*.

Her heart rate backed off full throttle, and as her ragged breathing slowed to normal, she swiped errant strands of her sleep-tousled, earth-brown hair behind her ears.

Before her stretched the seascape where tallow-colored sand edged a tidal pool and black rock monoliths stood sentinel along the shoreline. *Jooril Bay*. She was planetside, on Wysotti, north of Azilla. Safe.

Then what had ram-launched her out of a sound sleep?

A nightmare?

She searched her memory. No. Not a nightmare. Then what? She brought her knees up and hugged them. In doing so, moonlight sparkled across the rainbow pallet of nail polish on her toes—yellow, green, blue, pink, and violet. Eyeing the one tiny, white daisy decal gracing each big toenail, she felt her smile push back her cheeks. She'd been five summers old when her grandmother had introduced her to the wonders and colors of rainbow-painted toes.

How childish to paint her toenails. She was a grown woman now, a starfighter pilot, and regulations didn't permit painted nails. The polish would have to go. But not yet, not until she reported back to duty.

She looked up, peering deep into the star-spangled blackness. How serene the heavens. If only she were up there, among the stars, flying the voids, free of the shackles of duty to dyn and country.

And how quiet the night. *Like the eeriness of floating in space after ejecting from a starfighter.* What a strange thought. She was awake and firmly grounded, on land.

Yet, it was quiet. Maybe, too quiet. Perhaps she only imagined the silence, the stillness?

She cocked her head one way and then the other for a moment, listening intently. No chirping crawlers or flyers? No hunters and the hunted of the night prowling about? Not even a gnat buzzed. Why?

Then again, what did it matter? She sighed and let her gaze drift out, across the sea . . . Such still water . . .

Cloth rustled behind her.

Startled, she swiveled about, lost her balance, and dropped off the edge of the sleeping pad onto the sand. She righted herself and sat cross-legged.

An arm's length away under the lean-to, her atan — her husband — gargled a snore. He turned onto his side, his bare back facing her, and stilled. Moonlight wove shadows along his braid of dark brown hair, the end tied off with a black mourning band.

She stared at the band. *Mourning — And melancholy.* Two things she could ill afford to wallow in. She should snuggle up to her atan and go back to sleep, cuddling in his arms as she had hours ago. Only back then he'd instantly dropped off to sleep. She hadn't. She'd been kept awake by the infernal drum beats resonating in her mind. That drumming started this afternoon, after she lit her grandmother's funeral pyre. The drumming wasn't real, couldn't be real. Nor was it likely a malfunction of the neural net implanted in her brain. When that glitched, she would be dead, not hallucinating.

Yet, considering the past few weeks, the worry, the tears, the fatigue, the frustrations — and no real time to herself? Maybe it was logical to expect some kind of stress-manifestation. But why an auditory hallucination of her grandmother beating her Jewels of the Sky Drum? Even odder, the ghostly drumming ranged from loud war beats to gentle patting —

Starshine and shitfire! The drumming had stopped.

Would the beats renew?

Hardly breathing, she waited, hope tethered by fear. Moments later, she almost laughed with relief. What a silly o-lo-pii she was. She'd been woken by nothing more than the silencing of an imaginary drum. All was right with the world. Well, maybe not everything. Grandmother Zukaltay was dead.

The memory rose vividly in Darq's mind of the badlands canyon, the dyn's sacred burial grounds, and of her grandmother dressed in her white ceremonial dyn clothes, surrounded by flowers, reposed on her funeral pyre. Moc-ha-u-a burned in the incense pots at the corners of the pyre. The ghostly, blue-white smoke spiraled upward, releasing an earthy scent of pine resin laced with clover and wildberry roses.

Darq raked a hand through her hair, noting how cold her fingers were. Not as cold as her hands had been when she gave the eulogy, nor when doing her final duty, fulfilling her promise to her grandmother, and pushing the button that ignited the pyre.

Another image flashed of joining in the *eldic rondt*. During that farewell chant, the setting sun's flaring rays burnished the clouds on the horizon with crimson and gold, matching the flames licking up from the pyre. Among the dyn elders, someone had rasped out there was an omen in that sunset.

An omen prophesying what? Good or evil? Fortune or disaster? And for whom?

From the recesses of Darq's mind came her grandmother's deathbed words— *Embrace the ice of duty and the fire of courage, Darq, for they enable us to endure the adversities of life.*

Duty and courage? They were sorry bedfellows. Necessities in war. Necessities in dealing with death.

Damn the war. Damn death.

Darq inhaled a cleansing breath that sucked away the memories, but not her restlessness. She got to her feet and dusted the sand off her shorts. Feeling as she did, she wasn't likely to go back to sleep. So what should she do now?

She looked at the sea. *Water soothed the soul.* And so might a walk along the shore.

Her husband grumbled a snore.

She glanced down at him. If he woke and found her gone, he would activate Raytor to look for her. She eyed the automaton. Raytor had parked on the starboard side of the lean-to next to a dune. Spindly stalks of white-grass from the top of the dune had sprinkled seeds on his wheel base. She shifted her gaze up the automaton's boxy leg shaft, over the mauve-gray officer's tunic covering his masculine form, and checked his com-badge. No bar was lit. She checked his midnight-blue faceplate. No data line appeared. Then she zeroed in on the disk capping his globe-shaped head. A pinprick of light indicated a maintenance check in progress.

Should she rouse him? Tell him she was going for a walk? No, let him finish his diagnostics. She wouldn't be gone long.

Strolling toward the beach, her bare feet sank into the gritty sand, which was still warm from the day. Nearing the waterline, she heard the resounding thwack of wood on rock. She pivoted toward the sound and took a defensive stance, feet apart, knees bent, hands fisted and raised, heart racing, mind switching to hyperalert.

A cloaked woman, using her staff for support, carefully stepped off a tide pool's ledge. Once her feet were on the sand, she looked up, saw Darq, and abruptly halted. Her free hand slapped palm down on her chest, over her heart. Eyes wide, she stared at Darq.

A saalishani! *Great going, Darq, terrifying an old woman.* Darq stood at ease, hooked her thumbs at the corners of her short's hip pockets, and hoped she now looked nonthreatening.

Relief graced the saalishani's face, and she raised her hand, briefly waving hello. Bright moonlight cast its sepia glow over her frizzy-fine, white hair. Typical of saalishani, her long hair was parted down the middle with the temple hairs gathered, braided, and drawn around to the back of her head. Swinging her wooden staff in cadence with her strides, the old woman headed toward Darq. With each step, the moonlight burnished the diamond-shaped crystals atop the saalishani's staff.

Darq studied the four jewels — one for wind, earth, water, and fire. Which meant this was no ordinary saalishani. She was a healer.

A second later, Darq sensed the old woman's keen, piercing gaze and saw the woman's lips purse with dismay.

Saalishanies disliked public immodesty. Darq squared her shoulders. So what if her tank top had a plunging neckline or that her shorts hung lopsided off one hip? The clothes were her sister's, two sizes too big, but gratefully accepted. Besides, the clothes were more suitable for sleeping on the beach than regulation-wear. And why did she care what she looked like or what the saalishani thought?

The old woman looked down, her chin tucked against her chest, and studied the gnarled limb of driftwood blocking her path. She planted her staff, gripped it with both hands, and hopped over the limb. The landing not only jarred the fringe topping her boots and edging her shift but also sent her necessities bag swinging forward, out from under her cloak. That bag bore an embroidered white, four-legged dragon surrounded by a heavily-beaded medicine wheel. The plumed serpent represented purity, love, and goodness, which meant this healer served the Sisters of Ya'tal. That explained where the woman was headed but not what she was doing here at this time of night.

The saalishani stopped half a staff's length from Darq. "Adovee, daughter."

"Adovee, Wise Mother." Then, in a cooler tone, Darq said, "This beach is posted. It's private property."

"Ahh, yes, I know it is. In truth, I saw the sign but disregarded it." The twinkle in the old woman's eyes accompanied her widening smile, one that scrunched her cheeks and revealed the tips of her upper teeth. "You see, following the shoreline cuts off more than an hour on my journey. I did not think to find a soul about who would take me to task for my midnight trespassing."

"It's well past midnight." Why had she spoken as if she were reprimanding a cadet? Darq cleared her throat and softened her tone. "I take it you're headed for Ya'tal House?"

The old one nodded. "I am. It is my first visit to the priory. I do not want to miss morning prayers—or breakfast. I have been told they serve a wonderful breakfast feast."

"Yes, they do." Everyone raved about the buffet. A pricey meal due to rationing and shortages, but worth it because the Sisters' profits went to the local veterans' rehab center. As to prayers? The Sisters dedicated themselves to nonstop praying, nonstop beseeching of the Great Mother Spirit, J'Hi-inti, to aid the Wysotti in winning the war with the Doyons.

War. Soon she would be back on the *Dujaki*, flying patrols, fighting that war — and just why was she letting such thoughts circle like a buzzard waiting for something to die?

The old woman craned her neck to peer behind Darq. "Ahh, I see, in the lean-to, you are not alone." As her gaze swerved to Darq's left, moonlight winked golden in her eyes. "Oh, my— You have a droid?"

"He's not a droid." The saalishani should know better! Darq hardened her voice. "*He is a Na-ka-ta, an officer of the fleet.*"

"Oh, do forgive me, daughter, I did not mean to offend." No contrition resonated in the old woman's voice. "You are guardi?"

"Elpoccalli — space fleet. A fighter pilot."

One of the saalishani's eyebrows quirked upward. "And you choose to spend your leave under the stars?"

"Better under them than under my mother's roof." Had she actually said that?

"Families do tend to fuss when their daughters come home."

"They never fuss over me." Shitfire, why had she blurted that out? "I— I— "

"Didn't mean to express such a truth?" The saalishani raised her hand, gesturing Darq not to protest. "Be at peace, daughter, and do forgive me. People have always found me an easy confidant." The saalishani heaved a dramatic sigh, tilted her head back, and gazed steadily at the stars. A moment later she said in a soft undertow, "*How serene the heavens.*"

Like the fire-flash of a missile blast, the feeling of deja vu struck Darq. Only moments ago she had thought the very same words. Which was odd, and disconcerting, but likely just a coincidence. Right. Nothing but a coincidence.

A wayward cloud veiled the moon, delustering its glow.

"Ahh, the moon, how forlorn it looks." The saalishani sadly shook her head. "It brings to mind the distressing news I heard yesterday of raids into Doyon territory. It seems strange to behold such a tranquil sea and be reminded of a war." She leaned heavily onto her staff, and quietly, dispiritedly, said, "Whatever will be the Wysotti fate?"

The Wysotti's fate was only too clear, but no sense voicing that. Darq turned her attention to the sea where dawn grayed the horizon, and a splotch of rose-red marked where the sun would appear within the hour. The glow resurrected the memory of a Doyon missile bursting apart the stern of a Wysotti transport, of navigating her fighter, dodging dead crew and mangled Na-ka-tas tumbling in the vacuum of space. Darq heard herself mutter, "Will our fate be fire or ice?"

What was the matter with her? Being candid was one thing but sounding like an o-lo-pii certainly wasn't. Darq looked at the old woman and found her frowning.

"I'm sorry, Wise Mother," Darq said, "I spoke without thinking."

The old woman's frown vanished. "No reason to be sorry, daughter, though I must admit I am ever curious. *What is your meaning, this fire or ice?*"

There was no mistaking the tone of that question. The old woman wanted an explanation. The trick was to give a sane-sounding one. Darq eyed the sea, but didn't focus on any one point. "When the battle with the Doyons comes to our world—"

"That is not of a certainty, is it?"

Darq shrugged. "Who knows. Anyway, if the Doyons come to our homeworld, do we die by the destruction from Doyon missiles or do we die by their bombs spewing dust into the atmosphere and causing a planet-wide winter and ice age?"

"Have you no faith in the Elpoccalli fleet to stop the Doyons?"

Darq looked down to the tops of her toenails half-submerged in the sand. Faith required conviction. In truth she was not sure the fleet could hold off, let alone stop, a major Doyon offensive.

"You know," the old woman said, "you look familiar. Ahh, now I recall, the late-night news— You gave Ambassador

Zukaltay's eulogy. You are Darq, Zukaltay's firstborn granddaughter."

Darq squared her shoulders and met the saalishani's gaze head on. "Yes, I am."

"Dear one," the saalishani's voice gentled, "forgive me for intruding on your night of greatest sorrow. Please accept my sympathy for your loss."

The sincerity in her voice resonated in Darq and dredged up tears. *No more tears.*

Darq unhooked her thumbs from her pockets and closed her fingers tightly about her thumbs. She held her arms at her sides, muscles tense, and swallowed the tears in her throat. "There is nothing to forgive. Your condolences are appreciated." Then she half-whispered, "I've seen too much death to let another rankle me."

The look on the old woman's eyes said, *Liar, liar! Zukaltay's death is an irreconcilable loss to you.*

The saalishani's next words, although quietly spoken, rang with clarity. "If only the peace of this hour permeated all things."

"Unfortunately, Wise Mother, peace is not in a Doyon's vocabulary, nor favored by their power-mongering kungarike."

The old woman nodded. "True, but, tell me, do you believe this war with the Doyons is the Great Spirit's final revenge on the Wysotti people?"

What a strange question to ask. Stranger still was the imploring tone of the saalishani's voice, as if she needed to know. Darq released her thumbs and hooked them back into the corners of her pockets. "Moot point when you consider J'Hi-inti has forsaken and forgotten us."

"What if She hasn't? What if J'Hi-inti hears one voice? What if that voice asks Her to give the Wysotti the opportunity to prove they are worthy of continuing as a people, as a nation?"

Darq let out a bark of soft laughter. "You are a dreamer. We are nothing more than a world of women who survive on hope so as not to feel hopeless. For J'Hi-inti to hear one voice—any Wysotti voice—would be the grandest miracle of miracles."

"You do not believe in miracles?"

"I'm a realist. Besides, miracles ceased the day the *Tolamixi Mu* returned."

"Goodness, such cynicism in one so young."

Yes, she had become cynical, but truth was truth. Darq lowered her voice to a harsher, colder level. "We all know what that ship's crew did, and as the seers keep telling us, generation after generation, the sins of those fathers will forever be passed on."

"And in particular to you and your dyn?"

The knowing in the saalishani's voice had shame tying a double knot in Darq's gut. She would never be able to abolish the inherited disgrace, but that didn't mean she had to succumb to it.

Darq locked her gaze to the old woman's. "I do not deny my dyn heritage. I may be genetically linked to Kukulaan, but I am me — Darq of the Mayahi Dyn, granddaughter of Zukaltay, who was one of the greatest narans this world has ever seen."

The saalishani slowly nodded. "Yes, your grandmother was a wise dyn leader, and yet — What if one voice successfully entreats the Great Spirit to give the Wysotti an opportunity to undo the wrong the men of the *Tolamixi Mu* did? Would you not want that?"

"Yes, but — " Darq shook her head, sending her hair skittering across the tops of her shoulders and the shorter lengths flicking against her cheeks. "One voice or a billion, pray all you like, plead all you like, no miracle will happen because only death will free us from that mortal sin."

The saalishani tilted her head one way and then the other, in thought. Soon a wry smile curved the left side of her lips, and sympathy reflected in her dark eyes. "Grief has encrusted your heart. I assure you, for those who love and are loved, there is always hope."

The saalishani was too observant. Enough was enough. Time to end this absurd conversation. "Look, the hour is late." Darq pointed to the horizon, now a brighter gray. "You'll miss prayers and breakfast if you don't hurry on to Ya'tal House."

"Ahh, yes, I see I have tarried longer than I should have."

Darq turned to go back to the lean-to, but the saalishani reached out and touched Darq's arm, staying her departure.

"May the warmth of the rising sun bless your day, daughter, and ease your grief." She let Darq go and, before Darq could make a reply, the saalishani pointed to the bay. "Look!"

Darq studied the silent, still seascape. What had the old woman seen?

"Great joy of joys! Look at that. The first waves of the incoming tide." The saalishani turned her head and a breeze sent her frizzy hair fluttering. "Feel that? The wind has refreshed." She momentarily cocked her head. "Hear that? Creatures large and small now welcome the dawn tide and herald this new day."

The wind kissed Darq's cheek. Something buzzed by her ear. Then came the squawk of sea terns.

At Jooril Bay, a stillness and a silence came before the turning of a morning tide. How had she forgotten that? And what an idiot she had been to angst over nothing out of the ordinary.

"Adovee, Darq!" The grinning saalishani left, cloak swaying, the fringe of her boots and shift bobbing with each stride, and her staff thumping a quick cadence.

"Adovee, Wise Mother," Darq said to the old woman's back. Shortly, the saalishani entered the blackness of a monolith's shadow.

Seconds later, a vigorous wave swished ashore.

Darq turned toward the waterline where the sand had been newly saturated by the wave.

Incoming tide. What a sight to behold one last time before— Before what? Her death? Or the destruction of her planet? More likely both. But why dwell on such thoughts? This was the start of a brand new day. A day in which she had the strangest urge to play in the surf.

She padded forward, stopping, then wriggling her toes in the cool, wet sand until her rainbow-colored toenails glistened as if freshly polished. In the moonlight, the daisies on her big toes seemed brighter, and three-dimensional.

When the sky glowed a peachy-orange, Darq looked at the horizon. *The miracle of a new day.* Miracles? Not likely. But for a little while, couldn't she forget she had to fly back to the spaceport, board a packet ship back to the *Dujaki*, go back to a futile war?

From behind her came her husband's, "What are you doing?"

She didn't turn around. "Watching the sun rise."

He slipped his hands around her waist and nestled his chin on her shoulder. His smooth cheek warmed hers. She felt a familiar poke to her buttocks.

"Guess what, my love?" he whispered.

She chuckled. "I don't have to guess, Atlatl, I can feel your erection."

"It goes with an insatiable urge." His hands grasped the hem of her tank top. She raised her arms, and he whisked the fabric away.

A tremolo of joy pierced the air about the saalishani. She stopped, turning to face the way she'd come. In the distance, she spied two discarded pairs of shorts and a tank top—and a naked Darq with her legs wrapped about her atan's hips. Darq flung her head back and squealed another tremolo that urged her husband's hips to gyrate.

For the saalishani, memories flickered of the simplicity of ages ago on a blue, water-world planet. There the Vidarians' seedings had produced life that evolved into a human form. The saalishani recalled the pleasure of breathing souls into that stock, male and female alike.

Ahh, Darq, you are, indeed, the jungle beauty. And Atlatl? You are as fine as any of the Indian war chiefs to ever ride the Great Plains of the Americas.

An incoming wave splashed against Atlatl's shins. The saalishani watched him ignore the wave in favor of a binding kiss that cut off Darq's laughter.

All that had transpired in the past day flashed through the saalishani's thoughts, ending with Darq's words—*pray all you like, plead all you like, no miracle will happen because only death will free us from that mortal sin.*

You are wrong, Darq, Princess of the Misted Moon, granddaughter of the great naran Zukaltay. Miracles can happen for you and for all the Wysotti, if only you believe.

The saalishani gripped her staff tightly, released a surge of inner power, and ignited the four crystals, setting them aglow. With each step to the sea and into the water, the energy grew more formidable, brightening the crystals. When she was knee deep, she stopped.

Lifting her staff above the water, she focused on an incoming wave. She willed the wave to gather itself, build more forcefully, and race toward the shore. With a buoyant smile and inner delight, she looked at Darq and Atlatl. *I bless thee and this world with miracles.*

She plunged her staff deep into the sandy seabed, releasing the power of love and life in a bolt of energy that raced to the planet's core, burst, and spread out and upward to envelop the world. The old woman swiftly channeled the force of the incoming wave to strike Darq and Atlatl, sweeping the couple onto the beach, submerging them for their moment of climax.

The saalishani grinned, and the crystals of her staff emitted a blue-white glow. *Your heart's hope is the finest of miracles yet to be, my dear children.*

In a wink of iridescent light, she vanished.

✧ Chapter 2

Foolish, foolish woman, Zukaltay's conscience half-shouted, *what have you done?* She balled her hands, shoving them deep into the pockets of her ash-gray robe. The velvet noncorporeal wear covering her soul-body declared to all in the celestial qi that her soul required cleansing in the labyrinth of the Halls of Redemption. Even her transgressions were visible — and audible. The lengths of black links attached to the sin chain belting her waist jingled with each stride she took across the floor. A floor that glistened like snow in sunshine, its brilliance enabling her to ignore the sky-blueness of the chamber walls but not her conscience.

How had she let her temper flare so easily? Foolishness, that's what it was. An old woman's foolishness. *Stop castigating yourself. Own up to what you have done.* Own up? Those were words Darq and her generation spouted, not the words of a naran.

As Zukaltay passed Adrada on her way to the other end of the chamber, he said, "It won't be much longer."

She paused to look him in the eye. Being petite, she had to tilt her head back as far as it would go. She shot him her best quelling look. Yet, with the archangel's chiseled face surrounded by long, wavy, raven-black hair and abyss-dark eyes, he was more devilishly handsome than angelic. And his reaction amounted to his eyebrows of tiny black feathers briefly rising a fraction. She shifted her gaze to take in the full view of him.

Clad in a white shirt with billowing sleeves and wide-legged white pants, the Archangel of Departing Souls stood nonchalantly with his spine resting against a fluted column, one of a dozen supports for the Chamber of the *Book of the Future*'s vaulted ceiling. His immense gold wings bracketed the length of his body and, even tucked at his sides, the wing tips trailed on the floor. One other 'dark' aspect of this archangel was the purple outer feathers of his great golden wings. Some feathers were of such a deep hue that they seemed black, while others, particularly the feathers on the lower wing edges, were variegated, going from dark purple to the palest mauve before ending in golden tips.

She'd learned from a fellow sinner that the purpling resulted from Adrada's deep mourning—the sadness, the depression—from millenniums of service, especially from greeting the innocent souls of children who died at the hands of vile beings, most of them human or humanoid.

It had been Adrada who escorted her soul to the Great Spirit World of the Omega Qi and to the under chamber of the Hall of Redemption where a blond-haired archangel opened a console screen and read the list of her accountable misdemeanors. She honestly acknowledged them all, even the one, the most grievous sin. But sin or no sin, what did it matter once she'd found this room? Once she'd read the entries in the *Book of the Future*? Once she'd searched the records? The histories?

Zukaltay faced the wall screen on which the book had appeared when she had summoned it from the control console, an altar-like station that stood a few meters in front of the screen. Curiosity concerning who would win the war—the Wysotti or the Doyons—had overwhelmed her. Without considering whether or not she was allowed to look, she accessed the book's Wysotti texts. *Her curiosity may well have damned the Wysotti to extinction.*

Eyeing the blue wall, she recalled the giant, parchment-paged *Book of the Future* that had morphed into place. Writing filled the pages in a dialect she had to ask the console to convert into Wysotti Standard. She had not asked for the current date but for a look at the last moon-month of The Grand T'un, the last t'un of The Great Cycle, when on the winter solstice there would be an alignment of the planets. An omen some believed meant victory for the Wysotti against the Doyons.

After the shock of what she'd read wore off, she went to verify what happened on the planet Terra. Anger at the injustice of what she found kindled and burned into a hot rage. She'd held onto that rightful anger. Disregarding the edict forbidding Wysotti drumbeats in the celestial heavens, and to vent the tension coiling tightly about her mind and heart, she beat her drum, a spirit replica of the Jewels of the Sky drum she'd treasured all her life. Her drumbeats were finger-numbing, loud, and echoed.

She took her hands out of her pockets, turned, and eyed the spirit-drum. It sat at Adrada's booted feet, mere centimeters from the tip of the rune-adorned scabbard that held his Sword of Judgment.

Her gaze focused on the blue jewels of the starbursts on the front panel of the drum's base. On her deathbed she'd given the real drum to Darq for safekeeping—and with the prayer, and hope, that Darq would stop being the warrior and give birth to a daughter who would play the old drum.

"As much as you would like to pound your drum," Adrada said, no admonishment in his voice, "I cannot allow it."

"Yes, I know." Zukaltay clasped her hands to stop the tingling urge to bend down and touch the sleek skin of the drum, to lessen her anxiety. In life, the real drum had never failed to ease the turmoil of exasperating days dealing with Pyhanni, with politicians, and with whatever life placed in her path. Yet, there had been joys. Rare joys to be sure, but joys nevertheless.

Hearing the sound of sizzling energy, she pivoted and faced the iridescent, twinkling glow that heralded the return of the Great Spirit, J'Hi-inti. The glow suddenly morphed, spinning bizarrely into an upside-down vortex that grew larger and larger.

Zukaltay's mind flashed back to the day before. She had defiantly knelt with her drum between her knees, hands pounding a beat, but covertly watching Adrada speak in hushed tones to an old man wearing a white monk's robe. The old man had arrived in a similar burst of energy-light.

In the next moment, Adrada had glowed, and his angelic body re-formed into a black-scaled Doyon's. His golden wings darkened to ebony, and the edge feathers shimmered with purple highlights. His face became that of a snub-nosed lizard. First a black halo, replete with flecks of gold, crowned the top of his head, then a black headband, studded with silver and onyx, covered the blessed runes of gold tattooed across his forehead.

Later in the day, she learned Adrada shapeshifted like that because the Doyons called him Auc-Pon, The Ebon Warrior, who came for their souls. Adrada, as Auc-Pon, judged Doyons worthy of Ly'sienia, the eternal paradise, or of the Ghelmae Trench, a cold, dark abyss. She would wager not many Doyons got to Ly'sienia.

After the archangel had vanished in a whirlwind of iridescent energy-light, the old man waved his index finger, much like a magician waving a wand, and a vine bench materialized in front of her. He sat facing her and tucked his knobby-knuckled hands under the end of his thick beard. She ignored his dove-gray eyes studying her and became more and more curious why he didn't speak.

When she came to the end of her drum-song, he said, "It has been quite some time since I have heard a drum like yours, Zukaltay."

She let her ire sharpen her words. "Wysotti drums were banned in the celestial qi thousands of t'uns ago."

His brows furrowed in concentration, then the frown vanished. "Ahh, yes, so they were. And that drum of yours is the one dear possession from life that you chose to have with you during your penance?"

Despite her intentions to maintain her anger, holding onto it seemed pointless. She nodded. "Are you the envoy charged with getting me to see the light, to stop my protests and drumming?"

"I am the light."

"What?"

The old man looked down to where he had wound strands of his beard about his index finger. He released the hairs, then looked at her. "In your Wysotti existence, you were a mediator, a magistrate, were you not?"

"Yes, and eventually a naran—ambassador to the Kallian Federation." She'd spoken those last words with too much pride.

Pride accounted for eighty-five percent of the links on her sin chain.

His keen gaze, devoid of censure, studied her. "In your prime, you zealously found equitable solutions for difficult situations and championed the ordinary citizen and Na-ka-ta."

"It seemed to be my calling."

"Indeed. Your gift to seek justice for those who needed it was well used, and so I can readily understand the difficulty of your accepting J'Hi-inti's wrath and judgment."

Out of habit and to gather her wits, she took in a deep breath, then realized it wasn't necessary to breathe. Being dead, her spirit-soul-body didn't require air. Still, she had to make this envoy understand. "For the record, I believe the Great Spirit—who created all things seen and unseen, who placed the stars in the heavens, and who gave souls to sentient beings—is the loving heart of the Omega Qi." Feeling the escalation of temper, she gripped the drum with both hands, holding it as tightly as if it were her anger and she could keep it in check. She locked her gaze to the old man's. "However justified J'Hi-inti may have been at the time of the *Tolamixi Mu Incident,* the fact remains that the Great Spirit created a living purgatory for all Wysotti and, knowing what I know now, well, *enough is enough!*"

"The men of the *Tolamixi Mu* were depraved. They took pleasure in defiling nubiles and mature women, impregnating them in orgies that spanned a world."

"If the Great Spirit didn't want crossbreeding of human species, why did She permit that Wysotti scout ship to find that particular world and land on that planet?"

"There were extenuating circumstances."

"Extenuating—" She gave her indignation free rein. "Right. When they came to tell me the rule about no Wysotti drum playing, Rafael said the Great Spirit had too many things going on at the time of *the incident.* Mithra said the situation didn't become a problem until the bloodletting and the worship of the men as gods."

"Actually it was the hundreds of souls entering the qi."

She scoffed. "For a god who is supposed to know all and see all, I find the excuses unbelievable."

The old man scratched his cheek slowly, more in thought than to quell an itch under his beard. "Wysotti men investigating a new world did not cause alarm. Such is the natural flow of a species' curiosity about other races and other worlds, especially when they become starfarers." He stopped scratching and lowered his hand. "What became objectionable were the men using their superior knowledge and their scientific equipment to determine which females were ovulating, then anesthetizing and raping them, impregnating them to create 'superior beings.' Those Wysotti men irrevocably altered natural selection and evolution."

In her naran life, her government clearances had given her access to the *Tolamixi Mu* logs, but Kukulaan had destroyed most of them. Then there were the diary and testimonies of the few surviving *Onaja Toq*'s crew attesting to the devastation of the planet Terra's Mayan civilization. She had also read the official Board of Inquiry reports. "Only three of the *Tolamixi Mu*'s crew raped—the captain and his first and second officers."

The old man released a sigh. "The crew followed orders."

"Until they realized what the officers were doing—or are you saying the maintenance chief's diary is a fake? A wild yarn spun to defame the officers?"

"His words were true. You also know the military minds of that day, and beyond, sealed the records for the good of the space fleet."

To save their asses. "Yet," she said, "the facts eventually came to light."

One corner of the old man's mouth pulled back into a rueful smile. "Only after the maintenance chief died."

"True," Zukaltay replied. The chief's wife had found her husband's diary buried at the bottom of his old service rucksack. Even to this day, the controversy raged over the diary and the *Tolamixi Mu*'s nonexistent logs. Still— "The truth," Zukaltay said with determination, "it needs to be known."

He canted his head and eyed her, saying softly, "The truth? What might that be?"

"On that little blue planet the *Tolamixi Mu* landed on, great scientists, engineers, statesmen, and leaders were born of those

Wysotti-sired children. The planet's civilizations grew and flourished. They are now a significant starfaring legion of people who have colonized many star systems."

"And your point?"

"In the Great Spirit's wrath at the transgressions of those three Wysotti men, why were all Wysotti damned?"

"The punishment seemed fitting, quite proper at the moment. Just."

"Fitting? Proper? Just? Hardly! And for J'Hi-inti to decree only one male child be born of a man during his lifetime was uncalled for. It devitalized the population and economy. We women, *we innocent women*, have suffered and have struggled to keep our race alive."

"Adovee, Zukaltay," the Great Spirit's old voice jarred her back to the present.

She eyed the energy, now in the final stage of solidification into a saalishani. The wise-woman's necessities bag and staff indicated J'Hi-inti had returned as a healer, a Sister of Ya'tal.

Soul-heart pounding, dread weighing like ten worlds on her shoulders, Zukaltay watched the bag and staff vanish. Then the old woman's wrinkled skin gave way to a smooth, oval face that would have been beautiful on a man or a woman of any human race. The saalishani's clothing dissolved into a full length, voluminous, shimmering white robe with dagged sleeves skimming the floor.

Looking into the Great Spirit's dove-gray eyes revealed no emotion in them.

"Adovee, Great Spirit." As Zukaltay spoke the greeting, a shroud of doom closed in on her with such force that her knees buckled and hit the floor. She rocked back and sat on her heels. Hands clasped to stop their quaking and to steady her terror, she recalled having had the same sensation the day before when J'Hi-inti had been in the guise of the old man on the vine bench. She recalled her exact words to him, spoken with heartfelt conviction—"The Wysotti are not perfect beings, but I am confident that if J'Hi-inti walked among my people, they will prove worthy of redemption, of a second chance to continue as a race."

The old man had replied, "If J'Hi-inti walks among your people, will you accept the outcome of Her findings?"

Zukaltay didn't hesitate. She nodded and gave a resolute "Yes."

The force of the old man's smile had been enough to warm her soul. Then he revealed he was no envoy but J'Hi-inti.

The impact of who the old man really was, and the realization of what she had negotiated, had been a breath-strangling, heart-stopping moment — even for a dead woman's repentant soul. And now came the moment of truth. Whatever the outcome of the Great Spirit's visit to the Wysotti world, she must keep her word and accept Her decision.

"Zukaltay," J'Hi-inti said in Her solemn, ages-old voice, "quell your fears."

"Yes. Yes, of course." She couldn't look up, couldn't risk seeing the condemnation that might be written in the Great Spirit's eyes. Yet, she had to ask, "What did you learn?"

"What I have seen has softened my heart."

Zukaltay stole a covert look at the Great Spirit's face and found Her smiling. "What did you discover?"

"Yours is as imperfect a world as any other, yet, I was astonished with the ingenuity of the Wysotti women, their technology. Especially impressive are the Na-ka-tas, who are treated as citizens." A gleam brightened Her eyes. "Then to see firsthand that your breeding males were not enslaved and exploited but given equality and liberty? Now that was unexpected. As unexpected as finding their rights have been set forth in law so that, no matter what dyn the men are born into, they may have a career and lifestyle of their own choosing." A warm glow suffused Her eyes. "You were correct when you told me Wysotti women had suffered a living purgatory."

Even as a tremor of relief washed over Zukaltay, caution kept her hopes in check, as did a niggling suspicion. "And yet?"

The glow in Her eyes turned into a look of resolve. "As much as I doubt any Wysotti will again succumb to the godhood syndrome like that of the *Tolamixi Mu*'s officers, your race has evolved into a formidable and extremely powerful military force."

Terror dug talon-deep into her soul. "The Doyons attacked us! We were peaceful star-traders. *We fight only to protect our world.*" She calmed herself. "All right, I admit we have become a formidable military power, but according to the *Book of the Future*, the Doyons will savagely conquer our world, slaughter millions, enslave those who survive, and ravage our planet of every resource."

"This is true. Yet, never forget, Zukaltay, that among the gifts I bestow to sentient life are souls and self-determination."

What did She mean by that? "I don't understand."

The Great Spirit walked to the control console. Seconds later, the *Book of the Future* appeared. Pages flipped rapidly forward then three pages turned back.

Zukaltay staggered to her feet—and noted Adrada had remained standing where he had been, his back to the column.

The silent witness? Or was he the watchdog? And how odd—why did he hold her drum ensconced in his arms? *Foolish woman, why are you distracting yourself with Adrada and the drum instead of finding out what J'Hi-inti is doing?*

She went to the console and stood to J'Hi-inti's left. On the screen, everything below the second paragraph on the current page vanished. The pages turned, and every entry disappeared before the pages flipped back to the partial entry.

J'Hi-inti looked at the page, skimmed the text, and then pointed to the last line. "Zukaltay, from that point on, chaos rules until one Wysotti woman decides the fate of your people."

Surprise gave way to uncertainty. "One Wysotti will decide my people's fate?"

J'Hi-inti stepped back. "Yes." She gestured with a sweep of her hand for Zukaltay to go forward, toward the screen. "Read."

Foreboding sandstormed through Zukaltay, flaying her nerves raw, but she obeyed. Moments later, she came to the end of the passage. Why hadn't the name of the Wysotti woman, the chosen one, been written onto the pages? Did she dare ask? Yes. She had to know. "Forgive my curiosity, Great Spirit, but no name appears of who decides my people's fate."

"She is a young woman of courage and openness, of honor and integrity. One who speaks truth. One who survives on a shard of hope so fine that she does not feel hopeless."

That did not sound encouraging. "Why choose her if she has so little hope, so little faith?"

A droll smile nudged Her lips before J'Hi-inti replied, "Because the woman does not believe in miracles."

Stunned, Zukaltay stared at J'Hi-inti. Gathering her wits, she managed, "Are you saying it will take a miracle from this woman to redeem the Wysotti?"

"I imagine it will take quite a few."

The Wysotti were doomed. No. Foolish thinking. J'Hi-inti had decreed chaos rule, allowing the free will of Her creations — Doyon and Wysotti alike — to write their own destinies. Trouble was, one woman would be responsible for the entire outcome. *One Wysotti woman.* "What is the name of the Wysotti woman you've chosen?"

"She is Darq, Princess of the Misted Moon, first daughter of Pyhanni of the White Grasses — "

"My Darq? My granddaughter!"

J'Hi-inti grinned. Her garment hem began to shimmer, dissolving into a slowly swirling vortex. "A few things must first be put into place. As events unfold, you may observe, Zukaltay, but you are not to interfere, otherwise my original decree of annihilation will be reinstated. Do you understand?"

"Yes. I understand."

In a brilliant flash of sparkling light, J'Hi-inti vanished.

Zukaltay stepped to the console and, with a trembling hand, held the console's edge for support. A moment later, she became aware of Adrada standing in front of her.

"Take heart, Zukaltay," he said.

"Easy for you to say. It's not your granddaughter who will decide the fate of my people."

"Why so little faith in Darq?"

"Darq is Darq. I've never been able to figure her out. Why her? Why would J'Hi-inti choose her?"

"Possibly for that very reason."

"What reason?"

"J'Hi-inti couldn't figure her out. She is, as humans often say, a wild card."

Dread churned the spot where Zukaltay's stomach would have been if she were corporeal.

Adrada handed her the Jewels of the Sky drum. "I believe you have need of this and the East Garden."

She took the drum, noting her hands trembled. "Am I allowed to play it?"

"Anytime you like. The rule banning Wysotti drumming has been rescinded." He turned to leave but stopped. "Remember, you can observe, but you cannot interfere."

She nodded. "Yes, yes, I know."

He leaned forward to whisper into her ear, "Darq remembers you most for your drum playing. She has heard your drumbeats from the very first ones you pounded after arriving here." He stepped away and vanished in a flash of angel-light.

Now why would he tell her that? Zukaltay left the chamber for the walled garden at the far side of the Hall of Redemption. What good did it do for Darq to hear the drumbeats of a spirit-drum? The child had never learned to play a drum—nor any instrument. She couldn't even sing on key or carry a tune.

A memory rose of when Darq was five summers old, standing at the kitchen doorway, witnessing Pyhanni's spiteful words, "Darq was never my choice, mother. You needed a leader for the dyn, and I debased myself to bear her for you. *She's your trophy child.*" Then, in the haughtiest of tones, Pyhanni added, "The daughter I now carry is mine. A child conceived in purest love."

One look at Darq and it had been obvious she understood her mother hadn't wanted her. It took half an hour of sitting on the grass beneath an ancient daoka tree, holding Darq, softly drumming and chanting songs to soothe the child and end her tears.

Arriving at the East Garden, Zukaltay seated herself beneath a young daoka tree and stroked the smooth skin of her drum. The days ahead were going to be a trial, no doubt about that. She stilled her hands. *A period of chaos. One woman. One chance at redemption for the Wysotti.* And the outcome would be totally uncertain because — because Darq was Darq.

Ethereal tears of helplessness blurred Zukaltay's vision. She began to play the *Flowing Waters* rhythm, but the soft beat did not allay her tears nor vanquish a growing sense of doom.

✧ Chapter 3

Azilla Airfield Terminal, planet Wysotti

Atlatl clamped his jaw tight and his molars shattered the round piece of licorice candy. He relished the burst of intense flavor before he pulverized the remaining bits and swallowed. From the molded maroon bench where he sat facing the beige-framed departure boards, he caught the data streaming onto the lower left screen. At last, their flight had been posted. Soon he and Darq would be on their way to the spaceport half a world away. Their leave, such as it had been, was over. As usual, he'd split his leave. Half with his dyn and half with Darq. Only days into his time with Darq, he'd been called back to fleet HQ for a week-long special-ops briefing.

He sighed. He'd spent so little time with Darq, his lovely atan, his sexy wife . . . His thoughts drifted to that morning, dawn at Jooril Bay, the silken feel of her nakedness. He half-drowned in the memory of seawater and the explosive power of his climax. Feeling his penis swell against his fatigues, he silently swore. He needed a distraction. Any distraction.

Looking about, he settled his gaze on the small tan and green floor tiles and began counting the green ones. When he got to twenty-seven, he heard the squelch of fast-approaching spacer's boots.

Darq. She was back. He got to his feet and turned around to meet her, but instead of finding Darq, he beheld Rieeza.

As usual, her fleet fatigues were rumpled, and her rucksack bulged with clothing. A few of her favorite testers and mini-tool kits dangled from the sack's side loops. Though regulation standard, the rucksack had seen hard use. So had Rieeza's hair. Her crop of brown-as-mud curls looked more frayed than frizzed. Which meant frustration had gotten the better of her and she'd repeatedly raked her fingers through her curls.

The closer she came, the more aware he became of the strain lines furrowing her brow, her clenched teeth, her parted lips, her flared nostrils, and her labored breathing. He offered a welcoming smile, one she would realize showed his pleasure in seeing her. Oh, how proud he was of her, his most brilliant and youngest daughter. Yet, even now, when he looked at her, he was also reminded that he would never sire another child. Damn that radiation leak.

Rieeza stopped, her gaze lowering to the center of his chest, checking for his rank yokepiece. She looked relieved that he wasn't wearing it.

Between pants she managed, "Adovee, Father. Am I ever glad I found you. Can I hitch a ride with you and Darq to the spaceport?" She held up her hand to forestall his reply and to take a few breaths.

Typical Rieeza. He tied down the urge to grin and waited.

"Okay, don't scold. Here's how things went. You were right about Wichiwi. She is immature. Horridly immature. Do you know what she did? I'll tell you. Because she didn't want me going back to the spaceport, she erased my wake-up call. I overslept. When I woke and found I'd missed my connecting flight, Mom had me call Cousin Utina—she works here— Somewhere. Anyway. Utina said *Little Bit* had been moved into the refueling queue, but I had no way of contacting you— other than paging—and I know you don't appreciate people knowing a battlestation commander is on deck, and besides, a call would have guaranteed you'd say no." She paused to inhale a noisy, long breath. "I half-killed myself driving Mom's old flycar to get here. Then I jogged all the way from the parking garage to the terminal, and here I am, so please, PLEASE, can I ride with you and Darq to the spaceport?" She sucked in a lungful of air.

How fortunate. Only he must not allow Rieeza to know that. Spoiling her would not do. He rubbed his jaw, feeling the smoothness of his chin, all the while observing Rieeza's discomfort and the desperation darkening her smoky-blue eyes. So, he had been correct in his assessment of Wichiwi. The woman might be four t'uns older than Rieeza but, like Darq's mother, Wichiwi possessed the maturity of one twelve t'uns old. And why was he now comparing those two women?

"Father, if it helps you decide, you can tell me you told me so."

Forbidding any semblance of a smile to nudge the corners of his mouth, he replied, "All right. *I told you so.*"

She sighed. "Why is it I can understand equipment but not people?"

"Because, my daughter, you are an engineer, not a consuleir. You are much more valuable to the fleet as an engineer."

"Yes, well, my value to the fleet is now in jeopardy. Qelsey said if I was one nanosecond late in reporting aboard the *Dujaki*, she'd have the INS dismantled and shipped back to the institute with me in the cargo pod with it."

Good old Qelsey, his XO had a talent for threatening, cajoling, and wheedling the crew into performing their best. She'd told him many times that if Rieeza could respect a clock, follow a timetable, and be mindful of schedules, his daughter might one day become the *Dujaki*'s chief engineer.

"Well, Father? Yes or no? Do I ride with you to the spaceport or not?" She put her hands prayerfully together. "I'll get down on my knees and beg if it'll help."

"A little humility may do you good, Rieeza, but no need. You may accompany us — on one condition."

On her face, delight merged with relief. "What condition?"

"You copilot."

She took hold of her rucksack straps and reset the weight. "You always copilot for Darq. Geez, don't tell me you two had a quarrel."

"Nothing of the sort." He had better explain before she jumped to one of her erroneous conclusions. "Rieeza, HQ ordered me in for a week of briefings. When they concluded, I found flights were cancelled and air traffic grounded because of the Mount Senjo eruption. Have you listened to the news reports?"

Her cheeks turned three different shades of scarlet.

"Obviously not," he muttered.

"But you're here, Father."

"Yes, only because I rented a vehicle and drove all night. I arrived the day before the funeral service. With dyn protocols and the ceremonies of passage, family obligations—" He took a breath. "Look, I'm exhausted. I'm likely to nod off at the controls. If you copilot, you will ensure Darq stays awake."

"Why would she fall asleep? She's been on leave for a full moon cycle and then some."

"She had to handle Zukaltay's funeral arrangements and fend off the news media, not to mention dealing with Pyhanni."

Rieeza frowned. "Are you saying Pyhanni was grief stricken? No way. More likely she was eating up all the media attention and calculating how much her inheritance would be."

"True." More than once, Pyhanni's theatrics before the news people had nearly driven him to throttle her with his bare hands. Images from the reading of the will that morning flickered to mind. He glanced about. Although no one was near, he leaned forward and spoke so only Rieeza could hear him. "At the reading of Zukaltay's will this morning, Pyhanni set a new mark for melodrama and exhibited one helluva temper." Movement behind Rieeza caught Atlatl's eye. He glanced up.

Darq strode through the terminal's side door. Spotting him, she headed his way.

He looked at Rieeza and set his hand on her shoulder so she stayed put. In a low, commanding voice he said, "Darq is coming. Whatever you do, *do not stare at her cheek.*"

"What! Why?"

"Adovee, you two," Darq said before she stopped.

Atlatl released Rieeza, who turned, faced Darq, and grinned a welcome. He almost held his breath, waiting, watching for Rieeza's reaction. She didn't flinch at the sight of Darq's swollen cheek and the welted scratches. Relieved, the tension wafted out of him.

Rieeza spoke cheerily. "Father says I can copilot for you. He wants to sleep en route. That is, if it's okay with you."

Atlatl met the question in Darq's gaze and nodded.

Darq eyed Rieeza. "Sure. No problem. *Little Bit* is on taxiway one west, just outside and to the left." She pointed to the doors she'd just come through.

"Great. Are preflights done?"

Darq nodded. "You'll have to correct the flight plan and file it ASAP."

"No problem, glad to do it."

"Atlatl and I are about to get something to eat. Would you like to join us?"

"No thanks. I'll just stow my gear and get the flight plan updated. See you in the plane." She shifted her rucksack to rebalance it. "Adovee, Father, and thanks. You, too, Darq. Adovee." She strode off.

When she was out of earshot, Atlatl said, "Do you mind a change of copilots?"

"Why should I? We agreed you would nap, and we both know you hate *Little Bit's* seats."

"You built the copilot's chair for a teenager."

The uninjured side of her lips curved into a smile. "I was a teenager when I built *Little Bit*, and I did promise one day to refit it just for you, didn't I?"

He nodded. Military life and the war kept her from that promise.

Darq grinned. "My dearest atan, I have an insatiable desire for a trio of bean-and-maize hand pies. Let's go find some."

As she stepped away, he eyed her cheek. The nanobots in her bloodstream had been hard at work repairing the damage. By the time they got to the spaceport, the cheek might look almost normal. That is, providing Raytor hadn't fouled up the second nanobot dosage like he had the first. The idea that Raytor and Darq would get to know each other over the last half of Darq's leave and decide to bond had seemed a good one. The reality? One of the worst ideas he'd had in t'uns.

As Atlatl followed Darq, his mind drifted back to the reading of Zukaltay's will. When the solicitor handed Darq her inheritance, Zukaltay's rosewood puzzle box, Pyhanni immediately demanded Darq open the box and return Zukaltay's sapphires. Darq had opened the box, revealing it was empty.

Despite the solicitor telling Pyhanni the gemstones once housed in the box had been sold to pay for Zukaltay's medical treatments, Pyhanni didn't believe him.

Darq even explained Zukaltay chose to undergo the treatments so she could complete the negotiations with the Grier Cartels for shipments of ore and supplies for the war effort. Pyhanni became incensed and accused Darq of stealing the jewels. When Darq denied it, Pyhanni's temper erupted. Pyhanni slapped Darq's cheek, hard. As Pyhanni backhanded Darq, the large gemstones of Pyhanni's rings sliced Darq's cheek.

The image of Pyhanni's open hand, raised again for another strike, flared vividly in Atlatl's mind. Darq had grabbed Pyhanni's wrist, stopping the blow and twisting the arm, forcing her mother to her knees, shocking her to silence. Darq's words rang in the deathly quiet of the room. "I have put up with your bitterness, Mother, but no more. I now severe the umbilical cord that kept me thinking I should honor my mother for giving me birth." She released Pyhanni, who sat back on her haunches with enough force to tear the side slit of her designer-made skirt.

Clutching the rosewood box, Darq strode for the door. As the doors opened automatically, Atlatl followed his wife.

Now he again followed his wife, but this time he stepped through the airport terminal's doors and into the noisy hive of the food court. His nostrils quivered with the mouth-watering smells of deep-fried hand pies.

✧ Chapter 4

Aichi Three Fleet Recycling Facility in the Doyon Kungarike

Awareness of the sensation of drifting upward assailed Konuris Ippera. Weightlessness? Had the GFQs failed? Nonsense. The Gravity Flux Quellers never failed on the *Three E.* Yet, this weightlessness seemed heavier, like liquid, like rising through the waters of the lagoon from which he had been spawned.

Now why would he be thinking of his birthing? Weren't disconcerting thoughts a sign of old age? Why think that? He had a sharp mind. He was in the latter half of his prime, not his dotage. *Concentrate.* Yes, he must concentrate. He needed to take stock of his situation, his surroundings, make sense of this darkness and the floating.

He should start with an analysis of the darkness. The optic center of a Doyon brain abhorred darkness. It created its own light show to stave off the terror of the abyss. So, why wasn't there a light show?

Did it make a difference that he had never been particularly frightened of the dark?

What if he were aboard his ship, but it had insufficient power to generate light? Then again, what about the emergency lights? Why had they not activated? Could they have been on long enough for their power to deplete? Still, why did he not spy one pinpoint of light somewhere?

Maybe he should address the weightlessness.

He paused to clear his thoughts and feel. He was rising. No, moving. Difficult to determine precisely in what direction, yet, the sensation was one of weightlessness.

He must be aboard the *Three E*. If that were so, why hadn't he collided with a bulkhead — or something? And where were the sounds? Why no squeals or chirps of orders? Why no cries from the dying or injured? Why no whoosh of air venting into space? Why no buzz of the Madok units automatically patching hull breaches?

The vacuum of space was silent. The dead were always silent.

Was he dead or was everything and everyone around him dead? He strained every sense, probing for clues, lights, sounds. A moment later, the darkness around him yielded to a sallow glow.

His flag ship's AELUs gave off a copper redness. Perhaps the light came from one of those handheld Auxiliary Emergency Light Units. No, they had too small an output range.

A voice chirped, the brief sound frail and so far away it seemed a faint whisper. To his left, he spied a Doyon silhouette, but one with great black wings edged in darkest purple. A black halo crowned the entity.

Was that Auc-Pon the Archangel of Departing Souls, the mighty Ebon F'brig? It befitted a m'chi of rank and title to have the Black Imperial Warrior greet his soul. Provided, of course, he were dying.

Konuris felt himself being swirled about. Bright pinpricks of light burst around him, reminding him of the salvo of DGRBMs from the Wysotti frigate *Hercaal*. That destroyer had flipped upside-down in a close-quarters maneuver across the *Three E's* bow. Wysotti diggerboom missiles had pierced shields, hulls — one went decks deep into the *Three E's* bowels.

In the next instant, all went black.

More drifting.

Drifting.

Drifting.

The darkness again abated. No swirling now. No pinpricks of light. Just a brightening that transformed into the ash grayness of a hospital room — *his hospital room.*

An image coalesced in his mind's eye of that sterile gray room and of Vekka, her peach-yellow eyes looking into his murky topaz ones. Memories flared. Grief had turned her mottled snakeskin cheeks the dullest charcoal gray.

Dear Vekka, mate and mother. She'd served him well. Birthed him nine sons. Three of them now dead in the service of the kungarike, two more about to graduate from the war college—and likely to become corpses. F'brig bred and born to serve the empire, just like he had been.

Vekka's face shimmered and steadied into finer focus. He felt again her tiny hand, the smoothness of her fleshy palm covering his three, gnarled, wasted-to-bone fingers. He stroked his thumb across the back of her hand. Her smooth skin. His leathery and dry. She held on tightly when the death rattle left his chest and his heartbeat silenced. He died in that hospital bed, not from a battle injury but from a disease . . . Vekka kissed his cheek.

By the war god's ass, he had died! So what kept Auc-Pon from greeting his soul and escorting him to Ly'sienia? Or was it true what his officers said behind his back? That his soul had been damned by the legions he had slaughtered? What idiocy. He only followed orders. He killed righteously by those orders.

But that had been ages ago, when he had youthful pride—and arrogance—and the idealism of a true hero-warrior of the kungarike. He'd grown wiser, becoming a m'chi, one who came to understand he had been brainwashed from birth to serve.

He was also a m'chi who endured a humiliatingly tortuous death. Waiting for death had given him time to analyze his life and realize what the kungarike had manipulated him into becoming—and what the kungarike had devolved into.

A shudder overtook his thoughts and alerted him to the chill about his face and head. Then an even colder sensation encircled his neck and shoulders.

Cold did not bode well for any Doyon. Did the cold mean his soul was en route to the dark fathoms of the Ghelmae Trench, that demon-infested wasteland, one of never-ending cold and hunger reserved for the cowardly and depraved? Surely the trench was not for him. No. Never for him!

"Konuris?" The shrill squeak-whistle-wheeze held worry. "Admirid?"

Only one Doyon he knew wheezed like that—Nuzzi, Caprivi Ursk, captain of the *Three E*, who had faithfully served him for eight yils and whom he considered a friend. Friends were hard to come by, and to keep. The war had taken far too many comrades.

"Admirid Ippera, please, sir, answer me."

Desperation in Nuzzi's voice? That was not like the caprivi. Wait. Nuzzi had orders to take the *Three E* to Sector Two for refits. If that was Nuzzi's voice, then Nuzzi's soul must also be en route— Zzraa! *Nuzzi was dead?* How? When? Where?

"Please, sir, say something. Speak to me."

Konuris spoke his mind, his guttural words laced with reprimand. "Very well, Nuzzi, I will speak. When did you die? And *you had better not have taken my flagship down with you.*"

A cacophony of cheering whistles and chirps ensued before a female voice shrilled with authority, "Silence! Attend your posts."

All quieted. Then The Voice ordered, "Caprivi Ursk, continue reviving him."

Him? No one addressed Konuris Ba'dawl Ippera, Tor of Longbao, Admirid of the Fourth F'brig Stellar Fleet as HIM. *No one.*

A young female's clearly enunciated words came from a distance behind him. "Adrenalin levels on the rise."

A disquieting whisper flitted through Konuris's mind. What if he had not died? For the love of Auc-Pon, why would they revive him? He specified no medical interference or life support. Had Vekka—? No, she would never disobey him.

The young female chirped, "Countering. Adrenalin leveling off."

What was happening? Why couldn't he see anything? He listened more acutely. Mingled with the muted cacophony of computer ticks, pings, and humming came the chirps and squeaks of six distinct, but unfamiliar, male voices.

"My admirid," Nuzzi said, "I am not dead." His words held an undertone of anxiety. "The *Three E* is neither damaged nor destroyed. I have served you for many yils. You know I would never lie to you. The truth is—" He inhaled noisily, as if to fortify himself. "Admirid, you are dead—but *your brain lives on to serve our beloved kungarike.* I'm told you can easily serve another fifty yils. You will be a legend of legends."

The brain lives? Serve fifty more yils? Was Nuzzi insane? No. This entire conversation was insane.

Your brain lives on to serve whispered and echoed twice in Konuris's mind, and uncertainty nibbled like a katachin scavenging a beefy eomas carcass. Could it be possible that his brain lived on?

"Do not think me a fool, Nuzzi." Konuris heard the metallic twang in his voice, a voice not possessing the gruffness he intended. "I died. I stopped breathing. My heart stopped beating. I am dead. Quite dead."

"Not entirely true, sir. That is, you are correct, you did die, but— Do you remember telling me you had pictured a glorious death in service to the kungarike?"

With a sensation like drowning in clammy, cold quicksand, Konuris remembered that bedside conversation. He had said such nonsense because Nuzzi, like all lowborn protars, had been indoctrinated to believe Doyons lived and died to serve. It was the Doyon way.

By the war god's ass, this conversation was maddening!

Maybe not.

Could Auc-Pon be testing him? Hadn't he listened to the clerics espouse that the Archangel of Departing Souls often challenged a warrior before judging his soul fit to enter Ly'sienia's quiet lagoons—or be damned to the trench? Perhaps it would be best to assume this was a test and show himself a true F'brig, one eminently worthy of paradise. "I believe my exact words, Nuzzi, were that no greater honor befell an officer of the fleet than to die in service to the kungarike. However, I also said that to die abed, slain by a decimating cancer of one's bone marrow, was abhorrent."

"True enough, sir. True enough." Nuzzi's voice took on a proud, guttural note. "Your body is gone, but your brain lives,

Admirid. You live. And your desire to serve the kungarike with honor is at hand."

The self-assurance in Nuzzi's voice made Konuris flinch with revulsion. Death had been a godsend, the end of his service to the kungarike. It was outrageous to expect him to serve the kungarike again. No, no. Not possible. "*Zzraa!* Nuzzi, what are you talking about? Explain!"

"My admirid, within minutes of your death, a team of surgeons removed your brain and brought it here, to Aichi Three."

"A recycling center?" Damn the war god, he had been recycled.

"More than a recycling center, Admirid. Beneath the complex is a top secret R and D facility." Nuzzi spoke more rapidly. "Do not lament your passing. It was honorable. Your body was cremated, your ashes poured into the Roulag de F'brig Fountain. It was truly a most lavish funeral service. Full honor guard. Why, even the Hibizahn came. His speech glorified your service."

The supreme leader of the Doyon people had come and spoken at his funeral? Yet, his brain—

"Belay that nattering, Nuzzi. Why was my brain removed?"

"To become part of the future. Part of the greatest warship ever built. For weeks now, sir, you have been kept in a coma to allow the neural net to grow. Today all the links are operational and in place. *You have been resurrected.*"

Resurrected. *Resurrected?* NO! "I am dreaming that I am awake, but I am actually quite dead. And I object, Auc-Pon, to your tarrying in your duty to judge my soul and send me to Ly'sienia."

Nuzzi sputtered, but his stammerings were eclipsed by varied chirps and squeals coming from every direction. The Voice boomed and issued rapid commands mixed with a gibberish of terminology. In an instant, clicking of switches and protocol call-outs came as rapid as Stinger spacecraft off launch rams, with answering salvos by The Voice.

The fog parted around Konuris, and he found he had a one-hundred-eighty-degree view of his surroundings. Five Doyons wore antiseptic-white med-lab tunics with long sleeves, the cuffs tight about their wrists. The tunics' mandarin collars sported rank pips and caste slashes—all military medical corps. Each manned an array of monitor stations that filled the walls from floor to ceiling. Nearby, a narrow aisle separated him from a closed double-door hatch.

He was not on his magnificent *Three E*, nor on any Doyon ship. Nor in a hospital.

Sounds began to waft into escalating whisperings. To his left, a hushed argument between Nuzzi and The Voice ensued. Konuris went to turn, but he couldn't move. He strained to hear.

Something about keeping him alive without killing him?

In a gravelly bellow, The Voice ordered, "Everyone to the conference room. Now." A pause. "Except you, Ooots. You will monitor Ippera's vitals and keep him stabilized."

"As you command, Har Chingvee."

So, The Voice belonged to a doctor named Chingvee. And the soft female voice belonged to Ooots.

Ooots . . . Where had he heard that name? Ah, yes, ooots—his wife's favorite flower. Had the technician been named for that old-world swamp lily? Flashing to mind came one of the giant, lime-green lilies and its spidery plumes of outer petals.

With the loud, shushing closure of the hatch doors behind the last of the exiting horde, the image of the flower vanished and Konuris welcomed the silence. Not total silence. Computers and circulation fans droned like tiny swamp flies. From behind him came the clickety-click of switches and key taps. Was that Ooots? He swung his head toward the sound, but his head didn't move. Instead, vibrations assailed him and momentarily blurred his vision. He moved—mechanically. Slowly.

He gazed at the equipment coming into his line of sight, but he didn't have the clarity of focus to discern what the panels and their colorful spiking and winking dots or lines revealed. One unit's large red placard bore a stenciled NUTRITANK. The next, a larger, mirror-black unit reflected bands of twinkling lights circling a golden bust. That bust sat in the center of a meter-wide, matte, silver-and-black disk, sans lights. Bust and disk balanced on a half-meter-wide cylindrical pedestal.

Shifting his gaze, he stared at the golden sculpture, a classic Doyon visage.

The vibrations stopped. He stopped moving.

He focused on the bust's face. The usual chiseled bony structure of a male Doyon with the usual three nostril holes at the top of the snout. Although there was a masculine crest ridge running from forehead to nape, it looked narrower than average, and the mounded tips on the crest lacked a virile breeder's spikes. But what were those black spots on the bust? He blinked hard trying to clear his vision. When he blinked a third time, he saw a black speaker bar separated the upper and lower lips and a pair of small, glassy-black optical lenses stood in for the bust's eyes.

Into clearest focus came the welted scar that ran across the left slash of an eyebrow and angled back to the top of the left ear-hole. A forever reminder of a slip of a Wysotti girl's attempt to kill him —

Him?

He was looking at a likeness of himself!

Ping.

"Oh, no." Ooots' voice came from close by. "Please, sir — " Her voice squeaked octaves higher. "Don't panic!"

Ping.

He never panicked. Yet, as he stared at the macabre gold bust of himself, and knowing for a certainty his brain was encased in that golden sarcophagus, a trembling terror raced over every nerve fiber. His gaze lowered on the reflection to the base of the neck where a wide gold collar bore the raised reliefs of his admiral's starbursts, service insignias, military service slashes, and even his medals of honor and the glyphs of his noble-house and F'brig titles.

A collar. He wore a collar. Slaves wore collars. By the war god's ass! *He had become the slave of the kungarike.*

He stared at his reflection. Horror yielded to revulsion, and anger sparked to life the blood-fury lust to kill, only he had no body to carry out his rage.

Ooots stepped in front of him, blocking his view of his golden image.

She stood eye to eye with him. "Please, sir, do not panic. Calm yourself, or you'll trigger every alarm in this place, and they'll sedate you." Her voice nearly whined, "Your brain, the neural net, they might be damaged. You have to stay conscious a while longer."

He eyed her, or rather the optics he had for eyes focused on her young face. Her slender, arched brows were pinched with anguish. Anxiety shimmered across her mother-of-pearl skin and mirrored in her hazel-yellow eyes. Even her demure crest ridge seemed to quiver with dread.

"Please, sir. Please remain calm."

Didn't she realize he was helpless? At the mercy of scientists who cared only for the achievement of —? Of what?

Ooots' eyes glossed with unshed tears. She bit her thick, pointed thumb nail and held it for a few seconds before releasing it. "Please, Admirid, can you not compose yourself?"

Could this young female truly care about him? His eyes refocused, magnified her face, studied it, and found genuine concern. His thoughts raced. She had the right of it. He needed to be calm, in control — and to take control of himself. More importantly, he had to take control of the situation. "Ooots?"

"Yes, Admirid?"

"I do not panic. I was merely . . . *startled by my reflection.*"

She turned and glanced at the tank behind her. "Oh, yes, I see. Quite. Yes, of course." She faced him with a smile gracing her fine lips and revealing tiny sharp teeth. "No problem."

No problem? Idiot!

Then he remembered his father saying, *If there is a problem, there is always a solution.*

The most pressing problem at this moment was not knowing what was going on. Ooots could be an asset to gaining knowledge about this place, his condition, the truth of why he was here. Indeed, she could be a valuable asset. So, what should he do? Ah, yes, say something lighthearted. "In truth, Ooots, I could use a stiff drink. Mavriss, if you have any. Double up." It pleased him that his words came out lightly, if not softly.

"Oh, yes. Of course." She scurried to the right and out of his view.

What an odd reaction. He turned his head, and the banded disk he set on rotated so his gaze followed her. This time the vibrations did not affect his sight.

She slid onto a stool. With lithe fingers, she touched various spots on the large holograph screen.

He felt the kick of the liquor. The punch of sizzling fire ignite in his nonexistent veins. To her back, he said, "Ooots, how is it possible for my brain to ingest alcohol?"

She swung about and faced him. "Actually, it's not alcohol, sir. It's the synthetic chemical equivalent. It only required adding the mix to your biofeeds." Her face blanched. "Oh, pus!"

He would have laughed at that childish form of profanity had it not been for the whitening of her muzzle. "Ooots, what is the matter?"

She swallowed hard enough to flex the mandarin collar of her tunic. "Har Chingvee would never approve."

"I shall not tell."

She minutely shook her head. "The computers record the changes I make. If Har Chingvee reads it—" She almost gasped. "I'm doomed!"

"Nonsense. I will handle Chingvee." He had much to handle, and he would start now by aligning friends and identifying foes. "Ooots, summon Caprivi Ursk to me. Him and only him."

"But—"

"That is an order." Was he still able to give orders? "I am Admirid Konuris Ba'dawl Ippera, am I not?"

"You are, sir. Yes, sir. By your command, sir." She swiveled her stool around, then tapped a node on her desktop. "Captain Ursk, the admirid has ordered your presence—and only yours. He said at once, sir."

Konuris turned himself to face the hatch, noting that his bust-brain moved faster than the edge of the disk. Glancing down, he found he was centered on two independently moving disks. Why two? He needed information. He needed answers. Starting with the most pressing—Nuzzi's claim that he, Korunas Ippera, could serve another fifty yils as an enslaved brain.

But he must be vigilant, quick witted, and resourceful in how he garnered information. Someday, somehow, he would find a way to liberate himself and make those who did this to him pay dearly. Oh, yes, by the war god's ass, they all would pay dearly for resurrecting him.

✧ Chapter 5

Dujaki Battlestation

Darq stepped out of the turbolift and into the pilot's ready room, trying to ignore the clinking of her flightsuit's fittings, fasteners, and harness rings striking one another. One step later came the buoyant sensation of lesser gravity, which made her, the armored-vac flightsuit she wore, and the helmet she carried in her right hand, weigh half as much. Even the braids she'd plaited her hair into seemed to lift up, hovering a couple of millimeters away from her ears.

She paused and glanced about. Two dozen fighter pilots stood on their parked Na-ka-ta's wheelbases. Oh, how she missed riding a wheelbase. Well, maybe today luck would provide her with a worthy copilot. On this routine mission, she'd been given a possible copilot candidate, a Na-ka-ta named Phrys who held the rank of luten.

She turned her attention to the status board on the far wall. When half a dozen lights on the board flashed green, a half-dozen Na-ka-ta treads rumbled softly across the grate flooring. The automatons carried their pilots under the archways that led to the flight marshaling area platforms.

Darq checked the status board and found amber lights for her four-squad. The top bar bore their code name for today, ZEPHYR. The lines below listed the group's pilot identifiers and names—RAVEN Darq, CHANCE Jaqui, PEPPER Kunii, and MISTY Fahnia.

Seeing a familiar mop of kinky-curly short hair, Darq found Misty standing on El'gee's base, chatting with Pepper, who stood on Roq's base. Misty would fly the left-wing position. As for Pepper, she was fond of peppering Strikers up close and personal with short-range keg fire. Which was good because Pepper would cover the squad's asses.

From behind Darq came Chance's sultry voice. "Yoi, Raven."

Darq turned. Her roommate and best friend stood aboard Izzt. Following safety procedures, the Na-ka-ta's arms encircled Chance's waist, holding her in place. When Izzt halted, Darq took in Chance's shaggy, short, raven-black hair and wispy bangs that touched her dark brows. Chance's natural beauty always seemed at odds with the tenacity with which she flew. She also had the distinction of being among only a half-dozen pilots who could keep up with Darq's maneuvering. That's why Chance flew the right-wing position.

Chance's dark eyes flashed with merriment. She covertly wagged her gloved thumb to the right. "I think," she whispered, "what you're looking for is in yonder corner."

In that corner stood a Na-ka-ta wearing a blue and black, standard flight harness. He held a silver-gray cap in his left appendage.

Darq kept her voice low. "Is he Luten Phrys?"

By the tilt of Chance's head, she held a telepathic conversation with her Na-ka-ta. "Izzt says he's never met Luten Phrys. Oh, gotta go. We're up." Izzt's treads activated, and he sped for the nearest archway.

Darq took a deep breath. Might as well check out the Na-ka-ta. She strode for the corner and halted in front of the automaton. "Seeing that you don't have a pilot on board, I'm pretty sure what you're holding is for me. I'm Qtl-shi Darq. Raven."

His globe-shaped head angled downward, and she looked at her reflection in his faceplate. "Correct, Qtl-shi Darq. I am Luten Phrys, your copilot for today's patrol."

His soft, even voice held a congenial tone. Maybe that was a good omen, one which boded well for a possible bonding.

Phrys raised the cap, and she stood still while he placed it on her head. By watching the wink of the green lights on the bar across Phrys's chest-plate bib, she knew the moment the cap aligned with the nodes implanted in her skull. A second later came the tingling-hum, and when it cleared, Phrys's voice intoned in her mind, *Testing. One. Two. Three.*

Acknowledged. The volume is fine, Phrys. She waited to see if he would correct her using his name and insist he be address as Luten Phrys.

Qtl-shi Darq, now that we can converse privately, I wish to advise you that I am currently bonded to a pilot. My copiloting for you today is a temporary assignment.

Temporary? How strange. Then again, who was she to question? *Okay, no problem. May I mount?*

Affirmative.

Darq eyed Phrys's wheelbase where foot plates extended. She set her right boot onto the far plate and, in one easy movement, lifted herself up, turned, put her back against his chest, and planted her left boot on the other plate. Short rods twirled up like screws from the plates and into the channels along her boots' insteps. She lifted her arms and helmet. When Phrys's arms came around her waist, she leaned back against his chest. His fingers intertwined, closing the circle about her waist.

Not so tight if you please, she said.

Safety regulations require I hold you securely.

Secure yes, but you're crushing my suit against my diaphragm. Lighten up.

He obeyed, but she had little wiggle room. Darq rested her elbows and forearms on his arms and clutched her helmet between her hands. *Phrys, turn so I can see the board.*

She heard the soft laboring of his base motors engage. When she eyed the board, she spotted the number five-two. The light changed to green. *Our number's lit. Let's go.*

The Na-ka-ta steered a path across the room snaking around clusters of waiting Na-ka-tas and pilots. Once through the archway, Phrys slowed. *Qtl-shi Darq, safety regulations require you have your helmet on.*

I'll put it on in the airlock.

Regulations forbid me to enter the airlock with you aboard until all safety protocols are satisfied. Unless you comply by putting your helmet on, I must stop here. He stopped three meters from the airlock door.

Shitfire, she'd drawn a stickler for regs. But Phrys was temporary, only for today's flight. Better to go along and get along. *Okay. All right.*

Taking care not to disturb the neural-net cap, she tucked first her left and then her right braid behind her ears and down into the space between her leechsuit's crew neck and the pliable, spongy, protective flightsuit collar. After donning her helmet, the flightsuit's connecting rings locked around the helmet's base. She triggered the midnight-blue faceplate to descend and lock in place. As soon as the menu flashed, she eyed the icon, engaging the faceplate's virtual view mode, which allowed her to see the environment outside her suit in real time and with the existing lighting. Yet, no one could see her behind the midnight-blue faceplate.

A second later, she inhaled the metalicness of canned air being filtered through her suit. Next came the sensation of being wrapped in a thermal blanket, which was followed by cooling from the undergarment next to her skin. That leechsuit sucked away trapped body heat and sweat.

She eyed the inside of her helmet's faceplate. A tiny green square in the upper left corner indicated her suit functioned properly.

A menu icon appeared, but the tiny green square did not vanish.

A matching signal should have activated somewhere among the Na-ka-ta's monitoring systems for her and her suit. So why hadn't the Na-ka-ta moved? *Phrys, my helmet's on. Suit light is green — *

Affirmative, and thank you for your cooperation. The automaton moved forward.

A meter from the airlock doors, Darq glimpsed lights above the threshold twinkle from red to amber to green. The door snicked open. Once inside, the doors closed, and as the lift descended, the gravity compensators hummed to match the gravity of the exit level.

Qtl-shi Darq, may I speak frankly?

Yes. And my name is Darq, Raven when in the cockpit. Save the rank for protocols and when regs require it.

As you wish, Darq. I want you to know I did not volunteer for this assignment. I was ordered to serve you today.

Why such disdain in his voice? *Who ordered you to be my copilot?*

Majorn Varree. She was emphatic that fighters must patrol our borders. Spacecraft require pilots and Na-ka-tas.

Varree had said the same to her when she'd asked why she'd been assigned so soon after returning from leave.

Phrys's voice took on a bitter tone. *Since I am a qualified copilot and you were in need of a copilot, she ordered me to fly with you today.*

Varree was a crusty old majorn most of the time, but hadn't Phrys said he was bonded to a pilot? *Phrys, why would you have to be ordered to fly with me if you're already bonded to a pilot?*

Because the majorn believes I will change my mind about remaining bonded to Lingit.

Why did the name Lingit sound familiar? Ah— Squeeze Lingit. *I take it Squeeze is on leave?*

She is not. She is ill.

How ill? And from what exactly? Blunt as ever and far too curious by half. Would Phrys take offense?

She is ill. His even tone came shored up with personal resolve. *Lingit was exposed to toxic smoke, the result of an accident that occurred while maintenance repaired a biofeed line running along the back of her quarters.*

When'd that happen?

Two moons ago.

Two moons? *Oh, right! I remember. A fire. It sent two pilots to sick bay.*

Affirmative.

Surely both have recovered by now.

Lingit's roommate is back on duty. Lingit developed pneumonia and suffered an adverse reaction to the antibiotics. She is recovering.

Which begged the question of how badly damaged were Lingit's lungs? And did Phrys have a reasonable hope Lingit would recover and fly again? *Phrys, did D'ktr Enyeto say how long it would be before Lingit returned to active duty?*

Enyeto only says Lingit is making daily progress. His words seethed with frustration. *It is difficult enough having Majorn Varree assign me to flight duty, but to pair me with someone like you – I apologize, please disregard my last comment. I meant no disrespect.*

That's a tad hard to do. Partly because she was curious and partly because working with an unhappy Na-ka-ta in the cockpit could spell death in a dogfight. *Look, Phrys, I'll be the first to say I'm not perfect, so be honest with me. What bothers you most about flying with me?*

You are extremely finicky.

Finicky? Her? *In what way?*

You have currently refused four Na-ka-tas for bonding.

Yes, she had. *Compatibility is a necessity to me when flying my fighter. It's not easy finding a partner.*

According to Majorn Varree, your reason for refusing all copilots was – and I quote – 'unsuitable due to irreconcilable differences of opinion.'

Okay, so if she were being honest with herself, she used that excuse so it wouldn't reflect badly on the Na-ka-tas. The four she'd passed on had been good copilots, but they quibbled over her piloting decisions. Well, some days in the cockpit, not even she understood why she decided what she decided. Oh, to have a Na-ka-ta copilot as good as J.

A memory winked with the red glow of emergency lighting, of J grabbing her, holding her tight, shielding her from lethal shrapnel.

The lift doors snapped open and the bright lights of the platform forced Darq to shunt away the memories.

Phrys wheeled out of the lift and onto 'the ledge,' a balcony that spanned the central hub of this section of the battlestation's flight deck. She gazed out into the area below.

In that immense bay, fifty-eight V-shaped Pytak fighters parked wingtip to wingtip. Melded into the rumbling of several fighters' doige engines were the whup-whups of giant fans extracting heat and circulating air, as well as the putter-purr of tow-vehicle drones hauling fighters from parking slots into airlock chambers.

Strident bleeps warned of airlock doors closing. Over those airlocks, a myriad of lights glittered, banks of lights flashed signals, and strobe lights twinkled their messages and their warnings. Nearby the mellower tones of an airlock horn signaled the door opening, ready for another plane to enter. On the other side of the airlock came the vibrations of fighters being ram-launched into space.

In Darq's mind a blip sounded, notifying her that Phrys had linked to the flight command center. Soon he would be communicating with a crewmember or a Na-ka-ta for preflight and launch. She looked about and saw no line waited at pickup station C. With a rapid blink of her left eye to the faceplate menu, she cued the deck layout. Her fighter was parked near the center of the bay. Cable-lift C would get her to the *Ky*. A new screen winked on. Without being asked, Phrys had switched on the cable-lift graphics, which showed a pilot-lift coming toward them. Various check-off lists began scrolling.

With the completion of the main list, a green pinprick of light winked on her screen. Phrys moved forward and into alignment with a moving lift. As the lift's safety cables and lines dropped, connecting to Phrys's harness, then hers, light after light on two other checklists began winking green.

Phrys's hold about her waist tightened a second before the last pinpricks flashed. The lift motor engaged, moving the two of them forward and over the balcony edge, swiftly descending, taking them over the empty slots of fighters that had already departed. She peered down at her squad's three planes, all with canopies closed. One blue-striped tow vehicle pulled the *Zopa*, Chance's fighter, toward the airlocks. Two other tow vehicles backed and quickly locked onto Misty's and Pepper's fighters.

With a hiss, the lift's brakes engaged, slowing her and Phrys to a stop over the *Ky*. Lights flashed on Darq's faceplate indicating the lift's connections had released from her harness. Another light indicated Phrys had released her boot screws. Looking over her boot tips, she found the *Ky's* open cockpit. She was perfectly aligned to slide into the pilot's seat.

Phrys's fingers parted, releasing their hold about her waist, and his arms opened.

Darq stepped forward, off the boot plates, but instead of dropping to her seat, she was jerked back and stopped hard enough that her safety harness straps dug deep. She scrambled and got her feet back on Phrys's foot plates. "Shitfire! What happened?"

Phrys replied calmly, "You did not give the command for me to release your safety lines from the lifter. Safety protocols five one two seven, paragraph ten point nine six point two requires a verbal command be given by the pilot to the copilot—"

Darq muttered a few expletives and then took a calming breath. "Okay, let's try this again. Release for drop. On the count of three, I will step off."

"Affirmative."

"One. Two." Trying to ignore the little voice in her mind whispering she would be jerked back again, she said, "Three," and stepped off. She dropped into her cockpit, her butt thumping gently into the contoured seat. She recalled the next safety protocol. "I'm down. Secure. Release tether."

A click assured her the last safety line had released.

"Tether away and all clear," Phrys responded.

Behind her, on the other side of the panel separating pilot and copilot, she felt the thudding impact of Phrys's wheelbase on the *Ky*'s deck. A rapid pop of latches locked him from the thighs on down in his turret. The turret hummed and it spun him around, giving him access to the instruments and controls that filled every millimeter of the copilot's chamber.

Darq slipped her gloved hands into the tunnels on her seat's arm rests and clutched the balls beneath her palms. A second later, the tips of her fingers tingled, which they always did when the jacks activated, interfacing through the gloves' micro fibers to link her with the fighter's control network. She slid her feet all the way home into the foot wells where latches locked her boots to the *Ky*'s guidance systems. Her seat vibrated, activating, cradling to form-fit to her. Next came the *fffst fffst fffst* of connections inserting themselves into the sockets on her suit. Finally, the links of the neural cap plugged her into the *Ky*'s cockpit controls and Phrys's station. Since the cap's transmission speed was not as fast as if she were bonded to a Na-ka-ta, she made a mental note to take that into consideration while flying.

She activated the icon on her faceplate for an exterior view from the *Ky*'s various hull optics. For a few long seconds, the faceplate went blank. Then, as if there were clear glass between her and the world outside the *Ky*, she had multiple views of the bay. On the side edges of her faceplate, she cued checklists and data screens. By the dozens, Phrys went down the list of systems' checks and pinpricks of light switched from amber to green.

The canopy checklist popped into place. Overhead, the *Ky*'s shields and canopy began to close. The second after they locked in place, pitching her cockpit into blackness, she heard the copilot's canopy latch and Phrys's, "Canopies closed. Locks engaged. All secure."

Indicators on her faceplate verified the canopies were spaceworthy. She breathed in the drier, cooler air of the plane's systems. Another set of screens and lights at the top right winked onto her faceplate with a yellow light on the missile bay. "Phrys, what's the delay with the rack check?" She continued systematically going down the checklists.

"No problems. The new protocols take twenty seconds longer then before."

The light winked green on the missiles, then the kegs, and finally the 9EXSRs,the small thistle rockets.

"Okay, Phrys, my boards say we are good to go. Clear us with deck control ASAP."

"Affirmative." A moment later came, "Tow vehicle ready to attach."

When the tow vehicle connected, the *Ky* lurched. The engine start-up sequence checklists appeared on Darq's faceplate and a second later, with all lights green, Phrys said, "Zephyr Lead, we are cleared for taxi to the airlock. Start your engines."

"Affirmative. Activating engines." The *Ky*'s doige engines purred to life. On her faceplate, screens winked off, replaced by new screens. Through the optical viewers, she watched the *Ky* towed into and through an airlock. Once the tow vehicle aligned the *Ky* on the launcher, Darq gripped the guidance system balls under her palms. She cued the GNCS, and the guidance and navigation control systems came alive on her screen, followed by the STS, the star-tracker system. "Phrys, on my mark, revving engines for launch."

Phrys sharply replied, "Negative. Safety protocols require the tow vehicle be in the safety zone before increasing power for launch."

Damn the regs. With gritted teeth, Darq watched and waited. When the tow vehicle entered the white line of the zone behind the *Ky*'s port side and the lights winked all clear, she revved the *Ky*'s engines.

A series of lights signaled the launcher had engaged beneath the *Ky*. She took a long draw on the oxygen flowing through her helmet and fought the anxiety and excitement that increased with each digit of the countdown to zero.

The *Ky* went hurling down the flight deck.

The ever-increasing speed surrounded Darq with ambient noise and pressure until she was flung out into the vastness of space. Once clear of the battlestation, she hit full power to the *Ky*'s engines. Minutes later, she joined her squadronmates and led them away from the *Dujaki*. She accessed a rear view where the *Dujaki*, its shape like two small frame drums stacked one on top of the other, quickly diminished and vanished in the starscape.

Phrys sent a display onto her screen and said, "Course laid in for Joiz SOA."

"Acknowledged." She switched screens to a star map of the sector and saw the pip line up on the course. She set the autopilot. A boring, routine flight lay ahead. She sighed and switched optical views to gaze at the beauty of the star-blanketed heavens. A bright star drew her gaze. Stars were nurseries of life. Asteroids the graveyards of what never came to life. The Joiz station was a bit of both. What an odd thought.

An image of the Joiz surveillance and observation array station flitted to mind. The station had been placed on the far side of a break, known as The Narrows, in the Cypha-wee-ka Asteroid Belt. The Joiz had originally been a way station to Wysotti trade centers. Now the asteroids were both barrier and border between the Wysotti territory and the Doyon Kungarike. The Joiz station was also the last operating array spying on the Doyons. Being as far as could be from the Doyon homeworld, the station mostly watched trade-ship movements. Now and then its scanners glimpsed military ships en route to or from planets in the kungarike.

Scuttlebutt abounded that someday the Doyons would capture the Joiz Station and, en masse, come through The Narrows. The Doyons would then attack the *Dujaki,* proceed to take the Talragon depot, then *Ziital* battlestation. If that happened, nothing would be left to protect the Wysotti homeworld.

The soft beat of Zukaltay's drum broke through Darq's thoughts. A familiar rhythm. One of Grandmother's more emphatic ones.

But why those drumbeats now?

And just why was she letting her thoughts wander? Better pay attention to business. She checked various screens on her faceplate. All normal. Over the course of the next hour, the muted drumbeats haunted at the back of her mind.

A proximity alarm went off, startling Darq. She instinctively took manual control of the *Ky* and eyed her screens. Chance, on her right, had come within six meters of the *Ky.* Before Darq could issue a command, Chance's voice came over the com, "Sorry about that, Raven." Chance backed off.

In the ensuing hours, over the squadron's common frequency, chit-chat and poignant quips along with jokes eased the boredom of the flight. A blip noted the passing of another signal buoy, which would relay their position back to the *Dujaki.* Soon her faceplate's nav-screen winked, the grid highlighting the pumpkin. That rotund asteroid had a girth thirty times the *Ky*'s length, with light-colored mineral veins running up and down its dark-gray, gnarled surface. The pumpkin marked the entrance to The Narrows.

Zukaltay's drumbeats became louder and louder, the pounding strident and annoying.

"Raven," Phrys said, "why are you accelerating?"

Darq eyed her speed indicator. She had unintentionally increased speed. Not like her. Chalk it up to the drumming gnawing at her nerves. "We're fine, Phrys. I've flown faster."

"I wish to arrive whole and undamaged at the Joiz station. Safety protocols—"

"Enough with the protocols. If you don't throttle back on them, I might consider ejecting you to save my sanity."

"You cannot eject me. I am too valuable an asset to this aircraft and to you."

"Don't bet on it." She immediately regretted her words. Before she could utter an apology, another screen winked on her faceplate. Into the squad's comlink she said evenly, "Zephyr squad, single file." She watched a screen show the squad reform into single file. "On my mark, the time to turn is thirty seconds. Mark." When her countdown hit zero, she rolled the control balls beneath her fingers, adjusting the level with her foot controls, and made a crisp turn into The Narrows.

A comlink node flashed that she had entered the blackout zone. Neither the Joiz Station nor the *Dujaki* could read the squad's telemetry in The Narrows because of the makeup of the asteroids. It also meant not being able to pick up the Joiz beacon and home in on it. The squad was flying deaf, but the STS held them true to the course.

The drumming in her head abruptly ceased.

Darq heaved a sigh of relief. Silence, blessed silence. She did a routine check of her screens. Her squad followed, their spacing and speed consistent. Hours later, the first faint blinks of the Joiz beacon appeared on her screen. A large blip soon represented the Joiz station—dead ahead. Right on course, and her squad was right on time.

Leaving The Narrows, the *Ky* entered clear space, albeit flanked behind and on both sides by the asteroids.

"Raven," Phrys said, "contact made with Joiz tower."

"Acknowledged." Soon she would lead her squad in a single pass around 'the pincushion,' so called because of the Joiz station's dense collection of dish and rod arrays protruding from its egg-shaped hull.

Something flashed at the lower side of her faceplate. She looked at the blue pip. The ID scrolled into place—a Pytak fighter, one of four she and her squad had come to relieve. That fighter streaked out from behind a pockmarked asteroid.

How odd. Maybe not. Rooky pilots sometimes practiced darting in and out of the asteroids. She loved to do it when bored with the forever circling of the Joiz Station.

Behind the blue pip burst tiny red blips indicating the onslaught of a Doyon Striker's fang-rounds being blasted at the Pytak fighter. A larger red blip soon appeared, indicating the position of the pursuing Striker.

Darq's pulse surged. She cued a sector screen enlargement. Both Pytak and Doyon were coming toward Darq at max speed.

A dozen more red blips winked onto her screen where Strikers now emerged from various locations along the edge of the asteroids. One Striker surged forward and fired two copper-headed missiles at the Joiz station.

Oh shitfire!

✧ Chapter 6

Tokoray reset his visual sensors to ignore the reflection of his Na-Ka-ta face in the long viewport window of the superfreighter *Xultan Uxmatl*. Increasing his visual magnification brought the behemoth *Dujaki Battlestation*, often called The Dragon Lady, into sharp focus. Like a blessing, a sense of well-being enveloped him. He was finally here. At his new posting. The chance to regain honor.

The *Xultan Uxmatl* pitched downward, moving slowly and ever closer for docking. Tokoray tabbed the control on his environmental station. The turret his leg shaft stood locked into softly hummed, moving degree by slow degree until he stopped it. He viewed the *Dujaki's* flight deck and the massive, black, yawning portal of one of its two outgoing launchways.

Zooming out of the portal came one, then another Pytak fighter. Both burned engines and banked to port, then vanished from view.

Sensory memories flickered. He again felt the sensation of a ram-launch's thrust, the invigorating surge of doige engines, and the exhilarating acceleration of speeding into star-spangled space. What he wouldn't give to once again fly as a copilot.

Every pilot that flies with you ends up dead. The harsh, echoing voice of Na'zeakan sizzled through his brain, followed by her cousin Yasalan screaming, *You're a jinx!* In their grief, the two women had damned him and branded him a jinx.

But was he truly a jinx?

No. Wrong thinking. He was Na-ka-ta. An officer, a yojii. Soon he would begin his duties as the *Dujaki's* new Chief Flight Instructor and regain his reputation.

Lights winked on the *Dujaki*'s port side signaling the *Xultan* to stop and swing about, shifting so its main cargo doors were in line with the docking target on the *Dujaki*. Two cravlers approached. The tug-shuttles would finesse the freighter into dock, and crews would unload Pytak fighters along with supplies and ammunition.

Tokoray swept his visual sensors to the lower part of the *Dujaki*, pausing briefly to read the name *Marouser,* which was visible on the stern of the larger of the two Grier haulers.

Griers. Unconventional nomads who navigated the solar byways, mining the wealth of the universe. Merchants. Traders. Welcome because they had sounded the alarm of that first Doyon attack fifteen t'uns ago on the Wysotti's Qusaquit trade center.

"Well, what do you think of her?" came the raspy voice of Kaax Lek-lel.

He turned his turret to face the commander. "Once again you have managed to sneak up behind me."

"I try my best." A smile nestled at the corners of her thin, old lips. Impeccably dressed in a standard-issue mauve-and-gray fleet shipsuit and with her gray hair bobbed short, she was more regal than any other kaax he had ever met.

"Now answer the question," she said. "What do you think of the *Dujaki?*"

"The battlestation looks exactly like the *Ziital,* which is to be expected since they are sister stations of the same design. Same construction. Painted the same gunmetal gray."

Kaax Lek-lel chuckled. "My dear Na-ka-ta, they may look alike from the outside, but ah, the inside? Look." She pointed to the lower corner of the viewport where signal lights flashed along the *Dujaki*'s hull indicating docking of the *Xultan Uxmatl* had been completed. "Time to go. You too—and that's an order." She turned and strode with elegant ease toward the lift at the far end of the cabin, her spacer's boots barely thumping on the grate decking.

Quickly tabbing controls to release him from his turret's jaws, he powered forward, his treads making a soft zaahing sound on the grating.

Hours later, aboard the *Dujaki*, logged-in, quarters assigned, and orientations uploaded to his memory banks, Tokoray turned off a wide corridor, slowed, and then paused before the door to Majorn Varree's office, his new commanding officer. By the bright stars, let her be as open-minded as he had been led to believe.

He sent a data blip out through the disk-cap comlink on the crown of his head. The blip identified him and requested entry. A tiny light on the narrow black strip over the door frame lit in acknowledgment. With a muted wheeze of air, the door's pressure seals released and the door slipped aside. He entered, the door snicking closed behind him.

Seeing a bookshelf wall in front of him, he halted. Crammed behind the unit's protective synthglass doors were vases ranging from tiny pitchers to the centerpiece, a meter-tall, ceramic urn. The urn's shiny, ruby-red surface had been inlaid with a pair of white herons as well as silver and gold cherries. Had he erred? Was this the majorn's quarters and not her office?

A cheery voice came from his left. "Everyone stops to look at my collection."

Turning rapidly, his wheel-treads squelched on the tile floor. What a clumsy mistake to make gawking at knickknacks. The majorn would think him a lowly tyro. He was a yojii, an officer. He must act with officer pride, Na-ka-ta pride, and give a better account of himself.

He focused on the petite woman standing behind a narrow desk where a nameplate on the desktop bore MAJORN ETTA VARREE. He moved toward the space between the two dark-brown chairs in front of the desk. Although he aimed to keep eye contact, instead he looked at the silvery-gray hair at her temples and then to her closely shorn, nappy chocolate-brown hair. She appeared to be much older than her fifty-eight winters.

He stopped and saluted, fisting his right hand, knuckles down, and tapping the spot on his chest where a human heart would be. "Yojii Tokoray, reporting."

She nodded. "So, I see. I am Majorn Varree, but you already know that, after all, this is my office." Her voice and smile held welcome. "Come, come closer and let me have a look at you."

He maneuvered between the chairs and stopped centimeters in front of the desk.

Varree's bright hazel eyes studied him from disk-cap to midnight-blue faceplate and on down to the hem of his pristine tunic—a new tunic. Only why did she frown?

Her head came up, and she made eye contact with him. "I understand from Majorn Kasia that you prefer to be called Tokoray."

"That is true."

"I was told you had multiple doige-whorls, but I don't see them."

Dread crackled through him like a shorted circuit. "My tunic covers the scars, Majorn." He voiced his fear. "May I inquire who told you about the whorls?"

"Kasia did. She and I have no secrets. You see, your former commander and I go back to preschool days. We are more sisters than sisters, despite our postings. And you should know, Kasia lavishly sang your praises. I am ever grateful she decided to part with you." Her smile widened. "For the record, I don't care about the unfortunate circumstances that have befallen you. Aside from the *Dujaki*'s top brass, no one knows anything more than what can be found in your NPRs or in your duty jacket. And speaking of Na-ka-ta Personnel Records . . ." She picked up three data rods from her desktop. "Here are the files on the Na-ka-ta copilots you'll be training as well as those of cadets and pilots who need refreshing, advanced training, and testing. I made a few personal comments on various personalities, which should prove helpful to you." She handed the two longest rods to him.

A quick press of the end of the first rod to the socket terminal at the base of his thumb, and the data rapidly uploaded. He processed the second data rod and returned both rods to her.

"This one—" She handed him the third rod, a short one with a bright-green stripe around the tip. "This is a copy of a project of mine."

He took the rod. "What is the nature of your project?"

Her smile lit up her face. "We have a top-gun here by the name of Darq. Raven is her moniker. Some call her a loose cannon but—if you get my drift—her shots are always on target. Her kill record is envied. She has an uncanny ability for cleverly evading Striker fire. It's the evading part I'm most interested in. If we can figure out what she does, how she does it, and teach other pilots such skills and techniques, it will save lives. I am all for saving pilot lives."

"If you have the onboard data from her fighter—"

"Ah, there's the knot in the thread. Darq tends to come back from a foray with recorders riddled with shrapnel, fried, blasted apart, or crumbled beyond recognition—thus little salvageable data."

"I will do my best to assist you with your project." He hoped his voice carried the right tone of sincerity and willing cooperation. He uploaded the data and returned the rod.

"You also need to view this." She tabbed a control at the edge of the desk. A holograph screen came to life above the middle of her desktop. She touched the corner of the screen with a fingertip and guided the screen around for him to see. The large bold letters of the document's header read NA-KA-TAS QUALIFIED FOR BONDING.

Why did she want him to look at that list?

"Take a closer look," Varree said. "Fourth column, last entry."

He scanned to it and found *Tokoray.*

His name was on the list? For a millisecond, he felt as if all his powersticks had ceased output. "I do not understand."

"Kasia set a condition for releasing you to me. I had to promise to put your name on the list so when you, as you promised, told her you had met me, you could tell her I kept my word."

He was on the list. The list of lists. Wait. "If a pilot should pick me for bonding, you will lose an instructor."

"I know." Her smile morphed into one like a wily fox that held a plump quail in its mouth. "*You are last on the list.* Ahead of you are the best, top-of-the-line Na-ka-ta's. Improved models. Gallant, fearless officers. *And every one has seniority over you.*"

How devious of this majorn. He would be a flight instructor for two t'uns, likely more, slowly gaining seniority and moving up or notching up the list when one of the Na-ka-tas bonded to a pilot.

But did it matter? No. What mattered was being on that list. He could, in time, fly in a fighter as a copilot. Being on that list meant he had choice. He could say yes or no, accept or reject, a pilot. And as the highest-ranking training instructor on the *Dujaki*, he could secretly identify pilots he thought suitable for him to bond with. He could even pick a few good ones, train them and encourage one, the best of the best, to bond with him. Yes, being on the list was a good omen for erasing his past, erasing the stigma of being a jinx.

"One other thing, Tokoray," Varree said. "You have forty-eight hours to become thoroughly familiar with the *Dujaki*, then you begin your duties."

How odd to be allowed so much time. "May I inquire why I am not to go on duty immediately?"

Her grin crunched her cheeks back and the rosy hue of high spirits suffused her face. "I like a Na-ka-ta eager to get to work. However, most of the *Dujaki*'s decks are not laid out the same as her sister station, the *Ziital*, from whence you came."

Kaax Lek-lel's words came back to him—*My dear Na-ka-ta, they may look alike from the outside, but ah, the inside?*

"So far, Majorn," Tokoray said, "I have not encountered differences."

"You soon will. Fact is, a good many of the *Dujaki*'s deck layouts are scrambled. It was Kasia who suggested I give you time to unlearn the *Ziital*'s deck schemes." Varree tabbed a control and the holoscreen vanished. "War waits for no one, Yojii Tokoray, and time is vital. As we speak, the first of sixty new fighters are being off-loaded. All come with the latest technology and upgrades. Those fighters cannot go into service until pilots are proficient. Which reminds me—" She tabbed a desktop node. To her left, a small drawer slid open. She took out two maintenance coins and closed the drawer. She handed the coins to him.

Holding the coins in his hand, he noted each bore a single gold star. When he presented them to maintenance, he would have priority status in any repair queue.

"Have your wheelbase overhauled," Varree said. "Or, if need be, get the entire wheelbase replaced. Make sure it's up to the stress."

"What type of stress?"

"Forgive me." The timbre in her voice changed. Gone was the lightness. "My oversight. The flight simulator is at the far end of this deck, at the outer hull. The classrooms, on the other hand, are in section six—also located near the outer hull—at opposite ends and as far as they can be from one another. Consider it a prime example of the *Dujaki's* scrambled deck layouts."

He immediately accessed the orientation data and verified Majorn Varree's assessment. He also found other idiosyncrasies. After being dismissed, Tokoray cruised down the corridor toward the flight simulator bays to locate his assigned duty kiosk. En route, he heard the grating sound of his wheels over the decking. A normal sound but, perhaps, it would be wise to have his wheelbase checked.

Hours later, he left Na-ka-ta maintenance with a new, heavy-duty wheelbase with ultra-traction treads and such articulated wheels that, if he desired, he could soundlessly pirouette like a ballerina.

The work had cost him one of the two maintenance coins. A small price to pay to bump the work order to priority because the alternative was to wait a moon-cycle before maintenance could get to him. Tokoray rode a lift down to deck eight and the cadet classrooms. Moving along, he reveled in the soft glide of his wheels. No vibrations. Very little counterbalancing when going around corners, and no squelching when rapidly cornering.

Ahead of him stretched an empty corridor. Could he actually travel the thirty kilometers per hour that the wheelbase's manual listed for top speed? He revved the wheelbase motors and accelerated. Halfway down the corridor, a light winked that a maintenance lift's doors were opening. Exiting the lift and stepping into his path came a slender girl.

He activated an emergency stop. His tire treads issued tiny popping noises in protest of the abrupt halt. To his great relief, he didn't ram into the girl.

The young woman startled and quickly backed a step. The motion set the tangle of flight harnesses she clutched with both hands to jiggling and straps slipped down.

Her smokey-blue eyes focused on his tunic's shoulder patch with his insignia and rank bars. "My apologies, yojii."

He eyed her uniform's triangular shoulder yoke, pinged the ID node on it, and received information that this youngster was Mechnet Rieeza, a mechanical-systems engineer, age twenty-four, of the Haakon-Bayzit Dyn, fourteenth daughter of Atlatl, who commanded the *Dujaki*. The young woman also had the highest of security clearances. All of that data was at odds with what he saw—a young woman with frizzled, mud-brown hair, wearing rumpled coveralls and toting a dilapidated backpack bulging with tools and where testers dangled from side loops.

She looked right then left down the corridor. "Is there an emergency you need to respond to?"

He shouldn't stare. "It is I who apologize, Mechnet Rieeza, and no, there is no emergency that requires speed."

She eyed his wheelbase. "New." The corner of her mouth quirked up, and she looked at him. "Isn't exceeding the speed limit a safety violation?"

"It is." Then he added, "However, technically speaking, I was not speeding but testing my new wheelbase's functionality."

She grinned. "Obviously it stops on a kredi and gives nine senti change. Just like I—rather—my design team decided it should."

"You do not look old enough to be—"

"In charge of anything? Well, I've been certified a genius. My team's always upgrading equipment on the *Dujaki*. Last t'un we redesigned the Na-ka-ta wheelbases because the pilots said scramble times would be faster if their Na-ka-tas could peel down the deckways. Do you like the wheelbase?"

"I have had it less than an hour."

"Oh. Well, gotta go." She re-jumbled the flight harnesses she held, tangling the dripping straps anew. "The team's waiting, and it's a long hike to the shop."

He accessed the schematics of the deck. The shop she referred to was the last one at the end of the corridor, a long hike away. He could give her a ride. No, regulations forbid giving rides to anyone other than a bonded pilot or without direct orders of a superior officer. Then again— "Mechnet, I am en route to the end of the deck. Perhaps you would assist me in testing my new footplates by mounting and riding them?"

Her face lit up. "Boy, would I— I mean, yes, that would be terrific. Do I get to wiggle and squirm like a pilot?"

"Pilots do not wiggle and squirm. However, if you did move about, that would allow me to calibrate maximum speed and angles when cornering."

She giggled. "I like you. What'd you say your name was?"

"Tokoray. Yojii Tokoray, Chief Flight Instructor, newly arrived to the *Dujaki*."

Hours later, he exited a lift and stepped into the beehive atmosphere of the Flight Control and Command Center. Ahead of him stood the long, oval plot table, called 'the hub.' The comtar, housed in its base and the deck beneath, processed data for the two incoming and two outgoing flight decks. Data summaries were constantly channeled to the Chief Flight Controller, a kaax, a tall, slender woman with ragged-razored short, straight hair. The kaax had her head down studying readouts and screens along the hub's edge.

Across from her, the XO, a luten kaax, watched data streams from various small holograph bar-screens. Another officer, the Chief Flight Officer, stood at the far end talking into a com and using her fingers to manipulate various holoscreens, which, by her touches, whizzed and morphed from minimized to maximized and back again.

Beyond the hub stood a smaller oval plot board for Incoming Flight Deck Number One, with a controller talking into a com and watching a fighter being ram-launched. Along the bulkhead stood twelve terminal-stations, most occupied with women, but one Na-ka-ta occupied terminal-station number nine. All spoke into their coms, no voice dominating nor any voice holding anxiety or urgency. Business as usual aboard the battlestation.

Tokoray turned his gaze to the front of the center and its large rectangular viewport, which gave a vista of the massive incoming flight deck's rim and beyond, to starry space—and no approaching flights.

Aware that the CFC eyed him, he wheeled toward her and introduced himself.

"Glad to have you aboard, Tokoray," the CFC said.

"I am pleased to be of service to the *Dujaki*, Chief."

"Well then, my XO will give you a tour of the deck."

From behind the CFC stepped the XO who gave him a smile of genuine welcome. With her leading, Tokoray toured the facility, which had a different layout than he had been used to at *Ziital*. At terminal nine, occupied by the sole Na-ka-ta on the deck, the XO said, "This is our Na-ka-ta training instructor, Yojii Raytor."

Raytor buzzed through Tokoray's circuits with the power of a doige lightning storm. Raytor had been on *Ziital* when Na'zeakan and Yasalan publically damned him as a jinx.

No, wait. Raytor was a common Na-ka-ta name. By the bright stars, let this be a different Raytor.

The Na-ka-ta turned in his turret.

Tokoray scanned his ID node. It was the Raytor from *Ziital*.

"Greetings." Raytor's voice did not bear contempt or any other emotion.

Before Tokoray could utter a reply, the strident voice of the nearest controller overpowered the sounds on the deck. "Say again, Jaguar Two, say again!"

Tokoray instinctively turned and studied the young woman whose face had gone pale. Her hands flew across her control console, tabbing icons. Screens filled with information. At the corner of the hub, a red light began flashing. The controller spoke into her com. "Confirming, Jaguar Two. You are inbound with Na-ka-tas. ETA three hours ten." The controller triggered the comlink to the CFC. "Joiz station has been attacked. We have incoming fighters and wounded."

Alarms began to caw across the deck.

✧ Chapter 7

In his office adjacent to the back of the *Dujaki*'s bridge, Atlatl shook hands with the meter-and-a-half-tall, stocky Grier captain. "Welcome, K'pten Kheyser Marous," Atlatl said, careful to pronounce the man's entire name and rank. The Griers took pride in their names and considered it a dishonor not to be greeted by full name and rank.

One other odd thing about the Griers that led to confusion — they had similar first names, yet each name indicated the relationship within the family-clan. The name endings *-ar, -er, -ir, -or, -ur,* and *-yr* indicated sibling rankings. This Grier's first name, Kheyser, ended with *-er*, identifying him as second born and second in command. Regardless, his goodwill had become vital to the Wysotti. And everything depended on how this Grier felt about his younger brother, Kheysor.

Atlatl covertly studied the Grier's face. Its classically chiseled-to-a-point jaw, one of the distinctive attributes of the Grier race, was not so pointed that it made him look sinister.

"Your message," Kheyser said, "sounded most urgent, Azran Atlatl. I trust this is not about delays in unloading my ship."

"No, no delays. Please. Be seated." Atlatl waived his hand toward the upholstered chair in front his L-shaped desk, then stepped around the desk and took his seat. Atlatl watched the Grier's gaze sweep from the jar of black licorice candies at the corner of the desktop to the room's sparse furnishings. The Grier's attention lingered longest on a cluster of antique starfighter paintings hanging to the right of the narrow viewport.

While the Grier looked about, Atlatl studied the man to better gauge how to handle him. His k'pten's tabard draped over a tight-fitting, charcoal gray spacer's suit. The gray woolen tabard was belted to the waistband of his keld, a short skirt barely covering the man's groin and testicles. The keld's tightly woven blood-red, blue, and golden-yellow plaid were the Marous clan colors, a clan that ranked high among the Grier cartels.

Five rings of lavish cobalt-blue and silver thread circled the neckband of the Grier's tabard, indicating Kheyser took profit from five family ships. That made him a man of wealth — and power, influence.

The Grier wiped his hand over the six-centimeter-tall strip of sandy-colored hair that stood as rigid as a brush and ran from the top of the man's wide brow to his nape, where a long pigtail dangled. Though Griers were originally from human stock, they had colonized a heavy-gravity planet. Griers were miners and frugal master traders with a predilection for neutrality, which made them valuable assets for obtaining supplies for the war between the Wysotti and Doyon. When negotiating, one did not underestimate a Grier's intelligence.

This particular Grier had become an exceedingly interesting person to the Ichtaco. The Wysotti security force had been emphatic — the terms of these negotiations must be kept secret.

The Grier squirmed back in his seat, making himself comfortable and setting off a squelching from the friction of his spacer's boots against the inside of his intricately carved leather spats, the Grier's latest fashion craze.

The Grier's face held no emotion. "Azran Atlatl, is this meeting about my second mate flirting with one of your cadets?"

"No, it's not about that." But he made a note to himself to find out which cadet. No telling what the Grier had wheedled out of her, besides a romp in his bed.

Atlatl met the Grier's gaze and held it. "It's to be expected there will be a certain amount of fraternizing when maritime ships dock. However, I asked you here for another reason." Atlatl tabbed a control on his desk and engaged the room's security field. He leaned forward, placing his forearms on the desktop. "Good K'pten Marous, this meeting has to do with a priority message that arrived this morning. A message I have been instructed to forward to you. Certain aspects of the message must be kept in strict confidence."

K'pten Marous's bushy brows furled, tipping forward the brush of his hair. "Curious as I am, I do not know if it is wise to make such a promise until after I know what it is I must keep confidential."

"I realize that." Atlatl paused for effect. "Wysotti commandos have raided deep into Doyon territory."

Bewildered, the Grier cocked his chin a bit to the left. He leaned forward, setting a hand on the desktop, and lowered his voice. "I am now quite curious, yet I do not see how a Wysotti raid affects me. Nor do I understand why it necessitates my promise of secrecy or silence."

"The message carries intel about your brother Kheysor—spelled with an -or."

The Grier's startled reaction sent him to his feet. "You have news of my brother?"

The pleading tone of the Kheyser's voice left no doubt that the man cared a great deal about his brother. Atlatl nodded.

"Then by all means, azran, I shall solemnly pledge." He placed first his right hand palm down over the middle of his chest, then laid his left hand on top, also palm down. "In honor I am bound as I give my word, upon my beating heart and upon the blood of my forefathers that flows through me, I shall not reveal the Wysotti's raid to anyone nor reveal what we discuss here today." He removed his hands, and almost prayerfully held them clasped together. "Now, please, tell me— *Is my brother dead?*"

"No, he's alive. Please sit down. All will be revealed." Atlatl tabbed the nodes on his desk control pad.

The Grier hesitated but took his seat.

"This," Atlatl said, "is the message relayed to me from *Ziital* station."

The holograph screen in the center of the desktop flared upward. Its slate grayness soon gave a profile view of an emaciated, bald Grier looking to his left. A voice off screen said, "Record, now." The Grier turned, revealing his sunken eyes brimming with tears. He licked his crazed and cracked dry lips, took a breath, then spoke. His voice came out hoarse and wheezing. "Forgive me, dearest brothers. I was a fool. Not worthy to be alive, but I am. I beg you, dear Kheyser go to brother Kheysar and tell him I am safe among the Wysotti at *Ziital* station. Tell my wife and children I am free, no more the slave, no more their disgrace. I ask all to forgive me — please forgive me — allow me to come home."

Atlatl watched the Grier across his desk. Kheyser's eyes glossed with tears, then his expression hardened into a neutral mask.

In the holograph, Kheysor struggled to speak without sobbing. He held up a Doyon slave collar. "The Wysotti freed me. I am no longer a Doyon slave. Honor the Wysotti with honest dealings. Tell Eldest Brother Kheysar that he was right, and this time I have learned a lesson beyond all imaginings. Forgive me. Forgive me . . ." He broke into racking sobs.

The holograph flickered, then went blank, returning to its slate grayness. Atlatl tabbed a node on his desk and the screen winked off.

Emotions flitted in Kheyser's eyes. The expressions first drained then fired the planes of his cheeks with color. A smile slowly took birth on his fine lips. "My brother is alive." He eyed Atlatl. "How ill is he?"

"He's been starved, beaten, forced to do hard labor, but he should recover. It will take time."

"Thank you for bringing him to safety."

"You're welcome. However, you need to know that your brother, at considerable risk to himself and despite the stinging choke of his slave collar, aided Wysotti commandos to obtain valuable intel about Doyon military operations."

Taken aback, the Grier said, "My little brother is a hero?"

Atlatl shrugged. "I cannot say for certain. I am only repeating what I was told." He leaned forward. "K'pten, I need to ask you why the Doyons confiscated your brother's ship and took him prisoner."

"We do not know. We sent a representative to negotiate his release. However, our negotiator was unsuccessful. He returned with a warning that should any of our clan's ships enter Doyon space, they would be destroyed on sight. We had no choice but to consider my little brother and his ship lost to the family." K'pten Marous cleared his throat. "It is painful to admit, good azran, but my little brother always wants to get rich quickly and abhors working diligently to obtain honorable wealth. We have no idea what deal backfired on him."

"Perhaps being a Doyon slave has improved his attitude."

"One can only hope. So, what is to become of my brother now that your people have rescued him?"

"As you saw, he's malnourished. The d'ktrs are not sure of his mental state—he's been a prisoner-slave, gone through who knows what hell at the hands of the Doyons for more than four t'uns."

The Grier nodded. "It is amazing he survived."

"Yes, it is. I was told it may be two or three moon-cycles before our security people decide whether or not to release him."

The Grier squared his shoulder. His voice turned harsh. "He is your prisoner?"

"No. He's in protective custody. You see, the d'ktrs' fear Kheysor will lose hope if his family doesn't reinstate him and he'll commit suicide."

"Suicide is a dishonorable abomination for a Grier, and Kheysor knows this. Do you intend to lock him up forever?"

Atlatl shook his head. "Please hear me out. Your brother is smart. He told the Ichtaco he had been moved around, traded to different Doyon houses and locations, and he has vital information to give them."

A crafty smile softened the Grier's face. "I take it my little brother has set conditions for giving the information?"

"Yes."

The Grier's smile broadened. He now sat like a king graciously granting audience to a peon. "So you have asked me here to plead with my eldest brother, knowing that he, as head of our family, is the only one who can reinstate Kheysor?"

"Something like that."

"So, what do you offer? What incentive is there for me to beg my eldest brother to forgive Kheysor?"

"Something no other Grier has ever had."

"And what might that be?"

"For all ships owned and operated by the immediate members of the Marous clan — you and your brothers only — priority berthing at all Wysotti facilities. Priority load and unload. Priority repairs. Priority refueling and resupplying for your ships."

The glee at such a rich offering flickered in the Grier's eyes, but he remained silent, obviously taking time to consider the offer. The Grier leaned back in his seat, his fingers curling over and clutching the chair's armrests. "For how long shall this priority privilege last?"

"As long as Kheysor lives."

The Grier's smile dimmed. "So, when he dies, the deal dies with him. Such a clever way to encourage us to take him back into the family. And to do it quickly."

"The Ichtaco thought so."

"I shall be honest with you, azran. I see great merit in such a deal. I also shall admit I love my brother despite his possessing a mentality that frequently gets him into trouble."

"So you'll negotiate with your elder brother?"

The Grier nodded. "You may assure my little brother I will, as quickly as possible, be on my way to speak to the family." A twinkle ignited in his eyes. "You realize, of course, azran, that it will be *at least eight days before I am unloaded and can depart.*"

Clever bastard to insist for more. But, he'd been prepared for that. "I will authorize around-the-clock priority status so you can be homeward bound within, say, seventy-two hours."

Grinning with satisfaction, the Grier got to his feet. "A most excellent gesture, but to expedite my departure homeward, say within nine hours, I could unhook my cargo barge and leave it here with my son, who is my second in command. He can supervise its unloading until my return."

The Grier wasn't about to waste time, was he? "I'll have my XO expedite your hauler's departure."

The Grier nodded and turned to leave.

"One moment, please."

He paused and faced Atlatl.

"If you wish to send a greeting to your brother Kheysor, I can arrange that."

"Yes, azran, I do." He smiled. "I shall send one immediately, one encouraging him to be cooperative with the Ichtaco."

A buzzer sounded on Atlatl's desk, and the bar flashed the caller ID of the *Dujaki's* XO.

The Grier nodded and left. The moment the door closed, Atlatl tabbed the com node, "Yes, XO?"

"Sir, Joiz SOA has been attacked. Incoming fighters returning with wounded."

Atlatl laid his hand over his rank amulet, his heart thundering in his chest. "I'm on my way."

✧ Chapter 8

Blips of anti-missiles being fired from the Joiz station flickered on Darq's faceplate screen. Seconds later, bright flashes confirmed the destruction of two incoming Doyon missiles.

Because Na-ka-ta copilots could, in real time, track a horde of spacecraft from their TRAS, Darq cued up optical grids from Phrys's target recognition and attack station. She saw where her squad and where Jaguar squad's four fighters were—and the Strikers that outnumbered the Wysotti fighters six to one.

Darq rolled the controls under her hands. The *Ky* shot forward. She brought up targeting screens. Seeing sight lines converge on a Striker chasing Jaguar Four, she locked onto it, tapped the node, and sent out a burst of keg rounds. The shots hit and burst. The Striker peeled away with a heavily damaged port wing.

Jaguar Four flipped over and arced around, pursuing and firing on her attacker. The Striker and its armaments exploded.

At the corner of Darq's faceplate another screen popped up showing her squad had peeled off. Familiar voices chattered through her com.

"Incoming!"

"Locked on target."

"Multiple targets to port."

Darq steered the *Ky* toward a Striker, noting Chance covered the *Ky*'s approach.

"Zephyr Four—Pepper—where are you?" Misty's voice didn't sound rattled.

Pepper issued a profanity.

Checking her plot screen, Darq glimpsed Pepper diving and spiraling, then banking one hundred eighty degrees, attempting to shake off a Striker. Darq's attention switched to the nearby asteroids where another Striker emerged.

Misty turned about her horizontal axis and fired at the Striker pursuing Pepper.

Darq's faceplate systematically winked, updating targets and locations of the *Ky*, Chance, and the rest of the squad. Enlargements on one screen showed Chance taking out a Striker, but behind the Striker emerged seven more Doyon fighters from along the edge of the asteroid field.

A warning bleeped the *Ky* had been targeted. Darq seesawed, rolled, and dodged incoming fang-strikes. She veered the *Ky* sharply on a downward angle, turned wings up, and fired on a banking Striker. The *Ky*'s rear scanners verified the strike, and the flash of the Doyon's destruction.

Two Strikers sped toward her.

She cornered away from them and glanced at the optical vids.

On your six! Phrys's voice half-thundered through her mind.

Don't shout. I saw them. She sent the *Ky* vertical, flipped nose over tail, fired, and hit the lead Striker. Its destruction blasted debris into the other Striker, which hadn't been quick enough to maneuver out of harm's way. That Striker spun diagonally toward a chunky asteroid. The pilot ejected. On impact, the Striker's armaments exploded into a fireball.

"Raven—beyond the Joiz!" Chance's voice rose octaves higher. "Holy Mother of Heaven."

Darq swung the *Ky* about and aimed its nose sensors toward that vector. More Strikers emerged from the pitch-black morass of a dust cloud. Seven Strikers broke away from the line and became a V formation. The seven headed for the Joiz station.

Using her neural net to access Phrys's data, Darq found each Striker carried one Chelicera missile. Their course meant those enormously powerful bombs were intended for the Joiz station.

Spotting a Striker entering her targeting crosshairs, Darq surged the *Ky*'s engines for all they could give her.

Phrys warned, *You are exceeding engine output red line.*

Better to kill a Doyon than have him kill us. She keyed in the trace, acquired the target, fired. Her keg rounds blasted the Striker. Once again she brought the *Ky* around only to find incoming fang-fire from two Strikers flying side by side. Going vertical, she avoided being strafed.

Spotting a large asteroid, she swung around it, banked, and dove beneath its ragged bottom to come up with her crosshairs on the fuselage of one of the pair of Strikers. She released a volley of keg rounds, destroying the Striker, turned back, and used the asteroid to shield her fighter from debris.

A green light appeared on her screen. *Phrys. Why green on com six one six?*

Na-ka-ta chatter, he replied. *Relaying — Jaguar Lead retains command. Joiz station set to self-destruct when boarded. Jaguar Two docked to Joiz and has evac'd the station's Na-ka-tas. Data core loaded and secure. Jaguar Two proceeding to The Narrows and home. Jaguar Lead and Zephyr Four have engaged incoming Strikers. Jaguar Lead orders are for Zephyr Squad to cover retreat.*

"I'm hit—" came Chance's voice over Darq's com. "Ejecting!"

Shitfire. Not Chance!

Misty's voice came over the comlink. "I've got you."

Utilizing her neural net, Darq tapped into Phrys's WSTB. On the wide-screen tactical board, she found Misty had swung her fighter sideways and turned her opening missile load doors toward Chance's ejection pod. Misty did not lower her auxiliary ramp and that allowed the ejection pod to enter the fighter's missile bay like a fast ball into the sweet spot of a glove. The fighter's bay doors closed. Misty pivoted her fighter about, leveled out, and streaked for The Narrows. Misty's voice came over the com. "Chance is injured. I'm outta here. Somebody cover my ass."

Chance injured? How bad? No time to ask. *Mother of the Stars, watch over Chance – and Misty – see them safely home.*

A warning blip appeared on Darq's faceplate. A Striker barreled toward Jaguar Four, who had swung behind Misty to blast apart an incoming Striker.

Bursts of energy flashed on Darq's screen. One showed the destruction of the Striker, the other, debris engulfing Jaguar Four.

Phrys's somber voice came over the comlink. *Jaguar Four hit. Out of control, heading for the rocks. Zephyr Three, Misty, is gaining distance.* A long pause, then, *Misty is safely away.*

Relief washed over Darq. She tuned out the rest of Phrys's report and applied her attention to her faceplate screens, which tracked eight Strikers emerging from the dust cloud.

How had the Doyons moved so many Strikers so close to the Joiz station without being seen? And just how many more Doyon fighters were hidden in that dust? *Phrys, look inside that dust ball and tell me how many Doyons there are.*

Negative. Cannot do. Damage to our long-range scanner has cut its view to half-range.

Another screen lit with information. The Joiz station's automatic gun batteries had begun firing at the incoming V-formation of Strikers. The lead Striker was hit, but the others launched their missiles and dove aside. The missile trajectories were not aimed at the station's top or bottom arrays but at the station's girth.

The Doyons didn't want to take control of the station and board it? They wanted it destroyed? Why? It was not like the Doyons to destroy a sentinel they could repair and reuse.

A ghostly, chilling thought formed. This was the worst case scenario, the attack everyone had feared. The beginning of the end for the Wysotti nation.

The Adaptative Tactical Screen icon appeared on her faceplate. She tapped into Phrys's tactical arrays, noting the placement of Strikers and Wysotti fighters he was tracking. As her mind sped up, synapses fired faster than light speed so time seemed to slow and almost pause. Ideas swirled like a cyclone and all were transmitted to Phrys through the neural net.

Phrys's processors relayed to her mind likely vectors the Strikers would take to peel away from the exploding Joiz station once their missiles hit.

As she sorted or aborted ideas, Darq realized the dust cloud held the key to the Doyon's intentions, and an idea formed. The ATS screen winked a probability for her survival if she struck— Forty percent.

Not good.

As she lined up another target and steadied the crosshairs, she pushed the *Ky*'s engines for more speed, then fired on a Striker. Pulling away, another idea came to mind on how to see inside the dust cloud. The ATS screen relit with seventy-six percent.

Worth the risk. Worth dying for the chance, but she would need help.

Striker fire crossed her bow, and she broke contact with the Striker she'd been peppering with keg rounds.

She dove and sensed the disobedience of the *Ky*'s reaction. A damage report winked onto her faceplate. The diagram of the *Ky* lit with pink pips, indicating the *Ky*'s right wing edges to almost a meter in, toward the fuselage, had been badly holed. No warning issued. Nothing had penetrated the interior of the fuselage.

The pink pips quickly became light green, indicating Phrys had initiated damage control and triggered additional sealant to patch the holes.

Checking tactical screens, she found herself on the fringe of the fighting and that Pepper had banked, coming about for a rear strike to assist Jaguar Lead with a threesome of Strikers.

Jaguar Three, wings going over, dove steeply, and fired, taking out a Striker.

Jaguar Three was closest and likely best able to initiate her plan to attack the dust cloud.

Phrys, contact Jaguar Three. Verify she has viable DGRBMs.

A second later, Phrys replied. *Affirmative. Jaguar Three has four diggerbooms.*

Darq sent her idea to Phrys. *Call it Odd Man Out. Relay it to Jaguar Three.*

Have you lost your mind? That's suicide.
Over the comlink came the voice of Jaguar Lead, "Disengage. Repeat, disengage. Head for home." Jaguar Lead streaked away, with Pepper covering.

Darq bit back an expletive. She wasn't about to sacrifice this window of opportunity. *Phrys! I order you to contact Jaguar Three and relay Odd Man Out.* Before she could remind him she'd given him an order, Jaguar Three changed direction.

Phrys said, his voice growling with disapproval, *Jaguar Three acknowledges and is en route.*

Relay the plan to Jaguar Lead.

Affirmative. Message relayed, acknowledged. Jaguar Lead says you are go.

As if she needed Jaguar Lead's permission.

Raven, Phrys said, *Jaguar Lead and Pepper have entered The Narrows.* Disgust suffused Phrys's voice. *To die in service is my oath, but to die at the hands of a maniac pilot is debasing.*

Duly noted. Now arm three of our diggers.

Darq glanced at her faceplate screens. Jaguar Three had begun the arcing turn to come parallel with Darq's firing solution. Countdown numbers began to flash in the box at the top corner of Darq's faceplate. Targeting guidance systems locked in place, crosshairs lined up. Waiting for the green light from Jaguar Three to indicate she, too, had locked onto the middle of the dust cloud, Darq felt a constriction in her chest. She inhaled a deep breath. Why was it that when things got tense like this, she forgot to breathe? She took another deep breath.

The light winked green.

Darq said into the comlink, "Jaguar Three— Mark. Three. Two. One." Darq tapped the launch control with her pinky finger and felt the missiles roar out of the *Ky*'s belly. "Missiles away."

"Missiles away," Jaguar Three replied. "Oh, shitz—"

On Darq's faceplate, a Striker fired at Jaguar Three's tail. Jaguar Three spun twice, dove, flipped around, and got off a long burst of keg rounds, hitting but not destroying the Striker. The Doyon fighter went tumbling away, out of control.

Darq banked.

What are you doing? Phrys said.

Making a kill.
You are crazy.

She lined up her sights on the tumbling Striker. *Better to destroy a disabled Striker than have it rebuilt and kill another Wysotti.* She fired, and the Striker became a fireball.

From the left came another Striker, but this one banked, yawed unsteadily, and headed for the dust cloud firing, trying to hit the missiles Darq and Jaguar Three had launched.

The Doyon's shots barely missed.

Seconds later the diggerbooms vanished into the dust cloud.

Jaguar Three streaked for The Narrows. "Zephyr Lead, I'm outta here."

"Acknowledged Jaguar Three, thanks for the assist." Darq checked her screens. "I'll ride your six as soon as I come about." Two bright flashes showed on Darq's optical vids. At least two diggerboom missiles had hit something. Moments later, careening sideways out of the dust cloud appeared the prow of a Doyon battle fortress.

"Mother of the Stars . . ." Darq whispered. Not a measly destroyer but a Doyon battle fortress, one filled with Strikers.

Incoming data flashed onto Darq's faceplate screens. Diggerboom missiles had hit the right side of one of the battle fortress's flight decks. Yet, two more Strikers launched from an alternate, upper deck.

A huge explosion ruptured midway along the Doyon battle fortress's girth, taking with it the two outbound Strikers.

Darq held the *Ky* steady for its sensors to record the fortress's damage. In her peripheral vision, she watched Strikers head her way. "Jaguar Three," she said, not recognizing the calm of her own voice, "did you copy that?"

"Copy what?" came the reply. "I—have—my—hands—full!"

Darq's screen winked. Jaguar Three had taken out a Striker, but three more pursued her. Darq ordered, "Keep going, Jaguar Three. I've got your six. Don't look back. I'm transmitting data to you. Soon as you have it, burn for home. Get to the squad. Relay the data." Darq sent her next command through the neural net. *Phrys — *

Already sending data to Jaguar Three, he replied.
Transmission acknowledged. Raven! Multiple incoming Strikers to starboard.

The ironic thought flashed in Darq's mind that this had to be the first time the Na-ka-ta had done something without being asked.

Darq brought the *Ky* around, aiming the nose in the direction of Jaguar Three's retreat, and rolled the controls, asking the *Ky*'s engines for all they would give her.

Engines on redline, Phrys said. *Back off — or is it your intent to annihilate us?*

This is my bird and I know what he can do. Pay attention. Incoming on Jaguar Three. Those Strikers don't want either of us getting away to report that fortress. Ready two thistles.

A small screen appeared showing the location of the two 9EXSR energy-heat-seeking rockets mounted under her wings. A pip lit, indicating each was now armed.

Multiple lights of systems pushed to overload winked then returned to normal on Darq's faceplate. She checked tactical screens. She and Jaguar Three were the only Pytak fighter showing. The others were gone — they'd made it into The Narrows. She began the turn to come about.

Raven, Phrys said, *four Strikers closing.*

Don't tell me how many, tell me where they are!

Her screen lit with the four Strikers, all closing in on Jaguar Three. Darq headed for her first target, the last Striker in the lineup. The *Ky*'s sensors locked onto the Striker. Darq fired the two 9EXSRs. They locked on target. The Striker veered away. The small missiles followed and hit their target.

She pointed the *Ky*'s nose vertical, missing the debris, then dove, increasing speed. Seconds later, she fired keg rounds into the next Striker. Damaged, it spun like a whirligig out of range.

Darq swung back, leveling to chase the third Striker. Once she had him in her crosshairs, she ordered another pair of thistles and fired. One missile hit the Striker's engine output ring, the other hit the tip of the starboard wing. The Striker exploded in a ball of fire. Diving, Darq avoided the bulk of the debris but screens winked that shrapnel had splattered the top of her wings.

When nothing buzzed to warn she was in trouble, she breathed in, smelling the oxygen. That's what she liked best about the *Ky*, he could fly through hellfire. She checked her emotions and went back to the business at hand. *Phrys, give me an update on Jaguar Three.*

Phrys did not reply, but her faceplate screen lit with new images.

Jaguar Three had banked left toward a lone asteroid ambling on the edge of the asteroid field, missing the lead Striker's fang-fire. Only that lead Striker rode her tail and wouldn't be shaken off. Another Striker zoomed in, then both Strikers suddenly came sharply about and broke away.

The Strikers likely figured Jaguar Three would crash into the asteroids. Mother of the Stars, Jaguar Three had better not!

Blips indicated two Strikers coming up on the *Ky*'s tail. A warning buzzed. The *Ky* had been targeted. Darq dove and banked, laterally spinning on her axis and speeding for the asteroids. She pulled up the star charts of her position, seeking something to duck behind because it had been proven time and time again that Doyon fighter pilots had piss-poor skills when it came to weaving among asteroids at high speeds. She had no problem doing so. It was like flying low and fast through the narrow gorges of the dyn reservation to get to the high falls—and the best fishing hole on the entire continent. Well it didn't hurt either that, when she got bored on Joiz patrols, she regularly zipped about the asteroid field.

Warning buzzers and lights flashed on her screens—the lead Striker had her in his crosshairs. Other lights flashed. Three more Strikers were inbound on her.

A lefthand screen on her faceplate winked numbers for the huge asteroids ahead—familiar numbers—and the tight distance between them. She pushed the *Ky*'s engines for more speed.

Phrys's high-pitched voice resonated. *What are you doing? There's no clearance. No clearance!*

Warning bleeps from her wingtip proximity alarms resounded.

Darq ordered, *Kill those horns.* Holding her hands steady on the controls, she didn't back off the speed.

The alarms muted.

I said kill those horns! I can't think with them blasting in my head.

The alarms silenced, but a buzzer went off. A warning blip appeared counting down ten seconds to impact.

Phrys's shrill voice overrode the buzzer. *You are going to kill us.*

Shitfire, Phrys, I might kill you if you don't do as I order. Kill every damn noisemaker — NOW!

A flick of her hands and feet on the controls sent the *Ky* vertical, her profile at its narrowest.

The Striker behind her fired.

The rattle of fang-blasts hit. The *Ky* juked, trembled, slowed some, but still flew, still had power. Darq glanced at updating screens, noting the *Ky*'s strafed belly. The doors to her missile bay had been ravaged. One door dangled by a hinge, but the other door had protected her last diggerboom missile.

Concentrating on the asteroids ahead, she shot through the gap. The dangling door hit the asteroid and ripped off, tumbling into the weightlessness of space. The Striker swerved aside so it wouldn't be hit by the door.

Ahead loomed an asteroid, one larger than the *Dujaki*. She veered down, her mind racing, acknowledging that she now headed away from The Narrows. Checking screens, she found Jaguar Three emerging out from under an asteroid, streaking and turning into The Narrows — and no Strikers followed or seemed to notice her departure.

Seeing the blips of all the Strikers on her screen, her heart skipped a beat. Six of the nearest Strikers had turned and were converging on her. The others were headed back to the battle fortress.

That wasn't logical. Didn't they want to pursue Jaguar Three and the rest of the Pytaks in The Narrows? Why chase her?

A volley of incoming Stinger fire grabbed her attention. She dodged the most lethal fang-fire, but the *Ky* took hits on wing and tail. Her faceplate screen updated to show the Stingers closing fast.

Her heart raced anew, every nerve hyperaware of her surroundings, of the incoming Strikers, of the ever-changing data on her navigation screens — and of the numbers on the asteroids she approached.

Her thinking accelerated and time crawled.

Seeing Asteroid 004301 appear, a memory surfaced from her cadet days.

Phrys, how many powersticks will it take to mimic a self-destruct broadcast sequence?

*Mimic a self-destruct? I remind you that we are honor-bound to avoid capture and to self-destruct — *

I asked you a question. ANSWER ME.

Three.

Do it. She flooded him with her intent. The calculations on risk lit. Fifty-three percent. A smidgeon better than fifty-fifty.

Phrys's *You can't do that!* erupted into her mind.

I can and will. If I fail, we self-destruct. Until then, I'm going to grab a chance at life. Now, get that false destruct operational. That's an order!

Phrys replied bitterly, *Because of your erratic flying and the hits we've taken, our reserve powersticks are depleted. I can pull sticks from the long-range scans and the comlink array. You will lose ability to — *

I've flown deaf and dumb before. Get to it. Now!

If I survive, and we are rescued and returned to base, I will demand you have a psyche evaluation.

Already had one and passed it. Get going. It took less time than she figured for the Na-ka-ta to rig the signal device to broadcast the warning of a Pytak fighter's self-destruct countdown.

Phrys's voice solemnly intoned, *Digger armed. Engine locked for no start. Eight-second delay on warhead. All set for launch on your command.*

A yellow light on the missile panel held steady.

The ache in her chest had her sucking in air. If she got the timing right, the digger would launch, inertia carrying it forward. It would explode a couple of meters from her tail's engine output rings. Dangerously close.

She slowed enough to get the *Ky*'s engines under the redline and aimed for the chunky asteroid veiled with sweeping black shadows from the even larger asteroid behind it.

Her heart began to thunder against her ribs. *On my mark, Phrys, send the signal. Three, two, one. Mark!*

The false destruct countdown bleeped through the *Ky*'s auxiliary signal array and over her comlink, nearly deafening her. On the fifth blast of the countdown, the Doyons broke formation, hightailing it for safety and open space.

But one Doyon Striker stayed on her tail.

She angled the *Ky* under a projection on the asteroid where the shadows were darkest. She held the *Ky* steady and dropped the diggerboom. Momentum kept the missile speeding along in the shadow. With a gentle touch, she asked the *Ky* for more speed. The *Ky* surged, the marker going over the redline indicator, then above it, and higher still.

Phrys didn't make a sound of protest.

Six seconds.

In her mind, overriding the self-destruct signal came the beats of Zukaltay's drum. An odd, unfamiliar rhythm, but somehow encouraging. Which was weird.

Never mind the drum. Concentrate. Live!

Three seconds.

Into view came 004301 and, low to port, the oval hole in it. She held the *Ky*'s nose steady, aiming for the hole, then pushed the *Ky*'s engines for all the speed he could give her. Warning lights sprinkled across the inside of her faceplate, all indicating her doige engines were in danger of erupting.

One second . . .

The diggerboom hit. The blast pulverized the side ridges of the asteroid and sent the asteroid swinging about in a slow waltz. The Doyon on her tail didn't react fast enough and collided with the rock face, breaking apart in a burst of armament explosions.

At the same time, Darq tilted her wings, slipping through the hole of 004301. Chunks of cinders from the diggerboom's impact pummeled the *Ky*'s tail. The starfighter bucked. She fought the fighter back to steady. When clear, she dropped speed, swerved right and angled down, passing between two huge asteroids. Once clear of them, she continued to weave and lower her speed, going deeper and deeper into the morass of asteroids.

After a long while, she silenced the *Ky*'s engines. Engaging counter-thrusters, she set the fighter cruising in the shadow of a fast-moving asteroid. Her left wing tip grazed a boulder. Panic revved Darq's heart rate that a proximity alarm would go off, but none did.

Despite red lights flashing of damage to the *Ky*, no sounds came from any alarms to alert the Doyons that she had survived. Her heartbeat eased, but her hands, clammy-cold inside her gloves, trembled. She struggled to collect herself. She wasn't safe yet. She had to get to a garbage dump.

A tense hour later, her navigation screen, already littered with markers for countless asteroids, showed a cluster of white pinpricks. Drawing up a spectrum identification of the metallic pieces warmed her mind and soul. She sucked in a calming breath and let the tension go. She had found a Grier waste dump.

Well, Qtl-shi Darq, Phrys said, his voice unusually somber and low, as if afraid to speak, *we should be safely out of range of Doyon ears. What do you plan to do next?*

Glide.

To where?

Home. I know a shortcut.

Something akin to a scoff issued from Phrys, but he said nothing more.

She relaxed back against her seat. Maybe shortcut wasn't the right word. She knew the secret to how the Griers navigated inside asteroid fields. That secret had been one of the crazy bits and pieces of information she'd covertly picked up those summers she worked at the spaceport earning money to build *Little Bit.*

You do realize, Phrys said, *the Doyons will search to verify we are destroyed?*

Yes, but we'll be long gone by then. Besides, I have yet to meet a Doyon who can navigate an asteroid swarm, so I doubt they'll attempt to fly among the rocks, even if they pick up a doige vapor trail. Speaking of which, do we have any doige leaks?

Negative. Which is remarkable since you fly like a —

Give me the damage summaries. She didn't want to hear his opinion about her flying. If she made it back to the *Dujaki*, Phrys would never fill her copilot's seat again.

The sound of drumbeats echoed in Darq's mind. Zukaltay's drumming again? No. More likely it was anger at dealing with Phrys that had set her heart thundering in her ears and mind.

After listening to the rataplan for another minute, she knew it wasn't her heart. Perhaps she'd been a fighter pilot too long, and the drumbeats warned she stood on the verge of battle fatigue — or insanity. No. She was sane. Perfectly sane. She heaved a sigh to cleanse her lungs and her thoughts. What she needed was to calm down, or better yet, find a diversion. *So, Phrys, how's that assessment coming?*

There is much to thoroughly check, analyze, and compile. I am turning off systems which may allow the Doyons to discover we survived. Such conservation will also insure a slower depletion of our energy packs.

Then carry on. A long while later, a blip flashed on her faceplate followed by the ID of a Pytak fighter. Only the shape wasn't right. The silhouette had a bulge where none should be. *Phrys, are you reading this?*

Affirmative. Since we have no long-range scans or coms, nor would it be wise to use them if we did, I shall contact the copilot over the Na-ka-ta channel. After a few seconds, he reported with, *No answer from the copilot, only static. I will attempt secondary channels of communications.*

Darq waited.

Raven?

Yes, Phrys?

No answer back on any channels. Duty requires we not leave the fighter intact for the Doyons.

I know that. Nothing was more appalling then to have to destroy another pilot and her spacecraft. Something she had, so far, never done. But there had to be a first time.

Yet, the thought of doing so now brought to mind the words of countless flight instructors and officers, all reiterating that no Pytak fighter, its pilot or copilot, must ever fall into Doyon hands. Duty demanded she follow orders.

And follow orders she would.

Phrys, what weapons have I got left?

A screen on her faceplate winked and data flowed.

She had no diggerbooms, only four clips of keg rounds, and two thistles. If she tried to destroy the Pytak with either the thistles or the keg rounds, she would give her position away. Great. Nothing like being caught between a rock and a hard place—a very rocky-hard place.

A soft slow bleep sounded on her comlink.

"This is Jaguar Four, Beans," the tentative voice came laced with trembling fear. "Does anyone copy?"

Raven, Phrys said, *if she continues to broadcast, the Doyons will —*

Shut up. Darq cued the ship-to-ship com. "Beans, this is Raven, Zephyr Lead. Go to Na-ka-ta channel immediately."

"Can't, Raven Lead. He doesn't answer me."

Phrys?

She needs to switch to onboard Na-ka-ta channel two-niner-three, mark zero one four and keep the exchanges brief. I will integrate that channel so you and I can talk directly to her.

Darq relayed the message to Beans.

A moment later, Darq's comlink chirped, followed by "Beans here, do you copy?"

Darq demanded, "Yes, I copy. How long have you been broadcasting?"

"Actually, just the once. All my coms were down. I thought they were fried. Turned out the doige power cells were depleted. It took me a while to find a usable stick and swap it out for this one. Screens are sick, but I'm pretty sure my long-range scanners and coms are usable, that is, once I get out of these asteroids. I'm still in them, right?"

"Definitely, and we are not exiting."

"Why? Is there a problem?"

"A big problem. A Doyon battle fortress with sharp ears." She could hope one of the diggerbooms took out all or part of its scanning abilities, but that would take a miracle. And miracles were nonexistent.

A stammering came of "How— How soon before we're spotted?"

"Hopefully never. Stay put. I'm coming around to you."

"Considering the fortress out there and my *Serr*'s condition, well, maybe, Raven, you shouldn't. I'm blind. Not much is functioning. I— I probably should self-destruct."

"Negative on that!" Shitfire, the kid would get her killed too. "Look, Beans, you blow yourself up, and the Doyons will investigate and find me here. Absolutely no self-destruct unless I say so. Got that?"

"Loud and clear, Raven."

Some intricately fast gliding and maneuvering backwards and sideways, put the *Ky* alongside Jaguar Four's fighter, the *Serr*. Phrys sent imagery and schematics to Darq's faceplate from the *Ky*'s only operational close-range scanner.

"Beans," Darq said, "the *Serr* is banged up but intact, no engine leaks or obvious structural damage to prevent you flying."

"What about Ubon, my Na-ka-ta?"

"Don't know for certain. You have a chunk of Striker tail rammed upside-down into the divider wall between the two halves of the cockpit pod, with the bulk of the debris in the port side of the copilot's half. Sealant activated so the pod's calked."

"And Ubon?"

Likely he was dead. Should she tell the kid? Considering the shape of her own scanners, she couldn't verify that. "Beans, your Na-ka-ta might be impaled, injured, or pinned down by the debris—or the foam—or all of the above."

Beans stuttered out a whispered, "He's dead."

"Not necessarily. My fighters damaged. There's no way for me to tell for sure."

Phrys broke in with, "I would remind you, Raven, that we are trying to distance ourselves from Doyon detection. Too much chatter will get us spotted. I suggest we take the pilot aboard the *Ky*, set the *Serr* to self-destruct, and depart."

"No can do," Beans replied. "I tried to eject, nothing happened."

Darq reexamined the available scans of the *Serr*. "I see why. A twisted bit of that bulging piece of Doyon junk cut into the blaster unit. Likely the locks can't release."

"What if I manually crank back the cockpit canopy and exit?"

"Sorry, Beans. Scans say a corner of your canopy is fouled. Wreckage is lodged at the port corner. Foam sealed it to the fuselage."

"Darq," Phrys said, his tone a growl of condemnation, "you outrank Jaguar Four. Order her to take the nano-poison."

A gasp came from Beans.

Darq silently damned the Na-ka-ta for his bluntness but, in truth, that idea had already occurred to her. What it came down to was making the hard decisions, life and death decisions. Better to do her duty, save the *Ky* and herself, and get back to the *Dujaki*.

Only losing a good pilot when the war needed every pilot it could get? "Beans, ignore Phrys. We're not to the point yet that suicide is the answer. However, time is a factor. I need a list of your active systems."

Beans began a systematic report. Interior systems were sick. Her thistle target system remained functional but she had no thistles left. She had a full load of four DGRBMs, unfortunately, the targeting system for those diggerbooms was offline. A long pause, then "The DPEET is functional."

The Doige Particle Energy Emissions Tracer! "Bingo. We are in luck." Darq maneuvered the *Ky* so its engines faced the nose of the *Serr*. "Beans, turn on your bow DPEET. Does it pick up my engines' residual output."

A pause. "I see something. Hmm. I've got a wide bar. Okay. Yes, blue, doige blue—it's the outline of the engine output rings of a Pytak fighter!"

Darq turned on the *Ky*'s engines, holding them at their lowest power level. "Okay, Beans, watch your DPEET and stay on my tail. There will be a lot of twists and turns so pay attention. We'll go slow. Got that?"

"Affirmative, Raven. Engines on line. Ready when you are."

Darq moved the *Ky* to starboard. The *Serr* followed sluggishly.

Phrys muttered, *This is suicide. We have no star map. You will exit these asteroids in Doyon Territory – *

Your pessimism is duly noted, Phrys. Now cut the chatter, and let's get out of here.

✧ Chapter 9

Tokoray noted the activity on the *Dujaki*'s Flight Control Center's deck. As the red-alert horns faded, plot boards and screens became alight with streaming data. He assimilated the data being acknowledged and confirmed by multiple station scanner techs to the hub. The officers there studied, sorted, and forwarded the data to other deck stations, to the *Dujaki*'s bridge, and to Azran Atlatl himself. Yet, nothing gave a clear picture of the situation at the Joiz station or the fate of its two Pytak fighter squads.

As Na-ka-tas entered from front and back service lifts to take up vacant stations, the bustling and noise levels increased. Scrambled fighters were readied and processed for launch, all heading for The Narrows to stem the flow of a projected, incoming Doyon attack. Lights on databoards winked that doige tunnels had been set into place on the incoming flight decks. Other lights indicated rescue and medical teams were en route, with others on standby at their stations.

Tokoray said to the chief flight controller, "May I be of assistance? I have talked a number of pilots in when they have had heavy damage." Then he added, "All survived."

The commander stared at his faceplate for a long moment, then nodded and turned her attention to the ever-changing hub view in front of her. "Go to your assigned station. Link in. Assist Jaguar Two. She's damaged and has a load of Na-ka-tas from the Joiz station."

"Affirmative." As Tokoray rolled across the flight center, it momentarily occurred to him that volunteering meant not having to deal with Raytor. Then again, perhaps Fate smiled kindly, not that he believed in Fate, per se. Yet, the situation could be advantageous, giving him an opportunity to enhance his reputation, especially if he helped save fellow Na-ka-tas. *What if he could not save them?* No, he would not jinx his own thinking. Still, crippled fighters posed difficult challenges. Reaction times were critical, not only on his part but also on the part of the pilot and copilot.

He entered the station's turret and locked himself in. Facing the curved wall of data panels, he drew back his finger covers, exposing jacks, and plugged into the console controls. He activated his disk-cap's relays, receivers, and transmitters. His interior processing units strummed to life with sorting input, star maps, telemetry, and communications. He focused his faceplate's scanners on the upper corner wall panel where a viewscreen showed the *Dujaki*'s Incoming Flight Deck Number Seven and where Jaguar Two was to land.

Once linked to Jaguar Two, he gave instructions. As he did, it became evident she did not need any expert assistance. She landed her fighter safely. As the Na-ka-tas from the Joiz station rolled onto the *Dujaki*'s deck, they filled the comlink with gratitude to the pilot for their rescue and safe landing. No thanks were given to him, Controller One Two.

Tokoray's processors switched to standby mode. Job done. Nothing memorable. Yet, the disappointment of not receiving a thank you from the pilot or her copilot felt disheartening.

At the corner of Tokoray's faceplate, a vid screen with a neon-green border lit. The CFO's face appeared. "Controller One Two, assist Zephyr Three, incoming with wounded."

"Affirmative." Tokoray checked his incoming data. Zephyr Three had the ejection pod of Zephyr Two in its missile bay. The pilot, Chance, was injured but stable, and her Na-ka-ta copilot remained unresponsive.

In the lower left corner of his faceplate, an icon appeared, one with a thin red border that flashed intermittently, demanding attention. Accessing the icon's data revealed Zephyr Three had fang-strikes on both wings and on a large section of the port engine output ring. The screen's border tripled in width, the data indicating a doige leak on the starboard side. The leak lay behind the missile bay protecting Zephyr Two's eject-pod.

Another icon lit. Linking to it, he found the fighter had priority for landing and that medical personnel and Na-ka-ta rescue teams stood ready.

From the hub behind him, came the XO's voice, "Flight Deck Seven Doige Tunnel at the ready." Then, "Controller One Two, she's all yours."

"Zephyr Three," Tokoray said into the comlink, "this is Controller One Two, you are clear to land, flight deck seven. Doige tunnel is in place."

"Acknowledged, Controller One Two" crackled across his comlink. The XO approached and tabbed a screen above Tokoray's head. The screen's graph showed doige dust continued to spray out. At the rate of expulsion, less than nine minutes of usable dust remained. Which meant there would be no second attempt at a landing, and the pilot knew that.

A red pinprick of light appeared on the inside of Tokoray's faceplate. Figures rapidly spun on the little box giving the probability of a DLE – a Doige Lightning Episode.

Memories of flashing pinpricks of red light, the one hundred percent figure bright yellow, and buzzers going off bombarded Tokoray's concentration. With each passing second, anxiety intensified and coursed through him. Logically, rationally, what he dreaded was solely based on recorded repercussions, which occurred after the fact, after the DLEs he had experienced. *I am aboard the* Dujaki, *not a fighter. I am linked to a terminal, not trapped in a fighter cockpit. I am aboard the* Dujaki –

Next to that flashing pinprick of red light on his faceplate appeared a yellow 96.200 on a black background. A 96.200 percent probability Zephyr Three would have a DLE. The number winked to 97.150.

Tokoray fought the memories that strove to overwhelm his processing data and managed to state clearly, "Zephyr Three, DLE eminent. Repeat, DLE eminent."

"I see the numbers," Zephyr Three replied. "Two t'uns and I've never had a DLE. Only been through them in simulations. Man-oh-man, that was a long time ago."

"You will be fine," Tokoray reassured, then realized his voice may have betrayed his uncertainty. After all, no pilot could ever be adequately prepared for what a DLE was like because of the nature of the individual DLE leak or rupture. He had survived three DLE's, each different in cause and each of a different magnitude.

After extrapolating the current data from Zephyr Three's telemetry and from the scanners around the mouth of the incoming flight deck, Tokoray said into the comlink, "Inbound Zephyr Three, the docking target is lit. Four minutes to landing. Cut speed to one zero zero."

"Oh, shitz!" Zephyr Three said. "Every screen's sick. Docking target does not register. Repeat, docking target does not register. Switching on AFCS." Then she whispered, "Curse the luck. A blind landing on top of a DLE."

Tokoray linked to her onboard Auto Flight Control System. "Zephyr Three, I will guide you in."

Her voice went coldly even, businesslike. "Affirmative, Controller One Two."

In the recesses of Tokoray's mind, it registered that he had talked in pilots with worse damage and even without AFCS. "Zephyr Three, your port wing is too high, trim to level. Repeat, trim to level. Reduce speed to five zero."

Incoming data verified Zephyr Three used her quad-thrusters to level her wings, and her speed declined to five zero.

"Zephyr Three, you are aligned with the flight deck. You are flying true and straight for the tunnel. Two minutes to touchdown." As he examined the ever-changing data, he noted the *Dujaki*'s exterior sensors indicated a trailing ribbon of doige-dust still escaping along her starboard side and a 98.200 registered on the DLE screen.

Should her engines quit because there was no more dust to burn, there would be no DLE, but she would lose power. No power, no control of her fighter, no ability to guide her plane. She would crash. Then again, if the doige microfusion process kept the engines running, that process might reach the damaged area and, like fumes from an accelerant, ignite the escaping dust. Once lit, a lightning storm would crackle along the dust's path — forks would whip about, frying the fighter's hull, damaging the flight deck, then follow the particle trail into space. The dust would continue to burn violently until all of it was consumed.

"Flight Control One Two, what's my status?" Zephyr Three said, no fear edging her words.

"On my mark, cut power to zero." He did the countdown and noted her engines ceased. Seconds later, he said, "Your nose has entered the tunnel. You are level, straight and true."

He barely heard Zephyr Three's whispered, "Mother Sky bless this landing and save my wretched soul."

A large screen winked to Tokoray's left. The view from inside the doige tunnel showed Zephyr Three all the way into the tunnel. "Zephyr Three," Tokoray said, "apply retros— Now. The catch-net will grab in three, two—"

As the fighter crawled to a stop, a burst of blue-white erupted from the starboard side thrusters. In rapid succession, bolts of lightning crazed up and out, arcs and branches of lightning gobbled up doige dust, sizzling along the streaming trail past the fighter's tail.

The XO bellowed over her comlink to the doige tunnel chief on the flight deck, "Close that tunnel!" She then strode quickly back to the hub.

Tokoray watched the lightning strikes, watched the forcefield ripple into place, watched the swiftly descending door drop from the top of the doige tunnel, closing the fighter in, and severing the stream of dust.

"Controller One Two, what's happening to my canopy?" A triple booming shuddered over the comlink followed by crackling sounds.

Memories flared in Tokoray's mind of the crackling-boom of doige lightning strikes touching his fighter's hull. Then came the *zssst zssst zssst* of sealant foam sizzling and the patter of auto-repair units trying to plug the damage made by the strikes searing through the fighter's canopy and pod.

Other memories flared of getting out of his fighter, carrying his dying pilot toward the far end of the doige tunnel, toward the oncoming rescue crew, and the unexpected eruption of a DLE. Because his skin and body were designed to withstand such lightning, deflect and defuse it, he protected Citali.

Memories of another doige storm overshadowed the first. This time he dropped out of the belly of his fighter and, at top speed, wheeled across the doige tunnel's spongy surface to the safety cage, taking massive hit after scarring hit before the ship blew apart.

"Tokoray?" Raytor's demanding voice penetrated Tokoray's thoughts, and he jerked sideways to eye the Na-ka-ta now standing beside him.

Raytor's voice came out soft, but stern. "Your pilot needs reassurance."

Shame assailed him that he had, for the briefest of seconds, forgotten Zephyr Three. Rapidly checking his console and data, he said into the comlink, "Zephyr Three, do you copy?"

"Affirmative. There's a lot of noise around me."

"That is normal. To be expected." He checked specific data computations. "The storm should cease in forty two seconds."

"Then what?"

"Sensors will check to ensure no doige dust remains. If all is clear, a horn will sound. The rescue teams will enter the tunnel, and you will be given instructions to open your missile bay. The first units will get the injured out of the bay. Other teams will assist you and your copilot from your fighter."

"El'gee, my Na-ka-ta, he isn't in his seat. He's in the bay with the eject pod. Too much interference. Can't say what his status is or that of our passengers."

Tokoray checked the data streams flowing through his processing units. "The doige strikes are limited to the starboard side of your fighter. Your Na-ka-ta reports he is safe, and no change in pilot-copilot in the evac pod. All awaiting rescue."

"Good enough. Thanks Controller One Two for the assist."

"You are welcome."

Moments later, an all clear flashed across his viewscreen and crews entered the doige tunnel, their robo-carts racing at full speed.

Aware that Raytor still stood beside him, Tokoray glanced up at the Na-ka-ta. Was Raytor about to publicly comment on his lapse of attention to Zephyr Three?

Raytor said over the Na-ka-ta's private channel, *I have never actually been in a doige tunnel with a DLE, but I know you have survived three.*

And your point? Tokoray said, dreading what the reply would be.

All things considered, particularly in light of what has just happened with Zephyr Three, perhaps it would be advantageous to have the data of those DLE episodes erased from your memory banks.

Many times Tokoray had considered that. *To do so would erase the memories of my bonded pilots.*

Self-inflicted guilt does no pilot or Na-ka-ta any good.

Raytor turned and wheeled back to his station. *There are more incoming fighters. If you cannot concentrate on the job at hand, how good are you to any pilot?*

Judge not lest you also be judged was all Tokoray could think to say. He turned to his console feeling guilt sizzle through him like the crackling fire of a mini-DLE.

As the day progressed, messages were passed down from the last fighter that left The Narrows and sent on to the *Dujaki*. On receiving the fighter's message, the Chief Flight Controller contacted the *Dujaki's* bridge, demanding the azran. When Atlatl connected, she reported a Doyon battle fortress had destroyed the Joiz station.

An hour later, another message passed down the line from the incoming fighters. At receiving that news, the CFC's face paled. As the information circulated to the various officers, the flight control center went deathly quiet and all eyes focused on the CFC. "Bridge," she said, her voice holding an undercurrent of dread. "I need to speak to the azran again. Urgent."

Atlatl's voice boomed in the quiet. "Report."

The CFC almost hesitated, but said, "Incoming message passed down the line." She took a deep breath and intoned flatly, "Zephyr Lead self-destructed."

Silence ensued.

Tokoray looked at Raytor and spoke to him over the Na-ka-ta channel. *Am I missing something?*

Raytor replied, *Zephyr Lead is Raven. She is Azran Atlatl's wife. Her true name is – was – Darq of the Mayahi Dyn, her rank, qtl-shi.*

So the top gun was wife to the azran. She was a pilot who opted to self-destruct, going out of this life like a warrior should. Only now, with Raven Darq dead, Yojii Varree would not be able to complete her project to save other pilot's lives. What a pity he had never met Qtl-shi Darq.

Atlatl's voice, low and even, came over the comlink. "Is that confirmed?"

"No, azran. It can't be confirmed until the last fighter lands and we pull the recordings, and that fighter has engine trouble. It's making only half-speed. The Raven's *KY 52* will be listed as MIA until the self-destruct is verified."

"Acknowledged. Keep me posted and carry on."

The comlink chirped the disconnect.

Tokoray checked his terminal data. The *KY 52* would not come off the list until verification had been made of the self-destruct. That confirmation was seven hours out, locked in the data box aboard Jaguar Three, the last fighter to leave the Joiz station.

Chapter 10

The damaged Jaguar Three arrived and landed without a DLE incident. The doige tunnel chief's voice came across Tokoray's comlink with an "All clear," and minutes later came "Pilot-copilot clear." Tokoray set his terminal-station to standby, shut down his disk-cap relays, then pulled his jacks out of the control unit. Once the finger covers were back in place, he tabbed the node at the edge of the console top, sending his turret around, its jaws loosening their grip on his legs and wheelbase.

He scanned the flight center. Only a few people were left on duty because most were on a meal break. Although quiet, a ghostly tension gripped the deck and even the CFC and the XO, who stood side by side, spoke in hushed whispers. Which was logical because of unanswered, haunting questions. Had a horde of Strikers plowed their way through The Narrows intent on destroying the *Dujaki*? Could the *Dujaki* hold off an attack until reinforcements arrived from Talragon Station or *Ziital*?

Once his turret opened, Tokoray wheeled himself out. He spied Raytor activating his turret to depart his station. Was it wise to ride the lift up to deck seven and the Na-ka-ta barracks with Raytor? Would Raytor make more disparaging remarks? Better to speed up, reach the lift first, and get away.

Because lights on the tote screen at the far wall ahead of him blinked, Tokoray didn't speed up. He watched the background of the top entry, *KY-52-ZEPHYR LEAD-RAVEN/DARQ-PHRYS* change from its normal sky blue color to a dark orange. Which meant the recorders on Jaguar Three's fighter had been pulled and were now in the process of being analyzed to verify if the *KY 52* had self-destructed and the pilot and copilot were dead.

The lavender entry below remained unchanged. *SERR-06-JAGUAR FOUR-BEANS/XOCO-UBON*. Two hours ago it had officially been confirmed they were MIA.

The lift doors opened, leaving Tokoray a meter to go to avoid an encounter with Raytor.

A male officer exited the lift wearing a commander's yokepiece. Tokoray accessed the man's ID node. The officer was Azran Atlatl, commander of the *Dujaki*. As the lift doors snicked shut behind the commander, Tokoray paused so he would not impede the azran.

Heading for the hub, the azran said to the CFC's back, "Is the data in yet from Jaguar Three?"

The CFC pivoted about, facing Atlatl, and saluted. "It's being processed now, azran. Shouldn't be more than ten or fifteen minutes before confirmation is relayed here."

Atlatl stopped to the left of the CFC. "Very well. I'll wait. I have to know."

"Yes, azran. Understood."

The lift doors opened again, and out stepped Majorn Varree.

Both the CFC and Atlatl looked over their shoulders at her. Varree strode to the hub and halted beside the azran. "I hope you don't mind me coming down here, azran," she said. "I had to know what to tell Lingit about her Phrys."

Atlatl nodded.

Raytor now moved toward the hub.

Interesting, what was Raytor doing?

A ping resounded on Varree's com. "Varree here."

A woman's no-nonsense voice replied, "This is Ghonuni, from sickbay. D'ktr Enyeto wanted you to know he had an aid take Lingit to the chapel, to find comfort in prayer. She should be back in an hour."

"Understood. Thank you. End." Looking at Atlatl, Varree said, "When I assigned Phrys to Darq, it never occurred to me it would be possible for Darq to self-destruct."

"Nor to me . . ." He placed his hands behind his back, one atop the other.

Tokoray noticed the azran's fingers quivered. The azran's stance should have been indicative of at ease, but unmistakable tension stiffened the azran's spine and tensed his shoulders. Obviously, being commander of the *Dujaki*, the azran could not afford to let his personal concerns for his wife overshadow his duty — or allow the crew to see their azran overtaken by his feelings for her loss.

Atlatl eyed Raytor, who now stood an arms-length away from the azran on the other side of the hub.

Raytor's voice sounded strangely flat. "I am Raytor, bloodkin to Phrys. I am legally obligated to see the data confirming my bloodkin brother's death."

Atlatl nodded.

The CFC checked a screen, canting her head as if listening to something coming over her earcom. Standing more erect, she looked at the azran. "The data's in." Instead of showing the data streams on the holograph units over the hub, the CFC engaged a screen on the hub's tabletop. Atlatl moved to the edge of the hub for a closer look. Raytor and Varree stepped forward to the edge of the table.

The XO, who stood at the other end of the hub, suddenly turned and said, "Azran, Talragon Station needs to speak to you. The message is urgent, priority one, on SAT 461."

Atlatl went to the nearest terminal-station and said into the comlink, "Comtar, link me to SAT 461." A ding sounded.

A twanging female voice came over the link. After the acknowledgment of introductions, the Talragon's azran said, "Our long-range scanners have picked up an unidentified object drifting out from the asteroid field in the cross-over zone. Interference from the asteroids is hampering us getting a better look at it. It might be one of those new Grier ore ships. The blip's long enough to be one, but it might be a Doyon Marauder. Can you turn your long-range scanner on the area and identify it?"

"I'll get my people on it. *Dujaki* out." A ding sounded.

Atlatl ordered the comtar to connect him to the bridge. The connecting ding was followed by a gruff-voice female's, "Bridge."

Atlatl replied, "XO, swing our longest-reaching arrays to bear and check the double X vector. Talragon needs an assist in IDing a UFO. Report the results to Talragon ASAP. And, Qelsey, if it's nothing, swing those arrays back to The Narrows."

"Affirmative, azran."

"End." When the disconnect sounded, Atlatl returned to the hub and faced the CFC. "Let's get on with this."

The CFC tabbed a control panel with four sets of eyes looking at the tabletop screen.

Near Tokoray, the lift doors opened. A slender woman, wearing a standard-issue, medical-gray sleepsuit and booties, stepped silently onto the deck. Her dark-eyed gaze zeroed in on Varree's back. Her lips parted, teeth gritted, seething with rage, she padded forward at a jog. She raised her left hand, which clutched a knife with a white-knuckle grip.

Tokoray put full power to his wheels. The treads dug in, squelching and enabling him to intercept her. Reaching out, he grabbed the woman's wrist, pulling her knife hand around. He squeezed his fingers tight, jerking her sideways. She let go of the blade, and it flew toward the hub.

She screamed in fury and twisted, hopping onto his wheelbase with an ease that bespoke of having done so before. Fisting her free hand, she pummeled his faceplate, rattling his visual sensors.

"Let me go. I have to kill the murdering bitch." She pounded on his faceplate harder.

On her next descending blow, he grabbed her forearm and stopped her strikes. "Enough!" he bellowed.

She stilled. In the blinking of her tear-reddened eyes, he saw her anger supplanted by an awareness of her surroundings—and of him. Air wheezed from her lungs and her body began to tremble. Tears washed over her eyes. "You don't understand. She killed my Phrys."

In his clearest voice, Tokoray said, "Your Phrys? As in the Na-ka-ta copilot of the *KY 52?*"

She nodded. Tears dripped out of the corners of her eyes and down her flushed cheeks. "Varree ordered him to go with Darq—*that Na-ka-ta murderer.*" Her voice escalated to a wail.

"Phrys didn't want to go. Varree ordered him. She ordered him!" The woman's eyes glazed, her cheek color reddening.

How could he calm her? He chose a fatherly tone. "Hush. Calm yourself. What is your name?"

"Lingit. Ohti Luten Lingit. They call me Squeeze."

Her rank made her a second lieutenant, a junior pilot.

"I'm bonded to Phrys and now — " She gulped a breath of air. Her tears flowed more freely. *"Now, he's dead."* She began to sob, and the fight poured out of her.

Tokoray placed her hands onto his shoulders, cautiously released his grip, and lowered his arms about her waist, locking his fingers as if he were carrying a pilot.

Lingit hugged him and sobbed onto the left shoulder of his tunic. The microsensors imbedded in his skin registered her body heat. The numbers indicated her temperature above normal. Distraught, grieving, and feverish. No wonder she was irrational.

He checked another set of sensors, the ones on the palms of his hands, the ones he used to make sure his pilots were not under the influence of drugs, alcohol, toxins, or herbals which would impair their judgment when flying a mission. The readings confirmed a mix of drugs.

As her sobs began to ebb, Tokoray noticed that although no one approached him and Lingit, everyone watched them. He also noted Varree stood safely out of reach on the other side of the hub, whispering into a comlink.

Shifting his optics, Tokoray eyed Atlatl, who met his gaze and mouthed, "Med staff en route. Talk to her."

Talk to the distraught woman? He was no grief consuleir but, yes, talking invariably helped in situations like this. "So, Lingit," he said, using his fatherly voice, "tell me about your Phrys."

She sniffled and wiped tears off her cheeks, then wiped her wet palms on his tunic. She looked directly at his faceplate where his eyes would have been if he had been a human. "Phrys is the best Na-ka-ta."

She spoke of him in present tense. Which probably was not good. "Was he your first bonding?"

JEWELS OF THE SKY * Catherine E. McLean   103

"Yes. We've been together for eight moons." She smiled. "We survived three pancake landings with no DLEs."

"A remarkable feat." Recollection of words spoken to him after the loss of his first bonded pilot in a DLE surfaced. "Lingit," he said, "it is never easy to understand why one lives and one dies, whether it be pilot or copilot. Yet, we Na-ka-ta's, we give our oath to serve until death."

"But he didn't have to die. He didn't volunteer. Varree ordered him to copilot for that damnable murdering Raven!"

He chose to ignore the defamation of the Raven's character and said, "Do you recall when Phrys took his oath of duty to you after you two bonded?"

"Only pieces. My head ached from the neural-net connections. They said headaches were normal."

"Well, your Phrys would have said, *By my honor and free will, I choose to serve the Elpoccalli and the Wysotti people, to render the best of my talents, skills, and knowledge for the survival of the Wysotti race. Let me die in service, sacrificed if needed to save my pilot's life.*"

Tears welled anew in her eyes and she nodded.

"And do you remember him saying, *In bonding to my pilot, I will be a comrade and friend, doing my utmost to insure her survival and that of the craft she commands?*"

She nodded.

Then he lowered his voice a few octaves and said, "*By my own hand if necessary, I will terminate my pilot's life and self-destruct, insuring neither of us is captured by an enemy.*"

Her hands slid up to his shoulders and clutched the fabric of his tunic. With trembling lips and voice, she half-whispered, "*I hold blameless my bonded pilot if she, in good judgment, issues my self-destruct so I do not fall into enemy hands.*"

"Lingit, whether you believe destiny rules our fate or that J'Hi-inti, the Great Mother of the Heavens, picks the time, place, and circumstance of an individual's death, it is in how we live that matters most."

"Phrys didn't have to die."

Tokoray spoke softly. "Ah, little Lingit, the most honorable death for a Na-ka-ta is to die in service, in battle. Your Phrys had an honorable death. If you kill Varree, are you not shaming his honorable death?"

Realization of that truth had Lingit sucking in a noisy breath. She sniffled twice before slowly nodding. Leaning forward, she placed her forehead on his chest and quietly sobbed, all the while her hands kneaded the cloth of his tunic.

To his left, Tokoray caught the light flash over the lift doors and, seconds later, the door shushed open, revealing an elderly man wearing a d'ktr's medical tunic, a female nurse, and a hulking Na-ka-ta orderly beside a gurney.

A motion sensor alerted Tokoray to Atlatl raising his hand to halt the newcomers, and in his other hand, Atlatl held the knife Lingit had planned to kill Varree with.

Lingit released her hold on Tokoray and leaned back, putting the small of her back against his locked hands. She took in a shuddering breath. "I've made a mess of things, haven't I?" She glanced over her shoulder to where Varree stood and whispered, "Varree will have me court-martialed."

"I think not," Tokoray replied.

She blinked back the moisture in her eyes. "How come?"

"It will be difficult to prove you were of sound mind when you stepped onto this deck."

"How come?"

"First, you are grieving grievously. Secondly, my thermal sensors indicate your body temperature is two point five degrees above normal, indicative of a fever. My tox-sensors register a mix of drugs in your perspiration and tears that have been known to cause irrational thinking."

The d'ktr muttered a short expletive, then said, "Lingit has a history of adverse reactions to medication."

Atlatl walked up to Tokoray and stood where Lingit could see him. Compassion mirrored in his eyes, but he spoke with rank and authority. "Lingit, look at me."

When she did, he said, "We all grieve for your loss, but we are at war, and at red alert. There are certain formalities to be observed. One of them is to account for all fighters that come and go from the *Dujaki*."

She sniffled, swallowed, then nodded.

Atlatl faced the tote screen.

Lingit laid her cheek against Tokoray's shoulder, her breathing became shallow, raspy. Tokoray spun his wheels enough so she could better see the tote screen.

"Lingit," Atlatl said, his attention focused on the screen, "the data is in. It has been confirmed. The *KY 52* self-destructed. There was no ejection. Both pilot and copilot died in service to the Elpoccalli." In a softer tone, he said, "We shall honor them with the *eldic rondt* for their swift passage to the Great Spirit."

The screen winked. Only one entry remained, the one for the missing *SERR*-06-JAGUAR FOUR-BEANS/XOCO-UBON.

A hush settled over the deck.

Out of the depths of Tokoray's memory banks came the voice of his last pilot, whispering, *Grief is such an individual lament.*

✦ Chapter 11

Darq woke from her power nap, activated her faceplate, and cued the time. She'd slept twenty minutes, not the thirty she'd planned on, hoped for.

Ah, well. She shoved her hands deep into her pilot-seat's sleeves and felt the coldness of the control balls seep through her gloves.

"Oh, shitz!" wafted over her comlink from Beans.

Now what had happened. "What's your problem, Beans?"

"You awake?"

"Isn't that obvious?"

"Yes, of course. Sorry, Raven. I tried to pick up the sweeps from the Dragon Lady. Nothing but static. As Phrys said, it was a bad idea since we're not exactly in clear space yet."

Ah, the argument. When they spotted the edge of the asteroids, Beans's long-range sensors, now fully operational thanks to Phrys's help, had failed to pick up a Wysotti beacon signal or any scanner beams monitoring the edge of the asteroid belt. Which seemed odd considering that, from the day the war with the Doyons began, the Cypha-wee-ka asteroids had been under continuous surveillance from the San Hiphia binary stars to the Kallian border.

As positive as Darq had been that they would enter Wysotti space if they continued on, Phrys's muttering admonishments about an imminent incursion into Doyon territory made her question herself. So had the loud drumming.

Drumming?

No drumming now. At the oddest times during the flight through the asteroids, she'd heard her grandmother's hands rapping her Jewels of the Sky drum. Even odder, Darq recognized a couple of rhythms as Zukaltay's favorite anxiety busters. *Maybe she heard Zukaltay's drum because the drum was cursed.*

What a ridiculous thought. One brought on by what? She'd just napped. Okay, she might be fatigued, but she wasn't totally exhausted. Then why dwell on the drum? Because there had been times when she debated turns and the drumming had become loud and harsh, as if warning she was about to go the wrong direction. She had always had a primal instinct for navigating the cosmos. Maybe that was an absurd supposition. Or wishful thinking. *Instinct overrode logic to equal survival.*

She should be glad the drumming had ceased and not question it.

Whispering in her mind came the memory of Phrys yammering at her with *You currently have a fifty-fifty chance of survival. You are fatigued. You need rest. Nourishment.* As to Phrys and his nagging, the sooner they got back to the *Dujaki*, the sooner she would be rid of him. But, for the time being, she would endure.

Actually just after he'd said those words, they'd come into a clearing among the asteroids. It looked like a good place to take a break, a chance to eat, drink, and take a power nap. So, she linked the two fighters together by catching the *Ky*'s canards on the *Serr*'s tailfins above the *Serr*'s engine output rings. Doing so ensured the two planes remained together and drifted as one with the asteroids.

And speaking of drifting, why had Jaguar Four—rather Beans—even attempted to pick up a signal from the *Dujaki* if they weren't in open space?

Darq drew up a screen on her faceplate of the surrounding area and blinked twice. They were no longer among the asteroids but in clear space. How could that be? "Beans, when did you use thrusters and push us out of the rocks—and why didn't you wake me when you did?"

"I didn't use my thrusters. I thought Phrys moved us."

With a dusting of indignation in his voice, Phrys replied, "It was not I."

"Well if I didn't do it, and Beans didn't do it, and you, Phrys, didn't do it, how did we go from drifting with the asteroids to making a thirty-degree arc? And we are now gliding at two point six five percent faster than our original drift speed?"

"I do not know," Phrys said.

The only thing that might increase their speed was pressurized— "Phrys, check for leaks."

"Raven," Phrys said, twice as much indignation accompanying his reply, "while you and Beans napped, I ran scans on both ships with what functioning equipment we have. No depressurization has occurred, that is, none other than what was originally logged from initial damage, and that damage has been sealed. The engines are offline. No doige leaks. Nothing whatsoever that would produce thrust."

"Okay, okay. Then how do you account for us getting out here? Surely, you noticed us moving?"

"Negative. I did not. As I said, I was occupied with scans, doing calculations of supplies—oxygen, food, water, doige levels."

Beans broke in with a cheery, "Likely it was The Ancestor. She gave us a push out of the Chepha-wee-ka."

Had she heard right? Darq scowled. "What did you just say, Beans?"

"Sorry. My grandmother always said when I got an unexpected or unexplained assist in my life, one I couldn't rationalize or verify, it had to be because The Ancestor—well my great healer of an ancestor to be exact—had come to my aid. Sort of like a guardian angel. Our dyn has a history of healers and many benevolent ancestors. We do the Ghost Dance every new moon and praise them for watching over us." She said that with great pride.

The Mayahi Dyn didn't do the Ghost Dance. Too risky the devil might come calling with the crew of the *Tolamixi Mu*. "Look, Beans, help from your ancestors might have worked when you were a child, but as an adult? I don't think so. There's a logical explanation for what moved us out here."

"Raven," Phrys said, "look at your PS two."

Darq drew up the parsec screen.

A moment later, Beans said, "Raven, what do you see?"

"Several asteroids are crashing into each other. One's a huge bruiser. It's spinning slowly, but it's passing through where we originally stopped." She watched its trajectory. "Starshine and shitfire."

"What?" Beans demanded.

"If we had still been there sleeping, we would have been struck by that monster."

"A close call, right?"

"Too close for comfort."

Beans' euphoric voice rang over the com, "There you have it. The Ancestor was looking out for me—I mean—us."

Darq heaved a sigh. Just what she needed, a cheery little pilot. "Are you always so revitalized after you wake?"

"No. Not usually."

A tiny tremor of fear flicked deep in Darq's gut. "Beans, give me a readout on your C O two scrubber."

"Okay." A pause, then "Green to the top. Why did you want to know that? Oh! You think I'm suffering epoxia because I'm telling you about The Ancestor?"

"The idea crossed my mind." It surely had. "You're not exactly acting like you did en route here."

"I was terrified then."

"But not now?"

"No, of course not. And before you ask, that's because we're safely out of the asteroids, and I realized it's a miracle we are alive. Just a few things to rejoice about."

"It's no miracle. We're alive because of our piloting skills."

"If you say so, but if you don't mind, Raven, I'll call it a mini-miracle and give credit where credit is due—to The Ancestor and J'Hi-inti."

Darq stifled the growl of displeasure in her throat and decided not to argue with The Believer. She killed the screen view of the monster asteroid tumbling into another asteroid and drew up a wider perimeter of where they were. "Beans, I think I know why you didn't get any response when you tried to find Dragon Lady's signal."

"Oh? Why?"

"We were not quite clear of a tight band of small asteroids extending out from the swarm, but we should be now. Give it another go."

"Affirmative, Raven."

At least Beans' voice now sounded like a pilot's should—all business.

A minute passed, then two.

Unable to contain her curiosity any longer, Darq said, "Any response, Beans?"

"No reply, but hey—wait a sec. Weird. I just got a double pinging echo. It hit us again."

"What double pinging?"

Phrys broke in with, "Double pinging indicates we are in Doyon territory and two Doyon destroyers are en route to engage us."

Darq gritted her teeth to keep from screaming at Phrys. "For the last time, we are not in Doyon space." She took a calming breath. "Beans, can you get a fix on the origin of those pings?"

"Working on it. You sure it's okay to drift like this?"

"Affirmative. We are in no immediate danger, and we're together. The closer we are, the less likely someone can hear our ship-to-ship chatter. Besides, we need a direction, a beacon to home in on."

A loud ping sounded over the *Ky*'s comsystem, followed by a second, even louder ping.

"Gawd, what was that?" Beans said.

Darq's faceplate screen winked with a grid-map indicating the two signals came from different directions. "Oh, shitfire." They'd come a longer way then even she had thought possible.

Fear edged Beans's voice. "Doyons?"

Another double pinging resonated.

"No, Beans. We're in the cross-over zone of the long range scanners for the *Dujaki* and the Talragon station." Through the neural net she sent, *Can you determine our exact position, Phrys?*

Working on it.

Another round of pings nearly deafened her. A screen filled her faceplate. "Beans," Darq said, "get your long-range com activated. Send a message. Acknowledge the double pings. Tell them to tone down the signal and give us a beacon."

After two more loud pings, the sound muted to normal. The next single ping sounded normal.

"That ping," Phrys said, "is from the *Dujaki*'s longest-ranging sensor array. I am transferring coordinates now."

It certainly had taken Phrys long enough. Darq eyed her faceplate and the new screen. "Oh, great."

"I take it," Beans said, "you didn't mean great in a good way?"

"Affirmative. We're five and a half hours out from the *Dujaki*, six and a half from Talragon."

"Holy Mother of Heaven, Raven, that was some shortcut."

"Beans, are you picking up any replies to your hail?"

"Nothing but static so far. Still working on the reroute of connections Phrys gave me, but I'm not a tech."

"Okay, it's obvious they hear us but we don't hear them. Send a new message. State damage prevents us receiving messages, and if they understand, have them ping us three times in quick succession at normal tone."

The pings stopped. Tense moments passed before three quick pings.

"Wah-hoo!" Beans shouted. "Bless The Ancestor!"

"Tone it down," Darq sharply commanded. "Do you want to alert the whole damned Doyon kungarike on the other side of the Cypha-wee-ka?"

"Sorry, Raven."

Darq took a steadying draw of her oxygen. "Beans, we still need a beacon. Tell the Dragon—"

"To boost the homing beacon's signal?"

"Right." Darq eyed the chronometer flicker the time. As the sixth minute turned, Beans said, "Raven, how long does it take to boost a signal?"

"How would I know? Okay, so, yes, I would have thought they would have done it faster than this." To Phrys she said, *Give me your best guess where the Dujaki is and plot a course for it.*

That is suicide. Without accurate data we will deplete our engines and miss the station by many parsecs or not be able to reach it at all.

We only have to get up to speed and cruise. We'll have plenty of power left to adjust course when and if we get a better fix on the Dujaki. Now where is that plot?

Data appeared on her faceplate with three different settings before Phrys declared, *Those are the best estimates I can give you at this time.*

An indecisive answer at best. *Give me an average.*

That's ridiculous.

PHRYS! Give me the average.

He complied.

"Beans, heads up." Darq said. "We're moving out."

"You have a beacon?"

"No, but we can't waste time sitting around. We're taking a general aim for home. I'll separate our fighters, start you on course, and you can go to full throttle. Once you're up to max burn, kill your engines and cruise. I'll get in front of you and you can follow like we did through the asteroids."

Beans responded cheerily with, "Sounds like a plan." Then in the faintest of whispers came "Great and Noble Ancestor, watch over us."

Half an hour elapsed with Beans reporting sporadic single pings before the loud and welcome buzz of a homing signal sounded. Phrys sent Darq a sector map, which morphed to show the course adjustment needed to line up with the *Dujaki*'s beacon signal. She was four minutes left of the line.

Three and a half hours from the *Dujaki*, blips appeared on Darq's screen. *Phrys, I have four spooks – no ID coming up.*

That ID unit is fried. The four are friendlies. Pytak fighters. It would seem we merit an escort home.

An hour out from the *Dujaki*, a Na-ka-ta voice came over Darq's ship-to-ship com. "This is Flight Control Center Seven, Controller One Two, do you copy, Zephyr Lead?"

Darq's faceplate screens changed and filled with data – and a landing pattern. "Affirmative, Controller One Two. Data received." She made course corrections before the controller asked. At twenty minutes out, she said farewell to the escorting fighters. They broke away and headed for their landings on the flight deck on the other side of the *Dujaki*. Two fighters remained behind her and Beans, in case either she or Beans needed to eject.

"Raven," Beans said, "I've got a lower left bar trying to come on. It winks out before I can see what it's trying to tell me." Her voice didn't reveal fear but profound concern.

And the kid should be concerned. The bars in the lower left quadrant of a pilot's faceplate dealt with power output from a fighter's doige engines.

"Controller One Two, this is Zephyr Lead, we may have a problem with Jaguar Four and need a D-tunnel."

"Already anticipated, Zephyr Lead. Tunnel is in place."

Darq said into her com, "Did you copy, Beans?"

"Affirmative. My controls are going stiff. Hard to maintain level." Soft swearing ensued, followed by "To make it all this way and the *Serr* have a grumbler sucks big time."

"Considering what your fighter's been through and how badly his systems have been taxed, be thankful, Beans, that it's only a grumble." Then Darq tacked on. "Besides, don't you have an ancestor riding your wing?"

"Right— Oh, shitz!"

"Now what?"

"Warning light just came on. I've got eight minutes of O two left."

Raven, Phrys said, *in one minute ten you must veer to port so the* Serr *cruises the rest of the way in.*

I'm not blind. I saw the info on my screens.

You are not slowing.

We're not there yet. Does Beans have enough air to make it in?

She will require six minutes of air, provided she remains calm and does not panic-breathe. I will now remind you that you have only eleven minutes of air yourself.

"Oh, shitz," Beans whispered.

Darq checked her faceplate. The gap between the *Ky* and the *Serr* had lengthened.

"Raven," Beans said, a hesitation in her voice, "my engines died. They refuse to restart." Then the *Serr*'s nose drifted downward. Two ratcheting bursts of quad-thrusters leveled the ship, but the nose began to drift downward.

Darq banked sharply to port. "I'm coming around and under you, Beans. I'll piggyback you in." Darq contacted Controller One Two, told him what she planned—and that Beans was running out of oxygen. Darq mentally calculated and relayed time factors to the ATC. The little screen winked she had a seventy percent chance of success.

Phrys half-bellowed. *Those are insane maneuvers. You will crash this fighter into the* Dujaki's *hull, kill yourself—and ME. You have no right to—*

Shut up! On second thought, Phrys was right. Risking her fighter and her life was one thing, but a bonded Na-ka-ta who had a pilot waiting for him? A Na-ka-ta likely to pour out a litany of safety regs, allow proximity alarms to blast away, and cause her to lose concentration on the landings she was about to attempt? No way. "Beans, hang tight. I'll be right back."

Ignoring Beans questioning what she meant, Darq dove the *Ky*, revved the engines to max burn, and banked a steep arc, looking for lights over any shuttle bay indicating it was unoccupied. Finding one, she made course adjustments.

Terror raced through Phrys's voice. *What are you doing?*

I've had it with you, Phrys. "Controller One Two, inform shuttle bay four they have an incoming eject pod."

Controller One Two replied, "Acknowledging you are abandoning your fighter—"

Darq gritted her teeth. "I am not!" She reached for the switch to eject only the copilot's pod.

Then what are you doing? Phrys asked, bewildered.

Ejecting you. She hit the switch, heard the snapping pops and blasts, the shoom of the copilot's pod whipping away, and Phrys's outraged *You are insane!*

Darq pushed the *Ky*'s engines to the redline and sped back to the *Serr*. Braking her speed at the last possible second, she came up under the *Serr*, gently touched it, and carried it atop the *Ky*. She checked the time. Four minutes until Beans ran out of oxygen. Two minutes to the doige tunnel.

"Zephyr Lead" came the calm voice of Controller One Two, "Please advise. Do you intend to piggy-back land with Jaguar Four?"

"Negative. I'm going to push her in and break away."

"Understood. Adjust your angle. Six degrees up will allow the *Serr's* nose to drift down and come level for the net-catchers."

"Affirmative." Darq brought the *Ky's* nose up six degrees. A steeper angle than she would like considering what she had to do, but no one was going to suffocate to death — not if she could help it.

Darq switched her faceplate screens to a view of the yawning mouth of Flight Deck Seven and the bright winking lights of the doige tunnel inside it. She checked the rapid speed of her approach. Timing was everything.

"Zephyr Lead," Controller One Two said, "do you wish assistance to make a breakaway dive?"

"Negative." Darq concentrated on the view, all the while noting the descending readouts of the distance to the edge of the flight deck. "Hey, Beans," Darq said over the com, "I'm going to break away and you'll glide in. The second I break, kill all your power. Relax and hang in there until the rescue crews get you out."

"Thanks, Raven."

"Breaking away in four, three, two — one." With only meters remaining before the nose of the *Ky* touched the *Dujaki*, Darq became aware of frantic voices in the background behind Controller One Two. Someone was certain she would crash.

How odd. Controller One Two didn't question or speak?

Not that she was going to crash if she could help it, but — never mind. Fly. DIVE.

She put the *Ky* into a steep vertical dive, cut the engines, and let the fighter glide. Using thrusters, she followed the underside of the *Dujaki* and gradually opened up the distance between the *Ky* and the *Dujaki's* hull.

Minutes later came Controller One Two's "Zephyr Lead, Jaguar Four has landed. No DLE."

"That's a blessing." Then the thought flitted that maybe, just maybe, The Ancestor had kept Beans safe. Only no ancestor ever helped her, had they? And why was she allowing such thoughts? She had to land. She focused on the most important faceplate screen — and found it sick, flicking, only pieces of numbers flashing.

Over Controller One Two's comlink connection, from somewhere behind him, came a booming voice. "She's going to cream the arrays. Tell her to pull away."

"She cannot pull away," Controller One Two calmly replied. "She has little oxygen left to breathe and only one chance in ninety to pull off a switchback landing."

How did the controller know she intended a switchback landing? As a cadet, she'd ridden the copilot's seat behind Atlatl, who had been forced to make one after a Pytak crashed at the mouth of the landing bay. Back then, she'd thought it the grandest ride of her young life. And now? Now, she had decided to attempt the same landing. Maybe she was insane.

She shifted her attention to the assortment of comlink and scanner arrays ahead and hit the thrusters, moving laterally. *By the numbers — by the numbers . . .*

Once clear and sure her engines' output couldn't harm the arrays, she pushed for more speed. Soon she lined up with the belly lights at the edge of the mouth to flight deck one. She adjusted her rate of speed, checked angles, watched the calculations flicker, and noted less than three minutes remained before she came to the edge.

Controller One Two said, "Zephyr Lead, you may opt to eject after you clear the hull. Rescue is standing by to pick you up."

Nice of him to remind her of that option.

A red light flashed on her faceplate screen and a dull triple dinging ensued. Two minutes of oxygen left. She would be dead before rescue got to her. Shitfire, to survive the day and suffocate? Only she wasn't dead yet. Making a switchback landing got her closer to rescuers than any ejection. "Controller One Two, I'm landing on flight deck one."

Controller One Two calmly replied, "Zephyr Lead, you do not have sufficient oxygen left."

"The odds of surviving are better."

The second the *Ky*'s nose cleared the edge of the flight deck she checked the time—one minute fifty-one to land and get extracted before the air ran out. Was there any way to make the air last longer? Sometimes—no, a lot of times—in the heat of battle pilots forgot to breathe. She forgot to breath. Maybe she had held her breath long enough through this flight to have a margin of air left. A few breaths not taken?

She took in a long deep breath and held it. When her canards cleared the edge of the *Dujaki*, she pivoted the *Ky*'s stern horizontally, one hundred eighty degrees, brought the nose level, and throttled forward, into the mouth of the flight deck. The *Ky*'s mangled belly skimmed the deck, setting off vibrations which trembled through her.

Her lungs burned for air. She glanced at the oxygen reading. Zero.

The voice of Controller One Two came over her comlink. "You are in."

Rapidly she reversed power and shut the engines down, killing power to systems. *Dear J'Hi, let there be no DLE.*

She exhaled and took in a half-breath, heard the muted honks of warning horns within the doige tunnel, felt the jerk of the nets catching the *Ky*, pulling it down until it smacked the deck.

Her faceplate screens winked off leaving only the lingering echo of the screen colors on the back of her eyelids. She inhaled another half-breath.

Overhead came the pop of her canopy being opened. Robot extensions snapped onto her flight harness shoulder rig. Then came the clicks of her seat releasing its hookups to her flightsuit and the swift jerk upward, the pilot-extractor pulling her out of the cockpit and up, into the rescue room above the doige tunnel.

She let out the breath she could no longer hold. In the recesses of her mind the soft pattering of Zukaltay's drum began. She gave herself up to the light-headed, swirling sensations of a dance of joy—and darkness.

✧　✧　✧

Darq woke to the sharp hissing of an autozipper and the rustling of fabric. Into focus came her semidarkened bed chamber where the only light came from the starscape on the wallscreen. She tried to piece together the images of how she had gone from landing the *Ky* on the *Dujaki*'s deck to her bed-rack. Images flashed faster than keg rounds of her waking en route to sickbay with an oxygen mask on. Of passing Chance in a med-bed being taken to recovery after her surgery. Of remembering being told Chance would be all right. Fang-fire had ripped into the side of her cockpit and shrapnel had gutted the fleshy part of her upper arm and chest. By the blessings of the Great Mother, no blood vessels had been pierced. Chance's Na-ka-ta, Izzt, had taken a lot more shrapnel. He would be in the shop for a rebuild from hip to shoulder.

Funny how she recalled that information so vividly.

What else did she remember? Oh, right, a Na-ka-ta nurse who stood beside her med-bed injecting something cold into her arm that knocked her out. By the lingering aftertaste in her mouth, she had enjoyed a drug-induced sleep. Maybe those drugs still lingered, keeping her mind fuzzy.

A heavy thump in the darkness nearby was followed by a second heavy thump.

Boots?

Exiting the darkness and coming toward her was Atlatl, in his skivvies. He looked like he'd aged a thousand years. All that ripping, rustling, and thumping had been him stripping to present himself as husband, not commander.

His little-boy smile graced his lips. He said softly, "Move over."

She gave him a buoyant grin. "Waking me from a much needed rest, my dear atan?"

"Of course. Now, scoot over. I've got four hours to hold my woman, and maybe, just maybe, get a nap. And before you ask, D'ktr Enyeto says you're okay. Stressed but okay."

She chuckled and scooted over in her sleepsack, her tush bumping the wall, sending the rack swaying on its moorings.

When Atlatl had situated himself, she turned over, spooning against him. His warmth was as welcome as his musk-spice scent. She settled her hand over his, tucking his fingers under her breast. "Are you comfy now?"

"Indeed." He sighed with gusto. "And relieved, my dearest atan. Relieved to be holding you once more." His voice seemed to choke with tears. "You don't know the torture I went through when they told me your squadron was at the Joiz station. Then came word the station had been destroyed." He took a deep breath. "Then I was informed you self-destructed . . ."

"Well I didn't self-destruct. I had Phrys rig a false countdown."

"A countdown warning virtually identical to the real thing."

"What? Really?"

"Really."

"I guess I should thank Phrys for doing such a good job."

"If he did such a good job, why did you eject him? And don't say irreconcilable difference of opinion."

"He drove me nuts. He quetched away about safety regs and how I exceeded redline after redline, that I was insane, ad infinitum."

Atlatl chuckled, his warm breath gentle behind her ear. A moment later, with more somberness, he said, "You know, I kept thinking you were alive and had outwitted the Doyons. That lasted until I saw the data verifying the *Ky*'s self-destruct and no eject. Comprehending you were dead hit like a diggerboom to the gut."

Darq lifted Atlatl's hand away from her breast and kissed his palm.

His words came out half-choked, "And then I endured seeing your flight removed from the screens, confirming your death. *My soul died.*"

"I survived, Atlatl. I survived."

"Ah yes, that." He bit back a bitter chuckle. "There I am, in the throes of trying to suppress my anguish and be the *Dujaki*'s battle commander when a message comes over the flight control speakers, *Dragon Lady – this is Jaguar Four – and Zephyr Lead – do you copy*? I swear my blood froze in disbelief. When the message repeated, I nearly fainted."

"You never faint."

"Actually, your fainting scared the hell out of me."

"I did not faint." Had she? One of those memory puzzle pieces turned into place. She'd held her breath. Maybe for too long? "I ran out of air."

"You had no air left. Zero."

"Imagine that."

He harrumphed. "Just bless the stars, dear wife, the rescue crews got to you in time. Enyeto ran triple brain scans to be sure your brain wasn't deprived of oxygen."

"He did it to be sure I didn't have a glitch in my neural net."

"That too." Atlatl kissed her neck below her ear lobe. "I'm ever grateful the good d'ktr didn't keep you overnight for observation, otherwise I wouldn't have these precious few hours with you."

Another memory puzzle piece slipped into place. "And here I thought it was to keep Lingit from killing me as I slept."

He chuckled softly. "Ah, yes, Lingit."

"Did she really try to stab Varree?"

"Yes. I witnessed it."

"Ah, but you also gave the order that Lingit should be present when the *Ky* landed so she could greet her Phrys."

"Enyeto tell you that?"

"No, a very chatty Na-ka-ta nurse." An hour before being discharged from sickbay, that nurse had brought Darq a bowl of salty fish broth with a few skinny noodles in it and countless forms to sign.

"And you, Darq, my dearest atan, what do you go and do but eject Phrys into a shuttle bay."

"The exterior lights said the bay was empty." Darq let the chuckle bubble out of her. "It seemed the thing to do at the time."

"Well, I can tell you it was a mad scramble getting Lingit to the shuttle bay."

"But? I hear a but."

"Once Lingit got her arms around Phrys's neck, she wouldn't let go. She wept hysterically. Enyeto had to tranquilize her." He heaved a weary sigh. "And to think, the entire incident about Varree and Phrys could have been prevented if Varree hadn't ordered him to fly with you."

"I'll second that."

"Wife, you have no say in the matter."

"Ah, but I do get to fill out a report first thing I'm back on duty."

"Are you going to crucify Phrys? If you ask me, he suffered enough humiliation from being ejected."

"It'll be a good report."

"Oh, really?"

"Yes, really. He kibitzed about a lot of regs and safety issues but, considering he rigged the self-destruct countdown that saved us, I'm of a mind to be neutral."

He laughed. "A first."

"Oh, and as soon as I'm back on duty, I propose to have a few words with Varree about never pairing me with an already bonded Na-ka-ta."

"No need."

"Why?"

"I've already had a chat with Varree."

Darq squirmed and turned over to face Atlatl. "Did you crucify her?"

He ran his fingers over her temple, pushing her hair behind her ear. "I do not crucify my officers. Though the thought crossed my mind to chew hard on her hide, I did not. She was profusely contrite."

Darq beamed a smile at him. "Groveling, was she?"

He let out a bark of laughter. "Not quite, but close." His grin vanished, and his voice again turned somber. "She's frustrated, and with good cause. You have rejected four Na-ka-tas and ejected the fifth today." Atlatl gently placed his index finger on her lips and silenced her retort. "Varree has come up with a solution."

Darq pulled his hand down so she could speak. "Which is?"

"She's going to set aside simulator time for you to vet out Na-ka-tas and find one you can fly with. You have her — and my — permission to stop the flight-sims the instant you decide you can't work with a Na-ka-ta. No ejecting."

"Not even a simulated eject if I feel I'm under dire stress?"

"Be nice to the Na-ka-tas. After you ejected Phrys today, Varree thinks there won't be any volunteers."

"Ejecting Phrys seemed the right thing to do at the time."

"Be that as it may, dearest atan, Varree will be contacting Talragon and *Ziital* to see if they have any qualified Na-ka-tas and, more importantly, willing candidates. She's also going to have her brand new chief flight instructor go over all the *Dujaki*'s Na-ka-ta lists to see if he can suggest, or convince, a Na-ka-ta to fly with you — in the sim."

"A new CFI? He doesn't know me."

"Now there you're wrong. He talked you and Jaguar Four in."

"You mean — Controller One Two?"

Atlatl nodded. "He happened to be in Flight Control when the news of the Joiz attack came. He volunteered to assist pilots in. Did a good job of it. By the way, he stopped Lingit from stabbing Varree."

"A bona fide tin-suit hero?"

"Curb the sarcasm. The Na-ka-ta has only been here twenty-four hours, and already he's proved himself beyond Varree's wildest hopes."

"He's too good to be true."

Atlatl kissed her lightly on the lips. "Ever the pessimist."

Darq looked into Atlatl's darkening chestnut eyes where fatigue and love mirrored in their depths. She whispered, "I need a hug." In truth he probably needed the hug more than she did, but his strong arms were always a comfort.

He wrapped his arms about her, holding her as tightly as she held him. When his whole body trembled, she knew silent tears welled but would not be shed. She had, once again, scared the hell out of him. "I love you so much, Atlatl. You're the best thing that's ever come into my life." Hot tears surged, blurring her vision.

"I love you, Darq . . . If only there weren't a war . . ."

She kissed his neck, released her hold and pulled back enough to meld her lips with his in a kiss radiating the love in her heart. *If only there weren't a war* whispered through her mind along with *Someday there will come one last kiss.*

✧ Chapter 12

By the war god's ass, where was Nuzzi? It wasn't like him to be late for a game of bok'bon. Konuris Ippera eyed the giant CC's doorway. The only sounds in his cargo container were the docile hum of the surrounding life-support systems for the gold-encrusted bust that housed his brain. The only sensation he felt was the cold seeping off the collar around his neck. A collar that linked his brain to the primary computer housed beneath him. Forever constrained by gold and collar.

Currently demeaned and insulted at having to travel in a CC. Depravation. That's what it was. Chingvee exalted in lording her power over him. No admirid should have to endure such accommodations. He deserved better. Far better. Particularly considering the kungarike had grandiose plans for him and their new, all-powerful destroyer, *Ippera*. Thank the war god that Nuzzi had the balls and the security clearances that allowed him inside this CC. Nuzzi's daily visits included reports of what went on in the kungarike and, more importantly, details of Chingvee's machinations. So, where are you Nuzzi?

Konuris focused his optical lenses on the cargo container's doorframe. He magnified the view of the door's triple seals, searching again for the dot of a microphone, a sensor, a camera lens. Knowing Chingvee, that m'chee had installed something to monitor him during this voyage. She relished his discomforts.

Or had he succumbed to paranoia?

Nonsense. He hadn't. He was bored. Bored, bored, bored! What he wouldn't give for a way to hack into the *R'keyas*'s systems. Not that he wanted to know anything specific about the military long-hauler transporting him to the Aichi Two Ship

Center where the destroyer *Ippera* awaited. Still it behooved him to know how fast the *R'keyas* traveled and if the ship held to schedule.

The sooner he and his conglomeration of circuits and computers were installed in the *Ippera*, the more likely he would unearth a way to self-destruct. But he must be patient. Self-destruction must not happen until after he, or rather his brain and his destroyer body, were escorted to the farthest corner of the kungarike. There no one would witness the *Ippera* being tested.

Well, almost no one. The blasted Centauri outposts stood guard, but they had witnessed many a Doyon ship play war games and never reacted.

So none would be the wiser when he caused the destroyer *Ippera*'s end, preferably in a blaze of implosions and explosions. Whatever worked best to leave the destroyer — and his brain — in the tiniest of particles so no one could ever put him or the ship back together again.

He chuckled to himself. So many little things could go wrong when testing and stressing a new ship or a new ship's systems. Already he had a number of ideas to work with.

The cargo container's door opened and in strode Nuzzi who headed for the task chair bolted in front of Konuris's console.

Nuzzi did not greet him? How odd.

As Nuzzi took his seat, Konuris scanned him. "Hello, my friend, you look haggard." Konuris spun the outer ring of his console, bringing around the largest table-top screen the console had. He triggered the display. The bok'bon's gridded, pale green game board, edged in florescent orange, appeared.

"It's been a very long day." Nuzzi wiped a hand over his stub-nosed snout. "I am tired, sorely used, and abused. I fear, Admirid, you will easily win tonight."

"Doubtful, my friend. You are ever your best when under duress." He almost chuckled at his little rhyme.

Nuzzi scoffed.

"In truth, Nuzzi, my day has been utterly boring. So, I shall demand you enlighten me with the news of all that has transpired in your day, including your frustrations. Just how have you been used and abused today?"

"It's a mishmash of good news and bad. What do you want to hear first?"

"Start from the beginning of your day. I would like to take the news in chronological order. Choose your color."

"Black. I'm feeling like the proverbial privileged underdog."

Privileged underdog? Nuzzi had never uttered such nonsense about himself. How very curious.

Nuzzi eyed the various-sized, black, three-dimensional cubes appearing and lining up at his start side of the game board.

When the last red cube appeared on Konuris's side, Nuzzi said, "Black goes first." He tapped a finger to a cube then tapped the square on the board where a small, three-dimensional castle-fortress stood on a mountainside protecting a pass.

If Nuzzi could capture the fortress, it was worth a paltry five thousand units of land. The cube Nuzzi touched appeared in the square before the fortress's side gateway and quickly morphed into six fighting units that fanned out.

"Interesting first move," Konuris said.

Nuzzi shrugged. "I was woken this morning at the ungodly hour of 0400. Had to go to the captain's ready room for an urgent message from Supreme Command—one sent on an alphenus-secure channel."

An alphenus channel meant commander's eyes only. Although curiosity pricked Konuris, he moved one of his red cubes to the castle's parapet, opposite the black regiments below. He tapped the cube. It broke into twelve smaller cubes that dotted a defending line along the parapet. "Are you free, Nuzzi, to tell me what our beloved SC wanted of you?"

"Supreme Command didn't restrict me to silence."

Konuris met Nuzzi's gaze, a gaze that held unwaveringly steady. Softly the caprivi said, "Aichi Three was attacked by Wysotti commandos and Pytak fighters four days after we departed."

Despite not having a body, Konuris felt his stomach lurch. "A daring strike deep into our territory? How could they have gotten so far without being spotted?"

"Everyone is asking that very same question. And I mean everyone."

"And did we annihilate the Wysotti?"

"Far from it. They were in and out with minor losses — two Pytaks. Both pilot-copilots were retrieved by their own."

His nonexistent stomach flip-flopped again. "Impossible."

"Believe it. It happened. I saw the footage. An investigation is ongoing. Supreme Command has their best intelligence officers, *with absolute power*, seeking answers. Everyone involved in the I-Project is suspect."

"Even I?"

"Don't be ridiculous, Admirid, you are the least of suspects."

"Look on the bright side, Nuzzi, if the Wysotti strike was to harm me, they failed."

Nuzzi nodded, and his smile held a flash of sunshine. "We were fortunate in that." His voice lowered. "What troubles me, and from the whispers among the F'brig brass who have been told of the attack, there was no warning. No alarms were triggered, no satellite surveillance alerts issued." He lowered his voice even more. "Some say we have a high-level spy among us and a ring of traitors." His voice became a hoarse whisper. "Many say it is the work of rebels."

"Rebels? Really, Nuzzi — "

"What else could it be? After the attack, every ship and deep space StarNet scanner focused on egress routes but found nothing. Not even doige trace. The Wysotti came and went like vanshees."

"Neither of us, Nuzzi, believes in vanshees. I am safe so SC should be delighted."

Nuzzi shook his head. "Relieved is a better word." Then he whispered, "Some think the raid was not about you."

How could that be? "Then what were the Wysotti after?"

"The frozen Wysotti pilot and her Na-ka-ta. The ones that Grier trader aspired to make a fortune on by selling them to us."

A chill ran down Konuris's nonexistent spine. From those frozen corpses had come the knowledge about neural nets and how the net relayed information and telepathic conversations, linking the pilot, the automaton, and the Pytak's systems into one extraordinary weapon. The result now? A Doyon version of the neural net implanted in his brain, enslaving him for the good of the kungarike.

Yet, how ironic. He was no better off than the greedy Grier k'pten, now a Doyon slave.

"Your move, Admirid."

Konuris looked over the board and Nuzzi's latest move. After tapping a red cube, Konuris focused again on the caprivi. "Nuzzi, how can SC be sure the Wysotti only came for their own?"

"An eyewitness, a lab assistant who, though wounded, saw the commandos load the frozen corpses aboard an egress vehicle. She had the presence of mind to note the time the vessel departed."

"Were there no other witnesses?"

"Thirteen survived, all injured, some critical, but she was the only one to actually witness the corpses loaded."

"Three hundred are dead?"

"No, no." He shook his head rapidly. "The death toll amounted to a few dozen guards and sentries killed by the commandos. Another dozen were entombed underground when the Pytaks blasted the facility. Nothing left now but a kilometer wide hole and rubble."

"What of the scientific staff and techs? Surely — "

"They were granted leave. The minute you were secured in this hold, their exodus was en mass."

Konuris would have nodded like a wise sage if he could have. "To be expected since most of the techs had not been permitted any leave for upwards of two yils." Including Ooots. Another example of the slavery the kungarike had imposed on its loyal citizenry.

Nuzzi moved another block off the start and placed it closer to the fortress's wall.

Konuris chose the smallest of his cubes and sent it through the fortress's back gate. He tapped it twice. A line of tiny blue dots — assassins — fanned out and vanished. "So, tell me, Nuzzi, what of my nemesis, Chingvee?" He held his nonexistent breath that Nuzzi would announce Chingvee among the dead and not among the happy homeward bounds.

"They found her at dawn. Unconscious. Under rubble near the back of the facility. They rushed her to the hospital."

She survived? Damn that m'chee's soul. "When does she return to duty?"

"Unknown. Fractured skull, crushed vertebrae. If it cheers you, I'm told if she survives she'll be a paraplegic. As to her mind—well, it's scrambled."

Joy warmed Konuris, but he kept the delight out of his voice. "That cheers me, but her death would cheer me more."

Nuzzi leaned forward and half-whispered, "Careful what you wish for, Admirid. Even in death she may haunt you." He leaned back.

"What is that supposed to mean?"

A green dot lit on the board. One of Konuris's assassins had connected with one of Nuzzi's smaller units and had wiped it off the board. Nuzzi tabbed a cube on the board near the attack site. A six-dot squad soon trapped and killed the assassin.

"Well, Nuzzi, are you going to play or tell me how Chingvee, in death, can haunt me?"

Nuzzi rested his elbows on the console and laid his hands, one atop the other. "The day before you were loaded into this hold, Chingvee ordered me to her office. She interrogated me, insinuating you were suicidal and wanted to know why I had not reported your odd behaviors."

Damn Chingvee to the trench! Schooling himself, and in particular his voice, Konuris replied, "Ridiculous. What odd behaviors did she remark on?"

"She is convinced you are contemplating suicide because— *You are doing exactly as your predecessor did.*"

Predecessor? He had been under the impression his had been the first mind stolen and enslaved. "What predecessor?"

"Actually, there were six in all, Admirid. Six came before you."

"Six! Six F'brigs—"

"No, no. Only one was a F'brig—besides you, that is."

By the war god's ass, had a comrade, someone he respected, fallen prey to this ludicrous scheme to put a living brain inside a destroyer? "Who was the F'brig? Did I know any of the others?"

Nuzzi shook his head. "Their names were not familiar to me. The first two were idealistic computer technicians. Chingvee boasted how easy it had been to brainwash them into thinking they would live forever and contribute great advances in science."

"The two were short lived?"

"The first made it two hours before some system malfunctioned and curdled his brain. Number two lasted a week before being poisoned by a biofluid imbalance. Number three . . . ah, yes. A promising young officer who unexpectedly died. A freak accident, I think. Chingvee said he lasted nine weeks, nine days, nine hours."

Three nines. An ominously bad omen for any Doyon. "And number four?"

"A protar commander with a bad liver—cancer. No, maybe a genetic disorder. Definitely his liver had not been ruined by alcohol. Though he did drink. At any rate, he was in great pain, had only a few months to live. He made a deal, a rather good one. His brain for a lifetime income benefit for his family."

What captains did for their families. What admirids did for their families. *The sacrifices had become too great.*

"I don't recall, Admirid, how long the protar's brain lived or if Chingvee actually said how it died." Nuzzi took another cube out of the start line and set it in front of the castle-fortress's front gate. He tapped it four times and three massive catapults morphed into play and began slinging shots at the fortress. A counter appeared beneath each catapult indicating the number of hits remaining to collapse of the wall, with those numbers slowly descending.

"And who, dear caprivi, was number five, and what happened to him?"

"He came from one of the wealthy mining families. Rose to become an aid of Sector One's Admirid d'Coman Xenon. A short circuit within the collar electrocuted that F'brig's brain. Chingvee insisted a repeat of such an electrical problem cannot possibly happen again." He leaned forward and whispered. "The F'brig's death might have been a suicide, but knowing Chingvee, she would have covered up such a fact. Wouldn't do to have unwilling brains, now would it?"

So true, but enslaving F'brigs was unconscionable. Konuris moved another red cube. "And what of number six?"

"He commanded the destroyer *Yogevstov*. A protar by the name of Vuai. He lasted twenty months before going insane. Chingvee terminated his brain herself."

Ah, insanity, now there's a thought on how to die. Perhaps not. Being terminated lacked dignity.

Nuzzi cocked his head, his gaze seemed to focus on small details of Konuris's sculpted mask.

Konuris chose his words and vocal tone with care. "I assure you, Nuzzi, I am not contemplating insanity or suicide."

Nuzzi heaved a sigh. "I know, I told Chingvee so, but she isn't taking any chances."

"Perhaps she is the insane one. What makes her so sure I am in the throws of losing my mind?"

"The way you've been probing into subsystems. Particularly the incident a month ago when you hacked into her personal files."

"I did not get far. She had an effective firewall I could not easily penetrate. As to the subsystems, I merely wanted to see what was what. Computer systems tend to fascinate me when I'm bored."

"That's what number five and number six told her after they hacked into her computer. But I must tell you, your little recon was amazing."

"I know. Chingvee bellowed for an hour about my abuses to her privacy and assimilating top secret information I was not entitled to."

"Did you know your little foray resulted in the most sophisticated firewalls being installed on *every computer* working or associated with the I-Project to prevent access to subsystems?"

"Yes, I do. Chingvee took prideful delight in telling me so for days on end." What would Nuzzi do if he learned Ooots had shared how to bypass those new firewalls? No, that was his and Ooots' secret. And speaking of Ooots— "What of Ooots?"

Nuzzi's gaze darted to the game board. He remained silent.

Konuris felt his non-existent heart skip a beat. Nuzzi must be unsure how to break the news that Ooots had been a casualty of the Wysotti strike on Aichi Three. "It is all right, Nuzzi. I understand. The raid. I only hope little Ooots died quickly."

Nuzzi's head came up. "No, you have it wrong, Admirid. She wasn't killed in the raid on Aichi Three."

"She is alive? She survived?"

He nodded then shook his head.

"Make up your mind, caprivi!" The look in Nuzzi's eyes stilled every cell in Konuris's brain.

"Nuzzi, what has befallen her? Do they think she is the spy, a traitor?"

Nuzzi shook his head. "Ooots was one of the first to leave the facility. Her first day home, my wife introduced Ooots to our two sons, which I'd insisted she do, as we agreed. Two days later, my sons took Ooots and her cousin to a carnival at the seashore, next to the big water park—you know the one."

"I remember it. So what happened? An accident on one of the rides?" What a dishonorable way for Ooots to die.

Nuzzi shook his head. "No. That afternoon, the four met your son-the-genius, J'sein, and they all went to the boardwalk." He suddenly looked uncomfortable and swallowed hard enough that the thick skin rings on his throat contracted much like they would if he'd bolted down a whole rogg. He drew in a deep breath. "A riot broke out. A riot over—can you believe it—kakeli. A little cream-filled dessert!"

One Ooots loved and which she said cost a small fortune because of wartime shortages. "Nuzzi, what of my son? What happened to J'sein?"

"With violence bursting all around them, Ooots shoved J'sein between two ancient tapia trees. Then she and my sons helped him climb the tree." A smile flashed across Nuzzi's face. "The boy was probably more traumatized by the height they achieved than the riot, but he and my sons were safe, unscathed."

Konuris muttered, "Bless the war god for small favors."

Nuzzi hesitated, then firmly stated, "Evidently Sunatas has already blessed J'sein and Ooots."

"How so?"

"J'sein has taken a liking to Ooots, more so than either of my own sons." Nuzzi's again hesitated. "Perhaps I have erred. Was it not your intent she have a finer mate than some dweebel? Am I to discourage J'sein?"

"No, do not dissuade J'sein. My concern, however, is if Vekka will object to such an infatuation."

Nuzzi's eyes sparkled. His voice took on a lighthearted air. "Your Vekka has taken a liking to the little heroine. Vekka insisted Ooots enjoy her holiday and put her in one of your best guest rooms."

And likely pampered and fussed over Ooots in the bargain. Konuris wished he could give his nod of approval. "That pleases me, Nuzzi. I trust you will ensure Ooots never knows of our, shall we say, mating manipulations?"

Nuzzi nodded rapidly.

"Speaking of manipulations and manipulators, a thought occurs to me. How could my wanderings about the computer systems have triggered Chingvee's paranoia that I am suicidal?"

"She showed me the correlations between you and your predecessors, Numbers Five and Six." He paused as if recalling something. "You know, Chingvee admitted it was now impossible for you to kill yourself. Ah—I remember. They've installed failsafes. You couldn't kill yourself even if you tried."

Damn Chingvee's rotten soul.

Nuzzi wiped his hand over his snout. "Yet, what confused her most was—" He eyed Konuris. "Exactly what possessed you to count all the toilets and examine their schematics?"

Chingvee knew about the toilets? Did she suspect? No. Not possible. He had to gloss over this topic. "If you really must know, Nuzzi, reading anything mundane and technical often ends my insomnia. Being without a body that requires mandatory sleep makes it difficult to rest, and my mind does require some rest. So, I cope as best I can with the insomnia."

"According to Chingvee, you never suffered insomnia."

He lied. "That's only because I often discover fascinating trivia. Did you know the fleet specifications call for one toilet for every six Doyons? Doesn't matter if those Doyons have rank or are grunts. And only the caprivi, his second in command, and the various division chiefs have a private toilet in their quarters?"

A smile crazed Nuzzi's lips. "Perhaps it says more about their crap than them?"

Konuris chuckled softly. "Yes, I thought of that." What delighted him was discovering a way to short out the toilets when said officers sat on them. A possible way to remove someone who might be able to stop him from suiciding. He had certainly relished imagining Chingvee on her toilet and, many times, envisioned executing her.

A ping issued from the game board. Two of Konuris's assassins had killed the senior officers of Nuzzi's forces.

Nuzzi quickly backed his cubes into the forest area to regroup.

The board pinged again. A red crown appeared over the fortress, proclaiming it safe from further attack for two turns.

"Like bok'bon," Nuzzi said, "you have always played a skillful game, Admirid. It's how you've survived in the kungarike and risen up the ranks, but heed my warning. Chingvee means to ensure you willingly serve the fleet and you will never kill yourself."

"That sounds ominous."

"It is. Chingvee told me she had drafted a proposal to submit to Supreme Command. One guaranteed to keep you in line and convince them that, even if you did command a warship, you would never turn it on them."

So that possibility had been considered. "What could she threaten me with?"

"Not you. The threat is to your wife. Your sons. Your titles. Your wealth and property. Your reputation and good name."

Dread seized him. "What are you talking about? Explain."

"It's blackmail. Chingvee believes you value your family and heritage more than the service. Her fear, warranted or not, is that you'll kill yourself, or use the power of the destroyer you'll be operating to kill Doyons, and thus destroy trillions of romos that have been invested in this project."

"Not to mention her pension and reputation."

"That goes without saying." Nuzzi tapped his skinny index finger's thick pointed nail on the console. "Look, Admirid, we both know Supreme Command is desperate to end this war with the Wysotti. If SC gets her report, they won't take any chances. They'll agree with Chingvee. You make one wrong turn and they'll take everything away from your family, make them slaves or, worse, brand them traitors—kill them. Is that what you want?"

"No!"

Nuzzi took a deep breath and let it out slowly. "I'm also in that report, Admirid. Chingvee believes I'm aiding and abetting you. She's promised the same treatment will befall my family if I don't report signs that you're becoming a liability."

"I and mine have always been loyal, as have you and yours. She has no right—"

Nuzzi's fingernail struck the console with a loud click. He spoke quietly but sharply. "In these times, everyone's loyalty is being questioned."

"What are you talking about?"

"This war with the Wysotti was supposed to be a blitz, but it has dragged on. Some whisper the kungarike's coffers are empty, and the money spent on launching the new *Ippera* won't ensure victory." He paused, calming himself. "These are dark times, Admirid. There are shortages, hardships, sacrifices, more taxes. The discontent among the common people has led to clashes at mines and factories over working conditions and wages. In the past six months, there have been dozens of riots, all quelled with force. Now we're seeing spontaneous riots breaking out over such trivia as kakeli!"

Nuzzi drew in a deep breath, whether to fortify his resolve or to calm himself, Konuris couldn't be sure.

"There is, Admirid, the unspoken fear among the kungarike of an underground movement, one determined to overthrow the Hibizahn and take down the military aristocracy."

He must quell Nuzzi's fears. Clearly and precisely Konuris said, "Has Chingvee's proposal been submitted."

"I don't know. I don't think so, but Wosolek, her second in command, who was on leave when the Wysotti attacked, knew about it, helped her draft it. He's coveted Chingvee's job. You can bet he will use whatever it takes to guarantee you and your destroyer perform above expectations and he gets the credit."

"But you are not certain of him and his intentions?"

Nuzzi shook his head. "No."

"Will we arrive at Aichi Two on schedule?"

"Ahead actually. The *R'keyas*'s captain had orders to make all possible speed for Aichi Two. We'll arrive a day and a half early, if the engines hold. Oh, and I understand they're putting the final polish on the *Ippera* as we speak. Personnel are on standby to insert you. Likely we'll get underway for the testing two days ahead of schedule."

"What of the Joiz SOA? Have they decided what to do about preventing it from detecting the *Ippera*?"

Nuzzi smiled and the tips of his razor teeth flashed. "Good news on that. Under the cover of a virulent gamma storm, which blinded the Joiz sensors, the *Cocopaj Moji* made it undetected to the dust cloud, the little one — " He paused in thought. "Can't remember what it's called. Anyway, the storm and our newest stealth technology also enabled us to seed Strikers among the asteroids." His smile vanished, his tone hardened to disgust. "Unfortunately, one of the patrolling Wysotti fighters decided to do loops around asteroids. Only the war god knows why any pilot would do such an idiotic thing."

Konuris wanted to throttle Nuzzi for drifting off topic. "Nuzzi. What happened?"

"The Pytak fighter nearly collided with one of our hidden Strikers. Orders had been given that if any Striker was discovered, we were to attack. The war god knows we didn't want to deal with eight Pytaks but, in the end, we were triumphant."

"At what cost?"

Nuzzi seemed to deflate. "Enough. Mostly due to the Raven and her squad."

The Raven was a nemesis of nemeses. "How much damage did she do to the *Cocopaj Moji?*"

"How — How did you know she fired DGRBMs into the fortress?"

"I have, on two occasions, been the recipient of her DGRBMs."

Nuzzi looked contrite. "Reports say the Raven and one of her cohorts made a blind missile strike. Their missiles hit. One went deep, struck a power plant. Extensive as the damage was, there will be plenty of time for the fortress to make repairs."

"Don't count on it."

"Do count on it. Our missiles destroyed the Joiz station. We sent the Pytaks fleeing. The Wysotti are now totally blind and will not see our amassing the armada, nor the destroyer *Ippera*. The Narrows has been filled with mines. No Wysotti is going to penetrate it. And best of all, *the Raven is dead*."

"What? How?"

"The invincible woman was cornered by a squad of our illustrious Strikers. Those Strikers cut her off from The Narrows. In dodging fang-fire, she entered the asteroid field. She could not escape, so she chose the coward's way out. She self-destructed."

"Are you positive?"

Nuzzi chuckled. "Yes. Fleet's best ran her Pytak's self-destruct countdown warning blasts through the most sophisticated analyzers we have and checked the timing to the explosion. Absolutely no doubt. *The Raven is dead*."

Relief washed over Konuris. "All hail the benevolent war god's kindness."

"Indeed." Nuzzi leaned forward, eyes sparkling with delight. "You know what this means? It means the plans for the demise of the Wysotti homeworld are on schedule. We shall prevail. The asteroids we've seeded with rockets will go undetected." Nuzzi moved one of his largest cubes toward a town. After tapping it, an army of foot soldiers appeared, marching toward the city gates.

"Indeed." Konuris countered with a cube to defend the city. "Still one should not celebrate a victory until one is victorious. There are many months yet to the shock and awe of those asteroids being launched out of the swarm and impacting the Wysotti homeworld."

Nuzzi chuckled. "But only we few know the Wysotti's calendar End of Days will be their true end of days."

That he couldn't argue with. "We should never underestimate an enemy, Nuzzi. The Wysotti are unpredictable females. Clever in countering our Doyon offensives and tactics. Your turn."

More subdued, the two played on to a stalemate. Nuzzi left, and Konuris dimmed the lights that had been mounted for him on the cargo container's side walls. He triggered a soft melody, one from an album Ooots had given him, and contemplated everything Nuzzi had said.

Suicide had seemed such a grand way to end his existence, but now? He could not risk suicide because of what that would do to his sons, his wife. His dear wife . . .

He had been a soldier all his life, following orders, doing his duty, commanding men and ships, a fleet. He had been the conqueror. Now he was the conquered. The war would end. The Doyons would be victorious. Then what? More of same? An eternity of enslavement to the kungarike? No hell could possibly be worse and no problem so complex.

His father's voice echoed in his mind, *If there is a problem, there is always a solution.*

Yes. There had to be a solution. He must determine what that solution was, then be certain he covered his ass when he executed it.

✧ Chapter 13

Tokoray exited the main service lift on his way to the long central corridor, which would take him to the *Dujaki*'s outermost bays and the flight simulators. After passing three maintenance people and one Na-ka-ta, he checked his internal clock for the time. More than an hour remained until he met Luten Jaqui, also known as Chance. She was the first pilot of the afternoon scheduled for a refresher.

Ahead and to his left, the double doors of the Na-ka-ta repair center opened and out stepped Rieeza, with her half-full rucksack slung over one shoulder. Head down, she stared at her palm-sized datapad, mounted on her left wrist compatch, and thumbed through various icons and screens. She scowled a second before her head came up. Seeing him, she abruptly stopped. "Hi." Her gaze skipped to the flight harness he wore over his officer's tunic. "You look spiffy."

He halted. "Spiffy?"

"You know — nice, smart in appearance, stylish, up-to-date in the latest of flight harnesses. New by the look of it."

"It is new."

A frown scrunched down her dark eyebrows. "The flight deck is below us, so why are you in harness?"

"I'm headed for Flight Sim One to recertify a pilot."

"Oh." Rieeza's eyes went wide, her jaw dropped. "Oh, you mean Darq picked a copilot? Not fair!"

"What? I do not understand." His faceplate sensors registered movement. Four Na-ka-tas approached, two abreast. By their speed, they were intent in getting somewhere quickly. He wheeled himself at a right angle to the wall and parked, giving them room to pass by. Noticing the four, Rieeza scooted over and stood in front of him.

She kept her voice low. "What's not fair is that I was about to bet on the next candidate's fly-time."

The betting pool. He'd heard no one won the money yesterday because Qtl-shi Darq had not accepted any of the five candidates she'd flown with in the simulator. The money had rolled over to today. Half the wagering was on which candidate Darq would pick, and the other half on how long one would ride with her. "Rieeza," Tokoray said in his best wise-father-instructor's voice, "it is not prudent to gamble."

"I would bet on Darq any day, but I have to admit, figuring out how long she'll fly with today's choices is a turd-shoot. You have any insider info?"

"As I told you when we first met, I am new to the *Dujaki* and do not know many people or Na-ka-tas. However, before you ask, when Majorn Varree notified me that she had blocked in time for Darq to use the flight sims, Varree said every candidate she reviewed was highly qualified. The top six, exceptional."

"But they didn't last long, did they?"

"Evidently not." The first candidate rode with Darq for eighteen minutes. Hardly time for the simulated ram-launch and circling the *Dujaki* before heading out on a first mission test. As to the longest sim, candidate three lasted twenty-eight minutes.

Rieeza heaved a sigh. "Likely betting anything now is a moot point, but you're headed for the sims, so I'm thinking she picked one."

"Do not jump to conclusions. My scheduled use of the sim is an hour from now. I am early because I wish to ensure all is ready."

She smiled. "So I still have time to make a wager— See ya!" Gazing down at her datapad and tabbing its screen with her index finger, she strode away.

Tokoray engaged his wheels and resumed his journey. Nearing the junction of the main corridor with a secondary one, the sound of voices wafted about him. He upped his receivers to locate and judge how fast the voices were moving, the better to know if he needed to avoid a collision. From the right side section of the junctioning corridor, he identified Varree's pleading voice and her, "You agreed."

A baritone-voiced Na-ka-ta replied, "That was before I realized how erratic Qtl-shi Darq is and how better Na-ka-tas than I have not been able to meet her flying standards."

"Darq has no obvious standards!" Varree said.

Since he detected no sound of spacer's boots or Na-ka-ta treads, the two were obviously stationary and posed no problem. Tokoray rolled on and into the junction. In his peripheral sensors, he glimpsed Varree and the Na-ka-ta at the side of the corridor — and Raytor. That automaton stood at Varree's left, his back to the junction. Then Tokoray glimpsed Azran Atlatl exit the nearby lift and cross over to the trio.

Varree turned to Raytor. "Isn't there anything you can say to convince him to fly with Darq?"

"Perhaps." To the reluctant Na-ka-ta, Raytor said, "Cacma, you once told me your desire was to one day serve the best pilot in the fleet."

"That is true," Cacma replied, his baritone edged with certainty.

"So, tell me, how will you know who the best are, or what it takes to fly with the best, if you do not avail yourself of an opportunity — this opportunity — to fly with one of the best pilots the *Dujaki* has?"

"I concede your argument is valid, Yojii Raytor, but I have reservations."

"Name them," Varree demanded.

Tokoray continued down the main corridor. Would they be able to convince Cacma to fly with Qtl-shi Darq? Well, it was none of his concern. He had work to do, preparations to make for a pilot refresher testing, and he had better get on with it. He turned his hearing back to normal.

When he entered the quiet, cavernous bay, he glanced up at the cockpit-pod balanced on the machinery. Cadets often equated the unit to two long-legged spiders and an octopus fighting over a giant ball of yarn. The yarn-ball under the simulator's cockpit housed systems that could duplicate every conceivable maneuver of a Pytak fighter.

He halted and looked to the right, behind the protective, noise-dampening synthglass partitions. A row of gray-on-gray workstations had task chairs parked in front of them. A narrow aisle lay between the chairs and the beige bulkhead.

Where were the techs? Varree had assured him someone was always on duty and would show him the stations set aside to run his sims.

"Well, it's about time you showed!"

Tokoray spun his wheelbase toward the voice coming from the simulator's cockpit. He focused on the face of a young woman with a head of dark-brown hair parted down the middle and plaited into a braid over each ear. When the woman leaned farther over the edge of the cockpit, he spotted a silver-gray neural-net cap on her head.

"Well, Number Ten, just don't stand there. Get your ass in gear and let's get this over with." She shoved her braids under her flightsuit collar rings, brought up her helmet, and donned it. Then she slipped back down into the cockpit.

Was that Qtl-shi Darq? It had to be the Raven, the top gun whose secrets about flying Majorn Varree wanted to discover and incorporate into the training of other pilots. But Qtl-shi Darq had addressed him as Number Ten. Where was the real Number Ten?

The whir of the ceiling-mounted load-unload unit swiftly lowering its umbilicals resounded in the quiet. Tokoray moved toward the yellow-and-white pickup square marked on the mottled-gray decking.

What was he doing? He paused and checked the doorway, his sensors peering through the rectangular viewport windows of the double doors and finding no one—not even a servo-bot.

What if he rode with Darq? Observed how she flew? Ten minutes of flying with her could provide insights. And if Number Ten showed, he would exit the simulator. So, what was the harm in flying with Qtl-shi Darq? In this instance, assisting Majorn Varree in her quest for information outweighed the minor drawbacks. Didn't it?

Knowledge was power.

Wait. He needed the access codes to the qtl-shi's neural-net cap in order to interface with her mind. No problem, he could ask to verify them, thus obtaining them when he got aboard. He sped forward, stopped and centered himself in the lift zone. The descending unit latched onto his flight harness and quickly whisked him up, gently jostling him sideways before lowering him into the copilot's cockpit.

Atlatl strode behind the three, Varree leading the Na-ka-tas Raytor and Cacma, all heading toward Flight Simulator One.

Why had he succumbed to an impulse to walk over to them in the corridor after he exited the lift? Because he'd heard the strident twang of Varree's temper about to snap. She had a wicked voice when being thwarted.

So much for getting to the specialty workshop to pick up the hand-crafted backpack he'd ordered for Rieeza's birthday gift. Once again, azran duties overrode his fatherly duties.

And speaking of duties, how ironic Raytor's third reminder of a Na-ka-ta's sworn duties to Wysotti pilots finally convinced Cacma to fly with Darq. Likely the indecisive Cacma wouldn't last two minutes in the simulator with Darq. She hated indecisiveness.

The huge double doors opened to Flight Simulator One, releasing a calliope of hydraulic shushes, thumpings, and wheezings made by the simulator swiveling, pitching, and rolling the cockpit-pod about at high speed.

Varree stopped cold, causing the two Na-ka-ta's to squelch to a stop to avoid rolling into her.

Atlatl turned his attention to the twisting up-side-down cockpit and heard Cacma's "Obviously Qtl-shi Darq is still flying with candidate number nine."

"No, she's not." Varree replied. "He lasted twenty-two minutes." She swore. "Darq said she would wait for us."

Atlatl stepped up to Varree's side. "Knowing Darq, she became bored waiting and is flying a program or two to pass the time." He didn't voice, *and test the limits of the simulator.*

Raytor wheeled right and into the control center. At the first workstation terminal, he tabbed the console's nodes. Screens winked to life.

Varree strode over to Raytor and studied the screens. "What program is she running?"

"Ten three two six—a random assortment of skirmishers with Strikers, which, I believe, Darq set up yesterday for the copilot tests." He paused. "How odd."

"What's odd?" Atlatl felt a ripple of dread skim over him.

"Although the ID codes verify Qtl-shi Darq is piloting, *there is a copilot*." He tabbed node after node and screens flashed. "There is no ID entered for the copilot." Raytor shifted his head, aligning his frontal sensors to the upper left corner of the workstation. "Astonishing."

"What's astonishing?" Varree demanded.

Raytor continued to study the screen. "It seems the elapsed time of this simulation is now thirty-six minutes."

"That can't be. We couldn't have been that late getting here." Varree glanced at the triangular patch above her right sleeve band where the chronometer winked its digital display.

Raytor faced Cacma. "According to my internal clocks, Majorn, we are that late." The tone of his voice left no doubt he blamed Cacma for being difficult and delaying them getting here.

"Yes, I see." She eyed Raytor. "So, who's the mystery Na-ka-ta Darq's flying with?"

Raytor turned his head, his faceplate facing toward the upward spiraling simulator where the cockpit-pod made a vertical nosedive. "The only way to find out would be to stop the flight test."

"How long before the program ends itself?"

Raytor focused on the console and tabbed controls. "Six hours."

"What? I never scheduled that kind of time."

"People," Atlatl said loudly to gain their attention. "Isn't a tech supposed to be on hand for all simulator runs?"

"Affirmative," Raytor replied.

The bay's doors opened and in walked a mechnet, who saw the simulator bucking. She stopped and stared at the unit.

Above the noise of the machinery, Atlatl said, "Mechnet!"

The middle-aged woman turned her gaze to him, recognized his rank yoke, came to attention, and saluted.

Atlatl returned the salute. "Are you on duty here?"

"Yes, azran, I am."

"Why did you leave your post?"

"I didn't, azran. I'm the replacement. Mechnet Bennah took sick. Went to sickbay. I was sent over from Sim Three to man her post." She glanced at the diving cockpit, her eyes going wider than wide.

"We need to know who's in the copilot's seat."

"Yes, azran, right away." She strode to the control center. Raytor and Varree moved aside, allowing the mechnet to sit in the task chair. Her hands nimbly tabbed nodes. Screens and holograms flashed with data. Suddenly the woman's hands stopped moving. She leaned forward for a closer look at a screen. "Oh, no, no, no, no, no!" She tabbed a comlink button. "Chief, I have a disaster in progress. Sim One is locked into NOOM Pattern four-zero-four-zero. I've got a pilot and a Na-ka-ta about to be trapped in the cockpit."

"Help is on the way," came the reply. Echoes of an alarm bleeping sounded in the background before the signal dinged the disconnect.

"Mechnet," Atlatl demanded, "what's going on?"

The mechnet pointed to a diagram on the main console screen. "Last month we nearly lost a pilot in the sim because the life supports and comlink systems shorted out simultaneously. Those also locked the releases for the canopy. We had to dismantle the canopy to get them out."

There was a backup system for virtually everything including backup systems. Atlatl scowled. "Wasn't there a backup system?"

"Yes, azran, but it failed. Then the same thing happened again, only with a different program running. Different pilot and her Na-ka-ta were trapped. They ended up punching a hole through the canopy to get air into the cockpit. It took some time to get the pilot out."

Memories of a report flooded Atlatl's mind. Rieeza had spent two days troubleshooting the unit. Yet, the simulator hadn't been taken offline because Rieeza said it could safely run until—

"Was the new relay system controller installed?"

JEWELS OF THE SKY * Catherine E. McLean 146

The mechnet's fingers tabbed up information. "No, not yet, azran. We, that is, all of us techs were instructed not to allow four specific programs to run that Mechnet Rieeza said triggered the cascade failures." She began scanning down a list of a dozen items. Her voice went hoarse. "Qtl-shi Darq plugged in two of those four programs—*back-to-back.*"

Atlatl barked the order, "Shut the system down!"

"I can't, azran." The mechnet's voice trembled with fear. "The malfunction fries the coms, fries the override systems."

Both the bay's doors opened and four Na-ka-ta's, wearing maintenance uniforms, came in. Each pulled a gray chest behind them. Following them came four Na-ka-tas wearing bright yellow vests with RESCUE emblazoned in black. Those Na-ka-tas rode the front of their rescue-equipment pods. The pods forever reminded Atlatl of coffins. He shouldn't think such dire thoughts. His wife might be in danger, but she was not injured or dead—yet. Only she invariably flirted with death. One of these days, he was going to have a heart attack from the stress.

A shuddering vibration quaked the decking. Atlatl turned and watched the cockpit swivel at a ninety-degree angle. The cockpit paused precariously, nose chugging to vertical. A scream of metal against metal resounded followed by the pop of hydraulics and a burst of flame licked out from the simulator's base.

✧ Chapter 14

Darq swiveled the simulator's cockpit-pod one hundred eighty degrees and banked sharply. Adrenalin flamed the exhilaration coursing through her, heightening her delight at having a Na-ka-ta in the copilot's seat who didn't once mention the engine output had gone microns over the top side of the red danger line—and held there.

No doubt about it, this candidate was a winner, and that was as invigorating as flying free in space. But to be absolutely sure, the next simulation would be one of the two sims she had never managed to complete successfully. The first, a slingshot around the equator of a sun, which required avoiding erupting solar flares. If she got past that one, she'd punch in the second and see just how good this Na-ka-ta really was.

Screens burst to life on her faceplate, then a warning bar glowed red. The navigational balls under her left hand chugged instead of rolled.

Starshine and shitfire, another powerstick depleted? Okay, to be expected with all the maneuvers she was pulling. The nav-sys screens came back on, and the ball rolled freely in her hand. A flurry of joy assailed her. Once again the copilot had switched in a new powerstick without being told.

Oh, yes, this copilot was good! Her satisfaction morphed into a deep sense of jubilation that almost overshadowed the screen in the lower right of her faceplate blanking. The screen slowly came into crisp view.

Another power outage? So soon? Hadn't the optics system's powerstick been replaced before? She switched to a look at the status of all her power systems. Green lights filled the status lines. All normal.

"Raven," the Na-ka-ta said over her cockpit com, "we must end the testing."

"What? Why? This is the best ride I've had yet." She leveled out the craft and double checked her faceplate screens. No warning bars or red pinpricks.

"Raven, this has also proven a satisfying experience for me, but I have plugged in the last powerstick to the gyro system."

Sims only came with two backup sticks for inflight use.

Half a dozen screens winked off her faceplate and reappeared. "What's with the flicks?"

"I have used not only the spare powersticks but I have also raided five from my own service supply. You have eleven minutes until the WSTB's runs out of power and shuts down."

Na-ka-tas kept six powersticks on hand, using one a day but more if they needed extra strength or speed. Which meant this Na-ka-ta had sacrificed his own power just to keep flying with her?

Admirable. Really admirable, but— "Shitfire. You could have said something sooner." Her fingers rolled the control balls and their speed slowed.

A muted buzzing sounded for a few seconds then ceased.

Darq checked her faceplate screens. "What was that buzz? Nothing's showing on my screens."

"The buzzer is my internal monitoring system warning that eight minutes remain on my current powerstick."

And he had no backups? "Shitfire. Give me a countdown bar so I know when you run out of power."

"Affirmative."

A small gold and black bar appeared at the side of her faceplate with white numbers counting down seven minutes fifty-two. She brought up the simulator control screen. Before she could activate the emergency shutdown program, everything on the right side of her faceplate winked out, followed by a fade-out of her central navigational view. A shudder went through the simulator's cockpit followed by a hard twist at a one hundred ninety-two degree angle. Darq fought to compensate and level the craft. "What's going on!"

"Hold the vessel steady, Raven. Do not slow or turn."

Through gritted teeth she managed, "I'm trying." A moment later the cockpit-pod came level, then the nose drifted down four degrees. "That's the best he'll answer to."

"We are in trouble."

"What kind of trouble?"

"Serious trouble. A system-control motherboard has shorted, triggering a cascade failure to the second backup unit. A dozen circuits are fried."

"Shitfire." Darq hit the com control to the simulator bay console. Nothing chirped. No screen lit. Not even a whimper of static. Skimming through her screens, she found the problem. "The coms to the control room are fried."

"Affirmative. Override systems are also compromised."

More screens on Darq's faceplate winked out. She used the neural cap to access the copilot's WSTB. On that wide screen tactical board were two possible emergency evacuation protocols. The percentages for success were point two percent and one percent. The screen cleared and schematics displayed. Yellow circles indicated fried circuits and the progress of the cascade affect if it continued to flow. A bright red circle highlighted the mechanisms that released the canopy. Indicators flashed that without power, the mechanisms would remain locked. She'd have to await rescue crews to remove the canopy.

Another screen winked with the extrapolated number of minutes to rescue and the minutes of breathable air until rescue. A shudder of dread mauled Darq's stomach. She would be dead ten minutes before the rescue crews got her out. Starshine and shitfire, she would be killed not in the line of duty but in a simulator? No way.

A green circle marked a critical relay system, which the Na-ka-ta enlarged. She skimmed through the data. Superimposed over the view came another screen showing hydraulic controls to the canopy. Then another screen superimposed over the top of the two.

Why was the Na-ka-ta looking at those? An image flashed to mind. "Yoi, Number Ten, go back to the diagram of the canopy releases."

The image flipped to the top. Through the neural net, Darq instantly highlighted her idea. Seconds later the success rate appeared. Twenty eight percent.

Her copilot switched two elements on the diagram. The survival line winked sixty-nine percent.

"Let's do it," she ordered in a voice that did not betray the uncertainty gurgling in her guts.

Every screen blacked out on her faceplate, including the view of the WSTB. Seconds passed before one blue edged screen came back on, the flight viewscreen. Only it didn't show the test she'd been running, of threading through the edge of the Cypha-wee-ka Asteroid Belt, but a fast approach to the yawning mouth of one of the *Dujaki*'s landing decks. "What just happened?"

The Na-ka-ta replied, "In switching the necessary relays off to bypass compromised circuits, your flight test sequence reverted to a different program."

"Which one is this?"

A long pause, then a slowly stated, "A DLE landing."

"With or without lightning?"

Another pause. "A maximum nine firestorm."

The worst there was. Wait a minute— "Hey, not to worry. This is a simulator. There won't be any real lightning. We can do this."

No reply came from behind her.

"Did you hear me?"

"Yes." A pause. "I heard and understood."

He sure didn't sound confident. "Look, Number Ten, this is only a simulator. We are going to survive this cockpit. You will survive. I promise you will survive."

In a flat monotone came, "The odds may favor survival, but time is fleeting."

She glanced at the countdown node until he ran out of power— three minutes on the money. She needed forty-eight seconds. "Here we go." She cued the nav screen. When it lit, she rolled the controls to barrel straight and true into a doige tunnel.

As she triggered the rockets for an immediate stop, she heard the Na-ka-ta's "Releasing canopy hold downs, mark— Three, two, one."

A quadruple popping sounded above her head. Green lights winked. Hoo-hah! The mechanisms had released.

Another, though muted, quadruple popping ensued of the Na-ka-ta's canopy releasing. Both canopies would now open, that is, provided the cockpit-pod held level. The controls slowly turned, forcing her to push them hard into obedience and come to a full stop.

Her faceplate screens went black.

The acerbic odor of fried circuits snaked into her nostrils. "Check my OPU. I've got a smell." An amber light flickered for her oxygen-purification unit but the entire screen blacked.

Overhead came the rumble-scraping of the canopy sliding back and the jingling of the pilot-extraction unit beginning to lower. She hadn't expelled her sigh of welcome relief when the extraction unit connected to her flightsuit. Her chair's umbilicals released and the extractor whisked her up and out, swiftly depositing her onto the deck. Once released, she hit the control for the rings about her neck and took off her helmet. Her first breath held the strong odor of smoke, burned circuitry, and the rotten-fish odor of boiled biofluid.

She shook her braids out, and in the quiet of the bay, focused on the cockpit-pod above her. The Na-ka-ta had been extracted. A second later his wheelbase touched the deck.

Nothing like a landing you could walk away from. She removed her gloves, depositing both in her helmet, then tucked the helmet under her arm. She turned around, stopping when she saw Atlatl near the bay's control station door.

What was he doing here?

He minutely squared his shoulders, stood taller, in command.

He did not look happy. Not happy at all.

Movement to Atlatl's left drew her gaze to a firefighter Na-ka-ta packing up a fire-extinguisher-foam-sprayer unit. A slew of rescue and fire brigade Na-ka-tas were packing up hoses and tool boxes. She redirected her gaze to a half-dozen rescue techs and

Na-ka-tas, who also packed up gear. One departed carrying medical satchels. Although none had eyes, she had the distinct feeling they studied her.

What had happened here? She shifted her gaze back to Atlatl and found a cluster of onlookers. Varree stood to Atlatl's right. Beside her stood Raytor and a shorter Na-ka-ta in flight harness. Varree's face registered amazement that yielded to a scolding frown.

Atlatl raised his hand, palm out towards her, a silent signal to say nothing. He looked across the way, to his right, where Rieeza stood. "Is it safe to clear the deck?"

"Yes, azran," Rieeza replied.

In a loud, commanding voice, Atlatl ordered, "Clear the deck!"

A quick and orderly egress of Na-ka-tas, people, and equipment ensued. One of the bay doors closed behind the gurney, but the other door remained open.

Atlatl nodded to Darq, giving her permission to speak.

What did she say? Of course, she could find out what was going on later, but right now she had only one priority. She locked her gaze on Varree. "I'll take him. Number Ten."

Varree's eyebrows shot upward, her eyes went wide, then her features morphed into granite hard fury. "You can't have him."

Foreboding quelled Darq's spirits, and she brought herself to a military-perfect attention stance, feet squarely under her. Calmly she said, "Majorn, may I ask why not?"

"Because he's my new CFI. He's got duties. Cadets to run through simulations —"

Darq tuned out the rest of her list. Why would a chief flight instructor get in the cockpit with her when she had already been recertified for the t'un?

Hearing the approaching sound behind her of a Na-ka-ta's treads, she half-turned and looked over her shoulder, staring directly into the CFI's midnight-blue faceplate. "Why didn't you tell me who you were?"

"Why did you not ask?"

"Because I was pissed at having to wait. And, shitfire, there were plenty of times you could have corrected me when I called you Number Ten."

"That is true."

"Then why didn't you state your name and rank?"

"Because, initially, I was curious. In my short time aboard the *Dujaki*, I heard much about your flying ability, Raven. As we flew, I realized how good you were and, if I may be frank, I discovered how much I missed flying with someone my equal."

Equality be damned. Curiosity be damned. She turned toward Varree. "How am I to find a copilot when word gets out it took a master Na-ka-ta aviator, your CFI, to copilot for me?"

Varree's complexion paled. She broke eye contact and shoved her hands into her pants pockets.

Why did Varree look guilty?

Seconds passed with no answer from Varree.

Atlatl crossed his arms over his chest. He scowled at the majorn. "Varree, tell her."

She met his gaze. "Azran, I need him. He's the best—"

"Tell her." Atlatl lowered his voice to the deathly cold and commanding tones that cowed squadrons. "*Or I will.*"

Varree closed her eyes for a long moment, the expression on her face mirroring her reluctance and vexation. When she opened her eyes, she stared at the Na-ka-ta behind Darq. Her harsh tone amplified her pique. "He has choice."

Had she heard right? The CFI had choice? "Say again, Majorn?"

Varree's lips pursed and her tone remained harsh and clipped. "I said, Qtl-shi Darq, *the yojii has choice.*"

How could the Na-ka-ta have choice when he was a CFI? Darq faced the Na-ka-ta. "What is your name?"

"Tokoray. I am Yojii Tokoray."

Darq braced herself, waiting for him to say he chose to be a flight instructor, but he remained silent.

She had to know. "Well, Yojii Tokoray, what's it going to be? Fly with me or teach?"

A puttering bleep resonated from the Na-ka-ta.

"Oh, starshine and shitfire!"

Atlatl demanded, "What's the matter with him?"

"He's out of power." Darq heard the echo of frustration in her own voice.

That frustration paled to Varree's vexation. "He can't be!"

Darq wiped a hand over her eyes and down her cheeks, restoring order to herself, and said evenly, "Yojii Tokoray sacrificed his own reserve supply of powersticks to keep us flying. He didn't tell me that until the one he'd been using was almost gone." She turned an imploring gaze to Raytor. "Yojii Raytor, by any chance would you have a powerstick to spare?"

"Affirmative." He rolled forward. Once at Tokoray's side, Raytor lifted the hem of his officer's tunic and touched a black node at the top of his leg shaft. A triangular panel popped open and flipped down. From inside the exposed chamber, Raytor pulled out one shiny black, four-sided, powerstick. He slapped the panel closed. Once he triggered Tokoray's panel aside, Raytor switched out the used stick for the full one, and closed the panel. Raytor backed two meters and stopped.

A low hum sounded from deep inside Tokoray's chest. He became aware that his systems were again online and the last sequence action came out of his voice box. "Fly!" Realizing the volume he had used, he said, "My apologies. I did not mean to shout." Realizing everyone studied him, he said, "Who do I thank for the powerstick?"

"You may thank me," Raytor replied.

Tokoray focused on Raytor. Although grateful for the assistance, why would Raytor have done such a thing? Raytor was an officer, not a maintenance person. Did it matter? No. However, he should show good manners. "Thank you, Yojii Raytor."

Tokoray then turned his visuals to scan his surroundings, noting Varree looked pensive, no, displeased.

Coming through the bay door strode a slender women with shaggy short black hair, her bangs trimmed just above her dark eyebrows. The newcomer wore a flightsuit and harness and carried her helmet tucked under her left arm. The newcomer halted, glanced about at the state of the bay and seemed taken aback by the personnel and the officers.

On her way out, Rieeza passed the newcomer and said, soto voce, "Welcome to Raven chaos, Chance. You know—a little fire, a little disaster averted—Darq at her best."

Chance locked her gaze to Darq's but no emotion showed on her oval face. "And I missed all the fun?"

Varree placed her hands, knuckles down, on her hips. "What are you doing here, Luten?"

Chance brought her left wrist up and checked the triangular patch on her sleeve cuff. "I'm a couple minutes early for my refresher sim-flight." She eyed Varree. "If the schedule has been changed, Majorn, I wasn't notified."

Bitterness glazed Varree's reply. "Thanks to Qtl-shi Darq wrecking this simulator, the entire schedule will have to be changed."

Chance said, almost apologetically, "I'm supposed to fly tomorrow with Green squad."

Varree dropped her hands to her side and swung about, facing Atlatl. "Azran, we need Yojii Tokoray doing what he does best—training and testing pilots."

Atlatl wiped a hand ever so slowly over his chin, as if weighing the problem. A moment later, he said, "It seems more evident, Varree, that what Yojii Tokoray does best is fly."

"But, azran," her voice held a plea, "surely the needs of the nation outweigh personal preferences?"

Tokoray felt the azran's penetrating gaze. As much as he tweaked his sensors, Tokoray could not discern what the azran looked at specifically. Then the azran's attention shifted to Darq and her right hand.

Tokoray switched his visual sensors and increased magnification. The Raven's fingers curled around her thumb, which was tucked against her palm. He shifted his sensors to her other hand that clutched her helmet with a white-knuckled grip. Again he shifted focus, back to the commander, who keenly studied Darq's face.

Azran Atlatl turned to Varree. "We need pilots, Varree. Darq needs a bonded Na-ka-ta. Compromise. Find a way to make it work for you, for the CFI, and for Qtl-shi Darq. And make sure Luten Jaqui flies as scheduled. That's an order."

"Yes, azran."

"Carry on." He strode out of the bay.

"Well, folks," Darq said, "I'm obviously not needed here, so I'll take my leave, if that's all right with you, Majorn?"

Varree nodded curtly, and Darq exited the bay.

"Majorn," Raytor said, "I would like to offer a suggestion."

"Well, spit it out. I'm listening."

"Luten Jaqui can be re-certified within the next hour if she and Yojii Tokoray use Flight Simulator Bay Three."

Varree shook her head. "You have three Na-ka-tas flights this afternoon on that simulator."

"I did have three. Cacma was scheduled for two hours of practice but, because of the time it took to convince him to fly with Darq, and she flew with Tokoray instead, there is more than an hour open on the unit for Luten Jaqui. Once she's done, I can resume my normal schedule with the cadet Na-ka-tas. I will reschedule time for Cacma in a day or so."

Varree nodded. "Make it so. You and Cacma are dismissed." Then to Jaqui, she said, "Get a move on, luten. Sim three."

"On my way, Majorn." Jaqui followed Raytor and Cacma out.

Would the majorn order him gone? Or would she lecture him on his conduct? Likely the latter. Tokoray rolled forward and halted before her. "Majorn, may I be frank?"

She nodded but her stance, and the rigidness of her jaw, clearly indicated anger.

She had a right to be angry with him. "Majorn, I apologize for taking the initiative to fly with Qtl-shi Darq."

"Duly noted."

"With all due respect, Majorn, you did ask me to help you with your *little project*. It was with that project in mind that I decided to fly copilot to Qtl-Shi Darq."

Interest and curiosity now mirrored on her face. "What did you learn?"

"There may be no way to transfer how Darq flies to help other pilots learn her survival techniques."

"Why?"

"Because there are pilots and then there are pilots. With the good ones, flying is inborn. You cannot teach it, only hone the skills. And, especially with fighter pilots, they have to be willing to take risks. Qtl-shi Darq has a heightened instinct for survival. She thinks in terms of try something, try anything, but keep trying. Add to that my conclusion—the Raven does not fear death."

"I see. A one-of-a-kind talent."

"I believe so, Majorn, but let me assure you, I know where my duty lies. You can rely on me to continue as your Chief Flight Instructor."

Something like disgust clouded the majorn's eyes. "You flew the longest with her. You said you would chose to fly over teaching."

"It was an irrational reply, one not fully thought out. It has always been my desire to serve where I am needed most. In this instance, it is as your Chief Flight Instructor."

"Thank you. Dismissed."

He nodded and left the bay.

After passing the portal to Simulator Two, Tokoray spotted Raytor and Cacma in front of a lift, heads bent forward, talking. When the lift opened, Cacma entered and the lift departed. Tokoray swerved right to go around Raytor. About to pass, Raytor said, "A moment, Yojii Tokoray."

He stopped.

"I did not have an opportunity to tell you before now, but I was impressed with your assisting Qtl-shi Darq to piggyback Jaguar Four in for a landing. I was even more impressed that you did not panic when Darq cruised past the *Dujaki*'s arrays to make a risky switch-back landing."

Impressed? "I did not do much. I did not need to. Qtl-shi Darq merely took the shortest route to ensure her survival. Risky, yes, but she impressed me as an accomplished pilot."

"That she is, which is a positive. Unless you are a Na-ka-ta."

What did he mean by that? "Forgive my curiosity, but I do not understand your meaning. Is Qtl-shi Darq abusive to her copilots?"

"You witnessed her ejection of Phrys, did you not?"

"Considering what she was about to do, and the landing she made, I assumed she intended to save his life."

"Hardly. She is known to have murdered Na-ka-tas."

The shock of his statement yielded to a jolt of realization that Raytor had said Na-ka-tas—plural. "She has killed more than one of us?"

"Three. All bonded to her. Phrys is my bloodkin, and I assure you, he is grateful to be alive and not another of the Raven's victims."

"If she's killed our kind, why hasn't she been brought up on charges?"

"There were inquiries and investigations, but in the end, she was exonerated. We Na-ka-tas, however, know in our hearts that the Raven is a Hiack, The Raven of Death."

A Hiack? A destroyer of Na-ka-tas?

"Let me give you a little advice, Tokoray. No Na-ka-ta who has bonded with her survives long because of her unorthodox methods of flying and the risks she takes. I must go. I am keeping you from testing Luten Jaqui." Raytor sped down the corridor toward simulator bay number two.

Tokoray headed for sim bay three, mulling over what Raytor had said about Qtl-shi Darq. Was she responsible for the deaths of her three copilots? Most pilots only bonded to one or two at most.

And what did it matter? He would not be given permission to bond to her. He was here, aboard the *Dujaki*, to teach and train. There would be other chances to choose a pilot. Yet, finding someone with Darq's abilities, her intuitive instinct, and her intestinal fortitude would not be easy. Worse, he was likely going to compare everyone else to her. Shitfire.

How odd he would use that word. Qtl-shi Darq seemed to have a very unsettling affect on him. He must dismiss further ruminations. Luten Jaqui was waiting. He accelerated, speeding faster down the corridor.

✧ Chapter 15

Dressed in a regulation sleepsuit and a fuzzy russet-brown robe, freshly sonic-bathed, and her hair vacuumed squeaky clean, Darq stepped around the privacy panel of her tiny bathroom. Making her way to the kitchenette, the soles of her slippers sucked as the grippers adhered to the floor tiles and pah-pahed when they released.

Seeing Jaqui exit her bed chamber, Darq halted and resisted the urge to blink. Jaqui wore a piece of slinky electric-blue knit with cut-out holes that revealed more flesh than the fabric concealed. The handkerchief hem drizzled above the tops of her matching knee-high, spike-heeled boots.

"Well, Raven," Jaqui said in her deepest, most sultry voice, "do I pass muster?" Doing a three-hundred-sixty-degree turn, her heels never touched the floor.

Darq kept a straight face. "I suppose, Chance, you're as close to being naked as regs allow."

Laughter bubbled out of Jaqui and put starshine in her already glistening eyes. "I look that good do I? Well, it'll be worth it."

"Why?"

"Fahnia's bringing her hot new noviodo to my little party."

"Izzt will be jealous."

"He's never, ever jealous." Jaqui cocked a hip and placed her hand on it. The nail polish on her fingers matched the blue of her dress. "Darq, you should come with us. There'll be syaki beer, a few bottles of cheap, and not so cheap, wine—"

"You have something to celebrate." Several somethings actually. Jaqui had survived the Joiz attack, healed from her wounds, and been recertified to fly. Darq crossed her arms over her chest. "I don't."

Gaiety vanished from Jaqui's face. "You're depressed."

"Only a smidgeon and justifiably so." She dropped her hands to her sides and hooked her thumbs at the corners of her robe's pockets.

"Okay, Darq, I'll concede Varree won't let go of her CFI any time soon, but, I assure you, a good romp in bed and sex with a noviodo will do you ever so much good."

"I have a husband. I don't need a Na-ka-ta's programmed pleasures."

"Ah, but you had J, and when he wasn't your copilot, he bedded the minions."

His choice—and his personal calling. "But not me, Chance." Her conscience whispered she'd been mesmerized when J opened his wheelbase shaft casing and revealed legs. She'd been even more astounded when he switched out his faceplate for a face with the most exquisite lips a man's visage could bear. She'd kissed J, enjoying the touch of his pseudo-skin. But that kiss was all it took to know for a certainty that Atlatl was her true love and nothing would ever come of a personal relationship with J, except them flying as pilot and copilot. Her conscience tisk-tisked. Okay, so maybe J was more of a friend. A best friend.

Jaqui minutely tilted her head, as if something came over her neural net.

The door sensor chimed.

"Enter," Jaqui said before the room's comtar identified the caller. Jaqui grinned at Darq. "Speak of the devil, here's my Izzt."

Izzt wheeled in and down the short hallway to stop a meter from Jaqui. "I am now a devil? How did that come to be?"

Ignoring Jaqui's "I was trying to interest Darq in joining us," Darq unhooked her thumbs from her robe's pockets and headed for the food center.

"Obviously," Izzt said, "by her attire, she declined. And by your attire, I see you are not quite ready."

"I only have to grab my shawl. Be back in a flash." The click of Jaqui's heels across the flooring soon faded.

Darq placed her order, and when the food unit dinged, she picked up the mug of dark, auburn tea. She turned in time to see Jaqui emerge from her bed chamber wearing a bright-yellow shawl heavily embroidered with teal-feathered quetzals and silver-winged butterflies. Clutching the corners of the triangular shawl and stretching out her arms, Jaqui created pseudo-wings to twirl and swoop and flit about, to dance with the beat of some internal music while she made a circle. Between the electric blue of her dress and the yellow shawl, Jaqui had effectively dressed herself as brilliantly as any butterfly.

When Jaqui's second circle reached Izzt, she mounted the Na-ka-ta's wheelbase, and the pair went out the door. Jaqui finger-waved goodbye over Izzt's shoulder.

Mug in hand, Darq returned to her bed chamber. She looked at the large screen on the starboard wall where a serene starscape imitated a viewport window. No sense activating the screen and sifting through the thousands of selections for entertainment. She glanced at her comtar station in the corner. Why turn it on and find her mailbox full of condolences, jokes, and jibes, all dealing with the fiasco with Yojii Tokoray this afternoon. Shitfire, how could she have been duped by that CFI?

The patter of soft drumbeats began at the back of her mind. Zukaltay's drum. Again the drumming, drumming, drumming. Darq rubbed her temple with the fingers of her free hand. *Oh, dearest grandmother, why do you pound your drum?*

As Darq lowered her hand, she sighed, and a profound melancholy overwhelmed her. She went to the ceiling-to-floor unit beside her sleep-rack and peered through the protective plastiglass doors edged with a ribbon of faux stained glass. She ignored the model of *Little Bit* and the photo of her and Atlatl's wedding as well as the photo of her and Jaqui in front of their first Pytaks. Darq gazed at the image inside a plain pewter frame where her grinning-proud grandmother wore her tribal obsidian and pearls-of-all-colors amulet. Zukaltay's ruby-red dress, with a bolero jacket edged in black braid, matched the tiny ruby earrings she wore.

Darq glanced at herself in the picture. She stood with Zukaltay's arm around her shoulder. Her grandmother's reds a bloody contrast to Darq's dress whites. The picture had been taken the day Darq graduated top of her class from fighter-pilot training. Darq heaved another sigh. Zukaltay had been the only family there for the event.

Darq reached over and set her mug on the empty shelf of the recessed cubes that stood in for the headboard of the sleep-rack. Again facing the ceiling-to-floor unit, she dropped to her knees and keyed in the code, unlocking the bottom cupboard doors. The doors slipped aside.

In the right hand corner, Zukaltay's Jewel of the Skies drum took up half the space. Light glinted off the 'stars' spangled on the drum's blue-black base. The large stars were diamond-shaped sapphire glass. Shards of gleaming silver radiated from each, making the stars look ten times bigger. The smaller, round stars were faceted glass. Six pairs of feathers dangled from the stretchers holding the drum-skin tight. To the left of the drum stood her marriage basket. Tucked between the drum and basket sat the rosewood puzzle box with a sunstone carved into the top.

She eyed her marriage basket. Neatly folded in the basket rested her marriage sash, made not by her mother as tradition ordained, but by M'Tara and M'Tara's mother. M'Tara had been the best of friends and sister of sisters. Whispering through Darq's mind came the reminder that in her tweens she had wished M'Tara's mother had been her own birth mother.

On top of the sash lay three photo rods. The rods were old ones, the size and thickness of full pea-pods. The silver and black military-issue one held J's prerecorded goodbye message to her. The beige, wedding vids. The last one, the hue as turquoise as a tropical ocean, held all things related to Zukaltay's estate and a copy of her will.

The drumming beat quickened in Darq's mind but didn't grow louder. She gently patted the old drum with the tips of two fingers. No tune, no rhythm, just a gentle, deep-toned sound resonated. The drumming in her head ceased, replaced by images of sitting on her grandmother's lap, a child again, loved. Hot tears welled.

"Whatever are you doing down on the floor tapping a drum?"

Startled, Darq rocked back on her haunches. Rapidly blinking back her tears, she turned and looked at Rieeza, who stood inside the doorway, her hands gripping her bulging backpack to her chest. Something with a round-top pushed against a threadbare, twice patched seam.

"How did you get in?" Darq demanded, noting her gruffness but not intending to apologize for it. "These are private quarters."

"I overrode the door command. I can do that you know. I have the authority."

"You may have the authority, but you are not supposed to flaunt it. You should knock, request entrance. What if I was in bed with your father?"

"That'll never happen—" Her cheeks turned a bright red. "I mean, yes, you could be in bed with my father, doing you-know-what, and you have every right to privacy, and I would never interrupt THAT. Anyway, I asked comtar to make sure you were home before I opened the door."

"So, what can I do for you?"

"It's not what you can do for me but what I'm about to do for you." She lifted her backpack a few centimeters. "Inside this satchel is a pail of cacao-fudge, frozen solid, but likely melting. It's a present."

"Iced cream costs a small fortune. Where did you get the dovras for it?"

Rieeza beamed a grin bright enough to eclipse a star's output. "Thanks to you, I won the betting pool."

Darq got to her feet. "How could you win? How could anyone. I didn't fly with Number Ten."

"Ah, there's the rub. You see, I bet you would accept the *tenth Na-ka-ta you flew with* and the rules of today's pool stated you had to write in exactly what your bet was. I won eight-hundred and eighty dovras."

"And you're sharing your wealth with me?"

"Not exactly. I put all but eighty-eight dovras in my savings. The iced cream is a thank you. And from the look of things, I would say it comes at a great time to lift your spirits."

Why did everyone think she needed her spirits lifted? "I would prefer some alone time."

"You're depressed. I know depressed when I see depressed. Father looks depressed a lot. More of late. So does my mother, but she was born depressed. And grandmother— Anyway, c'mon, into the kitchen." She spun around and headed out the door.

Depressed was she? In truth, perhaps a little. But who in their right mind would pass up iced cream? And cacao-fudge at that? Darq followed Rieeza to the kitchen where Rieeza unloaded the pail. She shouldered her backpack, stepped to the utensil drawer and pulled out a tablespoon. Rieeza handed the spoon to Darq. "Nothing like pigging out on comfort food."

Darq took the spoon.

"Gotta go, Darq. See ya." She headed for the door.

"Hey!" Darq said to Rieeza's back, "You just got here. Aren't you going to share this with me?"

The door opened and Rieeza's parting words filtered through before the door closed. "Can't. Got a party to go to and celebrate my winnings."

Everybody seemed to be partying, except her. She looked at the iced cream. Tempting as the treat was, she didn't crave it. She tossed the spoon back into the utensil drawer, grabbed the pail by its handle, strode to the freezer drawer beneath the food unit, and deposited the pail.

The door chime resounded.

What was this, flight central?

The comtar's voice intoned, "Yojii Tokoray requests entrance."

What could he want? She stepped around the partition and faced the door. "Enter."

Tokoray wheeled in. When he halted, she sensed he scrutinized her attire and tousled hair.

"Forgive my late visit," he said. "I did not mean to interrupt your sleep. I know you need your rest."

"I was not asleep, and to what do I owe this visit?"

"I have come to talk to you about tomorrow, the bonding—"

"Bonding? What bonding?"

"Between you and I."

She felt the frown scrunch across her forehead. "What are you talking about?"

"Did you not get the priority message from Majorn Varree authorizing my bonding with you? She said she had notified you immediately after consulting Azran Atlatl."

"Starshine and shitfire." She jogged into her bed chamber, focused on her comtar terminal, and half-yelled, "Dayzee, on. Messages. High priority first."

The viewscreen lit and filled with data. Reaching the terminal, she grabbed her task chair, swung it about, and sat. Leaning close to the screen, she skimmed Varree's message then reread it slowly, letting the words sink in and staring at two words — *authorized bonding*. Joy gushed like spring melt cleansing her gloom. She spun around and looked at Tokoray, who now stood a meter away. "Getting Varree to relent on anything she's set her mind to is harder than defrocking a saalishani. But, I'm glad it's settled, and we're going to be flying partners."

He didn't immediately reply, which set off a ripple of unease through Darq and doused her joy. "You've changed your mind. Is that what you've come to tell me?"

"No, I have not changed my mind."

"Then why are you here?"

"I have — concerns."

Concerns. Plural. More than one. She rested each hand, palm down on the robe covering her thighs, and ignored her chilled finger tips. "Okay, it's logical you would have reservations, after all we only met today. So, what kind of concerns do you have?"

"I am not sure how to phrase this."

"Blunt is okay. Speak your mind. I promise not to take offense or get upset."

"Very well. Several sources have told me you have murdered Na-ka-tas."

Shitfire. Who had told him? Did it matter? No, because someone was bound to tell him. Nothing was sacred or secret aboard the *Dujaki*. She shifted her focus to her hands resting on her thighs, noting her cold fingers clutching her thumbs. Then she looked into Tokoray's dark faceplate. "I was never brought up on charges for harming or killing or murdering any Na-ka-ta."

"I know. Majorn Varree insisted I read the reports and realize what I would be getting myself into."

"And she pointed out you would likely die in the *Ky*'s copilot seat?"

"Affirmative. However, I must confess to a curiosity and uncertainty. Logically, knowing the facts surrounding the demise of your copilot Na-ka-tas will enable me to dispel any future murder accusations when they are presented to me."

He had a point. A very logical point. And being truthful, she appreciated his candor. No, what she appreciated more was him coming here, seeking to hear her side. It was never pleasant dredging up old memories but, if they were ever going to be partners in a cockpit, he better know the facts. She took an empowering lung full of air. "I'll be frank, Tokoray. I've had three bonded Na-ka-ta copilots. My first bonding was with J, just the letter of the alphabet *J*. He insisted the single capital letter gave him a uniqueness no other had."

"Was he unique?"

"In many ways." She shoved aside the memory of his collection of colorful little bottles of colognes—and the citric scent of him. "J was a noviodo, a pleasure giver. I liked J very much, but like— *Like a brother*. We never had a pleasure or sexual relationship. Technically, I was his second pilot. He often admitted how astounded he was at the strange maneuvers I came up with." Remembering his words, she smiled and said, "He concluded I had *a logically illogical female mind*."

Tokoray tilted his head in a nod, and the room's overhead light shimmered down the side of his dark faceplate. "He received a Silver Star."

"Yeah . . . that . . ." Memories swirled and flashed, forcing her to hold back the urge to let tears well. "We were aboard a transport catching a ride back to the *Dujaki*. Strikers attacked. A Chelicera missile hit the transport. J . . . He shoved me in front of him. Held me tight . . . The blast came from behind him. He shielded me from the explosion and the shrapnel, and I walked away with scratches. A shard sliced through his core, gutting his main CPU. He died." She heaved a sigh of remorse and regret. Her vision blurred. One tear escaped, hot and wet down her cheek. Then an image of Lucky popped into her mind.

"Darq?" Tokoray's voice held a fatherly timbre. "Do you smile because you are recalling a fond memory of J?"

"No. Sorry. I just recalled my second bonded Na-ka-ta, Luqeros." *Ah, Lucky, Lucky, Lucky . . .* " He insisted on being called Lucky. He loved jokes, had collected thousands. His repertoire of laughs ran from pipsqueaks to one helluva jovial belly laugh." More memories flitted, and through her tear-fogged vision, she found herself becalmed. "For a time after losing J, laughter helped get me through the days. Trouble was, Lucky developed these little glitches. It seemed once every week he ended up in maintenance. Which was bizarre considering that no matter how bad the skirmishes we got into were, he never got a scratch or developed a malfunction."

"What happened to him?"

"We had been through a trying encounter with Strikers. The *Ky* was peppered with fang strikes, his compartment had been hit three, maybe four times, but he assured me he was unharmed. He lied. He'd taken shrapnel to the head and shoulders." She chuckled, but there was no mirth in the sound of it half-echoing between her ears. "We managed to get the *Ky* home and touched down without a DLE, but a subsystem in his brain shorted next to the telepathic center on his neural net. That set off something akin to a DLE in his neural net, which fried his brain—and it would have fried mine had he not had the presence of mind to sever the connection between us." She took a deep, cleansing breath through her nose, the sound whooshing in, and she swallowed the clog in her throat. "He saved my life, my mind. I miss his jokes . . ." She gathered herself, shunting back the onslaught of Lucky's laughter.

A moment later, Tokoray's voice entreated, "What of your third copilot?"

She rubbed her hands over her face, discovered the wet tear tracks, and wiped them off. She had better take more control of herself. "Number three? He was Kamau, the quiet warrior. When I met him, and while bonded to him, he was a quiet, unassuming, poet-quoting Na-ka-ta. He taught literature, language, and poetry to both cadets and adults through a personal-enrichment program. In the cockpit, he was all business. Hindsight being what it is, when I look back on our relationship, I think he possessed a split personality."

A tiny white light flickered on Tokoray's disk-cap.

What records or data bases was he tapping into and what did he search for?

"The official cause of his death," Tokoray said, "was a malfunction due to the recycling of a defective part into his core analysis system."

"Which may have been true, but, in my heart—" Did she dare say it? "To be honest, I think he committed suicide."

"What do you base that on?"

"The last few poems he wrote. He created such eloquent poetry. No, I take that back. There were two other things that convinced me he was suicidal. One was the last assignment he gave his students. They had to read an ancient play about the madness, the insanity, of war and of brother killing brother. The second was Kamau had marked passages in his J'Hi-inti Book of Prayers. All those entries dealt with the murdering of innocents, the travesties of killing—and boldly highlighted was *Thou shalt not kill.*" She inhaled and let out a sigh. "I think he extrapolated that he had become a destroyer, a cold-blooded killer, even though, technically, I pulled the trigger. Maybe he felt it was guilt by association. I don't know. It's only speculation, my opinion."

The little white light blinked on his disk-cap a second before he said, "The psychological summations do not mention any mental health problem or suicidal tendency."

"The malfunction was blatantly obvious. I only made the connection when I helped Kamau's bloodkin, Raytor, pack up Kamau's things."

"Raytor has a number of bloodkin." Disgust tinged his voice.

"Yes, Raytor does. Last count I heard was an even twenty. His students are fond of him. Let me clarify that. It's usually the very best of his students who become copilots. Most of those he becomes bloodkin to."

"Qtl-shi Darq, may I inquire how the rumors started about you being a Hiack, the murderer of Na-ka-tas?"

A Hiack. Shitfire, he'd been told that too? "Branding me a Hiack resulted from Kamau's last poem. It delved into the injustice of Na-ka-ta's held prisoner in their copilot seats, of pilots who shouted triumphantly when a Striker was obliterated or its Doyon pilot floated dead in space. And before you jump to conclusions, no specific pilots were mentioned. Unfortunately, anyone reading the poem might concluded I was the *Sunatas Daughter who delighted in the kill.*" She put her cold hands in her robe pockets. "Looking back, it was soon after that when the rumors began, all distorting how my other bonded Na-ka-ta's died. The rumors twisted Kamau's death into my having a blood-lusting death wish." She stared beyond him, not really seeing anything. "His death sometimes haunts me. All I know is that my landing gear doors wouldn't open. Kamau went to check. Next thing I see him sailing out the left wing wheel housing, tumbling through the stream of doige dust we were trailing. Did he loose his grip or jump? I don't know. Then a spark winked on his chest. The dust exploded. I had my hands full trying to survive the DLE . . . Rescue had to haul me in." They'd also hauled in Kamau's charred remains.

Darq got up and strode for where she'd left her mug of tea. She lifted the cup and took a deep draught of the tepid liquid, letting it wash away the memories, then faced Tokoray.

"Thank you, qtl-shi."

"Call me Darq or Raven. Save the titles for when regs or protocols demand it."

"As you wish."

"I wish." She took another drink, wishing it was syaki beer, no, hundred-proof liquor, the kind Atlatl kept in his desk drawer for special occasions. She'd given him much too much anguish of late. If he became an alcoholic, she would definitely be a contributing factor. But such concerns didn't warrant pursuing now — Tokoray's did. "So, what are the other concerns you have?"

He looked at the doorway like a man desperate to escape, but he didn't move or speak.

Had her confessions and truths led him to believe he shouldn't bond with her? Maybe they needed more time to get to know one another? Pity there wasn't time. Majorn Varree's orders and her memo emphasized that it was *imperative Qtl-shi Darq be restored to duty status ASAP.* Yet, what did one say to this Na-ka-ta?

A memory of him standing powerless in the flight simulator bay that afternoon whispered to her. "Wasn't 'fly' your first word after Raytor inserted the new powerstick? You wanted to fly, not teach?"

"That is correct. It is still true. I would rather fly than teach. You are an excellent pilot, but—*I do not want to jinx you.*"

"Jinx me? How so?"

"I came to the *Dujaki* to erase the stigma attached to me by my fellow Na-ka-tas, as well as the pilots on *Ziital Station.*"

Shock zipped through her. "You're a jinx?"

"No, I am not. At least, I do not think I am. I sincerely pray I am not."

Obviously he wasn't positive. A jinx? She'd found a copilot worth his motherboards, and he was a jinx?

Feeling unnerved, she sidestepped to the bed, sat next to her pillow-roll, and held the mug with both hands. Schooling herself to look the epitome of unflappable patience, like her grandmother used to do, Darq's thoughts drifted. Images solidified of how, as a teen, she had stood before Zukaltay who sat, queenly-patient, waiting for an explanation of why Darq had upset her mother, upset her teachers, upset her sisters.

How odd. She never seemed to upset her flight instructors. Flabbergasted many of them, including Atlatl, but never actually upset them.

Realizing the silence had dragged on, she disciplined her voice to entreat, "Perhaps, Tokoray, you could explain why you were dubbed a jinx?"

"It is difficult."

"Is there a beginning place? You could start at the beginning."

"Yes, of course. The beginning. My life has been mostly spent on the *Ziital* battlestation. There I bonded with Citali. For three t'uns, nine moons, eight days, twenty hours, and seventeen minutes, we were friends first, pilots second. We were part of the squads engaged in the Qusaquit Trade Center Exodus."

"You were part of that first encounter with the *Cocopaj Moji* battle fortress? Outnumbered fifteen to one?"

"Affirmative. The Wysotti pilots prevailed but with heavy losses."

Darq recalled the incident and of being on Talragon, not knowing if she was to proceed to the *Dujaki* or if her orders would be rescinded and she would be heading for *Ziital* or the homeworld. Yet, hearing about those brave pilots and Na-ka-tas had humbled her.

"Our fighter had been crippled," Tokoray said, "but we made it home. Citali deftly landed us sideways in a doige tunnel, one that had already taken several DLEs. She needed medical aid immediately, so, I got her out. The rescue crews were halfway to the plane when an unexpected DLE erupted. Three of the rescue personnel died. I carried Citali through the lightning, to the nearest safety cage. A command-override signal by the d'ktr broke my link to her." He paused. "She died in my arms."

"You take to heart your Na-ka-ta oath?"

"I do. I felt honor-bound to die with Citali."

"But it was not to be?"

He nodded. "My next bonding was to Xami. She came from Talragon. After a sortie into Doyon territory, our fighter damaged, we made a hard landing. I could slow but not stop her bleeding, and there was radiation poisoning from a blown-away wing. A claxon blared, warning of an imminent DLE. Trapped in her cockpit, no time for rescue, she ordered me to save myself, ordered me not to self-destruct and die with her. I obeyed, exiting down the missile ramp. The DLE erupted . . . the fighter blew apart . . ."

The anguish in his voice cut deep into Darq's heart. Yet, she couldn't tell if his anguish was from not fulfilling his oath to die with his pilot or from the loss of Xami as a friend.

His voice lowered and, in an unemotional tone, he said, "My third pilot bonding was to Zafrina, who came from the *Dujaki*. We returned from an engagement, our fighter riddled. I had taken shrapnel. Sealant foam plugged the holes. Zafrina said she had only minor wounds, that her suit and nanobots were tending to them. Through the neural net, I read her med sensors, but the master relay had been damaged by a fragment, so I couldn't accurately monitor her or help with diagnosing what nanobots or drugs would be most effective. She passed out before we landed. I made the landing. I had to manually open her cockpit canopy. As I reached in to help her out, doige lightning erupted. I shielded her from the bolts of energy. When the storm passed and rescue got to us, the d'ktr said Zafrina was alive but in shock. They disconnected my neural link to her. I was carted down to maintenance for repairs. Zafrina went comatose and died four days later from an aneurism." In almost a whisper, he said, "Once again, I had been denied my death."

He'd been through much and lost much. Just like she had. They certainly were a pair. Only — "Have you ever thought your living may have had a purpose?"

"I've been told that by the consuleirs. I accepted that circumstances deemed I should continue on. I am a good flight instructor. I have always been a good pilot and copilot."

She grinned at him, hoping he saw her sincerity. "I'll second that." Then she vanquished her grin. "So, what happened after Zafrina?"

He rolled over to the wall screen and stood near the port edge, facing the starscape. "My fourth pilot was Quechua. Her name means Jewel, and Jewel was the pilot name she was given. She often joked she was gemstone quality, not rare and flawless. She had the distinction of having served both the *Dujaki* and the *Ziital* battlestations, as well as at the Talragon Ship Station and Refueling Depot."

Which meant Quechua had been a mature, older pilot.

"Many times," Tokoray said, "Quechua lamented she might not pass her next refresher and would be demoted to transports. But, I think, as long as she could fly, it did not matter what she flew."

Darq let him pause because she knew firsthand that some memories could not be denied.

When he spoke, his voice was low, subdued. "We had been on a recon mission into Doyon territory. About to enter the Cypha-wee-ka, a squadron of Strikers caught up to us. I still cannot account for how we held our fighter together and made it through the asteroid channel. We signaled a destroyer, who relayed our situation to a nearby Pytak patrol. They came and dispatched the Strikers. Because the data we had gathered was vital for the fleet, and we couldn't make it to *Ziital* or land even if we did, Jewel chose to eject us close to the destroyer." He paused. "Her ejection went badly. She was alive when they rescued her. Again, by order of the d'ktr, my self-destruct was terminated. Jewel, my dear Quechua, died an hour later."

Darq fought the hot tears rising. "I am so sorry for your losses."

"Thank you."

"I sincerely mean it. You've suffered more than I."

"Yet, we must let them go." He faced her. "Now comes the difficult part."

"The jinx part?"

"Affirmative. Back at *Ziital*, I found Quechua's sister Yasalan grief-stricken and angry because I lived and her sister died. The evening I returned, and before an entire rec hall of pilots and Na-ka-tas, she pointed to me and screamed that every pilot I flew with died in the sixth month of my service to them. Then her cousin, Na'zeakan, damned me as a jinx. I can still hear the pounding of fists on the game tables, the walls, the exercise equipment and the litany of *jinx, jinx, jinx*."

Darq felt his misery and understood his shame. But why hadn't that kind of scuttlebutt gotten around the *Dujaki* and to her ears? New people with histories were rumor fodder gobbled up by the bored masses. One of whom was Chance, and Jaqui would never miss a snippet of gossip about a jinx.

Darq got off the bed, set her mug back in the recess, went over to Tokoray, and stood on the opposite side of the viewscreen from him. "I take it, Tokoray, no one on the *Dujaki* knows of this jinx business?"

"Some do. Majorn Varree, Azran Atlatl, the XO . . ."

Interesting how he trailed off his voice like that. Which meant— "Is there someone aboard the *Dujaki* who knows of your jinx status and is likely to harass you?"

"No, no one . . . " He backed a little and faced the viewscreen, the twinkling suns of the starscape mirroring on his faceplate. "Raytor was there, in the rec room on *Ziital*, when Yasalan and Na'zeakan damned me. I am still trying to understand why he has not informed the Na-ka-tas here." He paused. "That strikes me as curiously odd because he was so swift to inform me that you were a Hiack."

Unwanted memories of Raytor slipped through her mind. "Chalk it up to typical Raytor."

"You know Raytor well?"

"Not exactly. When I was given emergency leave, Raytor was assigned to me so I could fly a packet ship to Wysotti. I found him rather passive-aggressive, but what got to me was how he let my mother use him like a servo-bot. And I wasn't happy when he fouled up a nanobot dosage meant to heal a cut on my cheek. The cut took a lot longer to heal." She heaved a sigh. "Sorry about the diatribe. Raytor is a sore subject with me."

"Obviously. Knowing that I shall endeavor not to inflame the wound. Pun intended."

She found herself chuckling and letting her gaze fall to a bright blue-white spot in the center of the starscape.

"Darq, which view-array does this starfield come from? I have yet to see a vessel pass by."

"The array is mounted among the *Dujaki*'s bottom spires. As an anniversary gift, my husband, Atlatl, the battlestation's commander, had a feed linked to this screen." She pointed to a cluster of white stars haloed with blue. "Somewhere out there, in that direction is the bane of my dyn. It's a little sun called Sol. The third planet orbiting that sun is the planet my loathsome ancestor, Kukulaan, destroyed."

"Kukulaan? The commander of the *Tolamixi Mu*? The devil himself?"

"So the history books decree and my dyn decry. I may be genetically linked to him, but, I assure you, I'm me. Darq. My own person."

"Ah, but some feel your bloodline is verification you are predisposed to being a killer, a Hiack, the murderer of Na-ka-ta's?" Tokoray's tone didn't hold censure. "Most unfair."

"Maybe not. After all, I'm having a conversation with a Na-ka-ta jinx." Seeing the irony, she chuckled. "What a pair of aces we are." Unbidden came a conclusion that flitted about her mind like a glider rising, circling a hot air vent. "Tokoray?"

"Yes, Darq?"

"If we bond, I agree, upon my honor, not to murder you if you don't jinx me."

He seemed to infinitesimally come to attention. "And I agree, Darq, upon my honor, should we bond, I will endeavor not to jinx you if you do not murder me."

She laughed, the sound and euphoria lifting her spirits. She extended her hand.

As he took her hand gently in his, a low rumble-chuckle emanated within him.

"I would very much like to bond to you, Tokoray. So, is it a go for tomorrow morning?"

He did not hesitate. "Affirmative. I will leave you now to get a good night's rest." He wheeled for the door and left.

Minutes later, she tucked herself into her sleepsack and ordered the lights off, leaving the starscape glowing on the wall screen. The satisfying thought that in thirty hours or so she would be flying with a bonded copilot, who knew his job, gave way to haunting memories of enduring previous bonding procedures. Bonding came with risks. Repeated bondings could be hazardous.

Thoughts flitted, the d'ktr's voice reiterating from the last bonding, *I do not recommend another bonding. There is a high risk of a stroke or an aneurism that would kill you. If you survive another procedure, it will be your last. I assure you, I will red-flag your medical records to that effect.*

One last bonding. Tokoray would be her last pairing. Absolutely the last.

Zukaltay's pat-a-pat-pat drumbeats lulled her to sleep.

✧ Chapter 16

With the wooziness quickly fading, Darq wondered why the intermittent ringing tones and the occasional bass hum wafting inside her head hadn't totally subsided. Then again, those noises were a lot better than Zukaltay's infernal drumming. Which had stopped.

On her next inhale, Darq caught a whiff of cinnamon that brought back memories of Jaqui's famous yam casserole. With her next inhale came the smell of fry-bread and limes. But no one was cooking anything. Once more she was experiencing skewed sensory perceptions, a side effect that lasted for a couple of hours after a neural-net bonding.

Bonding. She had bonded to Tokoray!

Memories rushed in like the *Ky* going vertical at max speed. She remembered a night of tossing and turning, reporting to sickbay ten minutes early and striving to hide her nervousness. Her worst fear had been that Tokoray would opt out of the procedure. Her stomach had been clinched so tight she dared not eat breakfast.

Somehow she held herself together, chatting easily with the Na-ka-ta nurses and attendants. Once dressed in a surgical cleansuit, she endured being strapped in the charcoal-black upholstered reclining chair. With a sense of dread, and a tight grip on the armrests, she watched the gleaming-white and polished-metal contraption lower over her head. The unit's pads clamped gently over her shoulders. More clamps tightened about her face and throat, immobilizing her neck and head. The last thing she recalled was counting backwards from twenty-five .

"Darq?" Jaqui's voice seemed close by. "Com'mon, open those peepers of yours."

Why was Jaqui here? Oh, no, not again! "What went wrong, Chance?" Hearing her own raspy voice made Darq aware of her dust-dry throat. She got her eyes to open, blinking twice to bring Jaqui's face into clear focus.

"It's about time you woke." Relief mirrored in Jaqui's smile.

Darq glanced about. She was in her bed chamber? Not sickbay? "Did they stop the bonding? What went wrong?"

"Nothing went wrong with the bonding. You're bonded. What went wrong was— Holy Mother of Heaven, Darq, how could you go into the procedure without eating?"

"I ate."

Jaqui crossed her arms over her chest and raised both brows, tweaking them into caret peaks. "Oh? When?"

"Don't remember."

"Well, D'ktr Enyeto had the comtar analyze your calorie intake for the past three days and found you had nothing since 1700 hours yesterday and only one cup of tea at 2350 hours."

"What time is it?"

"My lunch hour."

Which meant half a day had passed since the procedure took place at 0500 hours.

Jaqui leaned down and patted Darq's hand, a reassuring gesture accompanied by an equally reassuring smile. Then Jaqui stood and looked toward the doorway.

Darq tried to lift her head and crane her neck to see what drew Jaqui's attention, but her head felt six times heavier than usual. She gave up trying. Seconds later, she heard Na-ka-ta wheels approaching. Soon Tokoray came into view, balancing a covered tray between his hands. She stared at his attire—a deep-piled, pale-yellow tunic with a thick shawl collar. The garment's hem flared out around his knees.

A Na-ka-ta in a dress? Maybe she was hallucinating.

Jaqui gave Darq's forearm a double pat. "Hey, look. Tokoray's here."

She glanced to the Na-ka-ta and finger waved a hello. His head jerked a brief nod.

Jaqui grinned. "He's going to babysit you for a few hours. I've got preflight for today's mission and have to go. Oh, you're to eat and eat and eat. Stuff yourself." She's grin vanished. "I would make that an order, but you hate taking orders." She beamed a smile at Tokoray and left.

Food sounded good. A cold drink would be even better. Darq hit the switch that raised the top of her sleep-rack. As soon as she sat upright, she tapped the node which brought the narrow table out from the wall to hover over her lap. Tokoray set the tray on the table, removed the cover, and set it off to the side. He backed and stopped at the foot of the bed.

Darq looked at the maize-meal and yam soup reeking of cinnamon. Also on the tray were a slice of dark-brown fry-bread and Blue Crunch Pudding with maleet berries. Realizing how famished she was, she grabbed the spoon and dug in. By the time she'd eaten half the pudding, she felt sated. She leaned back into her pillow. "I'm full. You can take the tray."

Tokoray removed the tray and exited. Soon after she sent the table back into the wall, he returned and stood beside her bed. No data lines or lights showed on his faceplate or disk-cap.

Maybe he had tried using the neural net and she hadn't gotten his hail? "Is the psychic link working? Are we truly bonded?"

"The link is on, but I see no need to disturb you."

"Disturb me. Say something so I know the blasted connection works."

Testing, one, two, three. Will that do?

Nicely. Thanks. Now, tell me what went wrong in sickbay with the procedure?

*It was as Luten Jaqui stated. Lack of nourishment caused low blood sugar, and although you came out of the anesthesia, you blacked out. This the d'ktr had anticipated, however – *

My blackout was not normal. Which seemed the normal for her. Shitfire, she hated being sick like this. She punched the pillow beneath her head, momentarily relieving her frustration. She looked at Tokoray. "You don't have to use the internal channel anymore unless you want to."

"It matters not which. May I ask you something?"

"Ask away."

"Luten Jaqui told me you have had adverse reactions in the past to the bonding procedure."

"Some. Why?"

"The d'ktr became extremely agitated when you did not resume consciousness after forty minutes. It seemed impolite to trouble her for an explanation because she and the techs were scrambling to figure out if you had brain damage."

She'd better tell him. "It's never the procedure itself, Tokoray. It's always coming out of the anesthetic that does me in." She heaved a sigh. "At my first bonding, I blacked out for an hour and a half. Most first-timers pass out for up to thirty minutes. I also woke with one helluva migraine that almost triggered a seizure. The second bonding was a repeat with an hour's blackout and with the addition of me being woozy and nauseous for a few hours. Come the third time, the d'ktrs figured I should eat a full meal so I had something in my stomach and calories available to burn. That time the blackout lasted fifty minutes and generated a lower-grade headache. Only I puked and spent more than twelve hours fighting dry heaves."

"So," Tokoray said, "to avoid the puking this time you did not risk eating?"

She half-lied. "I prefer a migraine to retching until I can't breathe. Now, how about you answer a question for me?"

"Ask away."

"What's with the shaggy tunic you're wearing?"

"It is a cuddly. The d'ktr had me wear it to transport you here from sickbay. I was told Na-ka-ta nurses wear the garment when holding children. It is soft and protects youngsters from a Na-ka-ta's hard outer shell or the roughness of a tunic's nodes."

"There are no children on a battlestation."

"True. However, the cuddly is part of the supplies all sick bays are required to have on hand in the event of a civilian disaster or emergency."

"So I was being treated like a kid?" She felt the frown clamp hard between her brows. "Funny, I don't recall you carrying me."

"To be expected. The d'ktr had sedated you."

"Sedated me? If I was in that bad a shape from the bonding, why would they sedate me or even let me out of sickbay?"

"Because no one, including your atan, could calm you or make you understand you needed to rest."

"Atlatl was there?"

"Affirmative. I observed he was exceedingly concerned about you."

Hadn't she promised not to be a mental burden so he could focus on his command duties? Only lately it seemed she plunged him into new depths of worry and despair. Now she'd added this sickbay incident on top of the Joiz incident. What next? There shouldn't be a next.

"Darq? Did you hear what I said? If you have blacked out—"

"No, sorry. I was lost in thought. Not paying attention." Making Tokoray worry wasn't good either. "So, what were you saying?"

"That after the second time you tried to leave sickbay, the d'ktr—and Azran Atlatl—decided you would recover better in your quarters."

She winced. Why couldn't she remember that? "Caused a lot of bother, did I?"

"Affirmative, but you were most content when I placed you in your sleepsack. Of course the d'ktr and Azran Atlatl came along. I found their concern for you quite intriguing since both ordered me to stay with you and monitor your health. Tomorrow afternoon I am to accompany you to sickbay for a follow-up, to ensure your coordination and balance have not been adversely affected."

"When will I be flight ready?"

"I cannot say. I am not a medic."

She looked again at his attire. "Could you remove that cuddly? No offense, but it makes you look like a walking fuzz ball."

"No offense taken." He rolled back to the footboard and stopped. *May I speak frankly?*

Sure.

When we spoke last night about my concerns, it did not occur to me to tell you about my doige whorls.

She recalled snippets of their conversation and realized all but one of the pilots he'd bonded to were involved in DLEs. *So you have a few whorls, no big deal.*

Others do not perceive them as such. He triggered a node on his sleeve, and the soft zizzering of an autozipper reached her ears. A moment later, he shrugged so the cuddly dropped off his shoulders. After removing the garment, he set it over the footboard. He repeated the procedure and removed his officer's tunic.

Two large olive-brown and puke-yellow whorls, along with an assortment of smaller whorls in an ugly rainbow of variegated colors, splattered his shoulders and torso. Whorls angled over his arms, one reached almost to his elbow.

He turned around. A huge whorl set catercorner from his shoulder to mid-back. Under the room's lights, the scar took on an aspect of a pinwheel galaxy of olive-green grays. *The large whorl on my back is from the third DLE episode.* He came about.

Before her stood one helluva scarred Na-ka-ta. One helluva automaton. She suddenly felt small and inconsequential compared to him and what he'd endured. With vivid clarity, she knew she would be his last bonded pilot. He deserved to die a hero's death in the cockpit of her fighter, and she would ensure that she would die with him because she would never again bond to another Na-ka-ta.

"Darq?" His voice entreated. "Why the tears? Are you in pain?"

She wiped at the moisture leaking out of the corner of her left eye. "No, I'm not in any pain." She sucked in air through her nostrils and swallowed down the clogging tears. "I don't know what came over me, but you've been through more doige hellfire than any Na-ka-ta should have to endure."

"You are not repulsed by the scars?" His voice held his amazement.

She shook her head. "No. Not repulsed. I feel . . . I don't know, maybe sad because they look so—" Ugly came to mind, but that might be speaking too candidly. "Couldn't maintenance do anything about the damage?"

"Many washes were used. None eradicated the scars."

"What about a new skin covering?"

"That requires I be off-line and in maintenance for five moons or more. It is painstaking work to disconnect the numerous sensor jacks and links built into the underside of my skin-shell."

"I think your whorls are badges of courage." Speaking the words surprised her. She looked to see his reaction.

"I do not see them as such. They are forever reminders of good pilots lost, good friends gone."

"Time, as they say, heals all wounds."

"Perhaps. Yet, it has been a long time since I last bonded. I should check to see if anything new is available for treating the whorls." Tokoray put on his officer's tunic.

She gazed again at his whorls before they vanished from her sight and calculated the impact and the heat of the strikes—and remembered a favor owed.

He picked up the cuddly and began to turn toward the door to leave.

"Tokoray, wait. I know the chief of robotics. He owes me big time." She tabbed the wall node and brought up a small comlink with video-feed capabilities. Minutes later, she called in the favor.

When Jaqui returned, Tokoray departed for maintenance. Five hours later, he returned. What skin she could see peeping out from under his tunic had a soft, dove-gray matte sheen just like that of the shell covering his legs and wheelbase. One of his disk-cap lights winked and then her bedroom door closed. He wheeled up to her bedside. "Thank you, Darq." He removed his tunic. "The scrubbing compounds and a new polymer coating were most effective."

Darq smiled. "I'll say. A lot of your whorls are gone or so faint I have to squint to tell if they are or aren't there."

He turned giving her a look at his back. Only the one large whorl remained, a muted swirl, the pigments gold and silver, bronze and pewter. Like medals of honor given by the fleet for service beyond the call of duty.

When he donned his officer's tunic, she noticed his officer pips. "Have you been demoted?"

"No, but I will soon lose the title of chief flight instructor."

"Why?"

"Majorn Varree's is getting her second choice of CFI, a Na-ka-ta from the homeworld. Azran Atlatl had something to do with that, but I know not what exactly."

Atlatl came from a powerful dyn that had many connections on the homeworld. Likely he pulled in a favor, or made a deal or two.

The bedroom door opened, and in strode Rieeza, her backpack riding light and hanging off one shoulder. "Hi!"

Darq swore. "How many times must I tell you to request entrance?"

"Jaqui said I could come right in."

Rieeza glanced at Tokoray, then met Darq's gaze.

Exuberance twinkled in Rieeza's bright eyes. "It doesn't look like I'm interrupting anything. Well, that is, anything really important, now am I?"

Darq tried to maintain a look of indignation. "My peace of mind is important. So, why the visit?"

"To see how you were doing."

"I don't buy that, Rieeza. The glint in your eyes says you have an ulterior motive. Spit it out so I can get the rest I'm supposed to be getting." Darq squirmed down into her sleepsack and triggered the side zipper to close up to her elbows.

"Okay. You want blunt, you get blunt. When can I schedule you and your partner here to test the new and improved INS?"

"Mechnet Rieeza," Tokoray said, "what is an INS?"

Rieeza crossed her arms over her chest, not in a defensive manner but more of a joyous self-hug. "It's an Intuitive Navigation System, one that interprets a pilot's body and weight shifts and relays them a hundred times faster to a fighter's onboard systems. Kinda like a horse whose rider only has to tilt their head to get a turn. It's in the imperceptible motions and weight distribution—"

"Rieeza," Darq said, "have you had anyone fly the INS since I crashed it?"

Rieeza dropped her arms to her sides. "Yeah, four other qtl-shies, the ones you recommended. All loved it, actually loved it. Every one of them said if it passes your crazy flying, it would be the greatest thing since the invention of antigravity. So, when can you test it?"

Darq looked at Tokoray. *Ever done any test flying?*

Every time I ride with a cadet.

Darq choked on a laugh.

"What's so funny? Are you two talking behind my back?"

Darq stifled her merriment. "Actually, Rieeza, we're in front of you. Okay, as soon as the d'ktr clears me for flying and Tokoray has free time in his CFI schedule, I'll let you know, and we can set something up."

"Terrific! You'll make it sooner of soonests?"

"We'll certainly try."

Rieeza fairly skipped out of the room but stopped abruptly in the doorway to say over her shoulder, "Get better really, really fast." Then she left.

"Darq," Tokoray said, "are you good friends with Rieeza?"

"Sort of. I'm her stepmother. She's a genius mechnet with a talent for creating and troubleshooting machinery that's matched by none. Enough about her. You'll need to get up to date on the INS. Plug into my terminal over there." She pointed to the unit in the corner. "Everything I've got on the INS is in the link marked Rieeza Projects."

"She has more than one project?"

"She has hundreds, if not thousands. Her first project was an ejector-seat release, which is now fleet standard."

When Tokoray returned to her side, she had the bed in the sitting position, the table out, and the table top flipped over, exposing a comtar screen.

"You should rest, Darq."

"I'm not sleepy. Thought I would look up a few test flights to put the INS through. Got any you like?"

"I have several, two of which are useful in testing reflexes and reaction times, only . . ."

She stopped tabbing through the icon lists to look at him. "Only what?"

"It has been three and a half t'uns since I was in combat."

"It'll come back to you." She grinned at him. "I know just the test to reacquaint you with combat flight."

"One worse than the sim test we flew?"

"Oh yes, much, much worse — or better — depending on how you look at it."

She wasn't sure if what came out of his voice box was a sputtering snort or a derisive chuckle.

✧ Chapter 17

Ippera stared at his golden reflection in the black mirror of the nutrient tank across the aisle. Damn the war god's minions. What a fool he had been to think pushing the *Ippera's* engines, shorting a guidance system CPU, and forcing everything possible beyond tolerances would net a disaster to kill him or destroy the ship. Not even that jammed maneuvering rocket triggered a catastrophe. Was there no way to end his enslavement? "Pus."

"I believe that's my line, Admirid."

Startled, he spun his disks around and watched Ooots slip sideways through the silently opening blast door, giving him the barest glimpse beyond of the destroyer *Ippera's* semidark and abandoned bridge.

Ooots stopped in front of him.

He kept his voice neutral. "I would have thought you would be celebrating with everyone else."

"I did, well, sort of." She lowered her voice. "Between you and me, Admirid, things are getting, well, to put it politely — extremely boisterous with all the liquor flowing. Considering I have a transport to board at the top of the hour, well, I want to make sure I, um, well — "

"Escape an orgy?"

She nodded. "I also wanted to say farewell and wish you continued success with this vessel."

Too many well-wishers were wishing him success. He would be grinding his teeth in frustration at having to endure such platitudes, if only he had teeth.

Four settz ago, he had been taken aboard the *Ippera* and, under the tightest of security measures, uncrated. Thanks to Nuzzi, who used a portable display, he'd seen what the *Ippera* looked like—a helmet with two colossal horizontal pipes, its engines, one on its port side and the other on its starboard side. The vessel turned out to be the size of a cruiser, the lowest class of destroyer in the fleet.

Albeit the starship had a sleeker design. One with heavier armor, a lithe quickness of response to controls and commands, and an envious array of weapon systems. However, it possessed no new, impressive weapon of destruction in its arsenal. The equipment and weaponry were old technologies, ones that had stood the test of battle and time. Maybe that's why nothing failed. Zzraa! He wanted failures that would kill him. He wanted death.

"Admirid, are you all right? Did another filter clog?"

He should not let his thoughts digress. Nor should he alarm Ooots. "Yes, I am fine, but let me check the filters." He ran a quick diagnostic. All the while Ooots gazed at various panel lights turning pink-lavender and indicating no problems. "As you can see, Ooots, all is within parameters. No clogs."

Ooots' exuberant smile radiated in her voice. "I'm so glad, Admirid, to know you feel at home with being part of this ship."

He didn't, but he couldn't let her or anyone suspect that.

Ooots looked about the room of wall-to-wall tanks and equipment, then at him, centered on his pedestal, king of the room. Her smile waned when she gazed directly into his visual sensor-eyes. "Is it true, Admirid, what Caprivi Nuzzi said?"

"About what in particular?"

"That you exceeded the engines' tolerances until the entire ship vibrated, including your tanks?"

"Better to test in safety than in battle. After all, a commander must know his vessel's strengths and weaknesses, get a feel for pushing the limits of m'chi and machine." He couldn't tell her the truth, that if Nuzzi hadn't reached for the override to stop the speed test, something might have gone wonky. But to avoid Nuzzi panicking and thinking he, Admirid Ippera, was suicidal, it had been prudent to cut the power back and declare exuberant satisfaction with the ship's performance. Best to keep up the image and spout rhetoric the masses wanted to hear. "Yes, Ooots, I had indeed maxed the engines, and they held beyond my expectations."

"Beyond everyone's to hear Caprivi Nuzzi boast. Everyone is saying this destroyer can out-fly anything the Wysotti have, including Pytak fighters."

"That is likely true." Especially since the Raven, one of the Wysotti's best Pytak fighter pilots, was dead. Pity he had not been able to go up against her. She might have shot him out of the heavens. What a fitting end that would have been.

A smile nudged the corners of Ooots snout. "I also want to personally thank you for the recommendation."

"Recommendation? What recommendation? I'm dead to all and sundry, so how could I have possibly made a recommendation?" Was that bitterness in his tone? Had she detected it?

Her smile widened. "Caprivi Nuzzi told me you requested he send a recommendation to the university's board of admissions." Her smile beamed. "I got an acceptance. Once I get to the homeworld, I'll be working with the best bio expert there is. Thank you for making that possible."

"It was little enough for all you have done for me, Ooots, and also, in part, it reflects my gratitude for you saving my son. Speaking of J'sein, by the way, you do know he goes to the same university you're attending?"

Under her mother-of-pearl cheeks flushed a stricken, pale-yellow hue. "You do not approve of my associating with J'sein?"

"On the contrary, I pray the boy realizes what a grand match you would be for him."

Color returned to her cheeks and flushed her face. "Truly?"

"Truly, Ooots. If you decide to mate with my son, consider Caprivi Nuzzi your ally. The caprivi is aware of my feelings on the matter, and I have ordered Nuzzi to sit J'sein down and have a fatherly talk with him if it should become necessary. Nuzzi is to expound on your genius and your suitability to enhance the Ippera lineage."

Ooots sucked in a breath and grinned. "Oh, thank you, Admirid!"

"Now, when did you say you had to board your transport?"

She glanced at the chronometer on the wall above the blast door. "Oh, pus. I've got to go." She strode for the door, hit the open node, then paused to look back at him over her slender shoulder. "May the war god bless you with many victories."

The only victory he wanted was death. "And to you, Ooots, may the great war god grant you a long life and realization of your dreams."

"Thank you, Admirid. Farewell."

"Farewell, Ooots." With the blast door having fully opened during their exchange, Ippera now watched Ooots' hips sway all the way to the lift. The lift doors seemed to sneeze open, and he heard her say, "Good evening, Caprivi Nuzzi."

"Aren't you supposed to be on a transport?" Nuzzi's voice sounded slurred.

"I am. I came to say goodbye to the admirid—and did."

"Then be about your business."

"Yes, caprivi."

After the lift doors closed, Nuzzi ordered the bridge computer to halt the closing blast door. He walked unsteadily on, through the opening, and stopped at the edge of Ippera's outer ring. He staggered half a step. "Good evening, Admirid."

"You are inebriated, Nuzzi."

"I realize that. Everyone kept toasting you, this ship, everyone involved in its creation . . . Couldn't be impolite, now could I?"

"And why are you here instead of continuing the celebrating?"

"I am escaping said celebrations. They are stationwide. Boisterous revelings . . . " He paused, tapping a finger against his liquor-swollen lips. "You know, I came here for another reason. What was it? Oh, yes—to give you a warning."

"A warning of what?"

Nuzzi hiccupped and tilted to starboard. Realizing he was listing, he countered his stance.

Ippera triggered a seat that came up, out of the flooring. "Sit before you fall, Nuzzi."

"Thank you, Admirid." He eyed the seat, judged the distance to it, took two slow but straight steps, and sat facing Ippera.

"Now, my besotted friend, what is this about a warning?"

"Supreme Command insists I and my bridge crew remain aboard the *Ippera* for the war games."

Damn the war god. He didn't need a crew aboard. "Did I not demonstrate today how well I could handle this vessel and that I did not require a crew?"

"Oh, that you did." He paused as if trying to recall something. "Remember our conversation when we were playing bok'bon a few settz ago? Remember me telling you about Chingvee's blackmail scheme?"

"How could I forget that?"

"Well, they appointed that emaciated little assistant of hers, Wosolek, as her replacement. He presented her scheme as his own idea. Supreme Command had me on a secure channel for hours about it." He hiccupped. "I told them Wosolek was wrong. You are sane, and your genius would facilitate the quick destruction of the Wysotti."

"Did they believe you?"

Nuzzi shook his head. "Don't know." His lopsided grin held the blush of inebriation. "What I do know is they are not taking any chances."

"Meaning?"

"The war games begin in forty-eight hours. The *Xon Xun* arrived last night. Aboard her is the special attaché to the F'brig Space Fleet Overlord Commander, a fellow named Vytegravorg."

"He the one married to Hibizahn Xomott's homely daughter?"

"Homely? She's downright ugly. All that inbreeding—"

"Nuzzi, do not go off on a tangent."

"Sorry, Admirid. I— Now what was I saying?" He touched his temple with his index digit, as if to rub a thought forward. He lowered his hand. "Ah, yes. The ships that will be chasing you. The lead ship is the *Akeavosso*, Caprivi Mesk now commanding. I always liked him."

Ippera silently seconded that.

"The other is the *Bekrakaun*. Caprivi Eslatont has never lost a war game. Or a battle."

Shock trembled through Ippera, not because of Eslatont's devilish reputation but because of who Eslatont's XO was. "Is my son on the *Bekrakaun*?"

Nuzzi swallowed hard enough that Ippera's hearing sensors picked up the sound.

"Yes, Admirid, U'zan is aboard." Nuzzi leaned forward, both hands on the edge of the disk-top for balance. He lowered his voice. "Not only does Command figure Eslatont will give you one helluva battle but having U'zan aboard would come in handy should you go berserk."

"I go berserk? That's absurd!"

Nuzzi leaned back and hiccupped. "Agreed. But Supreme Command believes—thanks to Wosolek—that if I'm incapacitated or injured or dead, well then, you're more likely to respond to your son's voice and not do something stupid to destroy this ship."

"That's nonsensical garbage. Does U'zan know what's happened to me, that I am part of this vessel?"

Nuzzi shook his head repeatedly. "He isn't to be told until absolutely necessary. Eslatont knows. He confided in me he was appalled, and it's an abomination to remove a m'chi's brain from his body, especially one of your rank and honors."

"Eslatont is a hardliner."

"But realizing his brain could be taken from him has given him pause." He whispered, "It should give every officer pause. It has given me pause."

Astounded at Nuzzi's confession, Konuris remained speechless, yet pleased with that revelation.

Nuzzi hiccupped twice. "So, Admirid, like it or not, you're stuck with me and my crew. Oh, and I'm to self-destruct us if we are captured by the Centauri."

"The Centauri? Have they invaded?"

"No, no. They watch and patrol the neutral zone, but with more patrols and class two battleships."

If the Centauri had increased patrols with heavy destroyers, it meant some sort of incident had taken place. Should that incident kindle a war with the Centauri, the kungarike could not simultaneously fight both the Wysotti and the Centauri. Surely

Supreme Command realized that. "Nuzzi, what put the Centauri on alert?"

"How did you know they were on high alert?"

High alert! By the war god's ass— "Nuzzi, what has caused the Centauri to attack us?"

"They aren't attacking. Just sitting. Watching. Waiting."

"Nuzzi, you make no sense. Explain."

Nuzzi frowned like a man swimming through the thick fog of liquor and discovering a piece of driftwood. "Oh, right. The Grier."

"What of the Grier?"

"When they emerged from the asteroid belt near San Hiphia, right at the edge of the Centauri's neutral zone, the *Akeavosso* told them to heave to for boarding. The *Marousar* and *Marousir*—I hate the way they name their ships."

"Nuzzi, get on with it. What happened?"

"The Griers said they were headed for the Argo ship center. Our intel said they were bound for the Wysotti. Had to stop them."

"We captured the Griers? Is that why the Centauri are angry with us?"

Nuzzi shook his head. "The Griers abandoned their ore carriers. Flew their tow-haulers into the asteroids. No Doyon caprivi would risk losing a starship among those asteroids." Nuzzi smiled and swayed a bit. "We captured the ore containers, full ones. Didn't let them coast into Centauri territory." He blinked and his eyebrows rose. "I never realized how speedy those little Grier haulers could be, nor how agile. But, they are, aren't they?"

Ippera had an urge to throttle Nuzzi for being drunk, but to upbraid the man would not yield information. "Nuzzi, we have never stopped the Griers before when they had ore en route to Argo. Why now?"

"Supreme Command thinks the two ships might have discovered we seeded the big asteroids with rockets. Can't afford having the Griers get that intel to the Wysotti, now can we?"

"No, but, Nuzzi, if the two Grier ships fled into the asteroids, how do you know where they went and who they'll tell?"

"Not to worry. Our patrols. Long-range sensors. Reports came in showing both Grier ships emerged, streaking for Argo. Supreme Command doesn't care if they warn all the Grier cartels not to trade with us as long as they stay clear of the asteroids until the Wysotti End of Days."

"We need Grier traders to bring in goods."

"Couple hours ago, orders came down. No Grier ships are to be allowed into the area paralleling the asteroid belt. As insurance, you understand, because the Griers must not discover the rockets and tell the Wysotti about them." He chuckled softly. "We get to shoot Griers on sight and take their cargoes!" His self-satisfied smirk came with the heavy, slow opening and closing of his eyelids and the swaying of his head. "If we see any Grier ships, the *Ippera* can hunt them down and provide our gun batteries target practice."

"The orders included that?"

Nuzzi nodded. "But with my say-so."

Admirids did not take orders from caprivies. But that was a moot point since he wasn't technically an admirid but a ship's brain. "Nuzzi, is there any proof the Griers discovered the asteroids with our rockets?"

"Don't think so. No one's officially said." Nuzzi yawned. "Can't take any chances. Too close to the End of Days." Nuzzi yawned again, longer and louder. "We are F'brig. We do our duty to death." He slid off his seat onto the floor, curled up, and began snoring.

Ippera dimmed the lights and upped the heat along the floor to make Nuzzi more comfortable. Knowing Nuzzi and liquor, the m'chi would not remember any of this conversation.

By the war god's ass, the situation was untenable.

Yet, he could understand the Supreme Command thinking the Centauri were no threat unless attacked outright. As for the Grier ships, even if they discovered the rockets, the information could not get back to the Wysotti in time for them to launch an effective defense. And since, by all accounts, the Centauri and Wysotti did not know each other existed, worrying about the Centauri was pointless.

But what truly bothered him more was that his son, U'zan, would be on hand to witness the war games. His son had a great military future ahead of him. Only wasn't U'zan as brainwashed as everyone in the fleet? All believing duty to the kungarike was the only thing. *Duty be damned.*

Still, he would not shame himself in front of his son.

Suicide might be desirable, but it was one thing to kill ones' self and quite another to take Nuzzi's life—and that of seven others who would crew the *Ippera* during the war games.

An idea slithered into place. Perhaps he could find a way to get the crew off the ship, get them away in the life-pods?

Such complications. How was he to die equitably and end this slavery?

His father's words whispered in his mind—*If there is a problem, there is always a solution.*

Damn the war god's ass, there had to be a solution.

✧ Chapter 18

Darq stood on Tokoray's wheelbase, waiting for the lift doors in front of her to open. A yawn overtook her and emerged with gusto.

Tokoray's voice came out low, quiet. "Are you fatigued?"

"No." Contentment radiated through her, and she added, "It's a happy kind of tired. You have to admit that was one helluva flight test."

"Yes, I agree. Rieeza has developed a remarkable system."

"Even more remarkable when you consider what we put the unit through—and it worked almost flawlessly."

A ping sounded. The lift had arrived. When the doors opened, Tokoray wheeled forward, bearing left to diagonally cross the corridor to Darq's quarters. Once through the door, Darq spied Atlatl standing at the end of the narrow island of the food center. A glance at his tunic revealed no rank amulet. Yet, when she looked at his unsmiling, solemn face and anguished eyes, a deep-seated dread gripped her heart.

Atlatl lifted the small glass he held. Black chunks drifted at the bottom of the dark amber liquid in the glass. "Ek-musa."

Ek-musa, his favorite hard liquor with bits of licorice added. Which meant push had come to shove. Some crisis had gotten the best of him.

Tokoray stopped and released his hold around her waist. She stepped off his foot-plates. To Atlatl she offered a simple, "Adovee."

No emotion crossed his face. "We need to talk. In private." He took a swig of his liquor.

Knowing the liquor had the fiery kick worthy of a thistle missile, she waited for the sensation to pass through him. When his eyes again focused on her, she pointed to the doorway of her bed chamber.

He nodded once, curtly.

Tokoray's voice came over the neural net. *I will busy myself in the kitchen making you a calorie-laden snack.*

Make it a meal-worthy one. On second thought, make enough to share with Atlatl.

To take the edge off the liquor he has consumed?

Yes.

Once behind the closed door of her bed chamber, Atlatl set his drink on the recessed shelf of her headboard. The glass now held a mere two swallows.

Darq chucked her flight boots. She got out of her flightsuit and the underlying leechsuit, hanging both garments on the wall hooks designed for them. Instead of donning fatigues, she put on her old robe and slippers. Turning, she found Atlatl standing in front of her. His face seemed paler than she'd ever seen it. He slipped his hands around her waist and hugged her tightly.

She sent her arms up around his neck, her hands gliding under his long pigtail braid.

His body trembled.

She whispered into his ear. "Atlatl, tell me what's wrong. What's happened?"

His voice came out strangled, gruff, "The worst has come to pass."

Instant images of destruction flashed in her mind, and she whispered, "The homeworld has been attacked?"

He jerked back, lessening his hold on her. Anger momentarily flashed in his eyes. "No, not that, but as bad. Duty. That which a commander must do, what I, your atan, have feared most."

She lowered her hands to his chest, laying them palms down, one over his heart and sensed it pounding. "I'm being reassigned?"

"No." He closed his eyes, as if fighting an inner demon. When he opened his eyes, resignation hardened his chestnut-brown eyes to a rusty depth. "Orders came from fleet command. I am to pick the best, the very best pilots, to lead a sortie." He drew in air that flared his nostrils. "Darq, you are the best the *Dujaki* has. Maybe, just maybe, you can pull off a miracle."

She wanted to protest she wasn't the very best and that miracles were not in her providence, but she knew what he meant. His duty required he send her on a suicide mission. That duty now tore him apart.

He let out a shuddering breath and again hugged her tightly, burying his forehead against her neck and shoulder.

One hand she sent about his neck, the other lower, to the small of his back, pulling him into her embrace. She could find no words of comfort for him. *This was only the inevitable.*

The unspoken inevitable.

A long moment later, she gently pushed him back to gaze into his dark, morose eyes. Placing her cool hands on his warm cheeks, cradling him with love, she said in a low voice weighted with the pretense of bravado, "What mission would Fleet have that you think I cannot or will not strive to survive?"

"Not only you, six in all. The finest pilots the *Dujaki* has. You'll be going after —" He hugged her again, swaying her, and took a fortifying breath that shuddered out a second before he let her go. He stepped back.

Tears of empathy glossed her eyes and blurred her vision. "Atlatl, my love, from the beginning of our relationship and our marriage, we knew being Elpoccalli would make things difficult, try our patience, separate us, and — even kill us."

"I know, but it never sank in until now that I would have to order you to your death."

"I'm not dead yet. *Rejoice in life, in the now, in the moment.* Remember? We promised each other that."

He nodded. "It does not set well with me." He reached his arms out, and she stepped into them for another hug. "I love you, Darq. I don't want to lose you."

"And I love you." She kissed him, feeling the sorrow and the longing of hope — a hopeless hope — that all would turn out well.

Atlatl broke the kiss and feathered a line of kisses along her jaw and up to her temple before pulling back. She recalled one other time he had kissed her like that, just after she'd first come aboard the *Dujaki.*

"Atlatl," she entreated, "remember when I asked you to marry me the first time? We talked about our ages, you insisting you would be dead long before me from old age?"

He nodded and a faint smile curved his lips. "You cried because you couldn't convince me I was not too old for you."

"But, years later, the third time I asked, you said you truly loved me and made a promise."

"Ah, yes, the promise. I promised that if I died of old age, I would wait beside the gates of heaven for you."

Darq swiped a wayward tear from her right eye with the back of her index finger. "Well, my love, I now promise that if I die on this mission, I will wait for you by heaven's gate."

He kissed her cheek and held her for a long while before releasing her and going to her sleep-rack. He sat on the bed, clasping his hands prayerfully, and studied the decking.

When she couldn't tolerate his silence any longer, she said, "Atlatl, I get the feeling there's more to this mission than sending me to my death. Can you tell me what it is?"

He met her gaze, his eyes filled with misery.

"Oh, Atlatl . . . " She went to him, sat close beside him, and placed her hand over his. "Must I wait for the briefing to know what's up?"

He shook his head. "No, you're right. You need to know now, so it won't come as a shock."

That didn't sound good. "Hey, haven't you said a hundred times that I'm awfully hard to shock?"

He scowled.

"Please?"

By the rounding of his shoulders, she knew the moment he gave in.

"Darq, before we lost the Joiz outpost, *Ziital* launched a mission to a research facility deep in Doyon territory. With the assistance of anti-war sympathizers, our special ops got in and out undetected and destroyed the facility. They brought back a Grier slave. He had valuable intel to barter."

Griers, ever the bargainers. "What did the slave want in return for his information?"

"To be welcomed back into his family's cartel. Fleet agreed and so a lesser brother of the clan was contacted and asked to deliver an unprecedented offer to the Marous Clan. Just after the Joiz attack, that emissary headed for the Grier trade center to deliver the offer. The acceptance came back this morning."

"This morning? Was that the Grier hauler everyone was talking about, the one that came in with burned-out engines from running hot and fast?"

He nodded. "The *Marouser* brought word his brother is welcomed back into the family. The *Marouser* also brought bad news. The Doyons attacked and captured two of their ore carriers that had been heading for the Argo ore facility. The Doyons said any Grier ship trespassing in the kungarike or the Cypha-wee-ka would be seized."

"Greedy Doyons."

Atlatl briefly nodded, then the lines across his brow tightened, as if something puzzled him. "Fleet speculates the Doyons intend to mine the asteroids themselves." The puzzle-frown faded. "We're lucky to have that intel."

"How so?"

"The two haulers that were attacked didn't want to become Doyon slaves, so they jettisoned their ore carriers and escaped into the Cypha-wee-ka. Somehow they met up with the *Marouser*. The three captains had a powwow. They decided the *Marouser* would continue on to the *Dujaki* and the other two ships would streak for the cartel's home base, in full view of the Doyons — a deliberate distraction so the *Marouser* could get to us undetected and warn the other Griers docked here."

Darq squeezed Atlatl's hand. "That doesn't make sense. So what if the Doyons shoo off Griers to get their ore?"

He looked at her with his all-knowing smile. "It has to do with the information the rescued Grier at *Ziital* station has now given us." In a softer tone, one bound with foreboding, he said, "The Doyons have built a new destroyer. The ultimate destroyer of worlds. It's equipped with innovative technology, robotics, weaponry."

Shock gave way to a tremor of fear, which quaked Darq's guts, but she tamped down her emotions. "They've created a monster warship?"

"No, the intel says it's a class two destroyer."

Relief washed away Darq's anxiety. "A little-bitty destroyer?"

Atlatl shrugged. "Evidently they're starting small."

"Okay, so Fleet doesn't want them building bigger ones, and this mission you're sending me on is to hunt down and annihilate this war ship." Which meant the hunt would be inside Doyon territory. "Where's the ship docked?"

"It's not docked. Intel says it's en route for flight testing, which is likely going to be done in Sector Four, farthest from prying eyes."

"Eyes we no longer have because we've lost the Joiz outpost. Geez, Atlatl, star maps are spotty at best for Sector Four."

Atlatl shook his head. "No, not any more." He raised a hand to stay her question. "Remember the Grier slave?"

She nodded.

"He's been very cooperative. So have his brothers. Evidently they want the Doyons to pay dearly for taking their cargo. We now have Grier maps for you and the other pilots." Atlatl squeezed her hand briefly, then reached over and picked up his drink, wafting down most of the liquor but leaving the undissolved bits of licorice sloshing about.

"A swig for courage, Atlatl?"

He gave her a quizzical look.

"You still haven't told me what the shocker is."

He set his glass down. "The destroyer is a high-value target. Its name is—" He locked his gaze to hers, holding her with an iron grip. "*Ippera.*"

The deafening thunder of Ippera's name boomed through Darq's mind, roiling up a lightning storm of long-buried memories. Images flashed of Ippera, sword in hand, and of the ruthless Doyon commander lopping off the head of her classmate.

"Breathe, woman, breathe," Atlatl ordered, alarm in his voice. "You've gone stark white. Breathe!"

Darq inhaled, slamming down hard on the image of the bloody holocaust. She managed between ragged breaths, "The Doyons named a ship after that butcher?"

"Yes. Admirid Ippera died a few moons ago. To honor his illustrious career as a conqueror of worlds, they christened the vessel *Ippera*."

"Honor him? That's sheer insanity." Darq took a deep breath that helped vanquish the old memories. Ippera was dead, yet, his name lived on as a ship. If she couldn't kill the Doyon himself, the ship was the next best thing. She put a hand on Atlatl's forearm and squeezed once. "It shall be my honor and my duty to kill that bloody bastard's namesake."

The door to her bedroom opened and in came Rieeza, her ratty-looking backpack slung over one shoulder, her face alight with triumph and gaiety. "Hello, father. Hi, Darq."

Atlatl glared at her and in his sternest, most fatherly tone said, "Rieeza, it is considered polite to ask for admittance to a bedchamber. Especially one I am in."

"Yeah, I know, father, but I asked Tokoray if Darq had told him she didn't want to be disturbed, and he said no, adding you hadn't given such an order either, and therefore, no nookies, no sex going on. Ergo. Here I am."

Atlatl growled low in his throat, but his voice didn't betray his annoyance with her. "State your business."

Rieeza's gaiety waned slightly. She clapped her hands together and looked at Darq. "We, that is, me and my team of engineers, all our maintenance crews, plus all the pilots and Na-ka-tas and anyone else who willingly or unwittingly worked on or tested the INS, are getting together at 1900 hours for a celebration, and we want you, Darq, and Tokoray, to be there."

He hadn't heard of any celebration. "Rieeza," Atlatl said, "what are you celebrating?"

She propped a hand on her hip. "Why the INS being a success. Haven't you read the report I sent you?"

"I've been busy with fleet command." He did know Darq was to test the unit today but— "Are you saying your nav-sys is operational? Darq didn't crash and burn it?"

Darq stifled a chuckle behind her hand.

Rieeza's grin outshone ten stars. "Darq didn't bruise it at all. It's fully operational. Ready to go into the production phase."

The intuitive system. One touted as a boon to pilot survival. Pilots. Darq. Life and death in a cockpit . . . An idea percolated.

Atlatl got to his feet, reached into his tunic pocket, brought out his rank amulet, and attached it.

Rieeza stopped smiling.

Darq remained seated, looking at him with a questioning gaze.

He took a military square-footed stance, one of his more officer-formidable ones. "Mechnet Rieeza," he said with the power of his rank.

"Yes, azran?"

"How many operational INS's do you have that could be immediately installed into Pytak fighters."

She blinked. "Um — there's the one in the simulator, the one in the shop, and a prototype, which needs some tweaking. Two others are burned out from testing or malfunctions and will take moons to rebuild. So, I guess — three."

"Three are better than none." He turned to Darq. "If I have to order pilots to their deaths, they'll have the best equipment I can give them." He faced Rieeza, who looked shocked and curious. "Rieeza, by my order, there will be no celebrating." He held up his hand to stay her protests and pleading. "You and your teams have thirty hours to get those three nav-sys fully operational and installed in the *Ky*, the *Honon*, and the *Sunay*. Now hop to it!"

"Yes, azran!" Rieeza pivoted about and headed for the door. She began tapping her wrist datapad and speaking rapidly into her comlink. The door soon closed behind her.

When Atlatl again turned to Darq, he found admiration shimmered in her cacao-brown eyes. "It's the least I can do for you and the other qtl-shies."

"I know, azran." A smile pulled back the corners of her lips. "I'm grateful. The other pilots will be too."

"There's much to do." He studied her, drinking in every line of her face, to remember and hold dear the vision in case this would be the last time he saw her. He put his hand over his rank amulet, so she would know he, her atan, spoke. "Adovee, my love."

Darq broadened her smile of acknowledgment to him and put into her voice her love for him. "Adovee." She watched him exit and the door close. In her mind a soft drumming began.

Zukaltay again. Did her grandmother know her granddaughter would soon face death? Or was the drumming the fledgling warning of some sort of mental instability? A quirk of the neural net? Or the shock of having to confront Ippera again?

Ippera. Not the Doyon himself, but a destroyer. A machine. Technically, they were one in the same.

Her grandmother's words came to her — *Embrace the ice of duty and the fire of courage, Darq, for they enable us to endure the adversities of life.*

That day she faced Ippera, there had been an intense desire, a blood rage, to kill him, to kill the butcher. She was older now. Wiser. Now her duty demanded she kill the *Ippera.* Was that justice or recompense?

She eyed Atlatl's glass and grabbed it. *Death to Ippera!* She put the glass to her lips and jerked her head back, downing the last of the liquor and the bits, which burned her throat and stomach with the intensity of a DLE.

After the pilots' briefing, Darq returned to her quarters and pondered the coming mission and the likelihood of death. Not her death so much but those of the other Pytak fighter pilots and Na-ka-tas she'd known over the years who would be out there seeking the *Ippera.*

When she closed her eyes and hugged herself, the image of Atlatl winked into place. He had been devastated thinking she'd self-destructed at Joiz. What if she self-destructed in a Doyon no-man's land? She would die leaving no positive proof of her death.

Then she recalled Jaqui saying eighty-percent of the time, when a Pytak fighter self-destructed, among the debris was one or both of the pilot's boots — with feet still in them.

An idea flared to life. She went to the cupboard and took out the rosewood puzzle box that housed her meager collection of nail polishes. An hour later, she had triple-coated her toes with one-brush-strokes, making a rainbow from every color she owned. On the big toe nails, she applied shiny midnight-blue and dotted on the sapphire star pattern of the Jewels of the Sky drum. If her boots were found and her feet examined, Atlatl would know for sure those were her feet. Now all she had to do was not let anyone see her toes so she wouldn't be cited for violating regs. Definitely she didn't need Tokoray seeing them and having him register a note into his logs.

Once her toenails were dry, she took her time dressing for the Owl Ceremony. She painted her face according to the instructions Jaqui had given her. With half an hour remaining before reporting to the ceremony, Darq sat at her comtar station and pored over the star charts the Griers had supplied for the mission.

There were three possible areas where the Doyons might test the destroyer *Ippera* without having said tests observed. She and her fellow qtl-shies had drawn lots for the hunting grounds. She had drawn the farthest corner, where a dense, old cloud nebula still birthed a random star and where supernovas and mini-novas had pockmarked the cloud. According to the Griers, nothing existed on the other side of the nebula except a cartel trade terminal and their Argo ore facility. Her gaze shifted to the nebula's foremost edge and a lone binary, Alpha San Hiphia and its companion Beta San Hiphia. On the other side of those stars streamed the Chepha-week-ka Asteroid Belt.

A ping resonated, followed by the comtar's announcement, "Jaqui seeks entrance."

"Granted."

The door opened, and Jaqui walked in. "Are you ready?"

Darq turned off the comtar station. "As ready as I'll ever be."

"Geez, Darq, it's a blessing ceremony, not a funeral. Smile, woman, smile!"

"I know but, technically, we are not expected back."

"Don't say that. Don't even think that. Especially since you're the one with the advantage."

"I'll trade fighters if you like."

"No way. You are the best Doyon hunter there is. My job is merely to help you find the *Ippera* and cover your ass so you can blast it apart. Now, change of subject. Don't we just look like twins?"

Darq took in Jaqui's ceremonial white dress uniform, replete with fringed yokes, her hair decorated with white owl feathers, her face painted with red, yellow, and black symbols of valor, courage, protection. "Twins? Hardly, Jaqui. Have you forgotten the others? We six are sextuplets, thanks to our Na-ka-tas."

"Well, we are all on the same mission, so shouldn't we look alike?"

Darq shrugged. When she thought about it, it actually didn't matter what they looked like or whether they looked alike as long as they were present for the ceremony. She led the way out the door.

The attendees—friends, comrades, loved ones, Na-ka-tas—all gathered for the Owl Blessing Ceremony, filled the battlestation's main sanctuary, crowding together around the ceremonial circle.

Each of the mission pilots' Na-ka-tas wore a white dress tunic. Like their pilots faces', the sides of the Na-ka-tas' midnight-blue faceplates had been painted with symbols. Each wore a circlet of tiny owl feathers around their disk-caps.

The senior saalishani aboard the *Dujaki*, in full white ceremonial garments edged with black and red beadwork and with yards of long fringe, held a staff topped with gold and white feathers. The saalishani stood in front of the center circle's large fire pit, giving the invocation in Ancient Wysotti. Then she led the prayers, lit the fire and incense, and danced about the four directions, all to the beat of the massive powwow drum, which was encircled by twenty singers chanting and beating the drum.

Receiving the saalishani's cue, Darq led her fellow pilots to kneel under the crowned dome circling the fire pit. Centered high over the pit, the Holy and Perpetual Light flamed. Darq stared at the multicolored, shimmering sphere. The orb sparkled with facets of obsidian, silver, and gold. Only it couldn't sparkle. The glitter had to be an optical illusion. Maybe not. What if the incense had something more in it? Or was seeing the refracted light an omen? A good omen or a bad omen? Maybe a mix of both good and bad?

From the floor, jets of steam rose to symbolize purification of the body and spirit. Lastly, the saalishani lifted a fan of owl feathers decorated with beads and leather fringe. The beats on the massive drum changed, and she chanted in the old language, giving the ancient blessing, "The good warrior never makes excuses to Death. When the Great Huntress Death looks upon you, meet her gaze, be steadfast. The good warrior never makes excuses to death but says, 'I am ready.'"

Afterwards, Darq danced with the other pilots and a hundred others involved with the coming mission. But when the music of the Ghost Dance began, Darq maneuvered herself to the darkest corner and hoped she would not be noticed. The powerful choreography of pounding footsteps, drumming, and flutes went soul-deep and called upon the power of the forefathers, beseeching them to send the greatest of warrior spirits to aid, guide, protect, and grant pilots victory in their missions. The image of the pilot Jaguar Four, Beans, flitted to mind. For a brief heartbeat, Darq wondered if she might borrow Beans's Ancestor, not for herself but to watch over her fellow pilots.

It was after midnight when Darq returned to her quarters with Jaqui. Neither spoke on the way back. Darq entered their quarters first and headed for her chamber.

"Darq—" Jaqui said, "Wait."

Darq halted and faced Jaqui. In Chance's dark eyes the ice of anxiety shimmered. "I know we've gone through the Owl Ceremony a dozen times, but this time—this time it's unnerving. No one thinks we'll return." Never had her sultry voice betrayed such distress nor had there ever been such unshed tears brimming in her eyes.

"Jaqui, we've come back from worse."

She nodded once, quickly, her face reflecting more anxiety. "I'm being melancholy and melodramatic, aren't I?"

A sense of déjà vu struck Darq. "Being a true warrior is to balance sheer terror with a childlike sense of wonder, to shift harmoniously with the tides of time and circumstance—"

"And not to give in to death without the best fight we're capable of." A slender smile illuminated Jaqui's face. "We've had this conversation before, right?"

"Twice if memory serves." Darq opened her arms wide, and Jaqui stepped into them. Each hugged the other.

For a fighter pilot, it was a given that one lived with and accepted death, was expected to die but, deep down, death should come in a fair fight. She knew Jaqui expected a fitting end, an honorable death. So did she.

Jaqui began to sway and Darq moved in a dance of comrades. Simultaneously they stopped swaying and said, voices soft, thick with emotion, "Adovee."

No need to say anything more. Darq stepped back and headed for her bed chamber. She heard Jaqui walk away and her chamber door open and shut.

After Darq washed off the war-paint and changed into a sleepsuit, she gazed into the mirror at her own almond-shaped eyes, into the seemingly fathomless, dark, cacao-brown irises. "Duty before self, Darq. Do your duty to the best of your ability. Let the Fates decide what will be." Now why had she quoted her grandmother?

Zukaltay's drumming began, and the tempo beckoned a headache to life. Only this time Darq recognized the rhythm, *The Battle Song of the Nations*. She'd heard the beat half a dozen times this night. She rubbed her temples. Why did she continue to hear Zukaltay's drumming? Could it be stress?

Yes, that's what it must be. She needed a peaceful mind. Quiet reflection like she used to get when she went fishing. Trouble was, you couldn't fish anywhere on a battlestation. But there were quiet places. Yes. One particular quiet place.

She changed into fatigues and headed back to the sanctuary. As she made her way through the foyer area, toward the back corridor that gave access to the meditation garden with its waterfalls and ponds, she spotted Tokoray lighting a fat candle in one of the memorial wall nooks. In a low tone, she heard him utter the familiar words of *A Candle Prayer*.

She paused.

Hello, Darq. Were you looking for me?

Since he was using the neural net, he must want to be private. *Hi. No, I wasn't. I'm headed for the garden.*

He lit an incense stick. Curiosity got the better of her and she joined him. The scent of Moc-ha-u-a wafted in her nostrils. Ignoring the pale blue-and-white smoke, she read the name scrolled in gold leaf on the candle, Citali. *Your first pilot.*

Yes. He pointed to the nook to his left where three other candles burned. Each bore the name of the other bonded pilots he'd served. *Although I usually light one on the day of her death, it seemed fitting, since I may not be coming back, to honor her and the others as well.*

Touched and humbled by his words, she didn't know what to say.

Citali had no family to mourn her death. He set and lit another incense stick. *She was the last of her line, last of her dyn.*

Lines die out. Why had she said that? She, herself, was not the last of her line. She had two sisters. Only she had wanted children, but she never conceived one by Atlatl because he became sterile. Then again, how could she bring a child into a world she knew would be attacked and annihilated?

Darq looked over the memorial wall. A thousand nooks, most with gutted, burned-down candles. *So many remembered loved ones. Family. Friends. Na-ka-tas. One day, Tokoray, someone will light a candle for us.*

Indeed. As a precaution, I have made arrangements with the Sisters of Dujaki that, should I not return to light a candle for Citali on her death day, they will.

Again, Darq didn't know what to reply.

I hope you do not mind, Darq, but I have arranged for a candle for you. He pointed to the nook above and a saucer wide candle with the gold leaf of her name ribboned about an image of a Pytak fighter.

She stared at the candle, then blinked. How had this conversation devolved into the morbid? Enough. Time to lighten up. *Planning on jinxing me are you?*

Tokoray's soft chuckle wafted through her neural net. *Not unless you murder me first.*

She smiled at him. *Death is a certainty but life has its ups and downs. In case I don't get the chance again, Tokoray, I want you to know I feel as though I've known you for a very long time. Maybe in a past life we were friends.*

Na-ka-tas do not believe in past lives despite our parts often being recycled. However, Darq, the feeling is mutual.

See you in a few hours. She headed for the garden.

And tomorrow we die.

That phrase looped in Darq's mind all the way to the meditation garden and the dream-catcher's pond where white-and-gold fish swam about the pink lilies.

Zukaltay's subdued drumming renewed.

✧ Chapter 19

In flight gear, Darq stood beside Tokoray on the deck of the Grier hauler, *Marouser*. She fought mission nerves. No, double the nervousness this time around because of the nature of the mission and the *Ippera*.

Nearby Chance, riding Izzt, waited. Izzt had a finger jack plugged into a control panel, waiting for the go signal from the *Marouser*'s bridge.

Darq peered through her helmet's virtual-view at a narrow viewport window. Outside, streaks of asteroids zipped by.

A cord of uncertainty twined tighter in her gut and double knotted. A part of her didn't want to find the *Ippera*, didn't want to remember the Doyon, the vile monster.

Jaqui's sultry voice came over the comlink. "Raven, we've got a green light. Time to go."

"Acknowledged, Chance." Darq used the neural link to notify Tokoray. He activated and soon sped into the nearby airlock. Jaqui and Izzt followed. Entering the other side of the airlock, Darq felt the weightlessness of the vast U-shaped ore bay. A blue dot on her faceplate indicated Tokoray had engaged MIMs. Those magnetic mechanisms on his wheelbase let him trundle across the decking where the *Ky* had been chained to the massive port side door. Glancing over to Jaqui and Izzt, she found them nearing the *Zopa*, which had been bound to the starboard bay door.

A tackle-and-pulley system, added for the occasion, enabled Darq and Tokoray to get into their cockpits. Darq closed her canopy and began launch prep. Minutes later, over the comlink came Jaqui's voice. "All systems go, Blackbird Lead, *Zopa* ready to launch."

"Acknowledged, Blackbird Two." *Tokoray, signal the Marouser we are go for engine start and launch.*

A signal bleeped. A screen flickered with data. Darq studied an exterior view of the *Marouser* showing the ore bay doors parting, widening. On Tokoray's cue, Darq engaged the *Ky*'s engines. The opening door tilted the *Ky* on its wing edge. When the cable released, the *Ky* was freed of its bonds. As Darq shifted her hips and weight, the newly installed INS responded. Darq slowly glided the *Ky* down and away from the ore carrier, then smoothly under the nearest chunk of asteroid. Checking her screens, she noted Jaqui on her tail.

The Grier vessel remained on course, no speed change to alert prying eyes. If there were any.

True to the Grier star maps, Darq came up through the asteroids along the edge of the Turtledove Nebula, a dense black mass of cosmic debris, dust, and gas. To conserve her engines, she shut them down, letting inertia carry the *Ky* along.

On her screen, the nebula's shape resembled a bird about to take flight. She cued other screens and instruments. Moments later she relaxed. She was right where she was supposed to be. A glance at the chronometer showed her ahead of schedule by six minutes. Radiation readouts indicated nothing noteworthy happening in the nebula and no radiation penetrating the *Ky*'s shields. She checked other screens. Soon routine set in, and memories of the Ly-quetzel Incident flitted, like an unwelcome whisper, bringing a ghostly chill. Her fingers grew colder and colder despite her flightsuit readouts showing a normal body temperature.

Tokoray's voice came across her neural net. *Passive scanners continue to show no Doyon patrols or any vessels.*

Acknowledged.

The hours passed and the *Ky* went deeper and deeper into the Doyon kungarike. Like the undulations of the dust in the nebula she flew through, periodically the Ly-quetzal memories swirled with dark foreboding along the edge of her consciousness. Some time later, navigating an arm of dust to avoid residual radiation from a little star's death, the *Ky*'s controls momentarily went sick. The Intuitive Nav-System screen flickered, then held steady. *What was that all about?*

What was what? Tokoray replied.

The INS. The screen just flickered.

Checking. A few seconds later came, *All is normal." A pause. *Darq, perhaps you are fatigued. You should stop to rest.*

Did he hint she was so tired she imagined the screen flicker? Well, rest wouldn't hurt. And she was hungry.

Darq spotted a small void in the dust cloud that offered protection and had Tokoray use the Na-ka-ta command channel to relay a meal and rest break to Chance. The two fighters drifted, and to conserve power, the *Zopa's* long-range sensors took the first watch so no one snuck up on them.

Darq leaned back in the quiet of her cockpit. Through the food tube built into her suit and seat, she sucked down a hot nutrimeal. As she slurped the last of her fruity desert, her thoughts wandered to what would happen if she found the *Ippera*.

Tokoray's voice came over the neural net. *You have been unusually quiet.*

Hunger got the best of me.

I was referring to the entire flight.

Isn't this a stealth mission? Quiet's the norm?

It is. However, your medical sensors indicate anxiety levels that concern me. Are you worried about something?

Chalk it up to the mission.

I sense it is more than mission concerns. However, if you do not wish to confide in me, I will duly note that in my log.

Darq sighed. He was way too observant, efficient, and that log of his would be analyzed by the consuleirs when they got back. Shitfire. Perhaps it would be better to confess why she'd been so silent. *Tokoray?*

Yes, Darq?

My silence stems from some past history. Bothersome past history. Unpleasant memories.

Are those memories a threat to this mission?

I hope not.

You are not sure?

Nothing is sure in life but death.

Your agitation levels have soared.

She tried to tame her emotions, to silence her survivor's guilt, but the trauma of Ly-quetzal fought being caged. *Look, Tokoray, a long time ago, I met the real Ippera — and his commandos.*

*Yes, I recall a notation in your personnel file, but no details."

Just as well. *Look, I went through psyche counseling after the encounter but, shitfire, the memories still sometimes roar.*

She took a calming breath, then a second one. Neither helped.

Would you consider telling me what happened so I may offer assistance getting you through this mission and beyond?

The compassionate tone of his voice comforted and reassured her. The incident wasn't a secret, now was it? And if he remained clueless and she had some sort of retro post-traumatic event, she could inadvertently kill herself and him instead of completing the mission. That wouldn't be good. *You're right, Tokoray. You ought to know what happened.* She let herself drift back in time to that fateful night.

I was twenty-one summers old. A cadet. One of forty-eight who had successfully completed survival training at the Ly-quetzel DBSC. On our last night at the desert basin survival center, we celebrated the end to our grueling days living off the land. You know, an orgy of food, liquor, and merriment. All intent on dancing the night away. As for me, well, suffice to say, I was never into partying. I got permission to trek into the desert, to a plateau to watch what was predicted to be a magnificent meteor shower. I loved the skyscapes.

Memories shimmered into place. Again she saw the half-moon's silvery glow and the starry night sky ablaze with thousands of streaking meteors. None were considered a threat to the planet or to the base. A little after midnight, beneath the crescent moon, one bright-streaking meteor veered toward the base. She concluded it was a local supply ship coming in to land on the base's airfield and ignored it. An hour later, explosions thundered across the plateau. Looking at the source, she found a huge fireball blossoming above the southeastern side of the base.

She tried to raise someone on her comlink but got no reply. Foreboding and curiosity had her heading back to the base. Approaching the main gate, she found no lights on. None anywhere. Not even those of the airfield's com-tower that had a separate power supply. What disturbed and frightened her more was the silence. Except for the buzz of a bloodsucking gnat harassing her ear, she didn't hear any other noises.

Once at the main gate, she ducked under the striped bar across the roadway. Coming upright, she inhaled air suffused with the odors of acrid smoke and doige dust. She peered into the guard station and discovered two bodies. One guard's throat had been slit. The other's neck twisted, broken.

Terror sent her scooting away, heart racing, senses jumping to hyperalert. Every nerve, every cell screamed for her to run back into the desert, but her training stayed her flight.

Hearing muted tweeps and chirps growing louder, she ducked behind the guard shack. Heart thudding anew, she gazed into the darkness and spied two Doyons exiting the officer's club. Both were heavily armed. The pair were joined by two others, and all headed around the building toward the base's headquarters.

It took a long moment for her mind to comprehend that Doyon commandoes had infiltrated the base. Only why? What did they want from this out-of-the-way training facility? How many of them were there? And where was their ship? . . . Locate the ship and she might have a better idea of what was going on.

Slipping behind the vehicle garages and maintenance sheds, she headed for the airfield, encountering no Doyons. At the corner of the central maintenance hangar, she glanced at the end of the airfield's main runway. Across the runway, the base's shuttlecraft and two short-range transports bore blackened splotches from being strafed. From one of the two destroyed trainers, a low-grade DLE sizzled softly in the hot night air and spewed smoke, which wafted low to the ground.

She peered around the building's corner, looking northward at the base's headquarters. The back corner of the building had been gutted. Beyond stood the air traffic control complex where the dish-array tower lay toppled, the dishes smashed against the side of the building. To the right, a red glow poured from the lights of a Doyon marauder parked on the tarmac, its belly ramp down. The ship looked ready to take off at any second.

Shadows cut through the red light in front of the airfield's tower revealing four heavily armed Doyon commandos making their rounds, keeping watch over their ship.

She scooted back behind the maintenance shed, squatting, trembling with fear. Visions of the dead guards winked before her eyes. Her mind raced. She began assessing the situation as a fighter-pilot would, as a cadet with survival training had been taught. Likely the Doyons had taken out all communication venues. She couldn't signal or call for help. And she was, herself, helpless, weaponless. No, not quite weaponless. She had a dirk in her boot, and in her pocket, a tiny rodgun. The rodgun was for zapping snakes on up to poisonous lizards, but it was no match for what the Doyon commandos had. As for obtaining other weapons? No help there. The armory, such that it was, was in the basement of the headquarters building.

Yet, what she knew was that around noon a transport would arrive to pick up and drop off cadets. And because the local com-sats couldn't effectively scan through the meteor showers, those units were now offline until dawn. Which meant the Doyons must get what they came for and leave before dawn in order to stay undetected under the cover of the meteor shower.

She was one person, a pilot-cadet, not a soldier. She didn't know if anyone else was alive or if the Doyons had taken prisoners. Deep in her mind trilled the voice of reason that it was only a matter of time before the Doyons found and killed her. So, she needed someplace to hide, to survive, and to think of a course of action.

A breath of wind stirred up a dust devil, and she remembered the sandstorm bunker. Not the main bunker, but the one the cadets had dug in their training course and camouflaged. The bunker lay hidden three quarters of a kilometer away — on the opposite side of the base, but it offered the best shelter.

She backtracked to the main gate keeping to the heaviest shadows and soon jogged along the perimeter fence behind the officers' housing. After making sure it was safe, she sprinted across to the black, draping shadow of the gym-rec center. The front doors stood open, the interior dark. It would save time if she went through the building instead of going around. Did she dare do that? Yes, she dared.

She entered quietly, almost on tiptoes. When she came to the open center doors to the gym, where light glowed but no sounds came from within, she cautiously peered inside. Many of the psudo-candle table lamps set out for the celebration party still burned, casting a sickly-yellow glow on the carnage of bodies among mangled tables, chairs, food, and decorations. In the blink of her eyes, her mind tabulated that all her classmates and instructors were dead. The room seemed to spin. Her stomach lurched. She raced to the nearest waste receptacle and puked. After wiping her mouth on her sleeve and steadying her nerves, she listened, praying no one had heard her.

No Doyon footfalls or twirps or cheeps.

Trembling, feeling faint, she forced herself not to wretch anew and headed for the back doors, which were wide open. Warily, she sidled into the shadow of the right side door, searched deep into the darkness, and found the backs of two Doyons near the door of the headquarters building. Three more commandos came around from the front of the building and joined the two, then the five went inside.

She sprinted across the roadway to Training Center Number One, ducking into the blackness of its colonnaded entrance. Again, the front doors stood open. As she stealthily hurried down the corridor toward the back of the building, she passed Classroom C and remembered its supply room. She backtracked, went inside, and opened the supply room door. As fast as she could, she donned the demonstration unit, a one-piece camosuit of flexible armor that prevented sensors from detecting the body it shielded. Once she had the helmet on, she left the eye shield up, the better to see. She extracted powersticks from as many of the other suits as she could and, stuffing them in the suit's pockets, she left. En route out of the building, she stopped at the nook of vending machines. Using the camosuit's built-in wrist-cuff laser, she broke into the back of two machines, taking water and a handful of nutri-bars, then departed.

Anger at the Doyons needlessly murdering her comrades began to simmer and stew along with a desire to kill a Doyon.

Any Doyon. Then came the realization that since she wasn't likely to live long, instead of killing one Doyon, why not kill as many as she could? Her mind churned ideas which melded into a plan. She headed for Training Center Number Two to gather materials—and make weapons.

In the darkness before dawn, she arrived at the rec building's roof and rigged two crossbows. She loaded each with a cardboard tube three centimeters in diameter, scored to split on impact, and set the triggers. She descended and set up a booby-trap. In the twilight of daybreak, Darq stood in full camo-sensor mode, watching from the top-floor window of Training Center Two. Being up a story and a half gave her an excellent sightline to the Doyon ship while keeping her hidden in dark shadows.

A dozen Doyon commandos began returning from various directions, joining into ranks. All headed for their ship. Four guards remained on patrol outside the ship itself.

Seconds after the last of the commandoes marched into the Doyon ship, Darq triggered the signal that set off the timed release for the crossbows. She picked up the bow she'd made and reached down for the metal rods, which she'd fashioned into arrows. She got off two fast shots, which took out the ship's nearest perimeter guards. She wasn't quite quick enough in killing the third, so he had time to tweet a warning to the fourth.

Before that last guard sounded the alarm, the crossbows fired, lobbing deep into the gaping mouth of the Doyon marauder, delivering their shafts filled with the most aggressive, sting-crazy black bees the planet had.

Darq knocked an arrow. A Doyon came running out of the ship, swatting bees. She took aim, loosed the arrow, and killed him. Alarms sounded outside and inside the ship. A group of six came out of the ship running, weapons in hand, and all swatting at bees. They took cover by the gutted side of Training Center Number Three.

Darq loaded the special arrow and sent it away. The chemical on the arrow tip ignited the liquid cactus resin she'd laid down among the rubble. Stinking green-gray smoke began to billow, choking the Doyons, burning their lungs.

A bleep on her suit had Darq swapping out a powerstick. Looking up, she found half a dozen Doyons, all swatting bees, come out of the ship with handheld scanners, seeking but not finding her. With her arrows gone, she set the bow aside and departed for the top of the two-story-high Training Center One, safely out of range of the Doyon marauder's departure.

Twenty minutes later, the ship was still parked. The bees had been vanquished, and the dead Doyons taken aboard the ship. The rising sun shimmered golden rays over the forcefield engaged about the vessel. Minutes later, the forcefield vanished. In single file, three cadets, a mechnet, a maintenance tech, and the base's second in command came out of the ship. All had their hands bound behind their backs. Following them strode two guards with disrupters and a slender Doyon wearing a black sash that ran diagonally across his uniform jumpsuit. The sash connected to the black belt around his waist from which dangled a short sword in a scabbard. Obviously, an officer of high rank.

He tapped something at the shoulder of his black sash. His voice boomed, "Wysotti cadet, I know your name is Darq. I am Caprivi Ippera of the F'brig High Guard. If you do not surrender in ten minutes, I will kill one of your comrades. I will continue to kill one every twenty minutes until you surrender."

Her heart froze. There had been survivors. Prisoners.

But why had those few been kept in the Doyon ship? Were there more inside? If so, shitfire, she'd jeopardized all their lives. Maybe she should surrender.

Maybe she should fight to the death.

Surrender?

Fight to the death?

If she surrendered, she would become a Doyon prisoner. No, they would want to make an example of a Wysotti who dared to kill a Doyon. She would be killed. The solution was to force them to kill her outright so that the others might be spared.

Doing so would also delay the Doyon's departure, making it even more likely they'd be spotted either by the satellites or by the transport when it arrived.

She hurried to the ground floor, exited the building, and went to the highest point on the pile of rubble at the corner of the administration building.

Every few minutes, Ippera's voice boomed the time remaining until he killed.

Standing tall atop a tilted, white rectangle of stone, knowing no one saw her in her camo-suit, which worked its magic to blend her to her surroundings, she took out the slingshot she'd made. One like she'd used so many times as a kid. She brought out a small bundle of cloth from a patch pocket on her lower thigh. Unwrapping the bundle exposed three wads of mud she'd impaled with cactus quills. She'd soaked the quills in root-sap that would burn flesh on contact. In the center of the mud, she'd placed a sharp-edged piece of obsidian. Careful not to let a quill prick through her camo-suit's gloves, she loaded a ball into the slingshot's cuplike holder and set the other projectiles within easy reach.

Ippera's voice thundered out of the loudspeaker. "Time is up, Wysotti cadet!"

She looked up. Ippera had drawn his sword. The other Doyons came to attention but never took their eyes off their prisoners.

Ippera grabbed the nearest cadet by the shoulder of her fatigues. He ignored the girl kicking him in the shins and fighting against his hold. With the broadside of his sword, he knocked the back of her knees, forcing her to kneel. With one swift stroke, he lopped off her head. Blood splatted onto the mechnet, the next in line, who screamed her terror. Ippera shoved the headless girl's body aside. He grabbed the maintenance tech and yelled, "Shall I kill this one, or will you surrender, now?"

Shock gave way to an all-consuming rage. Darq flung off her helmet, breaking the camosuit's circuits, making her visible. One of the Doyon guards said something, and Ippera turned to face her. Darq's gaze met Ippera's head on, fury clashed with wrath.

Darq wound up her slingshot.

Ippera barked orders, then jerked the sobbing, pleading maintenance tech forward a pace, and kicked the back of her knees so she knelt in front of him. He raised his sword to strike. Darq released the slingshot.

A second before Ippera swung his sword downward, the projectile whacked him in the forehead, near his temple. He thrust the tech aside and staggered a step backwards. The tech toppled to the ground.

Ippera's whistling screech resounded with the decibel intensity of a doige engine whining past redline. He teetered but used his sword for balance and remained upright. With his free hand, he reached up to dislodge the splattered mud ball but howled anew when the sap-ladened quills burned his hand.

Four Doyons rushed out of the ship to Ippera's aid. One fired, but missed Darq, hitting rubble behind her head. She put another projectile into her slingshot, wound it up, and fired. The second ball struck the neck of the Doyon who seemed to be issuing orders. Two others took a knee stance to aim and fire at her.

A high-pitched screech resonated from the Doyon ship. A cacophony of squeals and squeaks bellowed from Ippera and the other injured Doyon. Suddenly, two Doyons ran out of the ship to either side of Ippera, gripped him under the arms, running, half-carrying, half-dragging him into the ship. The others followed. The kneeling commandos rose, backing, then halted at the end of the ramp. One fired at the captives who were dashing for cover. The other fired at her.

She grabbed the last mud-ball. Shots whizzed by her head. She ignored them, loaded the projectile, swung the slingshot, and sent it flying. The clod hit the front-most commando squarely in the jaw. He staggered backwards into the ship. The noise of his scream was instantly overridden by the marauder's engines and the rumbling of the ramp closing.

Seconds later the marauder was airborne, streaking into the stratosphere.

Darq's heart had pounded in her chest, threatening to burst, just as it did now. She took a deep breath. *Tokoray, I remember trembling, seeing in my mind Ippera's wrath, and the swiftness of him* *lopping off the cadet's head. My defiance had killed her.* I had killed her.*

Darq, Tokoray said, his voice calm and assured, *it is obvious you were not court-martialed for your actions or for her death.*

Actually, I got a commendation. Darq scoffed. *I never felt heroic.*

Did you ever learn what the Doyons were after? It seems rather odd they would attack an out-of-the-way school when there were better targets to be had on other planets.

Everyone wondered. The planet was one of those neat little worlds in its early evolutionary stage. Huge sea creatures, forests and bugs, extremes of heat and cold, volcanoes and earthquakes. You name it, you could learn how to survive it there. An ideal training ground. She paused to let a few of the more awesome vistas flit through her mind. *As to your question, Tokoray, what the Doyons wanted was star maps of our solar system, populations, locations of cities, defenses, and the moon mining colonies.*

Did they get it?

Yes, and a bit more. They managed to tap into the starcom and downloaded some data on ship placements.

Only you put a chink in their plans?

She chuckled. *I seem to have a knack for doing that.*

The com chirped, and Chance softly said, "Blackbird Lead, Spook approaching. Do you copy?"

Zukaltay, embraced by the aura of the archangel Adrada, held her drum tightly and waited for the archangel's glow to dissipate and his wings to draw back. She sensed him step to the side, yet he said nothing.

Looking about, she discovered herself perched above an immense, swirling morass of dust and matter—a tumbling, churning, bubbling nebula, one of the witch's brews of the cosmos from which stars took birth. The nearest star burned bright and had a smaller companion.

So, what precisely should she be looking at?

Adrada tucked his wings, narrowing his profile. "This is the hour, Zukaltay. J'Hi-inti thought you should witness the events unfold from the place where chaos shall begin."

She had hoped to watch the time of chaos, but now, standing here, fear of the outcome coiled like a six-headed serpent around her non-corporeal heart. She clutched her drum more tightly. The fate of the Wysotti rested on her granddaughter and what Darq did or didn't do.

Zukaltay gazed about the star-studded space, unable to orient where in the heavens she was. "Should I be looking at any particular spot? I see nothing but stars and star matter." She looked down. "And of course, this enormous mess."

Adrada stepped forward, waived his hand, sending a swirling spire of the nebula sideways, exposing clear space. "The Grier call this nebula the Turtledove. To the right, those bright stars are Alpha San Hiphia and its little companion, Beta San Hiphia. See that tail connecting the little one to the big one?"

"Yes. Looks like Beta is sucking material from the larger star. What's so special about that?"

"Look to the right of those two stars and you'll find the edge of the Chepha-wee-ka Asteroid Belt."

She eyed the river of planetoid boulders among tumbling rocks and rubble. What seemed odd were the scattered, lone clusters of asteroids moving toward the Turtledove. "And where is Wysa, the star of my home solar system? Or should I say in what direction?"

"Straight ahead, provided you are on the inner side of the asteroids. It's a considerable distance away, Wysa is merely a pinprick. "Now, look to your left, at the three little streaks coming this way."

She spotted them. Two reminded her of a round cooking pot lid set on top of a bigger pot that sat on top of an oval roasting pan. The third ship, the one in the middle, resembled a helmet with a huge pipe on either side of it. "What ships are they?"

"Doyon. The smaller, middle one, which is in the lead, is the *Ippera*. The other two are destroyers. The nearest to us is the *Bekrakaun*. It's captained by Eslatont, a fierce warrior who never liked Ippera—or any rival officer. Eslatont will take great pride in putting a direct hit on the *Ippera*."

"So many names. Am I to remember them?"

"Likely not, but of special interest is Eslatont's first officer." She had to ask. "Why?"

"He is U'zan, son of Ippera. A Doyon commander following in his father's illustrious footsteps."

"There is nothing illustrious about a Doyon."

Adrada quirked one of his feathery eyebrows up and glanced at her.

"So what ship is trailing the *Bekrakaun*?"

Adrada turned his attention to the ship. "That would be the *Akeavosso*. The captain is Mesk. He once served as second officer to Ippera and considered Ippera the best, most ruthless mentor he ever had."

"Are they going somewhere special in such a hurry?"

"Actually they are playing cat and mouse. A war game. One designed to test Admirid Ippera's ability to control the little destroyer that bears his name." Adrada stepped to the left and peered over the edge of a brackish cloud-mass. "The Doyons don't know two wolves await. Come, have a look."

She went to his side, searching for and finding a small clearing below where two Pytak fighters hovered.

"The one on the left is the *Zopa*, piloted by Jaqui, who is also known as Chance. Her copilot is the Na-ka-ta Izzt."

"And—" Zukaltay whispered out, "the one on the right is the *Ky* and my granddaughter, Darq."

"Her Na-ka-ta is Tokoray."

Zukaltay felt her breath freeze. Her heart grew colder with every moment she watched the Doyon ships approach the two fighters' hiding place.

The *Ippera* whizzed closer to the edge of the dust, coming nearer the Pytaks. The *Bekrakaun* fired tracers, which missed the ever-shifting, dodging *Ippera*. When the *Akeavosso*, streaking in the *Bekrakaun*'s wake, passed the Pytaks, the two fighters sprinted forward. The instant they burst from the nebula's cloaking dust, they fired on the *Akeavosso*.

The *Ky* went up and over the ship, firing two missiles that went deep into the destroyer. The *Zopa* went under, firing two missiles. By the time the fighters joined up, streaking for the stern of the *Bekrakaun,* multiple explosions ripped through the *Akeavosso*'s decking. The ship came to a stop, listing to starboard. Implosions pockmarked lower decks, breaching hull plating.

"One down, two to go," Adrada said.

Zukaltay looked at him. "Whose side are you on?"

"I can take no sides, and I remind you that for the duration of this encounter between Darq and the Doyons, you cannot play your drum. Neither of us must interfere during these next hours."

"Yes, I understand things must run their course when good and evil collide." Darq was good. Ippera evil. Good should triumph. What rubbed was J'Hi-inti's test. How could this confrontation be a test that would make it possible for Darq to decide the Wysotti's fate?

Zukaltay strode over to the edge of the nebula following the Pytaks attack on the *Bekrakaun.* That ship—and the *Ippera*—stopped playing their war game. Both actively engaged the Pytaks, spraying the heavens with fang-fire and small bursting missiles, some peppered the nebula and starscape, but none crippled the Pytaks. One Doyon missile's discharge ignited volatile gasses inside the nebula into a fireball behind Darq's fighter, but she dove out of harm's way and into the dust. Both fighters continued to duck into the cloud, then out, firing missiles and keg rounds that hit the *Bekrakaun's* shielding. A few broke through and exploded.

A missile launched from the *Zopa* narrowly missed the *Ippera*, which banked sharply.

The *Ky* angled across the *Bekrakaun's* bow, ducking fang-fire, and launched two missiles into the ship. The first missile burst, taking out a small area of shielding which allowed the second missile to penetrate the exposed hull and explode. The destroyer lost speed.

The *Ky* pivoted on its axis, coming about and firing four thistles at the *Ippera*. One of those missiles took out a section of prow shielding. The second punched through and emerged on the other side of the prow, then exploded. Numbers three and four hit the forward hull. The *Ippera* lurched but kept flying.

Zukaltay gasped to see the *Ky* wasn't flying away from the *Ippera*. The *Ky* swerved horizontally and fired a thistle point blank into the *Ippera's* forward hull and dove, streaking under the *Zopa*, which launched two missiles at the *Ippera*. The *Ippera* launched counter measures and took out both missiles.

The *Zopa* pulled a hard banking turn, coming about near the *Bekrakaun*. That Doyon's forward gun batteries opened fire at the *Zopa*. Salvo after salvo hit and the *Zopa* burst into a fireball.

"No!" slipped from Zukaltay's lips. She clutched her spirit-drum so tightly the base dug into the front of her thighs.

Adrada's voice pierced through Zukaltay's shock. "Fear not. The Archangel Gabriel has Jaqui's soul in hand."

Tears simmered hot along the rims of Zukaltay's eyes. "Jaqui and Darq are—were—best of friends."

"Yes, they were. Ah, now. The crisis. Take courage. Look."

The *Ky* streaked for the *Ippera*, which had come about and was barreling full speed toward Beta San Hiphia. The *Ippera* put out a hail of stern fang-fire. The *Ky* yawed and careened, then banked into the smokey cape of the dust cloud. The *Ippera* released salvos in a wide pattern, blind as to where the *Ky* had gone. Seconds later, the *Ippera* was cloaked in murky dust.

Bright spots flashed, revealing the two combatants exchanged fire inside the cloud. Then both emerged. Suddenly the *Ippera* spun, like a child's top, but slowly. The *Ippera* continued to spin, wobbling toward the small sun, Beta San Hiphia. Life pods broke away from the *Ippera's* hull, all aimed for the disabled destroyer *Bekrakaun*, which now began a slow arching turn.

The *Ky* came about, then suddenly swerved down, heading for the backside of Alpha San Hiphia.

"What's going on? Why didn't she go after the *Ippera?*"

"Because—"

Shockwaves and matter burst from the connection of the little star with the big star. Yet, both stars remained intact.

"Adrada? What just happened?"

"A mini-nova. Periodically there is a build up of energy close to where the tail meets Beta San Hiphia. Critical mass is reached because the little star cannot handle so much incoming matter, thus there is a mini-nova event."

"That can't be good." She searched for the *Ky* and found it tumbling, streaking away from the alpha star. Was Darq — Zukaltay could hardly breathe or move. "Is my granddaughter dead?"

"No. She is in trouble, fighting for control of her starfighter but, as you can see, she will soon be in clear space behind the stars, away from both Doyon and Wysotti territory."

"And away from this nebula, but what of the radiation from the nova?"

"The alpha star shielded both ships."

"Both!" She sought in earnest to find the *Ippera*. It spiraled drunkenly off to her left, into the darkest mass of the nebula's outer wing. "Adrada, what happens now?"

"Chaos rules. We wait. We watch."

✧ Chapter 20

With the *Ky* tumbling out of control, Darq fought not only the controls but also post-combat jitters. The warm musky-metallic perfume of her flightsuit and dried adrenalin-fueled sweat assailed her. Bile spumed in her stomach, eager to slosh up to her throat. She cued the puke-tube and clamped down on it. Only the odor of bile made it to her mouth.

Shitfire, she hated the taste of puke, hated even more the smell of it inside her suit and inside her cockpit. Better to let her mind dwell on something else. Like being alive. Staying alive and rejoicing that despite the weightlessness and tumbling in space, and the blackness of her faceplate, she was uninjured. So was Tokoray. And, as an added bonus, the life-support systems of her pilot's seat were functional. So, what else?

Radiation. How much radiation could she have received from the cataclysmic explosion of the mini-nova event? Flashes erupted in her mind of diving away from the *Ippera's* fang-fire and realizing the flashing screen on her faceplate warned Beta San Hiphia was seconds away from a mini-nova event. She had gone wings over, pushing the *Ky's* engines past the redlines to race ahead of the shockwaves and the lethal cocktail of deadliness being ejected. The leading shockwave struck at an oblique angle and propelled the *Ky* toward Alpha San Hiphia's corona. Hull temperatures had spiked. Circuitry fried, systems failed. The *Ky*'s engines shut down. Yet, the *Ky* had skipped off. So her fighter survived, albeit tumbling powerless out of control to who knew where.

But had the *Ippera* survived?

Now was not the time to think about that.

Over her neural net came muted peeps that Tokoray had attempted yet another reboot of some system and nothing had happened. For a fighter with so many redundant systems built in, leave it to her to be the one to fry 'em all.

Gazing at the darkest side of her faceplate, she prayed one system would make a liar out of her. Seconds became minutes with no screens or pinpricks of a light.

Tokoray's voice came over her neural net, *Intra ship comlink inoperative, but neural net clear. We have stopped tumbling.*

Realizing she sat steady and level lessened her queasiness as well as the dizziness. *Bless the stars for small favors.*

A bit later, feeling it safe, she released the puke tube. It snicked back into its place. *Tokoray, how about a status report?*

Do you want the good news or the not-very-good news?

Good. I need to hear something good.

We have stopped tumbling.

The urge to chuckle bubbled up, but Darq stifled it. *That's obvious, thank you very much. So, how about the bad news?*

The main systems continue to refuse to reboot. Extrapolations show seventy percent of our equipment is disabled from fried circuitry. Diagnostics indicate key systems themselves are operational, but no power is getting to them.

Why aren't we fried? We were close to Beta San's sleet and hail, not to mention Alpha's corona.

Skipping off the corona as we did put us behind San Hiphia in sufficient time to miss the barrage. Our superior cockpit shielding protected us, but the systems tucked around us, between us and the port side, were damaged. Because of compromised circuits, you cannot switch to a reserve O-two tank. I calculate you have seventy-two hours, depending on what transpires during that time, to live before your oxygen is depleted.

The *Ky* had been refitted with the long-range oxygen systems, which cut down by two the number of DGRBMs the *Ky* carried. Not that it mattered. Dying of asphyxiation wasn't exactly how she figured she would leave this life. No sense dwelling on that yet. And since they couldn't maneuver, move, or fight—
What's the status of the self-destruct system?

Functional. Perhaps the only thing that went unscathed.

Put it online. A small blue square with a yellow starburst in its center lit at the lowest line of her faceplate.

Light. She had real light. Light meant life. A wisp of joy delighted her, and then came an idiotic thought. *Tokoray?*

Yes, Darq?

I'm chalking this up to you not having jinxed me, so you're okay for the time being.

I am ever so grateful you have condescended not to murder me — yet.

Her chuckle crazed her stiff cheeks and joined his. Laughter was a good thing. A being-alive thing. *Any chance you can get a scanner up so we can see where we are, or where we're headed, or if there are Doyons coming our way?*

I continue to work on that.

Anything I can do to help?

Negative. No, wait. Although you have released your puke tube and may consider the chance of retching minimal, it has been hours since you ate. Please eat something, not only to keep your digestive system occupied but also to replace energy the skirmish with the Doyons has taken out of you.

For your information, Tokoray, the tumbling caused the nausea. Putting food in my stomach right now doesn't seem like a very good idea. How about I sip some tea and take a power nap? That usually works. When I wake, I'll eat.

As you wish.

Wake me in case you have something urgent to report or if Doyons attack and we have to self-destruct.

Affirmative.

Darq drank a cup's work of sweet, hot tea through her food tube, then closed her eyes, willing her tense muscles to relax. Swirls and splatters along with telescoping colors of light quickly graced the back of her eyelids. Funny how the eyes, the brain, didn't like total blackness. People trapped in the bowels of caves went mad when the light source ceased. Her cave was a cockpit, yet she didn't feel afraid of its darkness.

A series of red glowing splotches skimmed at the lower edge of her eyelids. Memories of Zukaltay's funeral pyre, engulfed in flame, played on the screen of her mind. Darq heard her own voice repeat words from the eulogy she'd given— *We Wysotti believe our creation and that of our world came from the seeding of life by the ancient Vidarians. Those star-mariners carried out the will of J'Hi-inti, the Great Mother Creator. Our forbearers believed we are the stuff of star dust. In death, we believe our souls return to the celestial Omega Qi, and J'Hi-inti welcomes the spirit of the righteous, the peacekeepers, those who loved and were loved.*

After Darq had spoken those words, in her mind the faint thrup-pa-pa, thrup-pa-pa of Zukaltay's drumbeats had begun. The next morning those slow, sad beats accompanied the spreading of Zukaltay's ashes into the pit where the family planted a daoka tree in her honor. *Ashes to ashes, dust to dust . . . out of dust comes forth new life.*

Only, for the Wysotti, life likely would turn to dust from Doyon bombs, and her own life would end as soon as the Doyons found the *Ky.* Just like Jaqui, the *Ky* would become dust.

Jaqui . . . oh, Jaqui . . . A deep sorrow tightly shrouded Darq.

Shitfire, this was no time to mourn her grandmother, Jaqui, or her own fate! Darq sought the thrup-pa-pa thrup-pa-pas that had plagued her mind at Zukaltay's funeral. The beats rose and soon looped in her thoughts. The rhythm quieted her mind, and the warmth of the tea she'd drunk soothed her stomach. Sleep soon hugged her as if she were a child again, held in her grandmother's arms.

Darq! blasted through her neural net like a ram-launch, startling her awake to find her faceplate replete with half a dozen lit screens.

What? She inhaled oxygen, desperate to fully wake, to clear her vision, to skim her faceplate to identify which screens she had. No screen winked a warning.

Trouble, Tokoray responded.

Be specific.

How long had she slept? *Yoi, Tokoray, how long did I nap?*

Eighteen hours.

What? That can't be.

It is. Change of topic. We are being actively scanned.

Her heart raced to life, blood pumping hard through her arteries. *Doyons?*

Negative. The signal is not one I nor the Ky's main comtar recognizes.

The Ky's comtar is online?

Affirmative, but it's a guess how long it will function since I jury-rigged a bypass to it.

Is the signal coming from a Grier ship looking to salvage us?

Negative. This is all I have so far.

A white square came slowly into focus in the center of her faceplate showing a dot representing the *Ky*. A sweeping gray line passed over the square so the *Ky*'s dot blinked. The origins of the gray scanner beam came from the one-ninety-six mark on the lower edge of her screen. No ID blip indicated what generated the signal because the source lay off the screen and out of range. The signal swept again but now held steady on the dot.

Tokoray, have we been targeted?

I cannot determine that.

How ironic.

What is ironic?

That you wake me so I can officially trigger the self-destruct.

It is too early to say whether or not we should self-destruct. First we must determine if those issuing the signal are friend or foe.

Which is more likely?

Foe.

A series of clicks and a bleep ensued.

Tokoray muttered, *Interesting.*

Darq checked her screens. Nothing had changed. *What's interesting?*

I think — yes — small signal bursts. Possibly we are being hailed in a number of different languages . . . That's it!

What's it? Shitfire, Tokoray, don't be so cryptic!

Grier. One of the bursts is Grier.

What are they saying? Put me in the loop. On her screen appeared a data line streaming THIS IS THE CENTAURI BATTLECRUISER CHENAULT VIKRAM. IDENTIFY YOURSELF.

The Centauri? Who were the Centauri? How did they know the Grier language? *Tokoray, can we reply? Should we reply?*

Give me a moment. I need to better align an exterior receptor, rather what's left of it. Seconds later, Tokoray said, *If the data the unit is giving me is correct, we are capable of a weak send signal. The Centauri may or may not be able to pick it up.*

Think positive.

Very well. What message shall we send?

A good question. What would be appropriate? And what was most pressing for her and Tokoray's survival?

Survival.

Tell them this is the Wysotti starfighter Ky, and ask if they are friend, foe, or ally of the Doyons.

Are you sure you want to send that? The Centauri may lie.

Won't know unless we ask, and, hey, what choice do we have? Don't answer that. Death is a last resort, unless, of course, we have any vid-links so we can see the Centauri and make a better judgment call.

Let me check the scanners again.

As the seconds dragged on, Darq put her hands to the controls, and found the self-destruct online. Maybe it had never gone off-line?

Tokoray came back with *We have no vid capabilities, and I think the Centauri realize that.*

Darq didn't bother to ask how he knew that because a blinking blue dot now appeared at the corner of the screen, indicating a large vessel accelerated toward the Ky. The vessel kept the sweeping signal over the Ky. Hardly daring to breathe, Darq waited, praying no additional blips appeared in the vessel's wake. None did. She closed her eyes for a second, letting relief wash over her that she was dealing with just one lone ship.

The cockpit comlink chirped. A burst of fizz ensued before a male voice said in Grier, "This is Captain Ian Warwick, of the Centauri battlecruiser Chenault Vikram. We are not—repeat—NOT allies nor friends of the Doyon. *Ky*, are you friend, foe, or ally of the Doyons?"

The intriguing male's voice, and the even tone of his query, made Darq smile and realize how fatigue-taut her lips and cheeks had become. She triggered the comlink and sent her Grier-translated words. "Captain Warwick, the Wysotti are at war with the Doyons. In a skirmish with three Doyon destroyers and a mini-nova event, my fighter was flung afield. I am Darq. My rank is qtl-shi. I am the pilot of the Ky." Then she tacked on, "My copilot and I come in peace." Which sounded terribly clichéd and o-lo-piish.

Darq, is it wise to tell the Centauri so much?

If they're scanning us, they already plotted where we came from and know we're damaged. Lies beget lies, and I'll not have a first contact turn into a fiasco, or have you forgotten the prime directives about first contacts?

After a long silence, and the Centauri vessel making even greater speed toward the *Ky*, the comlink chirped. "Qtl-shi Darq, we have a flight deck that can handle the landing of your spacecraft. We offer maintenance personnel and equipment for repairs so you may return home. If you are injured, we have medical facilities."

Before she could check her tongue, she heard herself speak her fear. "What a clever way of saying you're taking me prisoner and confiscating my fighter."

"Negative, Qtl-shi Darq!" The captain's affront was evident in his tone. "I am merely extending you sanctuary." His tone leveled out. "I would point out that at your present speed and course, in under ten hours, you will be caught in the gravitational well of a brown dwarf."

A brown dwarf? Ten hours away? Starshine and shitfire. How fast was she traveling? Darq eyed her faceplate, but her star map wouldn't cue on.

Darq, Tokoray's voice sounded unusually solemn. *I cannot determine the exact extent of our damage. Ten hours may not be sufficient to get engines online and avoid a catastrophe.*

Great. She looked at the self-destruct icon. She hadn't survived this long to push the damn button now. Pros and cons of believing the Centauri captain, his voice, his words, raced through her mind. She activated the comlink. "Captain Warwick, I will accept your offer of sanctuary and assistance in repairing my vessel with the understanding I will depart as soon as the work is complete." She checked the bull's-eye screen, noting the *Chenault* sped even more quickly toward the *Ky*.

At our speed, Darq, and the Chenault's *current speed, the Centauri will reach us in approximately one hour sixteen.*

Is that enough time for you to code the self-destruct so if we end up taken prisoner, either of us can use the neural net to blow the Ky and our minds apart?

Affirmative. I'm on it. What code word shall we use?

Darq said the first thing that came to mind. *Murdering Jinx.* Then she chuckled.

Tokoray's muted laughter filtered through her mind. *Done.*

Oh, and, Tokoray, can we rig the cockpit so no prying eyes and sticky fingers get their hands on our weapons systems, that is, if we do get help making repairs?

Affirmative. He began relaying to her how to set up the first of many cascade failures to destroy key elements of the *Ky*'s technology. They finished work minutes before the *Chenault* prepared to engage gravity lines. With trepidation, and despite not having power to steer, Darq gripped the steering balls under her hands. Tension had her curling her toes to the point her insteps were forced up against their boots' tongues. Knots tightened in her gut, and her breath went shallow.

She was so blind! What kind of vessel was the *Chenault*? How big? How much armament? Damn the *Ky*'s starboard scanners being offline. Damn her port ones being fried by the mini-nova.

The tractor grab of the tow vehicle sent a frisson of vibrations through the cockpit. Over the comlink droned the blow-by-blow description of what took place, in Grier, which the *Chenault*'s LSO spoke fluently. That Landing Safety Officer had a pleasant, clear, female voice. A voice devoid of emotion, a voice that curbed Darq's tension enough that she uncurled her toes.

Light gravity engaged, then came the noisy clunk of the *Ky*'s belly onto something called an LCFB, a landing-craft flatbed, which was then towed to a parking area in a shuttle bay. Softly booming thunder resounded, and a second later, she was told the *Chenault*'s blast walls had lowered and sealed behind the *Ky*.

She, Tokoray, and the *Ky* were well and truly imprisoned.

Over the comlink came the LSO's "*Ky*, you are parked and clear to dismount your vessel."

Darq set her faceplate for virtual-view and eyed the canopy overhead. While waiting those last moments for the Centauri ship to arrive, she and Tokoray agreed she would exit the *Ky* first, her instinct far better than logic. They had also agreed Tokoray would not arm himself. No sense in looking aggressive. However, if the *Ky* should be surrounded by squads intent on capturing her, she had only to utter the code through the neural net for the self-destruct to start its countdown.

Darq took a long, lung-deep, fortifying breath. On the exhale, she scolded herself that duty demanded no advanced Wysotti military technology fall into alien hands, particularly her neural net. She swallowed the rock-hard lump of her guilt and uncertainties. *Tokoray, I'm opening my canopy. Mark.*

To her amazement, the canopy opened smoothly, and she released the umbilicals between her seat and suit. At the corner of her faceplate, her suit functions blazed their normal greens. She used the handhold-rungs on both sides of the cockpit walls to leverage herself upright. Her legs went wobbly, which was normal for having sat for so long in a cramped cockpit. She flexed her legs one at a time. Then, with heart thundering in her ears and anxiety clawing the edges of her resolve, she stood on her seat. Her head and most of her torso cleared the cockpit. She made a quick check of her suit's environ-screen, noting the acceptable atmosphere had slightly more gravity then she was accustomed to on the *Dujaki*'s flight decks.

Glancing about, she beheld a square, gunmetal-gray bay with corrugated walls. Huge rib girders and ceiling I-beams had runs of silvery-gray and bright-white conduits. A look behind her revealed blast walls formed at a right angle not far from the *Ky*'s engines. The *Ky* had been parked cater-corner.

Hearing a chugging clang, she peered down past the *Ky*'s nose and discovered a boxy towing contraption moving away. The unit crossed a yellow line and stopped. The flooring lowered, taking the machine out of sight.

A quick look to the other side of the *Ky*'s nose and she found a wall where a round indentation held a triple circle device in the center. Likely an airlock — or an escape hatch.

Then she spotted a group of six who walked into view and stopped. All faced her. Each looked as human as she was, and none wore spacesuits or helmets.

She scrutinized the six Centauri, all military fit and trim in their brown jumpsuits. Tan piping decorated both the black V yokes and their black sleeve cuffs. Those cuffs ran from wrists to mid-forearm. Various sized gold pips and bars dotted upper shoulders and collars, which she chalked up to rank designations and ID bars.

Her gaze steadied on the tall male standing in front of the five, who studied her with unabashed curiosity. That male had short, graying black hair. Being the oldest, he likely had the highest rank and was the official greeter.

But what pleased her most was that none of them held a weapon in their hands. Only the two flanking the elder wore hip holsters. Bulging hip holsters. From the size of those hand-held weapons, they weren't capable of disintegration or vaporizing but likely packed quite a wallop.

Her environmental suit buzzed. Data flashed along the side of her faceplate telling her the biologicals, dust, and so on in the air wouldn't harm her. She could safely remove her helmet.

Overhead came a rumbling that grew louder.

Looking up, she found a red and yellow striped box traveled along a rail toward her. A modest-sized hook dangled from the end of a chain that was attached to the box. When Tokoray had explained there was no power to open the *Ky*'s missile bay and exit, he'd also told the Centauri that pilot and copilot were usually pulled out of a cockpit with special equipment. The Centauri had responded they would use a hoist. That unit now stopped to her left. The hook and chain descended, halting within easy reach.

Darq took one more look around the bay, where all remained quiet. The absence of an armed Centauri threat was reassuring but unnerving. Which was ridiculous. *Tokoray, you getting what I'm seeing?* As if she had to ask. Her neural net allowed him access to everything she saw.

Affirmative. What I have scanned indicates no armed legions beyond the bulkheads.

Okay. Come on out. There's only one hoist. We'll have to share it.

Affirmative. Tokoray's canopy slowly opened.

Darq covertly kept an eye on the group of six, who remained in place, nonthreatening, but obviously interested in her machinations when she climbed out and stood straddling the Ky's hull to either side of her cockpit. Into her com, which now had a separate link to the Chenault, she said in Grier, "I need a meter and a half more chain lowered."

A male Centauri voice replied, "Affirmative." The hoist whirred, playing out chain.

Darq grabbed the hook in her gloved hand. She carefully stepped to the crosspiece of the two cockpits and gave the hook and chain to Tokoray.

After much jangling, Tokoray said into the comlink, "Hook is securely attached. Lift away." Soon Tokoray's torso, then his wheelbase, cleared the cockpit. He dangled mere centimeters over the crosspiece. He'd fed the chain under the horizontal chest strap of his flight harness and caught the hook under the harness's belt.

Only two of the Centauri showed amazement at seeing Tokoray emerge, but both quickly resumed their passive miens.

Tokoray dropped his wheelbase flippers and offered his hand to Darq. Despite his slow twirl on the chain, she quickly found herself secure in his arms, her back to his chest and her suit padding the chain and hook.

Darq said into the comlink, "Lower away."

Her comlink chirped. A male voice said, "Lowering away."

Once Tokoray's wheelbase touched the decking, Darq's nagging conscience whispered that things were going too smoothly, too nicely, and in seconds she might have to trigger the self-destruct. And with those thoughts, her queasiness returned.

Tokoray released his hold on her. She leaned forward, enabling him to unhook and free himself from the chain. He gripped her anew around the waist and rolled forward, stopping before the senior officer.

Darq's queasiness intensified.

The older man offered a charming smile that dimpled his cheeks and said, "Welcome aboard the *Chenault*, Qtl-shi Darq. I am Captain Warwick."

The captain himself had come to greet them? That had to be a good omen. Or did it hide some trickery? Uncertainty churned her stomach anew and kept her heart doing a quick beat.

The captain stared into her faceplate.

She should remove her helmet, face him as being to being. She made one quick environmental recheck. Finding nothing amiss, she triggered the neck rings of her suit and removed her helmet. She pulled her braids free before resting the helmet between her hands and settling her forearms over Tokoray's.

The captain's gray eyes registered a moment of amazement before polite curiosity shimmered in his irises.

Her stomach grumbled its unrest. Fearful that bile would rise, Darq resisted the urge to close her eyes and try for a second of tranquility. She must focus, stay in control. She locked onto the captain's gaze. "Captain Warwick," she said, pleased her voice sounded normal, "I'm not much for formalities. Please call me Darq. My copilot prefers to be addressed as Tokoray."

Warwick nodded to her then looked at Tokoray. "Your robot is most welcome."

"I am not a robot," Tokoray replied, indignation skittering through his words. "I am a sentient Na-ka-ta automaton with full citizenship. My rank is yojii."

If Warwick took offense at being reprimanded, it didn't show in his eyes or on his face. "My apologies, Yojii Tokoray. Welcome aboard." Warwick turned to Darq. "Allow me to introduce my officers who will be assisting you." He faced the female in the center, who had dark skin and shaved, short, nappy black hair. Her dark eyes gleamed with excitement.

"This," Warwick said, "is my first officer, Robin Nicholson." In short order he introduced the others, beginning with the chief medical officer, a D'ktr Fulton, and ending with the *Chenault*'s chief of security. The chief and his second in command wore the holstered weapons.

A moment before the captain again faced her, a blood-cooling wave of dizziness assailed Darq. Since the deck didn't swim before her eyes, she dismissed the sensation, chalking it up to the tension she was under.

"Qtl-shi, I mean Darq," the captain said, "there are quarters available nearby if you wish to rest and refresh yourself, but if you would prefer, my chief engineer is ready to confer on the damage to your vessel and how you wish to proceed with repairs."

Now she felt trapped between decks. Was this captain genuinely helping her or was this a covert way to examine the *Ky* for its technology? Then again, some technology might be considered fair trade for the assistance, after all, she couldn't pay the Centauri with precious metals or coin or credits for their help, now could she? Still, she had to keep the *Ky* from being scrutinized.

Over the neural net, she quickly outlined a plan to Tokoray. After his reply, she said to the captain. "Tokoray will work with your chief engineer. As for me, I may be — " Why did her guts suddenly seem to spin in the opposite direction? What was with the feeling of weightlessness? What was going on? She leaned back against Tokoray, the back of her head knocking against the shoulder strap of his flight harness. Her hands felt cold, clammy. They minutely shook, and she lost the grip on her helmet. It tumbled onto the deck and rolled askew. Weren't these symptoms of — oh, Mother of the Sky — Radiation poisoning!

All went black.

When the blackness dissolved, Darq woke to find her mind functioning at a crawl and refusing to remember why she lay on a bed wearing an oversized, dull-brown robe with sleeves that went to her elbows. The thin, fuzzy-napped garment had no collar. Dark-brown snaps, evenly spaced on its wide front placket, held the robe closed, except the top snap was undone. Through the gap it left, she saw a brown V-necked tank top. She wiggled her butt enough to know she wore panties. Funny, the underwear felt silkier than she remembered regulation wear being.

She took in a breath of the cool air, its odor indicating the air had been recycled one time too many. Yet, she felt warm and comfortable. She pushed her head back, deeper into the spongy pillow. Above, the mottled ceiling reminded her of flattened seasponge someone had bleached white. Then she let the memories sort themselves out until *radiation poisoning* triggered her heart to thump faster, her mind to whoosh clear.

How much damage had the radiation done to her body? No, to her neural net! She sent both hands to her head and felt a soft, fuzzy cap. She wrenched it off and palpated her scalp. Her fingers found unbraided hair — and only hair. She picked up the brown cap. No nodes, metals, plastics, tubes, or wires littered either the inside or outside of the cap. As a matter of fact, the cap looked like the ones she'd worn as a child on blustery winter days. Then again, what did she know about the Centauri and their medical practices? Maybe she wasn't a prisoner but a lab rat.

Anxiety uncoiled anew and a bitter-tasting thought assailed her. What had been done to her while she had been unconscious? What if the Centauri had taken samples of her neural net and damaged sections? Worse, what if the Centauri had neutralized her neural net? What if she couldn't access Tokoray or trigger the net's internal self-destruct or the *Ky*'s self-destruct? Heart thundering, hardly daring to breathe, she accessed her neural link. *Tokoray?*

Ah, you are awake.

He sounded relieved, if not downright happy. The talons of fear eased their grip on her. *Tokoray, where am I. Where are you? What happened to me?*

To answer your questions in order. You are in the Chenault's *sickbay. I am in Maintenance Six, Section B, eleven decks below you and toward the bow of the* Chenault. *Lastly, what happened to you is that you fainted.*

Fainted? *I'm not being treated for radiation?*

Negative. You are being treated for the lack of nourishment, which caused you to faint in front of the captain.

Shitfire, and double shitfire. She'd fainted in front of a commanding officer. Not a good way to make a first impression. Which was the least of her worries. *Tokoray, are you positive-positive there was no radiation poisoning?*

Absolutely positive, and before you ask, I carefully observed the Centauri d'ktr examine you for said radiation. Since there was none to speak of, and I was at a loss to understand your unconsciousness, I authorized the d'ktr to, non-invasively of course, ascertain what caused your blackout.

I went from a faint to a blackout?

No. Forgive me for the poor choice of words. You fainted due to low blood sugar coupled with exhaustion.

That's it?

*Affirmative. I do apologize, Darq. Your not consuming nutrients is my fault. Aboard the Ky, I agreed to allow your request to nap because it would be beneficial. However, I became absorbed in repairs and neglected to note the time passing or how long you slept. Then we were being scanned, and – *

No time for eating because we had to rig the self-destruct.

Affirmative. Add to that the hours you sat in the cockpit unable to move about, and it is understandable you would be even more prone to faint once you got to your feet. I should have been more attentive to monitoring your health. I sincerely apologize for my oversight.

Acknowledged. Apology accepted. She had fainted from lack of food. As simple as that. She almost chuckled with relief. *So, I'm okay.*

It would seem so. The d'ktr intravenously gave you a nutrient mix to replenish your bodily needs. However, the d'ktr felt it would be best if you woke on your own.

I had eighteen hours of sleep in the cockpit. Why would I need more sleep?

I asked D'ktr Fulton that. She said she did not want to give any chemical stimulant to wake you since she did not know how your body would react. She did not want to do more harm than good.

How nice of her. So, how long did I sleep?

Three hours forty eight.

That certainly wasn't a long time. *So, what are you doing?*

I am waiting for the master machinist to finish the head-arrays for our long- and short-range scanners. By the way, two decks below you, a team of maintenance engineers has been assigned to replicate motherboard slugs and components so we have star maps and navigation screens working again.

What's the prognosis for completion of said work?

Twenty-four to thirty six hours.

What about the Ky? Are they swarming all over him and his weaponry systems?

As soon as you were on a gurney headed for sickbay, I closed and code-locked the canopies and missile bay. According to the sensors, which I am monitoring constantly, no one has touched the Ky. Darq?

Yes?

It is possible the Centauri have sophisticated scanning devices. We can only hope the Ky's hull composition minimizes penetration. He paused, then said, *No guards have been posted around the Ky or in the bay, so I am inclined to believe Captain Warwick is offering us nothing more than sanctuary and repairs.*

Maybe. Things could get dicey when we go to leave. I can't help but wonder what his real motive is for aiding us.

Such a pessimistic skeptic.

Better safe than sorry, but she didn't voice that.

Darq, the captain permitted me a download of the Centauri language. Via the neural net, I entered it to your brain's language center. You should be able to speak it fluently. Ah, the parts are ready. I must go.

Darq sensed the disconnect. She took another look about her silent cell. She shouldn't call it a cell. The walls were textured, like a course waffle-woven fabric that looked almost sunny-yellow. The two side walls extended from the back wall and met a curved rail at the ceiling where heavy curtains, the same shade as the walls, draped. She stared at the center of the curtain. Were there guards outside her cubical?

She listened. Nothing. Not even sounds of medical equipment working. Why no medical equipment noises?

She looked at the wall behind her. A half-meter-tall, black screen spanned the width of the bed above her. Obviously the unit wasn't monitoring her body, but did anything else? A visual check for gadgets focused on her turned up nothing obvious, other than a narrow panel on a rail at the top of the bed, which had six button-like nodes. Likely pushing one of those nodes would bring someone. Did she want anyone to know she was awake? No, better to get in as much recon as possible while she could. Which meant getting off the bed and finding out what lay beyond the curtain.

After locating and releasing the left bed rail, she shoved the cover aside and slipped her feet over the mattress edge. She stared at the khaki-colored socks on her feet. In vivid color came to mind what those socks hid — her painted toenails. Then came the realization that the person who put those socks on her feet had to have noticed her toes. That person would have been Tokoray. Her painted toes were now logged into the Na-ka-ta's memory, which would be analyzed when they got back to the *Dujaki*. Her cheeks flamed hotter than the *Ky*'s engines on takeoff.

Hearing the approach of heavy footfalls quelled her mortification. The footfalls passed by and veered away before stopping.

"Ah, there you are, Captain," a female voice said.

For a second, Darq relished being able to understand the Centauri language.

"I got your message, Fulton, and came as soon as I could."

So, the woman speaking with the captain was the doctor. Curious, Darq slipped off the bed, and since her legs held steady, she tiptoed to where she could part the curtain enough to see out. No one was about, definitely no guards. Yet, the sickbay lights were dimmed, as if no patients occupied the area. Had she been quarantined in case she held some kind of threat? Were forcefields in place to make sure she didn't leave sickbay?

Movement caught her eye, and she focused on the doorway of what looked like a central hub-station. Inside the open doorway, his back to her, stood Captain Warwick.

"Come in and see," Doctor Fulton said.

The captain stepped inside, where Darq could no longer see him. She strained to hear his voice, picking up only a few garbled words. Curiosity sent her tiptoeing across to the solid-walled front section of the hub. With her back to the wall, she edged near the doorjamb and soon heard the captain's voice.

"How's your guest, Qtl-shi Darq?"

"Considering the assortment of hardware in her—"

"Hardware?"

"Sorry, Captain, nothing dangerous. She has a mini-pharmacy tucked along her ribs. Every bone has fortifications of calcium. There are jacks implanted under her fingertips. Plenty of nanobots ranging through her blood."

"She's a cyborg?"

"Oh, no. Far from it. Yojii Tokoray assured me the elements in her are designed to help her survive. They also make her one helluva fighter pilot—an amazing amazon."

"I see you have succumbed to the rumors."

"Nonsense. Legends are based in fact, distorted most of the time, but with a kernel of truth in them."

"I'm sure, Doctor, you didn't request my presence to discuss Amazons. What did you find that has you so concerned about Qtli-shi Darq's condition?"

"Come with me, over here, and I'll show you the Amazon's brain scans."

They'd scanned her brain? Why? Darq accessed her neural net. *Tokoray, link and listen.*

The captain's voice resonated with awe. "That's a human brain. Is that a tumor? My god, it's huge."

Darq's heart skipped two beats. A tumor? They found a huge tumor in her brain?

Tokoray's, *Darq, do not panic. I am on my way to you.*

She wasn't about to panic. Breathe. She had to breathe. In. Out. Slow and steady.

The doctor chuckled. "No, not a tumor, captain."

Darq let out a whoosh of air and panted to regain her composure. Shitfire, how much noise had her panting made? Had she given her position away? With hands gone clammy with angst, she strained to hear. There were no footfalls or sounds from the office, so the doctor and captain were not coming to investigate.

The doctor said, "Now, here, as you can see by this view, it is no tumor but some sort of a, for lack of a better term, network. Much of it is deep-seated. Of note is this particularly long dark veining. In our human brain this area is the seat of telepathy."

"Are you saying Darq is a telepath who can read our minds?"

"Well, hello, there" came a male voice from behind Darq.

Startled, heart racing, she swung about, hands fisted, feet moving into a defensive stance. She looked straight into dark-brown eyes brimming with mirth that belonged to a human male who stood out of punching range. The man was not thin but hefty enough and with skin as dark as her own. He looked middle-aged.

The mirth never left his eyes, but it was soon matched by a disarming smile. "I see you're up and about." The smile grew wider. "Did you hear anything interesting?"

Footsteps behind Darq alerted her to the captain's and the doctor's approach.

The newcomer's gaze shifted to something behind her left shoulder, which put his face in profile for her to marvel at his raven-black hair. That hair had been pulled back and plaited from his widow's peak to go across the top of his head and over his crown.

His gaze remained steadfast. "I seriously doubt Darq is telepathic, doctor. She was eavesdropping on your conversation using auditory senses."

The captain replied, "As were you, counselor?"

"Guilty as charged, Captain."

The counselor shifted his gaze to Darq and his eyes seemed semi-brilliant with gaiety, but it might have been sexual innuendo. No way to be sure, but this was no time for her thoughts to dwell on the man's virility.

The counselor met her gaze, the merriment faded, his smile turning benign. "I am Doctor Paracles Dominicus Shu-sai-chong Yanti, but that's a mouthful. Call me Doctor Yanti." He glanced at her still fisted hands, and his voice softened. "I pose no threat to you, Darq. May I call you Darq?"

She nodded.

Yanti looked toward the captain and doctor, who now stood at the peripheral line of her vision.

"I sense," Yanti said, "that Darq is afraid we are planning some harm to her or have already done harm to her."

"We are not and have not." The captain's tone left no doubt he objected to the accusation.

Darq nailed her gaze to Yanti's and held it. "What are you?"

His voice gentled. "I am a human, having a heritage, as my many birth names indicate, of Old Earth ancestry. I am the ship's resident mental health advisor. I see by your frown you don't know what that is."

There was something unsettling about strangers. Even more so about these beings and her present situation. What should she do? Say? She put more effort into keeping her fists clenched and up.

"You see," Yanti said, "I help people with their personal, mental, and emotional problems. Sometimes I'm the resident shoulder to lean on or the friend to talk things over with."

Instinct prodded her not to trust him. She demanded, "What else?"

"I have a highly developed sense of empathy, but no telepathy." A smile coiled at the corner of his lips. "Coupled with said empathy is high intelligence and my somewhat droll sense of humor—or so I'm told. All of which enables me to assist this ship, its officers, and its crew in maintaining high moral and mental stability. I also assist visitors to orient to our culture."

"Which includes me?"

"Isn't that obvious by my presence?"

"What's obvious is how you came up behind me unannounced."

"And frightened you."

"So you admit you snuck up on me?"

Only his eyes betrayed his merriment. "I admit to no such thing. In truth, as I entered sickbay, I spotted you standing by the doorway and walked up to you. Although I must admit, I did wonder if I should stomp across the decking to catch your attention, but that seemed rather melodramatic."

"Yet, you didn't decide to make noise, did you?"

"No, and that's because I became curious as to what kept you so engrossed. I thought to listen myself and see."

He sounded sincere, but was he being honest? Had he heard the doctor talking about her neural net being part of her brain's telepathic system. Was he interested in that? Too many questions, not enough answers.

She looked from Yanti to the captain to the doctor. Both Fulton and the captain seemed relaxed, both taking their cue from Yanti. Eyeing the counselor again, he seemed content to wait for her to make the next move. Which should be what? Clobber Yanti and run? She needed an ally. Where was Tokoray? *Where are you? I'm trapped, my back to the wall, outnumbered by three aliens.*

Centauries, Tokoray replied. *They are Centauries, not aliens.*

I'm cornered. I have no idea where I am in relation to you — and just where are you when I need you?

The lift at the far end of sickbay opened and out came Tokoray, his motors revving to high speed. *I am here.*

Hearing the noise, the three Centauri's turned to watch Tokoray's approach.

Darq lowered her hands. Leaving her thumbs tucked to her palms and holding them tight, she straightened and stood with all the dignity of a qtl-shi she could muster.

Tokoray squelched to a stop a meter from her.

With Yanti in full profile, Darq became distracted by the sight of his long, tapering pigtail which dangled to his hips. Narrow hips. Shitfire, her mind had wandered.

Yanti smiled at Tokoray. "Ah, so this is the Na-ka-ta. Yojii Tokoray, I presume?"

"I am he," Tokoray replied. "Darq, are you all right?"

"Sort of." She looked from Yanti to the doctor and recalled why she had been listening in on the conversation between the doctor and the captain. "So, doctor, why did you summon your captain, and what were you about to tell him about my brain?"

Fulton eyes went wide for a second, as if taken aback. "It has nothing to do with your brain. I intended to talk to you when you woke."

"I'm awake now."

"So you are." She squared her shoulders. "You are in fine health for a woman who is seven weeks pregnant."

✦ Chapter 21

Darq stared at Doctor Fulton, the word *pregnant* echoing and triggering a lightheadedness.

Tokoray's voice filtered through her turmoil. *Hold fast. We will sort this out.* He turned, facing the doctor. "That is impossible, doctor." His words were spoken in his hard, yojii-officer mode, like the one Na-ka-tas used with argumentative cadets. "You have erred."

Fulton crossed her arms over her chest. "Darq is female with functioning ovaries, although one is damaged and scared from long ago. I assure you, Yojii Tokoray, I have not erred. I reran the tests to be absolutely sure."

Fulton was sure? How could that be unless— Shitfire! Darq's anger overrode her shock. "No, doctor, my being pregnant is not possible unless you implanted a baby in me while I was unconscious!" She turned to Tokoray. "How could you abandon me to them?"

Yanti raised his hand to stay Tokoray's reply and said to Fulton, "Darq is angry. Likely because she was not aware she was pregnant. Give her a moment to calm herself."

Calm herself? How could she be calm with such news?

"Doctor," Yanti said with a tone of insistence, "Darq saw the look in your eyes. Tell her what really bothers you about her being pregnant, why you are displeased and upset."

Fulton's gaze crackled with resolve. Her words came out low and harsh. "It angers me that your flight surgeon let you fly, jeopardizing not only your life but also that of your fetus."

Seven weeks of flying about space and not knowing a baby grew within her? Shitfire, all that radiation— "Is the baby dying? Deformed?"

The doctor's anger vanished. "No. Your fetus is fine. Normal. Ten toes, five fingers on each hand."

How odd to quote fingers and toes? Maybe in Centauri society such things were important?

"Doctor Fulton," Tokoray said, "according to my data files, Darq passed her physical nine weeks ago. There would have been no need for another examination despite our recent bonding."

"But surely she would have had some indicative symptoms—a missed ovary cycle, nausea, fainting, vomiting?"

Darq inhaled a quick, noisy deep breath. "My ovary cycle is hit or miss. I've felt perfectly fine."

"Except, Darq," Tokoray said, "you fainted after our bonding."

"Which stemmed from my not eating—like it did coming aboard this ship." She spoke more to herself then to anyone present. "How the hell did I get pregnant?"

The doctor scoffed. "Don't they teach you anatomy? It takes a male's sperm. A woman's egg. What were you doing seven weeks ago?"

Darq backtracked, seven weeks . . . "The funeral."

Fulton blinked. "You had intercourse with a corpse?"

"Of course not! I had sex with my husband, and he is very much alive."

"And no protection? You didn't employ any practices to prevent an accidental pregnancy?"

"Why would I? Atlatl's been sterile for eight years. There was no need."

The doctor's facial expression echoed disbelief. "It only takes one sperm and one egg to meet."

"I know that, but my husband is incapable of making sperm thanks to an accident. This can't be right. I can't be pregnant."

"Well, you are pregnant." The doctor spoke with a markedly no-nonsense tone. "No doubt about it." Then her tone dropped to one of composed evenness. "Darq, there is something else that you need to know. Come, let me show you." She headed for her office. "The rest of you might as well attend."

The captain followed the doctor.

Tokoray dropped his wheelbase flippers and Darq mounted, glad to be in the security of his arms but not glad that he still wore his flight harness, which lay against her shoulder blades, the rings hard and not cushioned by the fabric of her robe and tank top.

Tokoray followed Yanti, who trailed after the captain. Entering the large hub, she found every wall held medical data and view panels. Computer stations and desks set catercorner at the far back. Most of the equipment was idle or offline.

Tokoray wheeled up to the spot near the center of the wall screen that Doctor Fulton stood beside. The captain stepped to the doctor's right. Yanti seated himself on the corner of a workstation's desktop to Darq's left.

Fulton nodded to Darq. "Now, about this brain of yours—" She tabbed a node on the wall screen. It winked, filling with half a dozen three-dimensional views of Darq's brain.

Darq stared at the dark strands of the neural netting melded to her brain and whispered, "So massive."

"Darq," Yanti said, "have you never seen it before?"

She didn't look at him. "I saw it the first time, a moon after it was implanted. Standard procedure is a check one moon after it's inserted. They told me it would grow and become one with my mind, but I never gave a thought to what it might look like now."

Doctor Fulton touched the screen and a view enlarged. "Is it normal to cover so much of the brain and go so deep?"

"Tokoray, you answer that."

He moved his head so his faceplate's frontal sensors lined up for him to view the data. "Normal depends on the pilot," Tokoray replied. "Much also depends on how young the pilot is when the net is implanted, how many additional bondings they have. Comparing this view with my onboard data, all looks normal."

"What's not normal," Darq said, allowing the harshness to edge her words with meaning, "is others having access to my net, to its technology."

"Well," Captain Warwick said, "you don't have to worry about us using that net knowledge or caring about it."

"Speak for yourself," Fulton said. "I find it intriguing the way it's entwined about the brain and feeds off blood vessels with no signs of irritation, scaring, or rejection."

From his perch, Yanti said, "Captain, Darq doesn't believe you."

"Darq." The captain's voice demanded her attention. "Centuries ago, on our homeworld, the human race developed cyborgs and androids. We were nearly exterminated by a man who gained control of those automatons and began purging anyone or anything that thwarted his ideal of a perfect society. It took a world war to destroy that tyrant and his machines, at an enormous price in lives." Warwick's gaze went to Tokoray then back at her. "By the look of things, you and your Na-ka-ta have forged a bond of mutual respect and friendship that we were never able to achieve."

Somehow she believed the captain. "Be that as it may, Captain, the Wysotti have guarded the knowledge of the neural net for decades to keep it out of the hands of the Doyons, who are determined to destroy us."

The captain turned to Doctor Fulton. "Purge all documentation and scans of Darq's brain. That's an order. Do it now."

For a moment, Fulton looked as if she would protest. With dismay pursing her lips, she said, "Very well, Captain, as you command." Her hands flew about the control pad beneath the wall screen. The images winked out one by one. With the last vanishing, the doctor said, with a note of sadness, "Done."

"Captain," Darq said, "turning off a screen or exiting a file doesn't necessarily mean the documentation is gone."

"Ah," Yanti said, a lilt in his voice, "a cynic."

The captain eyed Yanti. "I would be skeptical too if I were in her boots." His gaze went to Tokoray's hands that were clasped in front of her, then to Tokoray's faceplate. "Yojii Tokoray, is that the link the chief engineer made for you that's attached to your pinky finger?"

Darq turned her gaze to Tokoray's hands and spotted the blue-black nub surrounding the tip of his left pinky finger.

"It is," Tokoray replied.

"Plug into this console and verify the records are gone. I'll give you clearance." Doctor Fulton stepped aside and the captain tabbed information into the console, then stepped away from the unit. "You can access this unit and the mainframe computer, and any other computer aboard the *Chenault*, but you'll be excluded from classified data banks."

"Thank you, Captain Warwick." Tokoray wheeled forward and Darq shifted herself to the right, to better stay balanced in his right arm while he plugged in. Once linked, she waited half a minute before asking, *Did you find anything yet?*

It took only six seconds to verify the doctor did, indeed, erase all files and images of your neural net and brain. The auto backup files were also erased. The doctor even deleted the brain images off your full-body scans, leaving you looking like a headless corpse. The doctor retains images of your body, organs, and your implanted med-systems.

Should we ask for those to be deleted?

It matters not one way or the other considering most of the technology you carry is as old as you are.

Thank you for saying I'm outdated.

My apologies. I am now checking redundant data storage systems to make sure nothing has been transferred or noted.

Darq let him work, all the while feeling three pairs of eyes on her and wondering why no one questioned how long it should take Tokoray to verify the erasures.

Interesting. Darq you should view this. He activated something and on the screen data flowed.

"What am I looking at?"

Doctor Fulton beat Tokoray to the answer. "DNA. Yours Darq and — " She pointed to the second image. "This is your baby's."

A third screen slid under the baby's, then an orange glow highlighted the same sections of DNA.

"It would seem," Tokoray said, "that all three share genes in common."

How could that be?

Yanti stepped up to the screen. "That's my DNA!" He scowled at Doctor Fulton. "What's going on?"

"I'm sure there's an explanation," the captain said, then, "Doctor, I take it this is what you called me down here to see?"

Fulton nodded. "Yes, it is."

"Enough with the chit-chat." Darq tried not to scowl at the lot of them. "How can Doctor Yanti have the same genes I do?"

"This DNA," Doctor Fulton replied, "indicates that you, Darq, are as human as we are. It also shows that Doctor Yanti and you share common ancestors."

"That's impossible. I'm Wysotti. I've never heard of the Centauri."

"And I, Doctor," Yanti said, "was born and raised on Earth. This is my first trip into space. I know nothing of any Wysotti."

Tokoray provided an answer, and Darq voiced it. "The only commonality we seem to have is the Griers." Darq raked her hands through her hair, pulling the strands tight over her ears and holding onto them for a second. "Damn them, why would the star maps they gave us to hunt the *Ippera* not include the Centauri occupying the backside of the kungarike?"

"What is the *Ippera*?" the captain's tone wasn't one of casual curiosity but one of command.

Maybe the Centauri should know about the ship. She leaned onto Tokoray's arm and faced the captain. "The *Ippera*'s a Doyon destroyer. Intel has it that the *Ippera* is the Doyon's newest, most technologically advanced destroyer. It could mean doom for my people, so a handful of starfighters were sent to find and destroy that ship."

Concern flickered in the captain's eyes. "I take it you encountered the *Ippera*? Where?"

"Near a binary called Alpha and Beta San Hiphia. We skirmished. Beta had a mini-nova event. I got clipped by a shock wave, which fried circuits and sent my fighter tumbling out of control."

The captain's brows minutely furled. "And what of the *Ippera*?"

"The shockwaves got the *Ippera,* but I don't know if it's space-dust. That's why I need my long range scanners online. I have to go back and make sure the *Ippera* was destroyed."

The captain headed for the door. Accessing his comlink, he gave orders to the ship's computer to link him to astrophysics and ordered deep space scanner beams to search for the *Ippera.*

Yanti said to Darq, "If the *Ippera* is out there, or the debris from what's left, this ship will find it." He pointed to Tokoray's finger still in the console port. "What else, Tokoray, did you discover of interest in the *Chenault's* computers?"

Tokoray responded with "Languages, cultural data." He paused for a few long seconds. "However, of special interest is the sex of Darq's fetus."

"The usual, a girl." Darq's sigh echoed her reluctant acceptance of that fact, which was immediately followed by a self-scold that any child of Atlatl's was a godsend.

"On the contrary, Darq," Tokoray said. "It is a male fetus, a boy."

For a moment, she couldn't breathe. "A male child? Are you sure?"

Doctor Fulton touched a screen. "See for yourself."

Darq read the enlargement, the highlighted XY chromosomes and muttered, "That can't be."

Doctor Fulton patted her arm. "Despite you wanting a girl, won't a son be just as welcome?"

"No, no. You don't understand. Male children are rare. Only one is sired during a man's lifetime because of the curse. My husband has never sired a son."

The doctor patted Darq's arm again. "Well, my dear, miracles do happen."

"No they don't. Not to me."

"Well what else would you call it? You're pregnant by a husband who is supposed to be sterile. You survived a battle with a Doyon destroyer that took you through a nova event, which, by the way, didn't cause radiation damage to your body or your fetus's." The doctor gave her that wisest-of-the-wise look Darq had often seen saalishani healers use. "Perhaps you have a guardian angel looking out for you."

Maybe an ancestor who cared about her? Nonsense. And just where had that idea come from. Beans. That kid was haunting her—or maybe her ancestor was.

The doctor blanked the screen and looked Darq in the eye. "You are alive, Darq, so is that baby within you. Not dead. *Alive*."

A headache began to beat, the pulse equal to Zukaltay's drumming. Darq rubbed her temple for a few seconds, willing the throbbing to go away and praying her grandmother's drumming wouldn't start. "Look, Doctor Fulton, I'm a starfighter pilot on a suicide mission. I have a duty to my people. The Fates have damned me. I cannot be pregnant!"

Fulton's voice held kindness. "Doctor Yanti will escort you and your Na-ka-ta back to your bed. You need to rest and keep up your strength."

"Strength for what?"

"To ensure the baby lives and you are capable of flying home. But, wait, perhaps I am mistaken. Do you want an abortion before going home?"

Revulsion scudded through Darq. "I don't want an abortion!"

The doctor's keen gaze nailed Darq's soul to her heart. "So, you want this baby?"

Did she? A baby. A son. Atlatl's son. Atlatl's child. Her child? Hadn't it been her dream to become pregnant and give Atlatl a son? The baby was a miracle of miracles.

Who was she kidding?

Duty came before self. Survival of her race demanded she do her duty, serve to the best of her ability. But what about her wifely duty? Her duty to Atlatl? After all, the baby was his child too—and she loved Atlatl to the depths of her being.

Would being a mother be so bad? Sure, no more flying. Well it didn't mean not flying forever, just not flying until the baby was born. Shitfire, flying or not flying was a piss-poor consideration. So, how did she really feel about having a baby?

Wonderful.

Terrified.

Overjoyed.

Motherhood! To be a mother—how strange and yet how right it felt to admit she wanted to be a mother. But could she live with herself knowing she had murdered this baby because her duty was to hunt down and destroy the *Ippera*? No. She was, once more, caught under a grinding stone. But this time, she would follow her heart. She took one long fortifying breath and on the exhale said decisively, "Doctor Fulton, I want this baby. I'll work things out."

Later, well-fed, released from sickbay, and dressed in the shipsuit Yanti had requisitioned for her, Darq lay in the port side cubbyhole beneath the back of Tokoray's cockpit seat and finished reassembling the WSTB. She could hear Tokoray in the missile bay below, clipping new fiber optic and crystal circuitry boards into their holders. Those boards had been made by the Centauri. The techs had laughed when they saw the boards because they recognized them as a Grier component, freely traded.

She pushed the last little circuit slug into place. Another Grier element. Somebody should really look into who the Griers traded with and find the real source of their technology. Yet, she shouldn't complain. That technology made for speedy repairs to the *Ky*. She lifted the loaf-of-bread sized unit and fitted it into its slot. The unit sat cradled like a babe in a mother's womb. *A baby.* She was going to have a baby. Tears began to well, blurring her vision. What was the matter with her? She sniffled.

Darq, are you all right? Have you breathed in fumes?

No, no, nothing of the sort. For some odd reason, my eyes just started tearing and plugging my sinuses.

She heard a whisper of static through her neural net, then silence.

In checking your bodily systems, Tokoray said, *you have not encountered anything that triggered a defensive response by your eyes, nose, or sinuses. However, according to the data I downloaded about pregnant human females, which Doctor Fulton provided, there is a slight spike in a few hormone levels. Hormone swings account for much distress in pregnant women, but they usually level off after the first trimester.*

Tokoray, if you're monitoring my hormone levels, you could at least warn me when a tear-inducing spike is going to hit.

It is not that simple, but I will endeavor to do so. However, on the subject of your health. I am reading brain activity indicative of a shift to a depressed state. Which, if I may speak plainly, I believe is caused by our situation, the uncertainties of returning to base, and how our mission goal conflicts with your desire to birth your baby.

And speaking of speaking plainly — *Tokoray, how do you feel about me being pregnant?*

Silence.

That silence squeezed her chest. Maybe he didn't reply quicky because he needed to couch his words, and she wasn't going to like what he had to say.

Darq, he said, *we are bonded. We have become a viable team. At this point in time, I do not know if I wish to remain bonded to you or not. I am a copilot, a flight instructor. I am satisfied with those duties. However, this is not the time to make decisions about such things. Our mission and duty is to hunt the Ippera and destroy it. That has priority.*

Duty first. Right. She wiped away the extra moisture in her eyes and replaced the panel cover. From somewhere inside the cockpit a ping resounded. *What was that?*

Tokoray's voice held satisfaction. *Good news. The WSTB is online and the diagnostic check indicates it is in optimum operating condition. You have done well.*

I can follow diagrams you know. She heard the exasperation in her voice and regretted it.

Darq, what is wrong? Talk to me.

She sighed. *I'm tired. Overreacting. I'm going to go to our quarters and lay down for a while.*

Very well — and do drink something.

She ground her teeth. Why did everyone keep telling her to drink and eat. Okay, she knew why.

Once she reached the quarters assigned to her, she went to the wall and triggered the wash unit. It slid out from the wall and unfolded. She splashed tepid water on her face, stood, and looked into the small rectangular mirror at a face dripping with water. Not so much the face, but the cocoa-brown eyes looking back at Her. Something shimmered in the depths of her eyes. Despair? Maybe desperation. Surely there had to be some sort of compromise between doing her duty and keeping her baby alive—but what?

Starshine and shitfire, this wasn't like her. How could she regain her equilibrium? Talking to Tokoray wouldn't help, he was programmed as a fighter-pilot's Na-ka-ta. He would record what they discussed, which meant their conversations would be reviewed by medical personnel.

Tokoray had proved to be a great Na-ka-ta. One who'd chosen a career as a flight instructor, chosen to bond to her, chosen to die with her. And, shitfire, now even his future was at risk because she was pregnant. Had he jinxed her? No, no, a baby was no jinx. Never a jinx.

If only she could talk things out with Atlatl. Wise Atlatl. Or, maybe, just maybe, someone as wise? Like who?

Yanti.

Yes, Yanti. She dried her face, tossed the small towel into the recycle slot, and triggered the wash unit closed. Once at the computer terminal nestled at the foot of her narrow bed, she requested a link to Yanti. Despite her stammering and sounding incoherent even to herself, Yanti agreed to see her immediately and gave her directions to his office.

When she arrived, the office door snicked open. She stepped through and onto a mottled pale-green carpet. Ahead, the lighting ended in a black abyss, indicating the room, rather offices, extended further. Since additional lighting wasn't needed, none were on. To her left, a forest green wall's spot lighting subtly graced framed paintings and pictures along with grotesque masks. Those shared space with short tiered shelves holding knickknacks. Or were they antiques? Artifacts?

She heard a door open and looked in that direction.

Yanti stepped out of the second doorway on the right. He smiled and greeted her with a simple hello. His gaze dropped to her hands, making her realize she had balled her fingers around her cold thumbs. She relaxed her hands and took an at-attention stance.

"Darq," Yanti said, "how about we go where we'll be more comfortable?"

For an instant she had the urge to turn tail and run, but she nodded.

He tabbed a node on his sleeve band and lights winked on, illuminating the abyss. "This way." He strode ahead.

She followed, pausing to marvel at a huge picture in an ebony frame.

Yanti reversed direction and came back to stand at her side. "That's the Great Wall of China," he said. "It's a copy of the northern portion of the wall. The picture was taken from orbit above Earth. One of my most ancient of ancestors was Mongolian. It's said he placed a stone or two in that wall."

Why did the word Mongolian sound familiar?

As they continued on, Yanti walked slowly, allowing her to take her time to look at the objects inside the glass-covered boxes on pedestals or the items hanging on the walls.

Was this strolling along his way of easing his patient's tensions? Not that she was tense or about to fall for such a ruse. Her gaze flitted to a painting of a building in ruins hanging next to a door that bore a white plaque with *Consulting* in black letters.

"Yanti?" she said, pointing to the artwork. "What's this building?"

He stopped. "That's the Parthenon. It's located near Athens, Greece." A faint smile softened his words. "I have Greek ancestors. A few distant relatives still live there."

"Did a war destroy the Parthenon?"

"Time and time again. And a few earthquakes. It's still standing. Preserved because of its historic value. It's a relic from Earth's ancient times. It's also considered a supreme example of Doric architecture."

He moved on and turned right, before a doorway with cream-colored faux wood grained double doors. Those doors shushed aside. Entering the room, where light came from around the ceiling molding, she spotted a starscape straight ahead, one that took up the entire wall. "That's some painting."

"It's not a painting, Darq. That's a viewport. Those are real stars."

Since those stars were not blurred, the *Chenault* had to be traveling slower than light speed, but why? And where were they headed? Without a reference star or constellation, she had no idea. Then again, being behind the kungarike, unfamiliar with any of the stars there, why did she even dwell on them?

Yanti stepped aside and waved a hand toward the plushly upholstered, russet sectional sofa that took up a wide swath in front of the viewport. Two matching chairs dotted the ends of the sofa and faced each other. "Please take a seat."

She glanced at the seating, noting the beige and green pillows tucked in the corners of the sofa, then decided to stand at the viewport. "I have always loved the stars. I've always felt at home among them. Safe. Secure."

"But now?"

"Now?" Her fears broke their bonds, and she half-whispered, "I feel as if I'm going to lose everything I hold dear." She hugged herself and focused on a distant pinpoint of a star.

"I see." His voice came from a distance behind her.

Momentarily shifting her gaze, she found his reflection in the viewport. He perched on the arm of the sofa, his hands clasped in his lap. The way he looked at the viewport, she knew he studied her reflection.

"And why is that?" He spoke with a friendly father-doctor tone.

She returned her focus to the star point. "Because my fighter is damaged. I'm stuck on this ship, in unknown territory, among aliens—I mean humans." She was mangling her words. "I'm sorry, I meant no offense."

"None taken. So, go on, finish your thought."

"Worst of all, or best of all—I can't decide which—*I'm pregnant*. My duty is to return to space, hunt down the *Ippera*, and destroy it if it is not already dust."

"Don't you want to go home, to your family?"

Zukaltay's drum patted a rhythm, one softer than a whisper. She ignored it. "Home? As my grandmother used to say, home is where the heart is. Currently my home is the *Dujaki*. As to family, that would be my husband, Atlatl. Him alone."

"What about your mother?"

Zukaltay's drumming paused.

"I came to terms with my mother and my relationship with her a long time ago. If you must know, my mother is selfish and self-centered. Hours after my grandmother's funeral, I officially severed myself from my mother. My sisters understood."

"You have sisters? Are they younger than you?"

"Yes. Two sisters. Both younger."

"Do you stay in touch with them?"

Darq nodded. Zukaltay's drum patted on, the rhythm short, repeating over and over like a litany.

"Tell me, Darq, would your mother be displeased if you had a child?"

Would she? Hardly. "I believe my mother would be pleased only if she can figure out what she could gain in the way of esteem, money, or merchandise from having my child about." She looked briefly over her shoulder at him. "Be assured, Doctor Yanti, my mother will never raise my son, or any child of mine." She looked back at the starscape. "I saw to that."

"How?"

Darq took a deep breath, one that quieted the patting drumbeats. "On my world, those who serve the E-calli may elect to have eggs harvested from their ovaries and stored. Later, when they desire it, a sister, another relative, or a volunteer becomes a surrogate. The surrogate often raises the child as her own and makes sure the child knows what the mother does, how important the mother is to the welfare of the Wysotti people. When on leave, the biological mother and child get together."

"So, to thwart your mother, you never had eggs set aside?"

How astute of him. "That's right. I figured if I died my mother would find a way to obtain my eggs, auction them to a wealthier dyn—one that valued brains and guts and military prowess—and make a fortune. And before you ask, yes, my sisters offered to bear me a child by Atlatl, but I declined. I thought I would get pregnant, but then Atlatl became sterile."

"That must have been difficult for you."

"At first, but over the years it has been enough to be with him."

"And now? I sense you have concerns about raising this child."

"I'm a fighter pilot, a good one." Again she looked over her shoulder at Yanti. "I'm not bragging, doctor. I'm not the best in the fleet, but if you ask Tokoray, he'll quote you where I stand in the ranks."

His smile reassured her that he knew she was good and not bragging.

"Look, doctor, I've been in the Elpoccalli since I was eighteen summers old. I never wanted to be planet-bound if I could help it."

"And having a baby will change that?"

She looked back at the stars. "My life will change. It is, I think, changing even now. How do I go from being a qtl-shi to a mother? I've always taken my oath of duty to heart. We Wysotti are a people at war, barely holding our own against the Doyons. How can I bring a child into such a world when I know that world may be destroyed, our planet taken and annexed into the kungarike? There are whispers the Wysotti will soon be like the Griers, straggling, struggling vagabonds. Traders in space with no home of their own."

"What makes you so sure your world is doomed?"

"The *Ippera*. It's a prototype. I flew against it, barely kept out of its clutches. A speedy devil. I never got a direct hit that did much good, and let me tell you, I don't often miss!"

"Are you angry about that?"

"No. Yes! Yes, I'm angry. I lost Chance. I mean, Jaqui." Now why had that come out? "Sorry, Chance is her pilot name, like Raven is mine."

"Did Chance-Jaqui die recently?"

"Yes. In the skirmish with the *Ippera* and two other Doyon destroyers. She watched my back, flew my right wing . . ." Like an undertow, sadness washed through her, threatening to drown her. She grabbed for duty and reality. "I'm bound by duty to go back, look for the *Ippera*, and if need be, give my life to destroy it."

"Have you mourned for your friend?"

She shook her head. "No time. Too many other things have priority. Later. Later I'll mourn her passing. She was the best . . . " A hot rush of tears volcanoed up, but she capped them off before they could reach her eyes.

"Why not fly back to the *Dujaki* and let others handle the *Ippera*?"

A tempting thought. The pat-ta-pata-pat drumbeat in her mind became more pronounced. Did guilt intensify the beat? Or did her grandmother scold her for asking a stranger's advice?

"Darq?"

"Sorry. Okay, facts. It's an extremely long-shot that I can make it back to the *Dujaki*. Doing so entails running a gauntlet. One that takes me into Doyon territory. One that might require avoiding another San Hiphia mini-nova. One that requires a fit fighter, and said fighter is low on armaments. Going back requires being able to navigate the Chepha-wee-ka and send a very long-range signal so I won't be considered hostile and my own shoot me down."

"Are you willing to die now that you're pregnant?"

"Until I learned I was pregnant, I had come to terms with dying. Being a starfighter pilot, one lives with and accepts death. It's me versus the Doyon."

"Ah, yes. Best one wins the fight and goes on to do battle another day."

He understood? Amazing. "Yes, Doctor Yanti. And death, after all, is nothing more than the cycle of life. Even Tokoray was, up until we found out about the baby, willing to sacrifice his life with mine or for mine, but now?" She shrugged. "It seems to me that to take the risks that duty demands equates to murdering the innocent life within me. I may kill Doyons in the line of duty and to save my ass, but . . ." She lowered her hand to her belly. Inside was a life. A new life. A baby. Hers and Atlatl's baby. Tears rose, blurring her view of the stars.

"And therein, Darq, lies the crux of your turmoil."

"No kidding." She hugged herself. "Got any answers?"

"One."

"Which is?"

"Time."

She sniffed back her tears. "I don't understand."

"You have been extrapolating worst-case scenarios, which is good in that you know the difficulties, the obstacles, and have looked at consequences. But what you need is time to find other ways to work things out. You never know when a miracle will offer enlightenment."

With the back of her hands, she wiped the moisture from her eyes. "I don't believe in miracles."

A tiny smile winked at the corners of his mouth. "Ah, yes, I recall you told Doctor Fulton you were an unbeliever."

The drumbeat increased in her mind. "Do you believe in miracles?"

"Yes. And I believe in the maker of miracles, the great power that can manifest itself in many forms, both corporeal and noncorporeal. It's said that entity has a billion names, but most simply call it God. Do you believe in god or a supreme being?"

"I believe in the great spirit J'Hi-inti. She is mother of all creation." Anger rose. "Only right now, if She took human form and came within reach, I would kick her in the shins for putting me in this situation."

He looked at her for a long moment and quietly said, "You wouldn't thank her for the child you bear?"

She would. *Shitfire — she would*! Oh, great J'Hi-inti— She really would thank Her. The tears oozed up, adding a shimmering blur to her vision. She was pregnant with a baby, a baby boy. She was going to be a mother. She wanted to be a mother.

Doing her duty would kill her child.

Hot tears gushed down her cheeks. Her knees buckled and thumped onto the soft carpet. She rocked back on her heels. Her right thigh butted against the viewport wall, providing support. She cradled her face in her hands and wept. When the storm of tears abated, she became aware that Yanti squatted beside her. He handed her a tissue. She took it and blew her nose and mopped up her teary face.

He reached over to the side pouch of the nearest armchair and pulled out more tissues. "You've held back many tears over your lifetime, haven't you, Darq?"

She nodded and took the tissues he offered. "Growing up was purgatory. Yet, there were happy times. Not many, but worthwhile ones." She let a watery smile bloom. "Like building my own airplane. Learning to fly. Getting my pilot's license." She felt the tears begin to clog her throat. "Life was pretty good on the *Dujaki*."

"What did you like about living on the *Dujaki*?"

Memories surged. "I met my best friend, Jaqui there. We became bunkmates. Flew together. She could get me to do the craziest things." Atlatl's grinning face swam before her for a second, and she didn't censure the joy of that memory. "Best of all, Atlatl, my atan, my husband—the soul of my soul—was there with me."

Yanti rose to his feet. "Life is what you make of it. Be patient with yourself, and you will find your way."

"There doesn't seem to be a way to reconcile motherhood with duty to my people. What of that?"

His smile radiated conviction. "Our people have a saying—*where there's a will, there's a way*."

She had the will but not the way out of the mess she was in. A lot of help he was. As she mopped up the remaining tears, the drumbeats quickened in her mind. She rubbed her temple trying to erase the sound.

"Do you have a headache?"

She dropped her hand away from her temple. "No. It's the drumbeats." Now why had she revealed that? Likely from losing control of her emotions.

His brows quirked upward a fraction. "What drumbeats? Are you talking about a headache or something worse? Is something wrong with your neural net?"

She heaved a sigh. "I didn't mean to say that."

"Obviously." He backed and sat on the sofa's arm.

The way he studied her huddled on the floor, he wasn't going to let her go without some sort of explanation. Worse, as an empath, he would likely detect a lie. "If you must know, ever since my grandmother died, I've been hearing her play her lap drum. Sometimes the beat has been loud and annoying, other times, like now, rudely distracting."

"Which grandmother?"

"Sorry. My mother's mother. Grandmother Zukaltay. She gave her old drum to me. It was everything to her, and it's all I have of her, other than her rosewood puzzle box." Now why had she mentioned the box? Such a little inconsequential item. Shitfire, she was being overly sentimental on top of being an emotional wreck. Darq looked up and met Yanti's patient, yet imploring, gaze. "I don't know why I hear her play her drum. I never played the thing."

"Did you love your grandmother?"

"Yes."

"Did you mourn her passing?"

"I thought I had."

"Perhaps you haven't."

She didn't believe that. She sucked in a deep breath. "Perhaps she's haunting me."

"Ah, so that's your fear, is it?"

"It's either that or I'm going insane."

He smiled and shook his head. "I doubt that. Consider this—your grandmother loved you, so why would she haunt you?"

"Good question. When I get to the Omega Qi, I'll ask her." She quirked a smile. "That's providing grandmother's soul made it there."

Yanti's chuckle was short lived. "I'm of the opinion you're still mourning her, Darq. Give yourself time to grieve."

"There's no time right now."

"I know. But there will be. Take the time. Don't keep it bottled up."

"Will you tell Doctor Fulton about the drumbeats?"

"Anything we discuss here is private. And as long as it's not life threatening to you or others, it remains between us."

"Thanks for listening."

"That's what I'm here for. Would you like some water?"

"Yes, please."

He headed for the back right corner of the room. She soon lost sight of him because the sofa blocked her view. She heard a panel slide back, then him say, "Glass, water, cold, three."

She got to her feet and strode toward him but froze at the sight of the back wall's collage and the subjects in it. Blinking brought the collage's features into sharper focus. Darq's heart began beating as if she were about to engage a Doyon Striker and her heartbeat overrode Zukaltay's drumming.

She resumed her advance, not toward Yanti but to the collage, and activated her neural net, half-yelling *Heads up!*

She stared at the view so Tokoray got a clear image.

✧ Chapter 22

Darq stopped a stride from the collage. She looked from the sky view of an earth-mound monkey and a spider to a flat mountaintop scarred with long parallel lines. Scattered about were a trio of stepped temples among jungle greenery. Everywhere she looked, she pulled out details that matched legends, stories—and history. Wysotti history. Her voice shock-choked, she demanded, "Where did you get this?"

Yanti approached with a half-full glass of water in hand. "That's a composite painting made by my great-grandmother, a renowned artist from a country on Earth called Mexico. My great-grandmother had an affinity for the ancient civilizations." He pointed to a temple on the painting. "Those ruins are near where she lived. They're still standing." A second later he said, "You're astounded by this collage. Why?"

Tokoray's voice intoned in her mind, *The border. Look at it. All of it.*

She started up at the top left corner and went around, recognizing symbols and glyphs. The first one she recognized was the sunstone, like the one on Zukaltay's rosewood puzzle box.

"Darq?" Yanti said with awe in his voice. "You can read that, can't you?"

Her gaze flitted to a glyph. "Yes. I can read most of the others, too. They are Wysotti, ancient Wysotti." She touched symbols. "Cozamalotl, the rainbow. Eztli, blood. Ixchel, the Moon Goddess." She looked at the collage and put her trembling finger near but not touching a spot. "This— This is his symbol. Kukulaan's. The Quetzalcoatl feathered dragon." She faced Yanti, dread and uncertainty shifting like a roiling sea within her.

The look on his face devolved into bewilderment and his frown closed the gap between his brows. "Darq, to me, to us humans, Quetzalcoatl is the feathered serpent, also known as *Kukulkan*."

A monsoon whirled in her stomach with realizations coming from the extrapolated possibilities and probabilities which she fought to deny.

Tokoray's voice intoned, *Logic must prevail. Seek the facts and you will uncover truth.*

She could hardly get the words out. "Are—are you Centauries from a blue, water-world planet with no rings? A planet orbited by a single moon?"

He nodded. "We're the third planet from our sun."

Third planet buzzed in her ears as if a Doyon had her in its crosshairs. But she had to be sure. "Is there another planet in your solar system, one with rings called Saturn?"

"Yes."

"Other planets, close to the sun?"

"Yes, Venus and Mars. We even have a gas giant, Jupiter."

His bewilderment plowed deeper furrows across his brow.

She took in a ragged breath and tamped down on the quivering rampaging through her body, threatening to put her on her knees again. The whispered words escaped her, "The stories are true." She looked again at the collage. Revelation and the reality of those stories roared faster than the *Ky* at full speed. Then with the impact of a diggerboom, the injustice hit. "You're supposed to be dead, your world destroyed!"

"Darq, please, calm yourself. Come, sit down." He cupped her elbow and led her to the sofa where she sat, her breathing as rapid as if she'd run six kilometers. She turned, forearms on the sofa's armrest, balancing herself to stare at the collage, listening to Tokoray, who had plugged into the *Chenault*'s computer system searching for Earth's history. With every passing second, he confirmed another truth.

Yanti set the glass of water down on the floor beneath the sofa's armrest. He bent forward and put his hand gently, but briefly, on her kneecap. "Darq," he entreated. "Talk to me."

She gazed from one image to another on the collage. "For what that one ancestor of my dyn had wrought, all the Wysotti were cursed. We've been suffering and struggling for eons when all along your people were alive, thriving. Your starfarers have colonies on other worlds — and you have armadas to protect them."

"Darq, I don't understand. Help me understand."

She looked into his dark eyes and shifted so she was seated with her back against the sofa. Tokoray blitzed her with input. Her heart skipped a beat at the importance of the newest data, DNA. Her hands trembled, her voice quivered. "Doctor Yanti, remember the DNA — yours, mine, my baby's?"

He nodded. The look on his face begged for more of an explanation, but he seemed willing to let her take her time giving it.

"That DNA isn't lying. We are related. Oh, we are so related. *You are Wysotti.*"

He frowned. "How can that be?"

"On our way here, we passed paintings — and you said you had Mongolian and Greek ancestors."

He nodded.

"The genetics you inherited from those ancestors stem from the genes of the officers of a Wysotti exploration vessel called the *Tolamixi Mu*. That starship had been following the old stories, the myths, the legends of the Vidarians."

"Who are the Vidarians?"

"A technologically advanced life form created by J'Hi-inti Herself, by Her own hands, out of mud and clay and the dust of stars. The Vidarians eventually became disciples of J'Hi-inti and, with Her blessing, seeded worlds with the essences enabling life forms to evolve. If those life forms became sentient, J'Hi-inti gave them souls." Darq listened to Tokoray. She wiped a nervous hand over her jaw, feeling the iciness of her shaky fingers. She put her hands in her lap, locking her fingers together to thaw them and to calm herself. When Tokoray asked, she took note of Yanti's facial features.

"Darq, please, speak to me. What's Tokoray saying that's upset you? Don't say you aren't talking to him because I sense it. And what are you searching my face for?"

She closed her eyes for a long blink to comprehend the logical conclusions Tokoray had drawn. "Doctor Yanti," she said, her voice not betraying her inner turmoil, "the seeding of other worlds resulted in you looking like me, I looking like you. *We are humans*, just like the Grier, and the populations of a dozen of the worlds of the Kallian federation, with adjustments because of the environment of our planets."

"All right, I'll buy that, but what's the Earth connection?"

Should she tell him? Someone had to know. The truth might sting but it was better than a lying cancer. "Kukulaan captained the *Tolamixi Mu*. His ship had been following the Vidarian startrails out of a cluster of stars you call the Pleiades to a planet called Terra." *The Pleiades was the design on her grandmother's Jewels of the Sky Drum.*

Yanti nodded. "Terra is another name for Earth."

"Yeah, Tokoray just told me that."

Realization flickered in his eyes. "Which accounts for you being shocked. You didn't know Earth is also called Terra?"

She nodded.

Amazement registered on Yanti's face. "So Earth really had visitors from outer space. Amazing. Here our race considered the stories of alien visitation fabrications. But how does that tie your DNA and mine?"

Her hands felt colder than before. "Kukulaan's crew first explored a region called Mongolia, home to primitive, brutal tribes of Mongols."

Yanti's brows unfurled and his eyes widened. "My relative, the Mongol?"

She gave him a confirming nod. "Somehow Kukulaan got the idea to improve the Mongol gene pool. He and his senior officers used their technology to capture and make females mate with them so they could get them pregnant with their own sperm."

"They raped women?" Distaste registered about the lines of his mouth.

"Yes. They justified the end results warranted the means. But their desire to upgrade Terra's human race didn't stop with the Mongols." Tokoray supplied her with more specific input. "They went to many other places, Normandy, the Ural Mountains—"

"Let me guess—Greece. Accounting for DNA from another of my ancestors."

She nodded only once. "Along the way, they killed crewmembers who tried to stop the orgies. Working their way westward, they took their ship to—" She pointed to the collage's corner map. Tokoray gave her the name. "The Yucatan Peninsula. They leveled that mountaintop." She pointed to it. "They used it as a base to fly in and out of and to continue their orgies. I don't know the specifics, and neither does Tokoray, but the history drilled into me and my dyn was that Kukulaan succumbed to the overpowering, natural pheromones, the raw essence of the primitive people."

Awed and seemingly humbled, Yanti slowly shook his head. "Thus I acquired the third match of DNA from my great-grandmother." A statement, not a question. He looked at her. "So, what happened next?"

"Kukulaan became a god, the Quetzalcoatl Dragon."

Astonishment registered on his face and in his voice. "Teotihuaca, where the gods came down to Earth." He staggered back a step, as if the revelation had punched him in the chest. "The chariots of the gods belonged to the Wysotti!"

"What?"

"There are those who believe aliens from another world came to the Yucatan, to the Mayan people, who treated them as gods. Chariots are—"

An image flashed in her mind. "Tokoray just gave me an image of a chariot."

He looked at her as if having another revelation. "The Mayan worshiped Quetzalcoatl, who they thought had come to life among them as the god-king Kukulkan."

Tokoray sent a burst of information. "Tokoray says the corruption of your Kukulkan and our Kukulaan can't be a coincidence. Nor is it a coincidence your race and mine have a

Quetzalcoatl, yours a serpent, mine a dragon—which is a kind of serpent."

He wiped both hands over his face before he took a deep breath. "This is a lot to take in. What else? What happened to Kukulaan?"

"Vanity coupled with narcissism coupled with technology. He and his officers wielded power that corrupted their minds and souls. Some reports say they partook of native hallucinogens. Kukulaan and his officers embraced and reveled in the natives' penchant for blood sacrifices and ceremonies, even encouraging it and taking it to bizarre extremes. They drank blood. Ate hearts. The orgies went on for days. They made those—" She pointed to the collage. "They used their gravlocks and antigrav equipment to move tons of earth to form the monkey, the spider."

"But those can only be seen from space."

Data came from Tokoray.

"According to Tokoray says there's a tale about a contest among the three gods to see who could make the biggest dirt animal in the shortest amount of time. There are stories about them using the ship's engines to sweep the roads of dust to prove to the Mayans that Kukulaan was master of the wind."

"My god, Darq, your ancestors— Wait. The Mayans. You said you were of the Mayahi Dyn. The Mayans existed before the *Tolamixi Mu* arrived. Your clan name—what's the connection?"

Darq let a rueful smile curve her lips for a second. "My dyn, my clan, were not given the name Mayahi until after the *Onaja Toq*'s crew returned home."

"You lost me. *Onaja Toque*? What happened to the *Tolamixi Mu*?"

"Give me a second and I'll explain. The *Onaja Toq* was another starship whose path brought them close enough to Terra to pick up an urgent plea sent by one of the *TM*'s crew—and he was killed for doing so. Anyway, the *Onaja Toq* investigated. They discovered what Kukulaan and company were up to and tried to stop them."

"Let me guess," Yanti said, "there was a fight?"

She nodded. "Kukulaan, with the backing of the Mayans, killed and took prisoner most of the *Onaja Toq*'s crew. A few of the crew got away to the *Tolamixi Mu* and took it to the backside of Terra's moon. They sent a distress signal. Kukulaan figured reinforcements were bound to come. He didn't want to be captured, held accountable. So, he held a massive blood sacrifice celebration. As the Mayan people and his two cohorts indulged themselves, Kukulaan brought the *Onaja Toq* over the site and, instead of a light display and show of his godly power, he triggered an overload of the engines that vaporized everyone."

Yanti muttered something under his breath that sounded like "My god!" then looked her in the eye. "To this day, Darq, archeologists have tried to figure out how the Mayan civilization vanished."

"Well, now you know. Kukulaan, the Wysotti, caused it."

"But why weren't the temples, the buildings, vaporized? The land laid barren?"

Another blitz came from Tokoray.

"The ship's engines. In those days, as the power cores imploded, consuming themselves in nanoseconds, the reaction sequenced so stone and dirt were seldom affected but anything with DNA burned up—animals, bugs, people. Mostly people."

"If Kukulaan destroyed everyone, how do you know what he did?"

"From the *Onaja Toq* survivors who were aboard the *Tolamixi Mu*. They were rescued and came home. One survivor, a maintenance chief, kept a diary and had copied some of the *TM's* logs. Only no one knew what those survivors had witnessed at the hands of Kukulaan until after the maintenance chief's death. His wife discovered his diary. She turned the data over to the news media."

"That must have been interesting."

Darq shrugged. "I wasn't even born then."

"Right, so go on."

"It's been drilled into us of the Mayahi Dyn that the night after the *Tolamixi Mu* landed on our homeworld, saalishanies everywhere dreamt of a furious J'Hi-inti damning all Wysotti for what Kukulaan and his had done to Terra. Those men had destroyed a civilization and a planet." Darq wiped her cold hands over her hot face and sighed. Nothing could wipe away the past, nor the knowledge of it.

"I take it there was an outcry by your people?"

She looked at him and his understanding gaze emboldened her. "A massive outcry. The government rounded up the families of Kukulaan and his two officers. Every one of them was stripped of their lands, their fortunes, their status in society. All were branded with new last names. Mayahi for those related to Kukulaan, T'zilotl for the second officer, Heeto for the third. They felt the sins of the fathers had blackened the souls of all their progeny and kin." She paused, remembering snatches of her dyn's history — the name calling, the disparagements.

She took a fortifying breath. "All kin were restricted to living in the deserts and badlands. Boundary fences were erected to keep them away from decent people." She leaned her head back against the sofa and closed her eyes. Images of the badlands shimmering in summer's heat assailed her. She opened her eyes and stared at the ceiling.

"I get it now," Yanti said. "Our DNA. You have the same markers I do because of inbreeding."

She lifted her head and looked at him. "Yes, I carry one from each of the three devil-families." She recalled bits and pieces of the elders, the old ones, of her dyn, their bitterness. "For the Mayahi, it was called the Time of Tears."

"I don't sense you're bitter about that."

"No. It's past history. My lot in life." And now her lot in life had taken a sharp left turn. She was pregnant. Life renewing within her . . .

"Why are you smiling?"

She shouldn't let her mind wander. She should tell him the rest. "Two generations after the roundup, it became obvious female births outnumbered male ones. Statistics verified men were siring only one male child during their reproductive years."

"Did that lead to enslavement of men for breeding?"

Darq tried not to scowl at him. "Almost. Everything conceivable by science was tried, but the population continued to produce more females then males. With a dwindling population, we didn't have the wealth or manpower to continue as space explorers. And no one wanted to risk the genetic pool by letting men go on long expeditions to explore the cosmos. Then, one day a great saalishani, a wise woman, a seer, dreamed a great angel of J'Hi-inti, one with immense white wings, had visited her because she sought enlightenment for the root cause of the Time of Tears. The angel revealed J'Hi-inti had turned Her back on the Wysotti and doomed them to a slow extinction for what the officers of the *Tolamixi Mu* had done."

"Did the saalishani believe that?"

Darq nodded. "Facts didn't lie. An outcry for repentance and prayers for forgiveness ensued and continues to this day. Yet, the population remained in serious decline." Darq reached down and picked up the glass of water, downing a few swallows to cool and clear her throat. She put the glass back down and eyed Yanti. "Redemption and forgiveness sound lofty, but in truth, J'Hi-inti long ago turned a deaf ear to any Wysotti prayer." Such a depressing comment. Too much remembering going on here. She looked at the starscape.

"Darq," Yanti said, "are your dyn and the other two still outcasts?"

"No. The advent of the Na-ka-tas boosted our world economy and, more than anything else, changed the worldview of us. It took time, but forgiveness led to tolerance, then acceptance, which led to equality. But it's not a perfect world."

"Let me guess—what helped was the Mayahi who developed the automatons, your Na-ka-tas. Right?"

Yanti was so perceptive. She smiled in acknowledgment. "None other. Soon we were doing really well, prospering, back in space. Star-traders, not explorers. Unfortunately, the Doyons attacked. Now we struggle anew to survive them."

Elation lit his dark eyes and a smile brightened his face. "So, we are, in a way, cousins."

She blinked before the connection registered, then chuckled.

"Darq, am I permitted to tell anyone about the Wysotti-Mayan connection?"

Tokoray broke into her thoughts. *Although I concur the Wysotti people have a right to know the Mayans still exist and the planet Terra and its star-colonies thrive, what effect will knowledge of* *our existence have on the people of Terra? Will they curse us? Hate us? Wage war against us?**

Yanti folded his arms across his chest, as if to shield himself from an expected, and unpleasant, reply. "What's your significant other saying?"

"He wonders what effect spreading the word among your people will have on us Wysotti. Will you hate us for what we did to the Mayans?"

"And your opinion is?"

Truth might hurt but secrets always fester. "I think — *cousin* — the truth will liberate us all."

Darq left Yanti, mulling over his parting suggestion that she seek asylum with the Centauri's until her child was born, then leave the baby with caregivers and return to her homeworld. She made Tokoray aware of that. He didn't comment.

Arriving back in her quarters, feeling physically drained from all she'd learned about the Mayans of Earth, she had no doubts now. She wanted to bear the child within her. She would go home, let her people know about the Mayans and the Centauri. Maybe even encourage establishment of diplomatic ties, become allies.

A sense of serenity assailed her. She lay down and soon drifted to sleep. When Darq woke, she found Tokoray parked with his back to the wall. She swung her legs over the side of the bed, yawned loudly, and stretched her arms.

"At last you are awake." Tokoray's tone was one of patience endured too long.

"If you had a problem with the *Ky,* you know you could have roused me."

"It is not about the *Ky.*"

"Then what?"

"Captain Warwick asked me to his ready room for a 'private conversation.' You must understand, Darq, he did not act on orders from the Centauri Fleet High Command. *He made a command decision.*"

Curiosity tinged with dread woke a swarm of gnats in her gut. "Okay, so what did he tell you?"

"He revealed there is considerable unrest and hardship among the various Doyon worlds. Riots and a few rebellions have been squashed. No one is sure what is behind those events or what they may portend."

"And now Warwick is sure it's because the Doyons are at war with us?"

"Affirmative. Warwick said the Centauri have been seeking ways to destabilize the Doyon economy, to tip the balance so the Doyons seek peace, not war, with *all their neighbors.*"

This time more dread then curiosity sent the panic gnats buzzing in her gut. "I take it Warwick thinks we can do something to tip the balance?"

"He is positive we can."

She shook her head. "I am not risking my fighter or my child to satisfy the captain's agenda."

"You have reached an erroneous conclusion."

"How erroneous?"

"We cannot speak of the exact details. I have classified maps and reports Warwick allowed me access to."

Darq felt the neural connection. Up came a star map of the Cypha-wee-ka a section beyond the San Hiphia stars. Six of the planetoids were marked. A dot at the bottom of the map showed that the Doyons had drilled into those six. The report stated a total of one hundred sixteen large asteroids had been drilled. Darq felt a puzzle-frown crimp her forehead. "Did they find gold?"

"No gold. A billion of a different worth."

"Don't be so cryptic."

"Very well." Tokoray lowered his voice. "The Centauri scanned those asteroids and found rockets had been planted on them."

"Rockets? What for?"

"The Centauri had no clue but, based on where the propulsion rockets were set, the time frame of when they were planted, the rate of speed those asteroids travel at, my conclusion is that the rockets will be fired so those asteroids change direction, increase speed, and hit Wysotti on the eve of the end of our Grand T'un."

The import of that information nearly stopped her heartbeat. "Our world will be destroyed by asteroids, not Doyon bombs?"

"Likely a bit of both."

"What do you mean?"

"Captain Warwick told me the Doyons are gathering an armada in Sector Four, which lies between the Centauri's Outposts Two and Three. The Doyons are not being discreet about the buildup."

"Which has the Centauri on edge. They think they're going to be attacked?"

"Indeed, but I dissuaded the captain of that."

"Why?"

"Because I made a logical extrapolation. The Joiz station was destroyed and The Narrows mined so we could not know about the armada. My calculations verify that once the asteroids are hurled toward the Wysa solar system, The Narrows will be opened, allowing the Doyon armada to attack the *Dujaki*, go on to Talragon Station, and take *Ziital*. It will be a massacre. We must return home and alert the Elpoccalli."

"Is that what Warwick asked you to do? Get me to agree to fly home?"

"No, it is not. I thanked the captain and said I must consult with you on our course of action."

She should be grateful for small favors — and the Na-ka-ta's wisdom. Yet, this news trumped her plans, didn't it? "So much for the idea of asylum and saving my baby."

"When did you decide that?"

"After having a chat with Yanti. In truth, it sounded like a plan. The reality is you and I took an oath of allegiance and have a duty, an obligation, to help our people survive. It's also now imperative the data Captain Warwick imparted to you gets to our fleet. You and that data are now more important than I or my baby."

"I am capable of navigating the *Ky* home. You may safely seek asylum for you and your child."

She shook her head. "I appreciate the sacrifice, but you know as well as I that there's a reason they put Wysotti's at the controls."

"Because the instinct to survive overrules logic."

"Exactly. Now, I don't want to hear another word about asylum. Go tell the captain we'll be heading home sooner if he can speed up the repairs to the *Ky*."

✧ Chapter 23

Eighty-two hours after the *Ky* had settled on the deck of the *Chenault's* shuttle bay, Darq sat in the cockpit, canopy closed and sealed, watching her faceplate light up with screens. Her fighter had been repaired—and refitted. She now had an additional supply of oxygen and Centauri-style keg-round units replaced her four forward guns, their magazines full.

Since she needed to travel swiftly and maintain maximum speed, she'd declined Captain Warwick's offer of additional missiles—and gambled she wouldn't need the few she had left, nor did she want to leave the one DGRBM behind for scrutiny by the Chenault's techs. Her intent was to run fast and hard, not fight.

She glanced at the time. Over two hours ago the *Chenault* had changed course for a cluster of wayward asteroids that had been propelled from the Chepha-wee-ka a few thousand t'uns ago and were now headed for the fringe edges of the Turtledove Nebula. The *Chenault* had done a series of drills, making fast, hard turns and abrupt stops among those asteroids. Warwick said the Doyons had watched the *Chenault* do such drills before and would think nothing of them. But there had been one clandestine maneuver—the *Ky* had been swiftly towed out of the *Chenault* and set down under the overhang of a stratified ledge on a peanut-shaped asteroid. On a return flyby, the tow vehicle was picked up by the *Chenault*. When the drills concluded, the *Chenault* returned to its patrol route.

With the asteroid the *Ky* rode on nearing the Turtledove Nebula's outer edge, she cued up her flight plan.

Zukaltay's drum revved up, the beat soft at the back of Darq's mind, as if each pat counted the seconds, tallied the minutes to fill the silence of helmet, cockpit, and space.

Tokoray's voice came over the neural link. *Darq, in all the preparations to launch us homeward, we have not discussed the Ippera and our original mission.*

There were too many other things to think about. With what we now know, getting home overrides hunting down the Ippera. Besides, there's a good chance it didn't survive the mini-nova.

We survived. The Ippera might have.

I'm hoping it didn't. She checked two successive screens. One green light remained amber. *I wonder what's taking the Chenault so long.*

I will inquire. Before he could connect with the Chenault's control center, a bleep sounded, and over the cockpit comlink came a male voice. "KY 52, this is Con One. Countdown begins on my mark. Three, two, one— Mark."

The amber light changed to green. "Affirmative, Con One. Countdown begun." The tiny box at the lower right of her faceplate began winking down six hours thirty six to Alpha San Hiphia at full burn.

Warrick's voice came over her com. "May fair winds take you safely home."

"Thank you, Captain. Adovee."

"Adovee, Darq, and to you, too, Tokoray."

"Thank you, Captain," Tokoray replied. "Adovee."

On Darq's screens, the Chenault engaged its star-drive engines and headed on a course for Outpost One which lay along the Centauri's side of the Neutral Zone separating them from the Doyons. At the appointed time, the Chenault would launch a drone into the dust cloud. Two hours later, the drone would send an intermittent, static-laced Pytak fighter's signal homeward to alert the Wysotti that it headed for a young star and would be destroyed. The signal bore the Ky's ID code.

Darq felt relaxed and optimistic. The drone was the main course for the Doyons to feast on—and choke. Provided, of course, luck rode the Ky's wings. The drone's purpose was to entice the two Doyon destroyers, the Akeavosso and the Bekrakaun, which the *Chenault* had identified, to turn around and leave their current search areas to seek what might be a better prize—the *Ky*, its pilot and copilot. It would take the two Doyon ships five or six hours to get past the Turtledove's leg and find the inlet where the drone traveled. At that point, the Doyons long-range scanners would not be privy to the *Ky* streaking full-bore for the safety of the Chepha-wee-ka.

Unease sobered Darq. Getting to the Chepha-wee-ka was the easy part. The hard part came when she arrived at the asteroids and had to choose how to get to the other side of them. The preferred plan was to find the Grier passageway the *Chenault*'s captain had mapped through the asteroids. However, two other options were available. One was to go over the asteroids, thus exposing herself to every Doyon sensor aimed that direction and doubling the time to get home. The other choice was to go under the asteroids. Under offered better protection but doubled the time getting home. And, of course, the main concern was whether or not she would have enough oxygen despite the extra tanks and cleaning units. The only boon was she had enough doige dust to make it if she didn't run into Doyons.

A signal shattered the silence of the cockpit. Her faceplate lit up with preflight engine ignition checklists. Then came Tokoray's "*Chenault* signal indicates all scans clear. We are good to go."

As quickly as she could, Darq got the *Ky* off the asteroid and with a swath of black dust as a shield, she headed for the darkest dustbin, hugging the swirling mass, and steering clear of a pulsar's emissions that would fry her equipment. Hours later, on time and vectors, her screens showed the backside of the star Alpha San Hiphia dead ahead.

A green square with a black dot winked, morphed into a bar where the black at the left edge spiked one third of the way across, then faded back to the left. "Tokoray, isn't the signal a bit loud?"

"Checking—it is what was agreed on and sufficient to catch the Doyons' attention."

Pity she couldn't see if the Doyons were taking the bait. The two Doyon battleships were on the other side of the morass from her. So if things were proceeding according to plan, why worry? Her hands became cold and clammy holding the *Ky* steady.

She'd been in worse spots—but not with a baby inside her. She had the urge to pull a hand back, to touch her belly, to reassure herself her baby was safe. Stupid thought. The fetus was too tiny to feel through her stomach let alone through layers of flightsuit. The baby was fine.

D'ktr Fulton had even seen to it that the baby had an extra layer of protection from radiation in the form of a specially designed powder-blue union suit. Although curious how the one-piece garment had come to be called a union suit, Darq didn't bother asking. She just put the garment on, wearing it over her leechsuit. Trouble was, with the two garments under her flightsuit, she felt fat.

Fat? Where had such an idiot thought come from? The extra layer did not impede her ability to fly, which was the important thing.

Another blip appeared on the nav-screen. Beta San Hiphia stood off to the left of Alpha San Hiphia, the tail pulling matter into the little star. The flight plan called for her to fly from right to left, going above the connection stream, and use the alpha star to generate a slingshot effect to boost her homeward. That meant getting close to the star. Very close.

D'ktr Fulton's warnings echoed—not only was the baby at high risk, but there could also be severe damage to Darq's nanobots and her neural net. Above all, there must be no close encounters with solar prominences.

"Darq? Do you propose to run us through that mess?"

Seeing the clawing paw of black, boulder-laden dust zooming ever larger, she swung the *Ky* to the wispy area at the lower left. Starshine and shitfire, she shouldn't let herself get distracted. Distracted got you killed.

The drone's signal bar on her faceplate spiked again, going nearly halfway.

"Before you ask," Tokoray said, "that was the correct signal."

"Fine. Keep passive recon engaged."

"Affirmative. All remains clear."

After nearly a dozen signals registered, a blip appeared on the left side of her nav-screen. "Tokoray, is that an S O?"

"Affirmative. Sinister object configuration identified. A Grier explorer. Likely the one Captain Warwick mentioned."

She recalled the briefing about ships in the area, which amounted to one. A month prior, a small Grier vessel had gone into the nebula after diamonds being burped by a gas giant. Easy riches if one could catch them and didn't get caught by Doyons or swallowed up by any of a dozen dangers inside the nebula.

"Odd." Tokoray's voice mirrored his bafflement.

She checked the movement on her nav-screen. "What's odd?"

"The Grier vessel started forward, turned to port, then turned to port again for an equal distance, and then serpentined through what appears to be a less dense gas-dust area. Interesting. The vessel is now on an intercept course for the drone."

"If you were a Grier, would you pass up a Wysotti fighter in distress, one that could be claimed for a reward?"

"A foolish Grier if he desires to claim the *Ky*."

"Greed is greed." Or was it? She drew up various screens but couldn't locate any diamond-burping gas giant nearby. What if the Grier had been salvaging something else? No. Couldn't be.

She linked to Tokoray's wide-screen tactical board, magnifying the location of where the Grier vessel had first appeared and its erratic course. She then pulled up the data from her dogfight with the *Ippera* and the mini-nova event. What the results implied, silenced her mind and made her catch her breath.

Tokoray's voice brought her out of her stupor. "Okay, Darq, I agree with your assumption that the Grier vessel may have been inside another vessel, but the likelihood that vessel was the *Ippera* — or what's left of the *Ippera* — is remote. More than likely the Griers were mining an asteroid or planetoid in all that dust."

There might be another explanation. "What if some of the *Ippera's* crew were left behind, and they ambushed the Griers when they boarded to salvage it? Once the Doyons picked up the drone's signal, they might have decided to use the Grier ship to get to the *Ky*, offering assistance only to capture us?"

"We are not there. The drone is."

"You know what I mean. Give me the ETA to the *Ippera* or whatever it is the Grier's launched from." She slipped the *Ky* sideways between two slivers of dense dust illuminated from within by faint starlight.

"Darq, ETA is one hour thirty."

She righted the ship and continued flying, all the while waiting for Tokoray to reveal what lay beyond the looming quagmire of dust hiding meteors and more than a few hefty asteroids. Ten minutes to target and she still had a wall of pitch black dust ahead. "Yoi, Tokoray, I hate to ask, but have you got any readouts on what's ahead?"

"Negative."

She waited until the last moment to alter course, to slow and glide downward.

"You are not going through?" Tokoray's voice seemed awed.

"It's safer to sneak up from below." Minutes later, she held her breath, felt her heart thunder in her ears, and, with gentle fingers on the guidance balls under her hands, nudged the nose of the *Ky* up. The nose sensors winked the view ahead — the bow of the *Ippera*. The reflective light from a star deeply imbedded in the dust on the other side of the *Ippera* gave Darq a silhouetted view of the destroyer, from the top to the horizontal engines on either side.

She let the *Ky*'s inertial drift take her forward. With every second, her heart thundered and every nerve tingled. It was almost like that night at the Ly-quetzel Outpost . . . She whispered over the neural net, *It looks dead, but you never know.**

I concur. Why are you whispering?

Sorry. Up close like this it's like looking death in the face.

The destroyer is a machine, not the phantom Death is purported to be.

That assessment didn't help.

Darq, passive sweeps completed. The ship does not emit any distress signals, nor are there any machinery noises, or life form signatures.

It still may be a trap. It's said that if Griers go aboard a ship in distress, they'll kill the crew and claim salvage rights. Or it might be the other way around, the Doyons killed the Griers and took their ship.

Darq accessed Tokoray's scanned data, her gaze flicking from one readout to another on her faceplate. The *Ippera*'s engines were intact but offline. No running lights on the outside. All viewport shielding was battened down.

Darq, Tokoray said. *Look at the hull radiation levels.*

She cued the screen. Brilliant reds mixed and tapered into yellows showed extreme radiation levels had penetrated the stern areas of the ship and the edges of both engine output funnels. The radiation went more than a quarter of the way forward, contaminating all decks it had reached. *The mini-nova dumped a lot of toxic garbage on her.*

Enough to kill the crew if they hadn't evacuated.

She switched to an exterior view of the *Ippera* and checked the vacant egg-shaped, deeply shadowed holes. Scans indicated all escape pods had launched. The crew had bailed, but had all of them left?

Darq, why do you hesitate to launch our remaining DGRBM into the Ippera and destroy it?

Why did she hesitate? Because something didn't feel right. *My gut says something's wrong.*

Scans do not indicate life forms or danger from any engine overload.

Maybe that's what bothers me. There isn't any clear and present danger. Remember Warwick showing us the telemetry after the mini-nova event?

Affirmative.

And didn't the Ippera drift for a while toward a cluster of stars imbedded in an arm of the nebula?

A tone of awe skimmed in Tokoray's voice. *Then the Ippera swerved in a slow arch, turning away from the danger. It spiraled, making smaller and smaller spirals until it vanished into the black ash of the nebula and contact was lost.*

Exactly.

Tokoray's voice changed pitch, no-nonsense, robotically factual. *The effects generated by currents and gravity from the newly forming star nearest the Ippera are consistent with forcing the ship to spiral.*

What if the Ippera had someone aboard, like the Grier, trying to save the ship for salvage and steering it to safety?

So, what do you want to do, Darq? And do not tell me you want to go inside and look around to make sure we don't kill any Griers. We do not have the time.

She stifled a chuckle. *Wrong. We have time. We can't emerge from this nebula until the Doyons are too far away to see us or, if their spy-stations detect us, too far away to be able to stop us from slingshotting home. What does it matter if we lay over here or at the rim?* *

Safety for one.

Okay, so it's risky, but my gut says we should take a peek inside that ship.

What about your baby? What if the Ippera is a ruse and there are Doyons – or Griers – hiding inside?

All the more reason to look and verify what's going on. But you're right, my baby is a factor. Another consideration is that we can't use our missiles to destroy the Ippera. Should wreckage be found containing Wysotti missile fragments – you do remember we never hit the damn ship hard enough with any of ours – the Doyons will suspect we are not dead. And, my dear Na-ka-ta, it is still a very, very long way home. I don't want the entire Doyon armada on the hunt for us.

What do you propose?

The Ippera's a warship with an arsenal of weaponry and damaged engines. We look around, rig something, make it look like it accidentally blew apart.

✧ Chapter 24

Fear turned the soul-energy within Zukaltay cold. She forced herself to continue peering down, through the Turtledove Nebula to where Darq steered the *Ky* up to the bow of the *Ippera*. The *Ky* slipped beneath the forward decks, skimming lower and lower along the hull, seeking an entryway. "Oh, no, no, no, please, Darq, don't go there. Think of the baby. Think about Atlatl. Go home, go home!"

"She cannot hear you, Zukaltay." Adrada faced her, the purpling of his great gold wings glinting with blue light from the starry emissions beyond a veil of dust. He stretched out his hand. "Come, we must go. The finale awaits."

"What finale?"

"You are to witness the moment of truth."

"I've witnessed a helluva lot of truths of late. Darq pregnant, the Centauri, the Mayans. What new revelations are there?"

His face and demeanor revealed nothing. "Come."

Resigned to his silence, she went to him, drum in hand. As comforting as it was to know Darq was pregnant with a boy child, and being privileged to learn more about the Mayans and that Terra had not been destroyed, it was no comfort whatsoever witnessing Darq take a detour.

That detour could cost Darq, and her child, their lives. Why would Darq place duty above her unborn child's life? Zukaltay wanted to pound her drum and drive Darq mad enough to reconsider, but she couldn't. She had to go with Adrada.

The archangel spread his wings and, in a flash of angel glow, swept her away to re-emerge inside a semidark chamber where black and matte-silver equipment filled every centimeter of the walls. In the center of the room, poised on a wide pedestal sat a disk-tabletop with many rings. In the middle of the disk was a gold bust.

Knowing yet wanting confirmation, she whispered, "Is that him? Is that Ippera?"

"It is," Adrada replied. "There is no need to whisper. Konoris Ippera cannot hear us or see us. Do not mind the crickets. It is Doyon music. Classical. He likes the old masters."

She looked about. Crickets? Then she heard the faint chirps. That was music? She met Adrada's gaze. "Will Darq make it this far?"

"She has already found the portal the Griers left open. Her instruments have verified no life forms await within and scans have shown the netted piles and pallets of scavenged items the Griers left. She has deduced the Griers will come back, provided, of course, that the Doyon destroyers don't find them first."

"So we wait and see?"

Adrada nodded. "It won't be long."

That was not much consolation. With mounting anxiety threatening to become a full-blown swoon, Zukaltay clutched her drum with trembling, noncorporeal hands.

In the weightlessness of the *Ippera*'s small shuttle bay, a rod gun in hand and her spacer's boots keeping her feet on the grate decking, Darq flashed her helmet light on the missile doors beneath the parked *Ky*. Anxious seconds later, the doors parted.

A whisking sound alerted her to the ramp lowering, followed by the barely audible hum of the MIM units on Tokoray's wheelbase allowing him to trundle down the ramp. Once on the decking, Tokoray's faceplate lit and the ribbon lines of his scanners winked rapidly, seeking environmental—and other—dangers. Attached to each forearm were his ML5 energy weapons. Tiny lights indicated a setting for rapid-fire bursts, enough power to overkill any Doyon—or a Grier.

"All clear," he said through the comlink. He dropped his flippers, she mounted, and as soon as she was ensconced in his arms, Tokoray sped forward at a cautionary speed. He stopped before the airlock doors. It took an anxious minute of tinkering before he could insert his index-finger jack and gain entry. Moving forward in the silence, his wheels seemed to thrum twice as loud over the grate decking.

And why did the ship have a modest level of gravity? A moment later, just inside a doorway, she noticed a jury-rigged, Grier-style grav unit's lights twinkling that it was at work. Why had it been left on? Had the Griers left in a hurry? Or didn't they expect to be gone long?

As Tokoray proceeded, passing a set of three open doorways, their interiors pitch black, a shiver of unease cascaded through Darq along with the feeling of being a fly walking the silk of a spider's web. Hyperaware and alert, she checked her faceplate readouts. All indicated a breathable atmosphere free of microbial threats to her life form. Feeling it would be best to conserve oxygen and her suit's power, she triggered her faceplate to slide up into her helmet. The breaths of cold, crisp air she inhaled were welcome, but the air seemed ultra-fresh. Without power, how could the destroyer maintain air circulation? Likely the Griers had rigged something . . .

And the quiet. It bordered on eerie.

Looking about, she spotted an access panel. *Tokoray, stop at the panel ahead. Plug in and figure out how much breathable air I have and how far it extends. Then locate the nearest ammo locker or bay.*

Tokoray plugged in and immediately pulled out his jack. *No power. There is a corridor junction ahead and what looks like a wall com-center.* He wheeled ahead, stopped, and plugged in. The oblong charcoal-gray unit winked to life long enough to show the deck layout and a large bay. *No info on air quality.*

Okay, proceed.

Arriving at the bay doors, Darq stared, appalled at the torch marks. *Looks like the Grier wanted in real bad but didn't get through.*

Tokoray plugged into the wall control. *The good news is this is indeed an ammo bay.*

And the bad news is the Griers got the door open and cleaned out the bay?

No, they did not. These doors open only when activated from a control center on the bridge.

Then let's find a lift and get to the bridge.

I doubt any lifts work.

Think again. The Griers were here. They installed gravity and air cleaners. I'll bet a bowl of maize there is one lift that's operational.

What if we cannot access the bridge's control?

Won't know until we get there. Now truck on. This place gives me the creeps. The sooner we are out of here, the better.

Tokoray located a working lift and, using Grier language, gained access, entered, and sent the lift up to the bridge.

Tokoray, when we get to the bridge, don't let the doors open automatically. I don't want to find any nasty Grier or Doyon surprises.

Affirmative.

Darq counted thirteen decks before they came to the bridge. She took a firmer grip on her rodgun, setting the trigger to rapid fire and turned on her wrist light. Its beam blazed onto the center seam of the lift doors. *Okay, open the doors.*

Tokoray raised his left arm's ML5 at the door.

With each passing second, an iron band of fear tightened about her chest.

With a soft shush, the doors broke apart, moving slowly, revealing blackness.

Darq swept her wrist-light into the darkness, revealing a deserted, silent bridge. Here and there, small databoards floated and ricocheted off the ceiling.

No gravity. Figured.

She let out a sigh of relief. Panning her light a second time across the deck, she squinted to identify the various workstations where computers screens and monitors lined the semicircular bridge walls. Near the rail marking the division between the workstations and the inner command center, several empty task chair seats slowly swiveled. Yet, nothing displayed a live screen or lights. The only sounds came from the swiveling seats and the quiet hum of Tokoray's wheelbase motors.

Tokoray, let me off. You go right, to the other side of the bridge, and look for that bay control. I'll go left. We'll meet in the middle.

Affirmative.

He released his hold and she stepped off, her spacer's boots keeping her deckbound in the weightlessness. When she arrived at the station in front of the navigation console, the deck's lights came on — and so did gravity. She dodged a falling databoard. Heart pounding with the fear of being killed or captured, Darq spun about, rodgun at the ready, and listened, straining, searching for where an attack might come from.

"It is all right, Darq," Tokoray said. "I found the grav controls."

"Shitfire! You could have warned me." She lowered her rodgun and waited for her fright to dissipate.

"My apologies. I have also found the deck layouts. In particular, the scorched bay doors we discovered. I do not know if I can break the code, but I am working on it."

She eyed the finger he'd plugged into a Grier style universal jack mounted on the console. "I take it the Griers were trying to break said codes?"

"Affirmative, but they did not succeed. Since they do not have my extensive abilities, and this is an encrypted code, quite sophisticated, it will be a challenge to decode."

She looked over the stations and made her way to the command center's tactical table, it's edges sporting green touch keys with white graphics. "I can't make heads or tails of these symbols." She touched a key with a diamond-like marking.

Up popped a holograph from the tabletop. She jerked back, then swore under her breath.

"I would advise caution before you push any buttons," Tokoray said.

"Wysotti women are curious creatures."

"Yes, I know, but you, Darq, seem particularly so."

"Is that a compliment or a complaint?"

"Neither. It is a fact."

"You making any progress?"

"Some."

She looked at the holograph above the table of a two-dimensional array of lines intersecting lines. She pressed the next green key. The current screen winked off and another appeared. This one, a star map of San Hiphia, the nebula, and the asteroid belt. No plot lines. No ship placement dots. Just a map of the stars.

One by one she pushed buttons. One by one images appeared. When she pushed the last key, a holograph with rows and rows of little squares, filled the screen. "Tokoray, what do you make of these?"

"Inconsequential. I broke the code. We have access to the bay door. Let's go." Tokoray's wheels revved, turning him. "We can—"

His cut-off sentence alarmed her. She turned, rodgun at the ready, damning herself for not paying attention and letting her curiosity get her into deep shit.

Tokoray stood, his back to her, focusing on a spot on the wall that was two meters from the lift's doorjamb.

The lift doors remained closed. No lights indicated they would open. No Doyon or Grier stood anywhere. No system had activated. Nothing.

"Shitfire, Tokoray, you scared me again. What's so fascinating?"

"Someone has been trying to burn a unit off that wall."

She went to him and studied the long, thin, burned-black panel on the wall. It didn't look melted or even damaged.

"Tokoray," Darq said in a low voice, "what's it made of that it can withstand such heat?"

"I do not know. This is, after all, the newest Doyon ship. One purportedly filled with innovative, hi-tech equipment."

She heard the tone of his words. "You say that sarcastically. Why?"

"Because my sensors are giving me such odd feedback. This is a false front." He pointed to the expanse of wall between the two bridge lifts.

"Lifts are lifts and bridges often have more than one."

"True. But these equipment panels go only twenty centimeters deep. They are devoid of circuits, except for a small box, likely a power pack, attached to the light circuits. All of this giving the impression of comtars at work."

"Why would the Doyons want the crew to think these are working units?" The answer raced to mind and she blurted out, "Unless they wanted to hide something behind them. But what? And where's the real access panel?"

"I do not know. My sensors have not located anything that looks like a door control except for this, which is blackened. *Where would you hide it?*"

"Why are you asking me?"

"Because Wysotti women are known as clever and secretive. Besides, your instincts are far sharper than my logic boards."

Darq took in a long, cool breath. "Right. Okay, if I wanted to hide something, I'd hide it in plain sight." She went to the middle of the wall, studying the units, looking for anything out of the ordinary. Then she saw a panel with dozens of horizontal and vertical seams. Those seams reminded her of Zukaltay's rosewood puzzle box—and other puzzle boxes she'd played with as a kid. What if . . . She put her rodgun back into its keeper. Beginning at the bottom edge of the seams, she pushed upwards, then sideways, first right and then left, before pushing down. With her last push, the seam parted and slid over, revealing the recessed edge of the panel next to it.

Tokoray stated the obvious, "Nothing appears to have opened."

"I think we have to move more pieces." By trial and error, she moved six panels. When the seventh yielded, she found a slender green bar. "What do you think, Tokoray? Push, pull, or slide?"

"You are asking for my opinion?"

"Why not?" She rested her hand on the green bar. "Guess. Just guess."

"Turn."

"Didn't think of that. Okay, clockwise or counterclockwise?"

"Counter."

She turned the bar counterclockwise. The bar swiveled easily, stopping when it reached an upright position. The hydraulic whoosh of seals ensued. The fake wall rumbled, then split apart horizontally, the upper section lifting and the lower one dropping into a floor pocket.

Darq stared at another wall, a pitch-black barrier.

Half-relieved and half-peeved, Darq commanded, "Scan this." Curiosity tempered her anxiety. Which wasn't good. Fear kept a person alive, curiosity often got one killed.

"Darq, I detect neither control nor seam."

"How thick is it?"

"I cannot determine that. None of my sensors will penetrate irziconium."

Using the ultra-polymerized composite was a given for the hulls of anything seeing duty in space, especially starships and starfighters. But why put that material inside a ship? "Are you sure this is irziconium?"

"Affirmative. I ran the analysis twice."

"Something really important must be behind this."

She took her rodgun in hand.

"Your rodgun will not affect the barrier."

"Don't be ridiculous. The gun's for protection should the door open unexpectedly, like what if this is a safe room for the ship's top officers? I really don't want to come face to face with trapped Doyons with weapons primed to blast me when I knock."

"You are going to knock?"

"Got a better way of hearing how solid this thing is?"

"No, but I will do the knocking. After all, I have weapons, which are fifty times more powerful than your rodgun, and I am built for protection, as well as assault. By the way, if there is a firefight, you must promise to save yourself and escape down the lift. Once you have flown the Ky into space, issue my self-destruct."

"Don't jump to conclusions. Let's see what happens."

"Darq." His stern tone left no doubt he was adamant. "Promise me."

"Okay, okay. I promise." She moved back to the lift and opened the door. Just in case she did have to exit pronto, she crouched down and aimed her rodgun at the center of the black barrier.

She caught the blink of the light on his left ML5, the setting switching to higher power.

"On the count of three." Tokoray lifted his other arm and extended the heel of his hand. "Mark, one two three." He banged on the door once, the sound a deep, dull thud. He knocked a second time. Same result. "It is a solid barrier. Next idea."

Darq stood up and stared at the wall. No ideas came to mind.

A rumbling was followed by the barrier moving aside, left to right, and light from the bridge spilling in a meter.

No Doyons rushed out.

No weapons fired.

No voices called out from the darkness within.

Nerves strung tight, terror cobwebbing in her throat and half-choking her, Darq went forward with her weapon ready. The chamber's lighting brightened. Once at Tokoray's side, she found black and matte-gray equipment lining the chamber's walls. At the center dais, a pedestal supported a multi-ringed disk. Her gazed settled on the backside of the gold bust of a Doyon that occupied the center of the disk.

A wide inner ring moved on the disk, bringing the bust around.

She held her weapon steady. Out of the corner of her eye, she spotted the green, glowing light on Tokoray's ML5. He'd reset the unit to impact power. A single blast could put a sizeable hole in a bulkhead, one big enough for him to walk through.

She turned her attention to the face of the Doyon coming into view. Her gaze locked onto the welted scar, one that began at the temple and went back to the left ear-hole. A frigid, soul-deep awareness and dread seeped through her.

The bust stopped moving. Tiny lights winked on one section of the innermost ring at the base of the bust.

The bust's features included a snubbed-nosed snout with three breathing holes, each a bit off-center. A black speaker bar separated the upper and lower lips, and two black optical lenses stood for eyes. Those eyes seemed to stare at her. A guttural male

Doyon voice with a metallic twang said in perfect Wysotti, "Why are you standing there? Fire. Blast away. Destroy your enemy."

She went to push the trigger on her rodgun, but stopped herself. Why would a Doyon encourage someone to kill him without putting up a struggle?

Movement at the corner of her eyes registered. Tokoray was taking aim. "No, Tokoray! Don't oblige him."

"Why not?" Tokoray replied. "He is the enemy."

"And," the voice said, "is it not the duty of a Wysotti Na-ka-ta to destroy Doyons?"

Darq scoffed. "Only when in combat, and this isn't a combat situation. Besides, you're awfully eager to die, so I'm thinking I shoot you and this chamber self-destructs."

The voice lowered its tone. "Nothing could be further from the truth."

"Since when is a Doyon truthful?"

"An officer must be."

So the voice belonged to an officer, but where was his body? Why this bust-machine thing? Was it a new kind of robot? "Someone went to an awful lot of trouble to put a robot in control of this ship."

"I am not a robot!" Bitterness and anger trembled in the voice. "I am Konuris Ba'dawl Ippera, Tor of Longbao, Admirid d'Coman, late of the Fourth F'brig Space Fleet. *I am your enemy!*"

Shaken by his name and his tirade, Darq leveled her gaze to the scar at the bust's temple. Memories flooded of the Ly-quetzel Outpost, of standing on the rubble, of letting fly the slingshot. Her vision blurred, white noise sizzled in her ears. Her heart thudded against her ribs.

"Darq?" Tokoray said. "Darq! What is wrong?"

She gulped in a breath and found strength.

"Darq?" Ippera said. "You are Darq — *The Raven!*"

She nodded and her mind raced. This was the voice she'd heard counting down the minutes over the booming loudspeakers at Ly-quetzel. The voice of Ippera the butcher. Only this time, she held a better weapon than a slingshot. She could kill him with her rodgun. She went to press the trigger, but the thought flitted that she would only be killing a statue and that stayed her finger. "They recreated you?"

Disgust permeated every word Ippera uttered. "Never! Inside this bust is my living brain. Me. Admirid Ippera. *Look closely — you scarred me on Ly-quetzal.*"

She looked and remembered her aim back then. "I intended to kill you."

His soft reverberating chuckle erupted but soon tapered off. "You have been the bane of my existence for many t'uns. I rejoiced when they told me that, during our assault on the Joiz station, you had self-destructed and taken the coward's way out of this life."

"I'm no coward."

"Then why not shoot your enemy? Why not kill me now?"

"I don't trust you."

"But you trust your instincts, do you not?"

She did trust her instincts and right now every instinct-alarm blared something was amiss. She didn't reply.

"You know, Qtl-shi Darq," Ippera said, "I was astounded when two Pytak fighters streaked out of the nebula and attacked the *Akeavosso.* I cheered when the *Bekrakaun's* batteries blasted your partner's fighter. But however did you manage to enter Doyon space unseen?"

He would mention Jaqui, dear Chance . . . Darq fought for control of herself and for a few seconds to figure out what was going on. She gripped the reins of her emotions tightly. "That's classified."

"Yes, I imagine it would be, but I had to ask. Duty and curiosity, you know." He paused, then said, "I truly hoped you had been killed by the mini-nova."

"Likewise." Darq watched closely but observed no response, no movement of his eye-lenses. Those eyes just stared, which, as the silence lengthened, became unnerving.

"I cannot understand," Ippera said, "if you are extremely lucky or highly favored by Sunatas." No tells echoed in his voice.

"I doubt your war god approves of me or any Wysotti. As for luck, it is as you make it." She let the thought burn into her smile and said for effect, "I see you've finally been beheaded, or did they just pickle your entire body and leave your head for posterity?"

Anger and insult ravaged his voice. "Yes, I have been beheaded! And yes, I now wear a slave's collar and, by the war god's ass, my brain has been encased in gold. Cold, icy gold!"

She glanced at the neckpiece anchoring him to the tabletop. "From the look of it, that's a rather fancy collar."

"Pure gold—" His abrupt stop had her staring into his black lens-eyes. His voice shifted to one of entreaty. "Qtl-shi Darq, take the gold. You will be rich. The gold can be yours with a mere pull of the trigger." More softly he said, "Kill me."

Her finger went for the trigger. Every instinct clanged louder than a dozen DLE horns asking why was he so eager to die?

A collar was a collar, a slave a slave. Or maybe not. What if— "Do you control this entire ship?"

"Officially I am the ship's supreme commander. Such rank should give me absolute control over every aspect of this ship. Unfortunately, I can only access what they permit me to access."

How interesting. Was he telling the truth or a lie? Truth. But maybe not the whole truth? "They don't trust you? Or don't the connections function as well as they hoped?"

He laughed, yet deep in the laughter burned madness.

Madman or not, Ippera deserved to die. Her finger trembled over the trigger refusing to fire the rodgun. She wanted to kill him. Needed to kill him.

"Clever, qtl-shi, clever!" His laughter vanished. "Do you seek confirmation to take back to the E-calli that I have a neural net?"

Starshine and shitfire! The Doyons had developed a neural net. Rattled, she struggled to keep her composure. She needed more details. "You actually have a neural net attached to your brain inside that bust?"

"See for yourself." From one of the panels along the outer rim of the ring about him flared multiple holograph views of his golden bust and what resided inside. Three images flickered, all showing his pale-gray brain with a blue-green mass of tentacles rooted deep into the tissues. Each image turned, providing a view of the various sections of the brain.

"Duly noted, you have a brain." Darq replied. *Tokoray, are you getting this?*

Affirmative.

"Excuse me," Ippera said, "it is impolite to use telepathy in a superior officer's presence."

He wasn't superior, no Doyon was, but he did have rank. Another round of unease attacked Darq, and she took care with her tone. "What makes you think my Na-ka-ta and I were conversing?"

"Static across my exterior neural sensors. It created a quivering sensation at the base of my non-existent crest ridge."

Tokoray spoke quickly. *I'm changing our link frequency. Our conversations will be private.* A whisper of a click made it over her neural net. *I am confident he cannot read us now.*

Trying not to stare anew at the scar she had given him at Ly-quetzel, Darq eyed the gold mask wishing something would move to let her know what Ippera was up to.

"Interesting," Ippera muttered, then said, "No more static. I wonder why?"

She shrugged. Let him wonder.

Silence prevailed.

"Well, ask me," Ippera said, his tone imploring her to answer.

"Ask you what?"

"A question. I am sure you have a good many questions, so ask one. Don't you want to know where the technology for my neural net came from?"

"Why don't you tell me?"

"From a Wysotti pilot and her Na-ka-ta copilot."

The whooshing shock of that froze Darq's mind, her breath, her heart.

Tokoray responded, saying, "You are lying."

"On the contrary, Na-ka-ta. The pilot and copilot were frozen in space, rescued by a Grier who thought to sell them to us for a fortune. Only it turned out to be his misfortune." Ippera chuckled, the sound ringing with a frost of his madness. "He was made a slave."

Darq's mind began to function once more. "And what of the frozen pilot and copilot?"

"Let us not discuss them."

"You said to ask you questions, so I'm asking."

"I did say that, didn't I." He remained silent for a minute. "Oh, very well, I shall answer. I was told Wysotti commandos raided the facility and fetched them back."

The moment of relief gave way to reality. If Ippera had a neural net— "I take it their rescue came too late, that the Doyons have the knowledge of our neural-net technology?"

"I am proof of that, am I not? But, you can and should—definitely should—destroy the prototype technology, don't you think?"

The eagerness in his voice alarmed her. "I think you're playing some devious mind game. Either that or something's wrong with your neural net and your sanity is questionable."

"I am as sane as I can be. I am not playing any mind games. Definitely none which could be deemed devious. Let me be quite frank and sincere. *I shall be truthful if you will be truthful.*"

How much truth he would tell was anyone's guess, but if he was in a talkative mood, she might get at the truth via a back door in the conversation. She lowered her rodgun but kept a finger at the ready on the ball trigger, just in case. "Deal."

"Let me ease your mind," Ippera said, "I am sane but suicidal."

"Right." Definitely insane.

His voice bellowed, "Don't be a fool! Do I have to spell it out for you?"

"I— I don't understand."

"Look around you. Look!"

She did, and as she did Zukaltay's words came to mind— *To sit in a room without light is to know the darkness of your soul.* Had Ippera been in this chamber's darkness too long? Still, it was best to keep him talking. She returned her gaze to him and used a voice she hoped sounded conversational and not confrontational. "I don't understand how you can be sane but suicidal."

"I am sane!" He paused. "Forgive me, I did not mean to shout. My frustrations got the better of me. I am a prisoner. I am enslaved to serve the kungarike for another fifty t'uns. Considering I've already served seventy-four t'uns, that's—"

"A total of one hundred twenty four t'uns."

"Yes. It's despicable to expect such duty. I would gladly give my life in service, but this—what's been done to me—is slavery!"

"Okay, calm down. I get it."

"Do forgive me. I have been unable to voice such an opinion since my incarceration in this bust." Bitterness sharpened his words. "I am F'brig. Bred and raised to be a loyal, blind and obedient soldier following orders, furthering the goals of the kungarike."

"What changed?"

"Dying." The bitterness left him. "I died, not in service like the legions of my ancestors, but of a bone-wasting disease that, over the course of more than a t'un, emaciated my body." He paused.

Had he realized he'd said too much?

"On my deathbed," Ippera said, easily, if not flatly, "I had time to reflect on who I was, what I had become, what I had done for the kungarike, and what the kungarike had devolved into."

That sounded like truth. So what had the kungarike devolved into? She recalled Tokoray's private conversation with Captain Warwick about the Doyon's civil unrest.

Ippera spoke, the tone catching her full attention. "Lying there dying, I looked back at my life, evaluated the toll my service took on my wife and children. Three of my sons died for the kungarike."

Sons . . . She touched her left hand to her belly. Inside her grew her son. Could she bear to know he died in service to the E-calli? Moot point. He'd have to grow up first and want to serve, not have to serve like the Doyons. Before she could stop herself, the words were out. "I am sorry for your loss."

"How kind of you to say."

She shrugged. "Losing one child would be hard, but three? I can't imagine losing three."

"I have nine sons. Can you imagine my astonishment when I, who had welcomed death, was not dead? Can you imagine my horror when they told me I would live and serve a minimum of fifty more t'uns? I will outlive my sons. I will see them serve and die for the kungarike. No crueler torture could befall a father."

More truth. *Sane but suicidal* echoed in her mind. "I can understand that. I suppose you considered committing suicide so you would be dead again?"

"I considered it in elaborate detail at times, but unfortunately my predecessor committed suicide. With a loss like that, the architect of this ship's systems could not take any chances with me."

"They installed failsafes?"

"Yes. Into every system and subsystem of this table-top command module as well as throughout this ship—and more."

"How much more?"

"I cannot trigger the ship's self-destruct without the codes of both the captain and a second officer of menotuz or higher rank. Facing the mini-nova event, the crew abandoned ship. There is no one left aboard!"

"Why didn't they set the self-destruct when they left?"

"Caprivi Nuzzi, the ship's official captain, could not find it within himself to do so. He felt it a dishonor to kill me, his friend, his mentor. Since this ship was headed for a protostar, we agreed it was a more glorious way to end my life."

"And to ensure this destroyer didn't ever fall into Wysotti hands?"

"Yes, that too, of course."

She remembered the spiraling maneuvers the Centauri had recorded. "But at the last minute, you decided you wanted to live, and so you took the ship out of harm's way?"

"No! The damn currents shoved me aside. I fought against the tides, but with so much radiation damage and failed systems, little worked. I had the glide angle of a brick, and every attempt proved futile. I could not get this ship caught in a gravitational well to turn it and myself into cosmic dust." He seemed to catch his breath—or was that some pumping unit behind him at work?

Ippera spoke in a hushed tone, as if he feared someone might overhear. "It was as if some force decreed I could not die." He paused. When he spoke again, he was the admirid. "The controls ceased functioning. I drifted. I am at the mercy of the nebula's tides. See for yourself." Holograms erupted from the tabletop showing the life pods breaking free, the mini-nova event, the *Ky* careening off the visuals, and the cockeyed path of the *Ippera* entering a billowing cloud of black dust and gas.

"Some," Ippera said with a hint of contempt, "would call my current existence a miracle."

"I don't believe in miracles" slipped out of her mouth before she could stop herself. In watching the spiraling of the Ippera, the flow of the nebulous currents seemed to be odd. The universe came filled with oddities and the heavens full of hells and purgatories. "Maybe this is fitting punishment for the lives you destroyed." She wished she'd held her tongue.

His chuckle ended with a "Tisk-tisk. We are warriors, soldiers, you and I. Our duty is to do whatever it takes to protect our worlds."

"Protect is one thing, attack and conquer another."

"What about all the Doyons you have murdered, Raven?"

"I'm not a cold-blooded murderer like you. I've killed — in dogfights. Never with malice aforethought." Except — "I take that back. When I faced you at Ly-quetzal, I truly wanted to kill you, with great malice. You on the other hand, have killed the defenseless."

His chuckle held a demented chill that filled her with dread. "Ah, Qtl-shi Darq, Raven, Raven, I have read the intel on you — Princess of the Misted Moon, Warrior Huntress of the Mayahi Dyn." His voice went coldly cruel. "You are blood of the outcast dyns, the blood of the destroyers of a blue-water world for which your god has condemned all your people."

He would throw her heritage back at her. Yet, she must not dignify that or correct him and reveal what she'd learned on the *Chenault*. "Yes, I am blooded to Kukulaan. Many generations removed. That's old history. I am me, Darq. Wysotti. A woman. A wife — " Her hand again went to her belly, but she bit back uttering *a mother*. And how ironic that, like Admirid Ippera, she found herself in a situation where duty to her country and love of family collided.

"Are you not feeling well?" Ippera said, his lenses widening.

"I'm fine."

"Then why do you cradle your belly so? Radiation poisoning?"

She removed her hand and looped the thumb under a flight harness strap.

Something pinged and lights winked on units about the wall opposite her. The lights winked out.

"How very interesting," Ippera said with relishing satisfaction. "You are pregnant."

"You're jumping to conclusions."

"You are lying. I scanned you. You are wearing a third garment, one between your leechsuit and flightsuit. One that does not permit radiation to filter through. I may not have seen the fetus, but I distinctly heard its heartbeat."

"Okay, so I'm pregnant."

"I was under the assumption the Wysotti valued children. So much so that those of the E-calli had surrogates bear their young."

"I didn't know I was pregnant until the Centauri rescued me." Damn her tongue.

"The Centauri captured you? You escaped them?"

"Rescued, not captured. They're all in favor of me taking my baby home."

"Then what are you doing here?"

"A regrettable detour trying to fulfill my original mission."

"Then by all means, do that duty. Fulfill your mission. Kill me. Destroy this vessel. You do realize you will be saving lives, Wysotti lives, and helping end the war between our races, do you not?"

"I do. But I get the feeling this ship is booby-trapped. I kill you, and I die too."

"No. As I told you, they did not trust me. No weapons were installed in this chamber nor on the bridge that reach past my blast door. Have your robot check."

"I am a Na-ka-ta," Tokoray said indignantly.

Ippera replied, "Semantics. No offense meant."

"Tokoray," Darq commanded, "sweep this place for weaponry."

Silent, agonizing seconds passed before Tokoray replied, "No weapons, no explosives."

"Qtl-Shi Darq," Ippera said with all the cunning of a fox with two dead quail at his feet. "As valuable as the Doyons consider me, think of the untold lives you could save over the next fifty t'uns if I were dead—Wysotti lives in particular."

"I think you'll go mad long before this ship can be repaired."

"I cannot go mad."

"Sometimes the insane think they are sane." She had a sinking feeling her words applied to her own sanity.

"I would agree," Ippera replied, "but I am sane enough that I am being blackmailed to continue serving."

Blackmailed? The idea almost made her laugh, but she kept herself in check. "You? Blackmailed?"

"Wosolek, the scientist who recently took over this project, was profoundly more paranoid than his predecessor. He unequivocally let me know if I commit anything remotely resembling suicide, or which could be construed as suicide, he would see to it that my wife and children become slaves. Generations of my families titles and wealth will be striped away. I will not do that to my family. But, if you should, in the line of duty, kill me, well, that isn't suicide, now is it?"

There was logic in that—and a flaw. "Who will survive to tell anyone the difference?"

"Meaning?"

"I'm here to blow this destroyer apart."

"Then destroy away. That will suffice."

"Only I can't let anyone know a Wysotti has been here."

"Meaning?"

"Meaning, Tokoray and I had planned to use your own bombs to blast you apart."

He was silent, but various boards flashed their little lights. "That will work, providing you act quickly enough."

"How quickly?" Damn her curiosity controlling her tongue.

"The currents are—" He flashed a star map up showing the *Ippera* in the nebula. "This is where we are now." A blue dot lit. "Here is where the *Bekrakaun* is, and behind it, the *Akeavosso*."

Her gaze took in the entire star map. "Starshine and shitfire—we're closer to the San Hiphias and clear space than we should be."

Tokoray broke in on the neural net. *It would seem the Bekrakaun is keeping watch for the Ippera as well as guarding the Akeavosso's back.*

I saw that. Had Ippera kept her talking to entrap her? To get her killed by the other two destroyers? She raised her rodgun, taking careful aim for Ippera's black, optical sensor eyes. Her hand shook minutely.

Darq? Tokoray said.

He has to die in order for us to blow this ship apart.

She must do this and get home—go home and become a mother.

Somewhere out of the depths of her mind whispered her own internal voice saying, *Killing in self-defense is one thing, but in cold blood? How will you justify that to yourself, let alone your son when he comes of age to question your duty years?*

Her son . . . Unbidden her free hand settled palm down on her belly. In Wysotti society, information like the death of Ippera at the hands of an ordinary fighter pilot would be public gossip and public record. Fodder for the news media and masses to dwell on for t'uns.

Was she warrior or woman? Was she a cold-blooded killer or a woman who would be a better mother than the one she'd had? Women were meant to be givers and keepers of life. As a warrior, a pilot, she had learned to be a master of death in her Pytak fighter. Yet, by not killing Ippera, wasn't she guilty of dereliction of duty? Was there no other choice?

Kill Ippera. Kill the enemy. The words echoed and the rodgun weighed heavy in her hand.

She went to focus on Ippera's inert eye-rings, to put the blast between his eyes. Instead, she looked at his golden bust.

Beneath that gold resided a semi-lunatic brain wearing a Doyon slave collar. Biofeeds and circuitry chained him to the ship. *A brain. No body.* A desperate-to-die being. Not a warrior. Not an enemy who could fight back.

What about her duty as a mother?

She should save herself, save her baby. There was a time to live and a time to die—a time to love, not kill. Not hate. She lowered her weapon. "I'm a mother-to-be, not a cold-blooded murderer like you." She holstered her rodgun. "Tokoray, let's go." She turned to leave.

"NO!" Ippera yelled with desperation. "*Kill me now.*"

She quickened her pace for the lift. About to clear the blast door, a buzz of static sizzled across the bridge and she halted. Tokoray's treads squelched him to an abrupt stop behind her. Chirps issued, more static, and then silence.

She spun around to face Ippera. "What was that?"

"The *Bekrakaun.*" His voice held the calmness of defeat. "They are trying to communicate with me. The last bleat attempted to turn on my locator beams."

"Did the beams engage?" Darq demanded.

"No. The first thing the Griers did when they came aboard was disable and remove my locator beams. Those were torpedoed into a roiling mass of energy. The *Bekrakaun* cannot find me in this dust-soup. You will remain undetected when you leave."

If the *Bekrakaun* was signaling, that meant— "How far away is the *Bekrakaun*?"

"See for yourself." At the tactical board on the bridge, the hologram of the star map lit up.

Darq went to the tactical board and looked over the viewscreen. The *Bekrakaun* had not moved, but the *Akeavosso* headed back toward the *Bekrakaun* and would soon exit the inlet it had been in.

"Admirid, do you have any long-range scanners that can look down this inlet." She pointed to it. "Is there a signal pinging away anywhere in it?"

The screen zoomed for a wider view. A dot appeared, pulsing a signal. Moving away was another icon.

"What am I looking at?" Ippera's voice came from a speaker at the edge of the tactical board.

"A drone that's supposed to give off a Wysotti distress signal and draw the destroyers to it."

"Looks like the drone is about to collide with a very hot young star and extreme gravity."

"I see that." The drone had somehow gotten caught in a gravity well.

"I take it," Ippera said, "the drone was a ruse to ensure both destroyers think you are dead and not search for you?"

"No, the drone was to draw them away so I could make a run for home—unseen." Now why had she told him that?

"Pity it didn't work. Now both destroyers will be returning to look for evidence of my demise. And the Griers will be returning for their salvage. That moving blue icon is their ship."

She checked the map and the blue dot. The Griers were not of concern, but the Doyons were. *Tokoray, how soon before those destroyers get here?*

Approximately four hours. However, their scanners are now actively looking for the Ippera and will detect us. We have drifted with the Ippera and now require an hour twenty to get to San Hiphia, where we will be out in the open and easily spotted. If we leave immediately, we may have a chance to go undetected.

How long will it take to rig a bomb?

Thirty minutes, give or take, depending on what we find in the armory's bay.

Not enough time. Shitfire, they had to abandon blowing up the *Ippera* if they were to have any chance of making it home. Her gaze drifted to the binary San Hiphia and to the tail coming off Beta San Hiphia. *When will there be another mini-nova event?*

Three or four t'uns from now depending on the incoming amount of matter.

Where was a mini-nova event when you needed one? No help there. What else could work to distract the Doyons?

"Darq," Tokoray said, his voice low. "Perhaps the Admirid is correct, you should kill him so this ship is useless to the Doyons."

The brain might be useless but the ship sure wasn't. *The brain!* "Shitfire, why didn't I realize it before." She looked at Tokoray, who had tilted his head as if wondering what she meant, but he didn't ask for an explanation.

She met his gaze. "If I kill Ippera, it's only a brain. All the Doyons have to do is plop another brain in and patch up the ship. There's nothing to be gained by killing Ippera except revenge. I don't feel the need right now to exact revenge. Okay, I do, but I'm pregnant, and I don't want my conscience haunting me or my kid ever deciding to hate me for murdering an unarmed person. Or thing or whatever Ippera is."

"Your logic is illogical," Tokoray replied.

Ippera's voice came over the tactical board's comlink. "Qtl-shi Darq, you should know destroying this ship will set the kungarike back twenty or thirty t'uns and bankrupt the empire."

Instinct questioned why he divulged such information, but curiosity won out. She left the table and went to the blast door and eyed Ippera. "What are you talking about?"

"On the deck below this, section one, cabin three six seven, you will find a half-meter-long by thirty-centimeter-wide, flat bronze case filled with datarods. Destroy those rods and you insure the kungarike's efforts to build more *Ippera*'s is devastated."

But obviously not ended. "What's the case contain? And if it's so important, why wasn't the case taken when the life pods ejected?"

"The quarters belong to Wosolek."

She remembered the name. "He's the paranoid guy in charge of this project who's blackmailing you?"

"The same. When your people raided and destroyed the Aichi science center, the data for the neural net inside my brain was destroyed, along with the key researchers involved. Wosolek had his own complete copy of the records. *The only complete copy.*"

Talk about paranoid. Maybe all Doyons were paranoid. Yet, how odd that Ippera stressed only one record remained.

"Do you know, Qtl-shi Darq, Wosolek never let that data out of his possession. He toted it with him everywhere he went. He didn't trust the ship's safe, or Caprivi Nuzzi, and I would trust Nuzzi with my life. I did, in fact, on many occasions."

Ippera was getting to something, but what? "Get to the point."

"Very well. I convinced Caprivi Nuzzi that Wosolek, being head of the Ippera Project, should be on hand to witness the war games and enjoy the accolades of my victory in said games. Nuzzi thought it a splendid idea and convinced Wosolek he would be safer on this ship than anywhere else in the kungarike."

Ippera was smart all right. Crafty too. Which didn't bode well for her, did it? She went to leave but a thought struck. She looked back at Ippera. "If Wosolek was so neurotic, why didn't he take the project data with him when he left in a life pod?"

"He never left the ship."

The prideful way Ippera phrased his words unsettled Darq. "Did you kill him, or did Caprivi Nuzzi?"

"The caprivi was tempted to on several occasions, but it was not necessary. There are a few subsystems no one realized had possibilities for, shall I say, other functions. Actually, I had planned the execution for my nemesis, the original project leader. However, as zealous as she was, she remained at Aichi and died of injuries suffered in the raid. By the way, I am grateful to the Wysotti for so thoroughly destroying that R and D facility. I only wish I had been there."

"You're welcome, I think."

"Darq!" Tokoray's warning echoed urgency.

She turned, finding him at the tactical board. "What?"

"The *Bekrakaun* is underway at seventy percent speed. That may give us more time."

She approached the board. "It doesn't change anything." She looked the star map over again. They needed a diversion. She put her hand to her stomach, over the baby as if to protect it. How could she protect her child if she couldn't protect herself? Damn the stars for taking Chance, she needed a wingman!

A wingman . . .

An idea emerged and grew. Over the neural net she sent the idea to Tokoray.

It could work, Tokoray replied, *but can you trust Ippera?*

She shrugged. *Get going, plant whatever explosive or bombs, or jury-rig something, anything that'll destroy this ship and then return to the Ky. And mind the time window. I'll meet you at the Ky. Don't question – get going. That's an order.*

Acknowledged. He sped across the deck to the lift. She headed back to Ippera and stood at the edge of the table in front of him. "Are you still intent on dying?"

"I am. If you wish, I will rotate around and you may fire your weapon to the back of my head."

"Not so fast. It pains me to say it, but I'm about to offer you a hero's death."

✧ Chapter 25

After a few tweaks, Ippera agreed to her plan and guided Darq to restoring bridge functions, activating the officer's lift from the bridge to the shuttle deck where the *Ky* was parked, and reinitializing the engines so they were online. As she worked, Ippera created a telepathic link to Tokoray, one exclusive to a neural net, one his fellow Doyons couldn't detect.

In a way she had to admire the *Ippera*—the ship, not the brain for the ease with which systems worked. When she left the bridge, she stepped into the officer's lift. As the doors closed, she checked the time. She had fifteen minutes to get to the *Ky*. Plenty of time.

Reaching her hand out to press the symbol for the descent to the shuttle bay, a thought wormed to the surface. She hit the button for the next deck down, exited the lift, and stepped into a dark corridor with no gravity. Using her wrist light, she quickly found cabin three six seven. The door opened easily enough into a spacious cubical. She inhaled the stagnant air, which held the faint odor of chicken manure. Opening cupboard doors and drawers didn't reveal a case like the one Ippera had described. She pressed the release to a door, and it opened partway. She shoved the door back into its wall slot and flashed her wrist light into the narrow room. The beam glistened on the dead eyes of a Doyon sitting on a toilet.

She jumped back, heart racing, breath rasping. She calmed herself and looked about the room, avoiding the corpse's eyes, and spied a thin bronze case against the wall near the corpse's calf. A mag-clip kept the case anchored.

It figured the prize would be in some gawd-awful, narrow, hard-to-get-at place. And worse — next to a corpse. An emaciated-looking Doyon corpse.

Alert for any signs of danger and knowing she had to hurry, she squatted and reached under the corpse's floating arm, tripped the switch on the mag-clip, and grab the case by its handle. In doing so, her light flashed on the wall behind the toilet and the lightning crazed lines traversing to the flesh fried to the seat.

A part of her mind interjected that this gave a whole new meaning to the term 'hot seat.'

She shivered with revulsion, then exited with the case. In the other room, she set the case on a workstation top, took out her rodgun, burned off the latch, opened the case, and fired, turning the datarods into vinegar-smelling blobs. She rushed out the door and took the lift down. Stepping out of the lift, she accessed her neural net. *Tokoray, what's your ETA?*

Look behind you. I am en route.

Seeing Tokoray, relief washed over her.

As Tokoray sped along the center of the corridor, he passed the middle door of the trio the Griers had left open. Suddenly a booming recoil sounded from the darkness within. Red-hot, rod-like projections shot out the doorway a half a meter above the floor and slammed into Tokoray's wheelbase and leg shaft before striking the wall. The shots sizzled and rattled on the cold surfaces they struck. In a cacophony of screeching motors and tearing metal, Tokoray careened sideways, spun around, and his left shoulder rammed against the wall. Smoke and fire blazed out the bottom of his wheelbase. Unbalanced, Tokoray's wheelbase tipped. He went backward, falling and crashing onto the decking.

Darq spotted a fire-suppressant tank, sprinted for it, yanked it off the wall, and raced to the Na-ka-ta, ever thankful for the low gravity that let her run in a flightsuit. She rammed herself to a stop and sprayed the area, dousing the wheelbase and what rods lay about.

Over the corridor's comlink came Ippera's "What happened?"

Darq shouted, "Damn Grier booby-trap! Why didn't you warn us?"

Ippera replied indignantly, "Because I did not know about it. Are there others?"

"How should I know?"

"Are you injured?"

"No, but Tokoray is down." She dropped the fire-suppressant tank, stepped gingerly across the debris field, and grabbed Tokoray's harness. It took all her strength to pull him clear. She looked over his mangled wheelbase.

"Darq, go," Tokoray said. "Leave me. Save yourself."

"No way. I am not murdering you, unless of course you've jinxed me, but I think the Griers did the jinxing—on you. Shitfire, how did your sensors miss that trip beam?"

"I do not think it was a trip beam but a motion sensor. According to my database, the Griers have been known to set a motion detector to arm explosives. When the field is crossed a second time, the explosives go off. Be thankful it was me and not you."

Ippera's voice intoned, "ETA to your departure is six minutes. What is your status?"

"Not good, but not hopeless. Tokoray's wheelbase is toast. I'm going to have to drag him to the ship."

"No need," Ippera replied.

"What do you mean?"

"Behind you, left door, a machine shop. Get a grav-cart."

It didn't take long to find a cart, load Tokoray onto it, close her faceplates, activate screens, and go through the airlocks to the *Ky*.

At the *Ky*'s ramp, Tokoray said, "Go, Darq. There are enough handholds and empty missile hangers for me to pull myself into my cockpit."

"Duly noted." As soon as Tokoray cleared the ramp, she triggered the missile bay doors closed. Releasing her boot grippers, she leapt through the low gravity, scrambled along the *Ky*'s wing, and got into her cockpit. Three minutes behind schedule, she took the *Ky* out into space and slipped ahead of the *Ippera*.

As unsettling as it felt to be in front of Ippera's guns, what unsettled her more was her conscience scolding that despite Ippera's sacred oath to follow her plan, and regardless if Ippera were sane or insane and contemplating suicide, she was an o-lo-pii to trust him.

On a sigh, she spoke her heart, *Dear Ji'Hi-inti, let Ippera keep his word and let me get safely home with my baby.*

The comlink crackled. Ippera said, "One min."

She checked the chronometer on her screen—00:59.

"Affirmative. Die well, Admirid." Idiot, why had she spoken to him as if he were a Wysotti warrior?

"I intend to. And Darq, keep the solar winds to your back."

Was that a Doyon adage? Or a reminder? "Affirmative." She lifted her hands off the controls for a moment, stretched her fingers, then reconnected. When the zeros of the countdown winked, a blast of fang-fire sailed overhead, close to the fuselage, and she rammed the *Ky*'s engines to full speed. She ducked and swerved, the *Ippera* staying on her tail, his fire missing her at every turn—as planned—but since she still didn't trust him, she wasn't about to give him a chance to hit her.

Tokoray's voice came over the comlink. "Ippera reports the *Bekrakaun* spotted us and is now coming our way at eighty-five perscent speed. The *Akeavosso* has also increased speed, but they must be severely damaged. They are making half speed. Wait—another incoming message from the Admirid." After a pause, Tokoray said, "We have a third destroyer—in line with Beta San Hiphia, at full throttle, heading this way. Ippera says it's carrying the attaché to the F'brig Space Fleet Overlord Commander—and reporters to witness the war games."

"Someone must have forgotten to tell them about our little skirmish and the mini-nova event." As inane as it sounded to actually want to be seen, the *Ky* must be seen, and the more eyes the better. "Tokoray, are we in full view of the three ships?"

"Only the *Bekrakaun* and the *Akeavosso* will be near enough in ten minutes. Even at full speed, the third vessel won't come into range for twenty two minutes."

Which was a good thing, considering all three Doyon vessels would be on one side of the little sun, unable to see the other side of Alpha San Hiphia, where she intended to be by then.

"Darq," Tokoray said, "make the following course correction and begin the death run."

Death run echoed in her thoughts until she focused on the nav-screen. It was to be Ippera's death run, not hers. With the coordinates locked, her hands nimbly rolled the controls, and she shifted her hips. The INS reacted, helping her bring the *Ky* crisply and swiftly about.

The Ippera fired another round. The fang-fire nipped near her port wingtip. Wings over, she turned and burned, zigzagging away—but she didn't push the engines to max.

Tokoray calmly intoned, *One minute to launch. Changing scans to Alpha San Hiphia.*

Her screens lit with a massive orange ball spewing vibrant fire colors indicating an enormous eruption on the equatorial plain. Two colossal, fiery-hot solar prominences were erupting simultaneously. Megatons of molten star matter spewed nearly two hundred thousand kilometers upward. The spouts' tops joined together to form one towering inferno that crested like a giant tsunami with a shockwave of energy. She ignored the prominence, held course, and headed horizontally across the star.

Tokoray broke into her concentration. "Ippera has allowed us to listen in on the communications between him and the *Bekrakaun*. I can pipe it to you."

"I'm kinda busy." Dodging fang-fire, she yawed the *Ky* then dove and came up. *Ippera,* unshaken, kept the *Ky* in his crosshairs.

She checked her position. The *Ky* had gone a third of the way across the equator. She glanced at the time. "Here we go—five, four, three, two, one." She swung the *Ky*'s nose to tail and fired a pair of missiles, one right behind the other. The first missile hit low on the *Ippera*'s underbelly not doing much damage. The second missile hit its prearranged target, the port engine. The *Ippera* began to careen, then leveled off, losing speed, allowing it to be caught in the sun's gravity. A second explosion ripped the back end of the damaged engine.

A string of high chirps screeched through the cockpit. "What was that?" Darq checked faceplate screens for a calamity, yet the *Ky* felt fine under her.

"That explosion," Tokoray said, "was the insurance I planted. The squawking is Ippera protesting we did not trust him and how foolish to damage his engine like that."

She hit the neural-net com, *Admirid, that engine was supposed to fail. We just guaranteed it.*

Yes, yes, of course. I'm relaying damage reports to the Bekrakaun. *Losing power, being pulled into the star— Listen in.*

A click was followed by a masculine voice with a wheezing quality. "Ippera, my friend, we cannot get to you in time."

Darq, Tokoray said quietly. *Ippera says the voice is Caprivi Ursk.*

In reply, Ippera's voice boomed with resolve. "Nuzzi, I'm throwing everything I have at the Raven before I go down!"

Darq's tactical boards lit up. The *Ippera* now opened gun ports and missile ports, making ready to fire.

Oh, shitfire! Tokoray, he's not supposed to do that.

Not to worry, Tokoray said. *While I was on the bridge, I tweaked his target vectoring systems. They should miss.*

The shots Ippera fired went under the *Ky*. Yet, she had to dodge his next two rounds of fang-fire. He had compensated. And Ippera had way too much ammunition at his disposal.

She looked at the star map and her position. She wasn't past the horizon where the *Bekrakaun*'s scanners couldn't see her race for the Cypha-wee-ka.

A spot ahead on the sun's surface turned a bloody red. A solar prominence shot upwards.

"Double shitfire."

"Darq, what's wrong?"

"Remember when we were in the simulator, when we first met, and I told you about the two simulations I never could beat? Well here comes sim one. The real-life version."

"Don't dwell on past failures, Darq. Think." Tokoray spoke in a steady, resolute tone. "We must get over the horizon, or the Doyons will know we survived and come after us."

"I'm trying. Hard to evade the *Ippera*. The beast sure can fly." She shifted her weight, thankful the INS system's intuitiveness gave her an edge. Her screens lit up with multiple incoming missiles—two copperheads and one big Chelicera. Why had Ippera fired those? Maybe for show? *No, of course not!* He needed to unload weight in order to pull free of the star's gravity and save himself. Shitfire, why did she have to go and trust him?

Crackling fear heightened her senses, enabling her to evade the missiles. A warning flashed. Another came on. Two more. She checked the nav-sys screen, the view of the sun's chromosphere. Ahead loomed the belching inferno of one helluva mass ejection.

Fang-fire whizzed by the *Ky*. She swung to port, banked and swerved.

"Darq," Tokoray said, "the *Ippera's* good engine just winked out."

Ippera's strained voice, half-panicked came over the com. "The magnetic fields are playing havoc with navigation controls. I can't hold her, Nuzzi. Starboard engine failing. Hull temperatures critical."

"Try, Admirid, try." Nuzzi's voice. "Get away from that star!"

In the tense seconds that passed, Darq watched a port battery on the *Ippera* blow out. Ahead of her, the solar flare leapt higher and higher. She flew straight for the column. Every scenario she'd flown in the simulators had never worked. She had to get to the horizon on the other side of that column and out of the range of the *Bekrakaun's* scanners.

Darq, Tokoray said, *as agreed, Ippera has issued the countdown to fire our DGRBM.*

She spun the controls and, when the light went green, fired her missile toward the solar flare. She rose above the missile's trajectory and leveled out.

From the mid-deck battery of the *Ippera* launched six missiles—all running true toward the DGRBM she'd fired. When Ippera's missiles hit the diggerboom, the Doyons would think Ippera had destroyed the *Ky*. At least that was the plan. And from the look of things, Ippera had kept his word. The trick was to veer out of the way of the explosion and not be seen doing it.

Tokoray's voice broke into her thoughts. *Ippera says to stay in his shadow as he goes down. Look at the WSTB.*

His shadow? She eyed the WSTB, astounded at the ninety-two percent chance of success but more astounded that Ippera had offered the opportunity — and ashamed to have doubted the Doyon's integrity, his sincerity about dying.

The *Ippera's* nose rose until the destroyer stood vertically. It seemed to stand motionless, then succumb to the gravitational pull of Alpha San Hiphia and slowly descend toward the star.

In the blink of her eye, Darq realized the *Ippera* had become her shield, blotting out scanner beams so the other Doyon ships couldn't see the *Ky*. Almost like an eclipse.

A bleep sounded. Her attention switched to the warning. Ippera's missiles hit her DGRBM, and it exploded.

A flashing indicator reminded her of the rising prominence ahead.

Shitfire.

Her thoughts hit hyperdrive, and the idea emerged of who said she had to keep to the equator? She had room on either side to angle left or right of the prominence. Why had she never thought of that tactic before?

A quick check of the WSTB confirmed she had plenty of maneuvering room and could remain in Ippera's shadow — but just barely. She shifted her weight. The intuitive navigational systems met her demands. She put the *Ky's* engines past the redlines. About to go over the horizon, she checked the *Ippera's* location. The outer edges of the *Ippera* had begun to flame, but the ship held vertical, continuing to shield her.

Only a little way yet to go—

Ippera's voice came over the com. "U'zan, my son, know that I did not die a withered old man but a true F'brig. Ask Caprivi Nuzzi to tell you everything. Tell Vekka my heart has always been hers." Static sizzled, then "Caprivi Eslatont, do your duty. Inform the F'brig Supreme Command that I, Konuris Ippera, Admirid of the Fourth F'brig Fleet honored my oath as an officer of the kungarike. *I destroyed the enemy and served unto death!*"

The link crackled to silence.

Darq refused to imagine the inferno consuming Ippera. She pushed the *Ky*'s engines for all they were worth, ignoring the heat building in the cockpit, the flaming tinge to her shielding about the *Ky*'s nose and wings, and the ghostly pat of Zukaltay's drum at the back of her mind playing a death dirge.

"We are clear!" Tokoray's euphoric shout startled her. Then more calmly, he said, "We are clear. No active scans. No pursuit. We are clear."

The *Ky* shuddered from the buildup of such speed, and she wondered how long the fighter would tolerate it. She shifted the *Ky*'s nose, slingshotting around the remainder of San Hiphia's girth, going beyond Doyon sensor range. Soon the Cypha-wee-ka came into view on her nav screen. A moment later, she spied the indicators marking the blackest rocks, identifying them as bubbly material, not solid boulders. *Lacy cinders*? Yes. Lacy cinders. She made the course correction.

"You are going under?" Tokoray asked in a normal voice. "That will take us longer to get into range of the *Dujaki*."

"Maybe not. Remember Captain Warwick telling us about the lacy route? The shortcut?"

"I do, but how can we be sure this area is the shortcut?"

"Warwick said there was only one spot of black lace. Are you trying to jinx me with self-doubts?"

"No, but don't murder me for asking."

She grinned, feeling her strained jaw relax and her tight cheeks crinkle. "By starshine and shitfire, Tokoray, we are going home!" The nav-sys hiccupped, and she sobered. She wasn't home yet. Still a long way to go. She steadied the *Ky*. The cranky nav-sys pinged a warning. Moments later she entered the quietness of black lace with three more warning lights on, one for an oxygen tank.

Standing on the bridge of the *Ippera*, Zukaltay watched Admirid Ippera. Chirping music played around him. The ship shuddered. The music grew louder.

With tears heating her eyes, she knelt and patted her drum in a death dirge's cadence. When she came to the refrain, she heard the sweep of wings across the decking and glanced up.

Adrada stood a meter away. "Why the tears, Zukaltay?"

She stopped playing and looked at Ippera. "Because that Doyon, that bastard of bastards, did a good deed, a kindness in his dying." She looked at Adrada. Her voice crazed with a mix of amazement and soul-deep appreciation. "He gave my granddaughter and her baby a chance to live."

Angel light spun brightly beside her, and the Archangel Rafael appeared.

She met his blue-eyed gaze.

"Zukaltay," he said, "I'm here to escort you back."

His great white wings closed about her. Before her view was cut off, she glanced at Adrada, who had transformed himself into Auc-Pon, the mighty Ebon F'brig.

When Rafael's wings opened, she found herself in the Chamber of the Book of Fates, standing near J'Hi-inti, who once again appeared as a saalishani, but dressed in a gold–and–white monk's robe. J'Hi-inti wrote in the book. Rafael vanished without a word.

Curiosity gouged deep. Would the curse be lifted? Would her people be allowed to continue as a race? Or had she been a foolish, foolish old woman to hope so. Standing as tall as she could stiffen her spine, she said, hating the trembling in her voice, "May I know the fate Darq has wrought?"

J'Hi-Inti twirled the shimmering opal writing stick with Her fingers several times but did not turn or look at Zukaltay. "Despite your granddaughter having the traits of Kukulaan—"

"What traits?"

"Being independent-minded, a daredevil. Having little fear of flying and danger. No fear of death—"

"I thought all space pilots had those qualities?"

"Come to think on it, I suppose they do, at least to some extent." J'Hi-inti began to write again. "And yet, Darq is singularly an enterprising and surprising young woman."

"Yes, Darq will be Darq."

J'Hi-inti nodded. "Indeed. She had enough hate to kill Ippera without a second thought, yet she decided it was wrong to kill in cold blood, to murder an enemy who could not defend himself. Whereas the men of the *Tolamixi Mu* murdered in cold blood." J'Hi-inti stopped writing and faced Zukaltay. "You had a good influence on Darq."

Fear raced through Zukaltay—J'Hi-inti knew about the drumming! "I only played the drums a time or two."

J'Hi-inti chuckled. "That was not what I meant. By the way, you must realize the passing of time will help your granddaughter come to terms with her grief for your loss, and she will no longer hear your drumming."

It was to be expected, but a part of her had hoped she would remain connected to Darq by the drum. She nodded.

A smile nestled at the corners of J'Hi-inti's lips. "I must say, Zukaltay, I did not expect your reaction on the bridge of the *Ippera*."

Remembering Ippera's sacrifice, tears rose anew to heat her eyes. "Admirid Ippera did a brave thing. I know he's a black-hearted Doyon, and his soul is rot, but he did something remarkable. At least it was remarkable to me."

"Yes, quite remarkable. As remarkable as loving his wife and children. He even showed kindness and concern for a young Doyon female far below his caste. In his younger days, that would never have been. He had a seed of kindness in him, though he did not permit any to know it."

"You knew."

"I am J'Hi-inti, the One Who Sees All." Her serene voice did not carry a reproof.

Only Zukaltay felt the impact, felt chastened. "Yes, yes, of course."

"Be assured, Zukaltay, Auc-Pon judged Ippera righteous enough to enter the moat about Ly'sienia. In due time, purgatory will cleanse him. One day he will join his good wife in Ly'sienia." J'Hi-inti stopped writing and looked at her with a glint of pride in Her eyes. "You, too, child of mine, showed an unexpected compassion and kindness to Ippera. For that, I have decreed you shall be the ancestor your dyn may call upon for guidance."

Zukaltay felt the brilliance of grace brighten her soul, followed by the snapping of a dozen sin-chain links as they vanished.

J'Hi-inti set the writing stick down and stepped aside. "Now come, Zukaltay, see the future you and your granddaughter have begotten for the Mayahi Dyn, for the Wysotti, for the Doyons, for the Centauri — and for Earth's Mayans."

Aboard the Dujaki

Through the fabric of his uniform, Atlatl felt Rieeza's cold hand touch his forearm.

"Azran, are you sure you don't want me to come with you? To help?"

He patted her hand, then removed his rank amulet and slipped it in his uniform's pocket. "This must be done. You go take care of Jaqui's belongings. If I need you, I know where you'll be."

"Yes, father." She stepped away from him, pulling a small cargo-chest behind her and entered Jaqui's bedchamber.

Atlatl stared at Darq's chamber door, swallowed hard enough to remove the choke from his heart, then pushed the node, opening the door. He stepped through and commanded the light on.

He had put off this duty too long. Made too many excuses. A Grier ship had reported two Pytak fighters — the *Ky* and the *Zopa* — had engaged three Doyon destroyers. They'd also reported the *Zopa* had been shot outright, the *Ky* a victim of a mini-nova event of the San Hiphias. In his grief, he'd then given orders no one should disturb Jaqui and Darq's quarters until after the court decided who had legal claim to Jaqui's belongings. Why Jaqui had not made out her death requests, no one knew.

He knew. Some pilots figured doing so jinxed them, so if they didn't fill out the forms, process the paperwork, they would not die. But die Jaqui-Chance had.

Unlike Jaqui, Darq had long ago faced the probability of her death in a cockpit. She'd made sure her paperwork was always up to date, with him as her heir. Now his wife was dead. Gone. Time to sort her things, pack them away. With no child to give anything to, what he kept was his. All else Darq had insisted he give choice to his sisters and daughters—or sell. Nothing was to go to Pyhanni. Nor to her sisters. Both sisters had insisted they get nothing so Pyhanni couldn't needle them until they gave in and turned over whatever had belonged to Darq.

He opened the cupboard beside Darq's bed and gazed on the model of *Little Bit*. He remembered meeting Darq for the first time when she brazenly landed *Little Bit* in front of the base hospital because her passenger was in labor, about to birth a male child. He recalled Darq professing t'uns later that she had fallen in love with him on first sight, then and there.

His gaze went to the wedding picture in which Darq held their marriage basket. Beside tthat picture stood one with Darq and her grandmother. The day Darq graduated from the academy, and he'd overheard Zukaltay say, *Execute all your duties to the best of your abilities, and you will thrive wherever you go.*

Now he must execute his duty and pack away Darq's things, but he would not thrive without his beloved atan.

Wiping aside the moisture from his left eye, he reached for Zukaltay's drum and pulled it out. He sat cross-legged on the floor and patted out a rhythm, soon losing himself and his tears in flashes of Darq's smiling face, her laughter, her unruly tongue.

"Father!" Rieeza yelled from behind him.

Startled, he quickly wiped his tears with the heel of his palms but did not turn to face her. He let his crackling anger bellow out. "Rieeza! When will you ever learn to knock? I want privacy."

"Oh, no you don't. Qelsey's here, huffing and puffing!"

What the devil? He turned to look with tear-blurred vision at Qelsey. His XO's flaming red cheeks and heaving lungs bespoke of her having run her stout body hard. "Azran—message cascaded down—from Gray Lead—on patrol—The Narrows."

His heart rate tripled. "The Doyons are coming?" He half-threw the drum aside to get to his feet. When he faced his XO, her smile was as wide as a flight deck.

"Azran—Raven is on her way home!"

✧ Epilogue

Song of Springtime

Again the sun warms, the birds return with song,
    flowers bloom.
My heart flies, my song resounds, joy and hope
    renewed.
    — *Ancient Wysotti Drum Song*

Darq stood at the water's edge of Jooril Bay, watching the
dark, glassy seascape where ebony rock monoliths dotted the
waterline and the beach's tallow-colored sand edged the tidal
pools. The late spring breeze had subsided, and the water giggled
each time it lapped the beach. She was on the homeworld
enjoying the last two days of a month-long leave before returning
as flight instructor to the E-calli island base half a world away.
Going from flying ace to teacher had been a profound change of
lifestyle. Almost as profound as the tide about to change now.

She glanced at the water and caught sight of her rainbow
painted toes. She'd left the *Chenault* with painted toes, reassured if
things went wrong there would be evidence of her demise. Oddly
enough, Tokoray had never brought up the subject. Nor had
Atlatl. Nor had she been cited for disciplinary action. Ah, well, as
curious as she might have been and might still be, it was best not
to question and accept the kindness of Fate.

Movement out of the corner of her eye had her swinging
about, but not in a defensive stance. To her left a saalishani
emerged from the dark shadows of a rock formation. Watching

the old woman advance, Darq recognized her. "Adovee, Wise Mother," she said. "Trespassing again?"

The old woman planted her staff, stopped, and chuckled softly. "Guilty as charged, and adovee to you, Darq. I have the correct name, do I not?"

Darq nodded.

"We met here, what—? Ahh, yes. Six t'uns ago."

"You have a good memory. Are you making another pilgrimage intent on a world-famous breakfast?"

"Partly yes, partly to sing and dance in an honor circle and commemorate the valiant warrior-princesses of the war t'uns who gave their lives."

A memory winked of Jaqui but quickly flitted aside. "It's fitting. More fitting now that the Sisters of Ya'tal offer thanks for our deliverance from the Doyons."

The saalishani nodded. "I have it on good authority that J'Hi-inti heard not their voices but one particular voice and listened. That voice was your grandmother's."

Darq didn't believe it, but she let the smile hover on her face. "I wouldn't put it past my grandmother, but I'm still a realist. What the seers purport and what the news media report are not necessarily one in the same. Only J'Hi-inti knows the truth."

"Yes, indeed She does." The old woman glanced inland. "I see you are sharing your lean-to with more than a husband."

"Yes, my son and daughter."

"Is the little one clutching a drum?"

"It's my grandmother's. He and it have become inseparable."

"I enjoy a good drum-song, don't you?"

"Sometimes." And sometimes when her son patted the drum, it brought back memories of those weeks after Zukaltay died and the audio hallucinations. The internal drumming had ceased soon after Darq visited the daoka tree planted above Zukaltay's ashes. The ashes had nurtured the roots, making the tree's leaves the darkest of greens. A sadness wafted through Darq, and she recalled weeping and saying farewell. Gaining closure . . .

"Goodness," the saalishani said.

Darq looked at the old woman who now faced inland, her gaze on the sand-castle from which Tokoray protruded. In his hand, he held a purple-and-green-striped paper flag.

"That Na-ka-ta doesn't look like the one you had before. The uniform—then again, they do tend to look alike."

"It's not the same one," Darq replied with pride. "This one and I are bonded." Still pilot and copilot, but holding higher ranks now, teaching and challenging cadet pilots. Outflying everyone.

No Na-ka-ta was like Tokoray, a friend forever. And who would have thought Tokoray would like playing in the sand with her kids? Okay, so Rieeza had made him a wheelbase that was impervious to grit, wet or dry.

The old woman's gaze shifted to Darq's abdomen.

Darq put her hand to her slightly rounded belly. "Yes, I am pregnant. Another son."

"Seems a good many sons are being birthed these days. Oh, dear me, you brought back the revelation that Terra—I mean, Earth—and its Mayans were not destroyed, did you not?"

Darq nodded.

"Do you think, as many say, J'Hi-inti withdrew her curse on the Wysotti?"

Darq shrugged. "One could hope so."

"Ahh, yes, hope." The saalishani looked up at the sky. She pointed her staff heavenward, toward the constellation the Doyons called home. "To think that not so long ago, we were facing the end of days, the demise of this world to the Doyon Horde. Who would have guessed the tables would be turned, that asteroids would break free from the Cypha-wee-ka and threaten the Doyon homeworld?"

Darq smiled to herself. After she made it back to the *Dujaki* and the Elpoccalli were informed of the rockets planted on the asteroids, teams of commandos secretly went in, located, and reset the asteroid rockets to send the rocks in different directions. When the Doyons ignited those rockets, the asteroids sped into Doyon space. The Doyon armada, which had been poised to enter The Narrows, scrambled to stop the asteroids that threatened not only military installations and space-fleet ship yards but also their homeworld. One asteroid got through and hit near the kungarike capital.

That calamity hastened the overthrow of the military government. One t'un after that, Ippera's youngest son married the technician who had served Ippera's brain. The couple led a movement, no, a grassroots revolution, for self-sustaining terraforming. For the time being, the Doyons had no need to conquer and rob other worlds. Even the Griers were back to trading with them.

Darq looked over the peaceful sea. She felt at peace. Was that because she no longer felt duty-bound to her dyn or to the service? Her duties now were those of mate, mother, teacher, and friend. "Peace is a good thing for a society."

The saalishani scoffed, but her grin said she wasn't serious. "Is this the same Elpoccalli fighter pilot I spoke to who said peace was not in a Doyon's vocabulary, or favored by their power-mongering kungarike?"

Darq chuckled. "You have a good memory. Yes, the same. Wiser minds rule now."

The saalishani nodded. "I particularly like the new ambassador, Vekka Ippera. Such a stalwart woman. An amazon when you consider her F'brig heritage. A Doyon with enough courage to expose the atrocities of the military regime."

Darq nodded.

"And then, a moon ago, what happens? We have a Centauri ambassador arrive by Grier ship to seek friendship and trade. We have allies bearing no ill will for what the *Tolamixi Mu* wrought. That is simply amazing." A knowing twinkle appeared in the old woman's eyes. "So many things have changed in so short a time span. It makes me believe all the more in miracles."

Miracles? Darq hugged herself and looked out at the first wave building to announce the tide coming in. Memories swirled of surviving the Joiz attack, finding Beans, and getting home to the *Dujaki*. Another memory flashed of flying with Number Ten, who turned out to be Tokoray, and of how a pilot's jinx and a Na-ka-ta murderer bonded—instant friends, comrades still. More images winked to mind. The mini-nova of the San Hiphias.

Rescue by the Centauri. Truths revealed about the Mayans, Terra, her pregnancy—and Ippera.

For a long while after Ly-quetzal she'd dreamt of revenge, and yet, when face to face with Ippera, she hadn't killed him. Who would have guessed Ippera would turn out to be an honorable Doyon who made it possible for her to get home? Such an unexpected event.

So many unexpected events. And yet, each and every one had been miraculous. A profound realization fluttered within her. *Divine intervention . . . miracles.*

"Darq?" the saalishani's voice entreated.

She eyed the old woman. "Sorry. I was lost in thought."

"I gathered that."

Darq held the old woman's gaze and smiled. "Wise Mother, I stand corrected."

"Oh? How so?"

The first wave of the incoming tide struck the beach, nibbling at Darq's painted toes. She grinned. "I have come to believe in miracles."

THE END

✧

✧ About ✧

Catherine E. McLean

Catherine writes "Women's Starscape Fiction"
because she enjoys a story where characters
are like real people facing real dilemmas,
and where their journey (their adventure-quest,
with or without a romance) is among the stars and solar systems,
and where there's always a satisfying ending.

Writing as C. E. McLean, Catherine has sold short stories
in science fiction, paranormal, and contemporary (romance)
to hard-copy and online anthologies and magazines.
Her novel Karma and Mayhem,
(a paranormal fantasy romance) is available at
https://www.soulmatepublishing.com/karma-and-mayhem/
(And other online e-book outlets).

~ ~ ~ ~ ~ ~ ~ ~ ~

✦ ✧ Catherine is also a writing instructor and workshop speaker (both
online and in person) who believes craft liberates and enhances talent.
Her workshop and course schedules are posted at
www.WritersCheatSheets.com

✦ ✧ To book the author for your event or to do a workshop online or in
person, go to Rimstone Concepts at www.rimstoneconceptsllc.com
and use the contact form there

~ ~ ~ ~ ~ ~ ~ ~ ~

✦ Interested in being notified of Catherine's upcoming story releases,
workshops, interviews, blogging, or public appearances?
Then join her at Twitter -
https://twitter.com/#!/CatherineMcLea7
Her Website is: www.CatherineEmclean.com

See Darq's avatar (a doll!) by going to
Http://jewelsofthesky.wordpress.com